"I THOUGHT IT WAS JUST ME." IT COMES OUT IN A WHISPER.

I glance over. Her eyes are big, big enough for me to see in them, the innocence and longing she hides so well. It touches me in places I walled off, long ago. She knows who I have been and wants me still. "Oh hell." I unsnap the seat belt, and it retracts with a clang. I slide across the seat and take her face in my hands. She doesn't draw back—doesn't shutter the want in her gaze. When I lower my head, my hair falls, curtaining us. Our lips touch, a tentative bird's-wing brush. *Sweet.* I trace her lips with my tongue and she rises and takes me in. I fall into her, taking what she gives, and trying to give back.

When I realize she's crushed in my arms, and our breathing is loud in the enclosed space, I loosen my hold and force myself to back up. "That shouldn't have happened. Sorry."

She gives me a Cheshire cat smile. "I'm not."

Praise for Laura Drake and her novels

THE LAST TRUE COWBOY

"Drake takes readers on a beautifully imperfect journey with two people who can no longer have their ideal future, but learn that the real one might be even better."
—*Publishers Weekly*

"Brilliant writing, just brilliant!"
—Lori Wilde, *New York Times* bestselling author

THE SWEET SPOT

"Drake is a fabulous new voice in romantic fiction; this is a first-class Western!"
—*New York Times* bestselling author Linda Lael Miller

"Poignant, heart-wrenching, hopeful...this realistic contemporary zeroes in on issues of trust, communication, healing, and forgiveness. A cut above the rest."
—*Library Journal*

"A sensitive, honest look at a family destroyed by loss... Drake's characters are so real, so like us, that you will look at your own life and count your treasures."
—*RT Book Reviews*

"Lovers of western settings will enjoy debut author Drake's detailed descriptions of bull riding and cattle ranching."
—*Publishers Weekly*

NOTHING SWEETER

"Drake writes excellent contemporary westerns that show the real American West—not a dude-ranch fantasy...This one's not to be missed."
—RT Book Reviews

"A sweet, passionate, at times heartbreaking romance set in picturesque Colorado with two very strong-willed protagonists, each recovering from their own recent setback."
—HarlequinJunkie.com

SWEET ON YOU

"*Sweet on You* is a wonderfully written book and one I wholeheartedly recommend to fans of just about any genre."
—The Romance Review

"A bittersweet romance contemporary that deals with grief, heartbreak, and forgiveness. Drake's ability to work past the trite and hit on the cusp of the matter with beautiful prose and a genuine empathy for her couple made that book a winner for me."
—Smexy Books

HOME AT CHESTNUT CREEK

LAURA DRAKE

FOREVER

NEW YORK BOSTON

Home at Chestnut Creek copyright © 2019 by Laura Drake
Excerpt from *A Cowboy for Keeps* © 2019 by Laura Drake

Wild Cowboy Ways copyright © 2015 by Carolyn Brown

Cover photograph by Claudio Marinesco. Cover design by Elizabeth Turner Stokes. Cover copyright © 2019 by Hachette Book Group, Inc.

Forever
Hachette Book Group
1290 Avenue of the Americas, New York, NY 10104
read-forever.com
twitter.com/readforeverpub

First edition of *Home at Chestnut Creek*: July 2019
Wild Cowboy Ways was originally published December 2015

Forever is an imprint of Grand Central Publishing. The Forever name and logo are trademarks of Hachette Book Group, Inc.

The publisher is not responsible for websites (or their content) that are not owned by the publisher.

The Hachette Speakers Bureau provides a wide range of authors for speaking events. To find out more, go to www.hachettespeakersbureau.com or call (866) 376-6591.

ISBNs: 978-1-5387-4645-5 (mass market); 978-1-5387-4644-8 (ebook)

Printed in the United States of America

10 9 8 7 6 5 4 3 2 1

OPM

AUTHOR'S NOTE

My husband and I have crisscrossed New Mexico on a motorcycle several times, and I fell in love with its harsh beauty. But it wasn't until we did a bicycle tour across the state that I *felt* New Mexico. A bicycle is much slower, so you have hours and hours alone on the road to notice: the huge expressive sky that can change moods in minutes; the crumbling walls of rock with striations of color from off-white to ochre; the lonely wind, ruffling the grasses. The land spoke to me in ways no other has; it left marks on my soul.

Along the way, we learned of the rich history of The People; the Navajo. We rode our bicycles 75 to 100 miles a day, visiting ruins, missions, and pueblos. At night, we met the local tribe. Several shared a meal with us, danced, and imparted some of their rich culture and history. I came away with a deep respect for their wisdom, how they live, and how they view the world.

I wanted to honor them in some small way, and this book is my attempt at that. I had help from Laurelle Sheppard, a Diné who lives on a reservation in Arizona, who's writing children's books in Navajo to preserve the language. I owe her a big debt of gratitude. Any errors in this book are mine alone, and I only hope that my respect and admiration for this amazing culture shines through.

HOME AT CHESTNUT CREEK

CHAPTER 1

Nevada

The bus blows by a wooden sign:

WELCOME TO UNFORGIVEN, NEW MEXICO
HOME TO 1,500 GOOD NEIGHBORS
AND A FEW OLD SOREHEADS.

I knew Carly lived in the boonies, but dang.

The bus turns onto an old-fashioned town square, with a peeling gazebo plunked in the middle of a bunch of dead grass. Most of the store windows are covered in butcher paper. Snowflakes drift from gray flat-bottomed clouds to melt on deserted sidewalks.

This place is the dead end of civilization. A good place to hide.

I hope the haircut and dye job help keep me safe. I roll my shoulders, and my neck pops. I'm tired, and my shoulder is killing me. It was hard to sleep last night, worrying about somebody stealing my backpack.

The bus turns, and I see it: an old train station with the sign CHESTNUT CREEK CAFÉ above the door.

I know the owner, Carly, from when she ran away to the rodeo, preggers and scared. I was cooking for Cora on her food truck, when she went to visit her newest grandkid and left me and Carly to handle the business. It was rocky, but in the end, we didn't kill each other. Carly told me to come see her if I ever needed a job. Hope she meant it.

I pull the cord, lift my backpack, and stumble down the aisle as the bus comes to a halt.

The driver watches me in the long rearview mirror over his head, and the door opens with a squeal.

I step out into three inches of slushy water, and the bus pulls away with a roar and a choking cloud of diesel. My tennies are soaked, and the wind whips right through my denim jacket. Cora tried to get me to buy a heavier one before I left, but that'd just be one more thing to carry. I don't need the weight.

Warm light from the café spills onto the cold sidewalk. There are people inside. It looks welcoming.

I don't care about a welcome. I need a job.

My shoes squelch all the way to the door with old-fashioned gold lettering. Metal bells jingle against the glass, and I step into a hug of heat and the smell of grilling beef. Shaking off the shivers, I wipe my freezing feet on the mat and look around.

Red vinyl booths, mostly occupied, line the windows on three sides, and in front of me, a counter with round stools covered by locals. Behind it, a serving window with a long chalkboard above, declaring the daily special, meat loaf. My stomach snarls, reminding me I skipped breakfast *and* lunch.

The room is full of voices and laughter. I walk across the

old black and white patterned tile floor to take the last open stool at the counter.

A tall black-haired woman in jeans, a checkered blouse, and a food-spattered apron steps up, holding up a steaming pot of coffee. "Cold night for a light jacket. Want some?"

"Oh, heck yes." I flip over the mug in front of me and she pours. I'm about to ask about Carly, when the bells tinkle behind me.

In walks Austin Davis, in a Marlboro man shearling coat, one arm weighted down by a carrier full of blanket-wrapped, kicking baby. Carly follows, laughing and shaking snowflakes out of her crazy red curls.

Patrons call to them.

"Hey, Austin."

"There they are!"

"Carly!"

A frail old lady with fire-engine-red lipstick bleeding off her thin lips waves bony, talon fingers. "Austin Davis, you bring that baby over here right now. I need to give her some sugar."

"Yes'm." Austin stomps off his boots then walks to the booth and sets the carrier on the table.

Carly sees me, and her mouth drops to an O of surprise.

She rushes across the floor and wraps me in a hug. "Nevada Sweet, I hardly recognized you! Why didn't you tell me you were coming? What did you do to your hair?"

My fingers go to my new dark brown pixie cut, and I untangle myself. "Back up off me, Beauchamp."

"Davis."

I look down at the small rock on her hand. "Cora told me he finally made an honest woman of you."

A lightning flick of pain crosses her face, before her smile amps again.

I always say the wrong thing, even when I mean well. Not that I often mean well, but I wouldn't hurt Carly on purpose.

"Why didn't you call?"

"Because, if I owned a phone, I'd have to talk to people."

She laughs. "Same old Nevada." She looks around the room. "Where's Cora?"

"Wintering in Oregon, same as always."

"But I thought you were going to stay with her until the rodeo circuit starts up again."

"Hang around a bunch of squalling kids? Not hardly." That's at least partly true. The other part, Carly doesn't need to know about. "Thought I'd stop in and see if you had any work until then." I'm not going back and putting Cora in danger, but I'm not saying that, either.

I can read Carly's face like the *Houston Chronicle*. Her lips turn south, and one cheek lifts in a wince. "I don't—"

"No problem. Just thought I'd check before I headed to Albuquerque." I push off the stool.

"Wait, how'd you get here anyway?"

"Greyhound."

She frowns, studying my face. "Hang on. Let me see what I can do..." She waves at the blond waitress.

"Hey, forget it, okay?" I knew this was a mistake. I'd fit in this cozy place like a coyote at the kennel club. I shoulder the strap of my backpack and reach in my pocket for a couple bills to pay for the coffee.

"Dang it, Sweet, would you stop being so stubborn?" Carly nods to the kitchen door when the waitress walks up. "You. Sit." She glares at me and points at the stool. "Stay."

"Marriage made you even bossier." Might as well sit. Maybe my feet will warm up before I have to head out again.

I take a sip, and the coffee burns its way down, warming me from the inside out.

Austin is now in the middle of a crowd of people wanting to pet the baby. The cowboy I saw last summer would have never put up with not being the center of attention, but he looks as proud as if he pushed that baby out himself. She has her hand around his little finger, but it's clear from the sappy look on his face that it's really the other way around.

I order the meat loaf from a young waitress who stops by. When she brings it, I dig in. It's not just that I'm hungry—I know good cooking when I taste it. Green peppers, jalapeño, and some spice I can't quite name make it the best meat loaf I've eaten. I look through the serving window. A tall, rangy, broad-shouldered guy has his back to me at the grill, a long black braid trailing to his waist. Nice butt.

I'm mopping up gravy with a piece of homemade bread when Carly and the blonde come through the swinging door.

"Nevada, this is Lorelei West, our manager. Lorelei, Nevada Sweet."

I nod.

Carly looks around, and when she finds her husband, a smile lifts the corner of her mouth. "What with Faith, and our new business, I don't get in here much. Lorelei would be your boss. But you need to know, we've already got a cook—a good one."

"Yeah, I found that out." I wave at my empty plate. "That's okay; I'll just—"

"But we *do* need a busboy, and someone to waitress in the busy times," Lorelei says. "Carly vouches for you, so that's good enough for me."

Carly hasn't stopped looking me over. "I know you can do better, but I want you to stay. Will you take it?" She names an hourly rate that's better than the job deserves.

I don't do charity. But I'm tired. Tired of running. Tired of worrying. And I'd be near invisible here in the butt crack of America. Besides, it's too cold to be on the road. Maybe I'll stay 'til it warms up. I hold out my hand to Lorelei. "Okay." I can't meet Carly's eye, but I pull the word from my gut and spit it out. "Thanks."

"Come with me." Carly clamps onto the sleeve of my jacket and pulls. "I want you to meet Fish."

"I'm not a fan of tuna. Besides, I just ate."

She laughs that tinkling laugh I remember. "No, silly." She pulls me through the swinging door to the kitchen. "Nevada, this is Joe 'Fishing Eagle' King. Fish, to his friends."

The name makes sense when he turns around. He's obviously American Indian: long burnished face with strong bones, crow-black hair. One fine-looking dude. His eyes...they're calm and steady. It's like they see *into* me.

"Fish, this is my friend, Nevada Sweet."

He takes his time, looking his fill.

"What, do I have gravy on my chin?"

He smiles like he knows something I don't. He's got a mouthful of startling white teeth. "Welcome, Nevada."

"Whatever."

Carly says, "Nevada's going to be busing tables, helping out cleaning up in the kitchen, and waitressing when we're shorthanded. But she's a heck of a short-order cook by trade, so if you want to take some time off for a change, you can."

"We'll see." He turns back to the grill. "Nice to have the option."

Carly tows me back through the swinging door. "You'll come home with us."

I stop, and pull my sleeve out of her grip. "I'll just get a hotel room."

She puts her hands on her hips. "Did you see a hotel anywhere around? The nearest is five miles down the road to

Albuquerque, and how would you get back for your shift in the morning?"

"Hitch a ride." I don't want to be the flat spare tire in their home sweet home.

"Oh, shut up, Sweet. You look beat. You're coming home with me. Austin will bring you back in the morning."

I don't have anything to say to that.

"Come on, we'll rescue my husband and baby, and get on home."

She's not going to give up, so I follow.

"I'm sorry, everyone, but we've got to get this princess home. Past her bedtime." She touches Austin's sleeve. "You ready, babe?"

"Ready, Tigger." He looks down at his wife, smug as a dog by the fire.

I'm *not* jealous. I'd never get married, much less have a baby. But the reminder that I'm alone in the world...it gives me a lonesome ache sometimes. I shove it back down.

"Nevada's spending the night. She'll start work in the morning. Thought you could bring her in when you go to the hardware."

"Sure thing." But from his corner-of-the-eye look, he's not thrilled.

Well, I won't bother them long. I'm not taking the chance of bringing trouble to their door. Besides, I'd probably have a blood sugar problem, from all the sweetness flying around. I follow them out the door followed by diners' good-byes and blown kisses.

Turns out, they live a ways out of town in a big rambling old house with a shake roof and a porch all around. Austin opens the front door for Carly and me, then carries the baby in.

"You forgot to lock the door." I glance around to see if the furniture is gone.

"This is the country, silly." Carly unzips her ski jacket and hangs it on a hook by the front door. "No one locks their doors out here."

I reach behind my back and, coughing to cover the noise, twist the deadbolt. I wouldn't sleep a minute, imagining somebody turning the knob, and—

"Come on. I'll show you the guest room." Carly lifts the sleeping baby out of the carrier and leads me through the kitchen—a modern room with shiny appliances, made to look like old stuff—through a hall, to a small room behind the stairs. She snaps on the light. "Here you go. We have more bedrooms upstairs, but if Faith cries, it'll be quieter here."

The room has a whitewashed dresser, a rocking chair in the corner, and an iron bed covered in one of those old-fashioned nubby bedspreads. "This is nice." I drop my backpack right next to the bed.

"You're going to need blankets. Here." She hands over the sleeping baby before I can tell her no. "I'll be right back." She walks out.

The baby frowns in her sleep and squirms, so I settle her in the crook of my arm before she starts yelling. Doing the math from when I met Carly, the baby is around eight months old; all legs and head and she weighs a ton.

Her eyes open. Seeing who's holding her, two little commas form between her eyebrows. This is clearly going south.

I walk and bounce her. Where the heck is Carly?

The baby's lower lip pops out and she pulls in a breath.

"Hey, hey, hey, little girl."

Her look shifts to undecided.

"You got nothing to complain about. I'm bouncing you. You're warm. You have a whole bunch of people who think you're the bomb. You have a nice house, and all you can eat. What's the problem?"

Her face clears, and she looks up at me with wise eyes, waiting to hear what else I have to say.

"I'll bet there's not one rat in this house, and I'm fairly sure your dad's drug of choice is a longneck on the weekend."

She reaches a pudgy hand up and pats my face.

"Trust me, kid, it doesn't get better than this."

She grabs my nose and squeezes.

"Ow, ow, stop!"

Carly rushes in, dumps a heavy American Indian pattern blanket on the bed, then pulls the baby's nails from my nose. "Sorry. I should have warned you. She's into noses this week." She takes the baby and lays her on her shoulder.

"Kid's got a grip."

"Yeah, wait 'til she gets hold of your hair." She rubs circles on the baby's back. "Nevada, what happened? Why did you leave Cora?"

I shake my head. I can't tell her I'm on the run. Not yet. Maybe not ever.

"Hey, you can tell me. I've seen your butt, remember?" She smiles.

Carly probably saved my life that day, riding me down the mountain on the back of her motorcycle. "That was your fault. How'm I supposed to know to look for rattlesnakes when I pee in the woods?"

She winks. "But you know it now, right?"

"Hell, now I watch for them in a bathroom."

She snorts. "Okay, you're tired, so I'll leave it for tonight. But tomorrow morning…"

"Yeah, yeah, so you say."

She turns and walks away. The baby's face is soft in sleep, her fat lips puffing a little on the exhale, relaxed, trusting that Mom has got her.

Lucky kid. I close the door, kick off my wet shoes by the old-fashioned floor grate, and strip out of my jeans. Mom's NA "welcome chip" falls out of the pocket and rolls. I pick it up and rub my thumb over the Serenity Prayer on the back. It's cheap plastic, more like a Vegas poker chip than something special. They probably give out better ones to people who go to more than one meeting. I tuck it back in the watch pocket.

The door is old-fashioned, with a hole for a tiny key. I pull open the drawers of the dresser, but there's no key. I pull the rocker over and shove the top under the door. I'm pretty sure I'm probably safe here, but taking chances isn't what's kept me alive so far.

I fall onto the bed, pull up the blanket that smells of cedar, and drop my head on the feather pillow. It's good to get off the road; to be warm and safe.

I'll decide in the morning if I'm going to stay.

* * *

Joseph

"Come on, Awéé. You move like a tsisteeł." I slow my jog until I'm abreast of the fourteen-year-old girl who's lagging. The rim of the horizon is the color of a dove; sunrise is minutes away.

"Who're you calling a rat, Fishing Eagle?" She pants.

"I called you a tsisteeł."

"What's that?" She picks up the pace a bit.

I smile. "You'll have to look it up."

She groans.

I run ahead on the path my feet have trod hundreds of

times. "Only a half mile left to go. Pick it up. Do you want the Zuni girls to beat you in the Wings Competition?"

The girls in the front of the pack sprint away. They may not be fluent in Navajo yet, but they have tribal pride. And I have pride in them.

The reservation itself is ninety miles from here, but a good percentage of this county's population is Navajo. I do what I can to teach our young ones the old ways. It's not easy, when the modern world is as close as the Internet on their phones, but I owe it to my grandmother to try.

The sun tips over the horizon just as we reach the mishmash of old adobe houses, hogans, and trailers. I'm breathing hard, but not sweating. I gather the girls in a group as the last stragglers run in. "It's always a good day when you get to greet the Gods in the morning. Yá'át'ééh abíní."

"You have a good day, too, Fish."

I get in my battered truck and head for my place, and a shower. If I don't hurry, I'm going to be late for work.

A half hour later, hair still wet, I pull up behind the café. I unlock the back door, flip on the lights, and when I walk to the dining room to raise the blinds, I see Austin and the new girl, Nevada, arguing on the sidewalk. I unlock the front door.

"You're not carting me back and forth to work every day."

"Just until you find somewhere to live. It's not a problem."

"Not happening."

"Okay, then at least..." He reaches in his back pocket, grabs his wallet, and pulls out some bills.

Nevada puts her hands on her hips and gets in his face. "I don't. Do. Charity."

When Austin backs up a step, I grin. Spunky little thing, backing up a rough stock rider. "You want to continue this inside? I'm freezing here."

"We're done." She flips a hand to wave Austin off, and pushes her way past me.

"Jeez." Austin watches her stomp her way to the kitchen. "I was just trying to help."

"The proud ones are the prickliest."

"Don't matter to me, but for some reason, Tig has a soft spot for that girl. Darned if I can see why." He shakes his head and dons his cowboy hat. "See ya."

"Later." I close the door and lock it.

"What do you want me to do?"

She's standing behind me in one of my extra-long aprons that almost brushes the floor. But doesn't cover the slogan on her T-shirt: *Sarcasm: it's how I hug.*

I'll let Lorelei deal with the dress code. I step past her and reach to lift the apron strings.

"Hey!" She spins, her face mottled red.

I hold up my hands. "I'm trying to show you how to tie that so you're not tripping over it."

"I know how; it's just that this is really long."

She allows it, but I can see from the taut muscles in her forearms, she doesn't like it. I pull a horizontal pleat in the apron, cross the laces in the back, reach around her sides to hand them to her. "Tie them in the front, or you're going to be stepping on those, too."

Head down, she pulls it tight and ties a bow. "I just don't like people touching me, that's all."

"Noted." She reminds me of a Chihuahua my grandmother had when I was a kid. It snarled at everyone but her. When I asked why she kept it, she said, "It is not angry. It is afraid, acting the big dog to cover it up." Man, I miss my shí másáni.

"You want me to fire up the grill?"

Easy to see the job she really wants. "Why don't you

pull up the shades, sweep, and then come back and unload the dishwasher? Our early waitress will be here in a sec." There's a knock at the back door.

Sassy Medina bounces in, pink cheeks and all. "Hey, Joseph. Nice day, huh?"

"A beautiful day."

"I think today should be—" She stops when Nevada steps into the kitchen.

The two couldn't be more different. Sassy's all curves, with bouncy blond hair and enthusiasm while Nevada has a rectangular, athletic frame and short brown hair. Her facial bones are as sharp as her snark.

"Sassy Medina, meet Nevada Sweet. She's our new bus-boy...girl...person."

I clear my throat and shoot a look at Nevada. She doesn't look like the sensitive type, but you never know nowadays.

Sassy's face lights up. "Oh, good. The high school boys we had busing were gross."

Nevada rolls her eyes. "I'll get to work."

I glance through the serving window. A couple people are standing on the sidewalk, stamping their feet to stay warm. The day has begun.

* * *

After the lunch rush, Lorelei says through the window, "Nevada, why don't you take your break?"

Nevada pulls the silverware tray from the industrial dishwasher. "Nah, I'm good."

Lorelei sighs. "You have to eat. Meals are on the house while you're working."

"Oh. Okay." She sets down the tray and wipes her hands on her apron.

"What'll you have?" I ask her. "I'm making a BLT for myself. Want one?"

"I'll make my own lunch."

I am about to object, but the look of longing on her face when she steps to the grill stops me. She looks like a little kid peering through the window of an ice cream parlor. "On second thought, I need to check inventory. You mind making mine, too?"

"Sure. You want fries?" A not-quite smile dances around the edge of her lips.

"Heck yes."

"Then move."

I watch her out of the corner of my eye as I pretend to go through our paper stock.

Without a wasted movement, she drops in a full fry basket, puts bacon on the grill, and cracks two eggs, then scrambles them. "You need some music in here." She glances at the order wheel, then at me.

I shake my head. "They can sit for a couple minutes. You need to eat."

"Like I'm going to starve in the next ten minutes?" One last longing look at the wheel, then she turns back to the grill.

"Where'd you learn to cook?"

She looks at me as if I asked if she were wearing underwear, then she shrugs and pulls bread out of the toaster. "Here and there. Why?"

Lots more to this prickly girl than she shows on purpose. "Just wondering. You clearly know your way around a kitchen."

She doesn't answer, just pulls up the fry basket, gives it a practiced bounce to shed oil, while scraping eggs off the grill with a spatula.

In a minute, I pull out two plates, and she fills them—mine with a BLT and fries, then hers with a breakfast burrito and fries.

We lean our butts against the counter to eat.

"You know, I probably shouldn't tell you this, but the Lunch Box Diner, down the square, is looking for a cook."

Her brows rise, and her eyes light. Then the scowl that seems to be her normal expression falls again. "They've got to be the competition, right?"

"Yeah, but—"

"Not doing it." She shakes her head and brushes a crumb from her mouth with her sleeve. "I owe Carly. I pay my debts."

"Yeah, I heard about the rattler butt-strike."

She whirls to me, face red. "It wasn't my butt. It was the back of my leg."

I smile. "I know. I'm just teasing you."

She slaps her hand on the stainless counter. It sounds like a gong. "Why don't we have a few chuckles at your expense, then?"

My face heats. I, of all people, know what it's like to be the brunt of jokes. "You're right. Sorry."

A glacial silence fills the kitchen, dampening sound like a heavy snow.

My grandmother's Chihuahua has nothing on this stray. The question is, what is it that Nevada Sweet is afraid of?

CHAPTER 2

Joseph

Night, Fishing Eagle." Booger Rothchild, Unforgiven's night cop, crunches out into the frozen slush on the sidewalk.

"Night, Booger. You stay warm now." I close and lock the door behind him, then lower the blinds on all the windows. The tables are spotless, the floor is swept *and* mopped, and there are enough coffee setups to last through the lunch rush tomorrow. She may be socially challenged, but Nevada is a good worker, I'll give her that. I push through the swinging door to the kitchen.

"Oh, come on." Nevada stands, talking to Lorelei; her body is as stiff as her tone. "People can't see my T-shirt through the apron."

"It's not only that. You've got to stop swearing." Lorelei sighs. "You have to understand. Unforgiven is a small town. We offend people, they'll go down the sidewalk to the Lunch Box Diner."

Nevada's eye roll and dramatic sigh speak volumes. I

walk over to clean the grill, but it's been done. The crappiest job in the place—she must've done it while I was out front. Efficient, sneaky, and fast...I'll have to remember that.

Lorelei rubs her forehead. "Look, you did more than I expected today, and you did it well. Is this too much to ask?"

Nevada glares for a few seconds. I can see her weighing options. "Oh, all right. I'll try, but I'm not promising I won't screw—mess up now and again. How did this dump get the name *Unforgiven* anyway?"

Deflecting to cover defeat. Interesting.

Lorelei releases a breath that, from the sound, she's been holding. "Depends on who you talk to. The story I heard was from Manny Stipple, the town drunk, so take it with a grain of salt. Things were pretty wild in these parts up to the turn of the century. You know, bandits, Indian raids..."

She blushes and shoots a glance at me.

I pour dill chips into the big jar. "Probably Apaches. My people were on the Long Walk." After the Navajo were starved into submission, Kit Carson and his troops forced them to walk from the land they'd lived on since the First Man and First Woman. Eighteen days, three hundred miles, in the dead of winter. Women and children, too. Of the thousand who started, two hundred died. But I'm not bitter.

"Um, sorry. Anyway, the day after the railroad spur opened, bringing lifeblood to Unforgiven, people were still partying. The train came in, and a dandy from back East got off. He rented a horse at the livery, but apparently didn't know much about riding. The horse bolted, ran over a cowhand's dog, killing it. They were not a forgiving lot. They strung up the city-dweller for 'killing an honest and forthright citizen.'"

Nevada made a sound in her throat, softer than a snort. "Cool."

"Well, like I said, the story depends on who you talk to. Ask around, people will tell you different ones." Lorelei walks to the hooks by the back door and takes down her coat. "Fish, do you mind locking up? Momma's not feeling well, and I've got to stop at O'Grady's and get milk on the way home."

"You go. We'll be fine."

"Thanks, I owe you." She pulled the door open. "I meant it, Nevada: you're a great worker. I'll see you in the morning." She steps out and pulls the door closed behind her.

Nevada turns to see me watching her. "What?"

"Where are you staying tonight? Carly told me she offered to pay rent on a room over a store on the square for you. Why did you turn her down?" Even if Carly hadn't called and asked me to check on this one, I would have anyway.

Her chin comes up. And out. "None of your business."

She reminds me of a scorpion, who ends up stinging herself as often as others. I walk over to the first aid kit, retrieve a couple of aspirin, and try to hand them to her. "Maybe not. But you can't stay here."

"I don't do drugs."

"I've watched you. Your shoulder is hurting. It's aspirin. Take them."

She holds her hand out, then tosses them back and dry-swallows them. "I'm not taking charity from anyone, including Carly. Why can't I stay here?"

"This is a diner. We don't have showers, not to mention a bed, or anything resembling one. The county would shut us down if they found out." I put the lettuce on the cart along with all the other condiments and roll it to the walk-in fridge.

Nevada is wiping down a counter. "Oh yeah, like they're going to know."

I open the door. "Do you want to take that chance? Carly and her grandparents depend on the income from this place, you know."

I hear a muffled curse after the door falls closed. I let her think on that while I put away the garnishes.

When I come out, she's scrubbing the sink like it's guilty.

"I have a place you can stay." Why am I going to the effort? But the lesson my grandmother taught rises in me. Kindness is never wasted.

Her head whips up. "I'm fine."

"Really?" I cross my arms and lean against the grill.

"I don't need help."

"Okay." I walk to the door and take down my peacoat, shrug into it, open the door, and hold it open. "Out you go."

Her lips disappear into a thin line. She walks to the rack, pulls down her thin Levi jacket, and shrugs into it. She buttons it, looking at the frozen tracks in the slush outside. The wind whips past me, and she shivers.

"Come on, I gotta lock up." When I see her steel herself to step into the cold, I take pity. "Look, my grandmother passed a few months back. Her RV is parked behind my house. It has heat, water, and electricity."

Her eyes rise to mine. "How do I know I can trust you?"

"You don't. Do you want to rent it?"

She squints up at me. "Does it have a lock?"

"It does."

She grabs her backpack hung on the hook under her coat. She loosens the top and pulls out a thick wad of bills. "How much?"

"Whoa. If you had that kind of cash, why didn't you look into renting a room over a store?"

She looks at her holey tennis shoes. "I thought I could stay here until I got my first paycheck. And it's none of your business."

I don't have time to figure out this girl's logic, or her psyche. It's getting late, and I have animals waiting at home. I name a weekly rental rate that won't make her suspicious that I'm offering charity.

"Deal." She peels the bills off the wad, hands them to me, then stuffs the money back into the backpack.

"Do I need to charge you for the ride into town tomorrow, too?"

The edges of her lips curl a fraction in what could, for her, be a smile. I wouldn't know, having never seen it. "Nah. I'll do chores for that."

I shake my head and lead her outside, unlock my truck, and wave her in, while I go lock up the back door. In two minutes, we're on the road out of town and the heater is blasting lukewarm air. "It's going to cost you one more thing, to stay at my place."

She jerks taut as a twisted rubber band.

"Tell me how you got the sore shoulder."

I feel her gaze on the side of my face.

She sits long enough that I think she's not going to answer. "Some chick in the bus station in San Antonio tried to steal my backpack. She was tougher'n she looked."

"Where'd you get all that money?"

"If I don't tell you, you gonna leave me by the side of the road to die?"

I smile at that. Carly trusts her. And despite her attitude, I do, too. I learned too late to trust my gut. "No. You can keep your secrets."

"Damned white of you."

When I look over, she's blushing. So, she does have manners, she just chooses to disregard them. To shock people, I think. Interesting.

* * *

Nevada

He drives out of town five, six, seven miles. He's way too cute for me to call him "Fish," like everyone else. "Fishing Eagle," now that's way cool, but too long. Fish? He looks like a fish like I look like Mariah Carey.

The last of the sunset shows a landscape in taupe, sage, and tan; dead grass, scrub brush, the snow-covered mountains in the background. And rocks—boulders to gravel, everywhere you look. I glance over at his long, burnished face. It's a strong face. Carly vouches for him, but still, we've been driving forever, and you could leave a body out here and no one would find it for years. "How far away do you live?"

He spins the wheel and we bump off the road, following two tire tracks in the dirt. "About a mile out this way."

I look out the window. The lonesome country strikes something inside me, like a flint on a rock. Tears prick the back of my eyes. Man, I must be tired. "They did leave you guys the crappy land, didn't they?"

I expect him to be pissed, but he chuckles instead. "The reservation is ninety miles that way." He points down the road away from town. "I paid for this land."

"You got screwed."

"Why do you do that?"

When I turn, he's doing that stare-into-me thing. "What?"

"Go out of your way to try to piss people off."

I shrug, so he knows I couldn't care less. "It's my superpower."

We pull up to a weird-looking building. It's a log house,

but it's got like five or six sides, with the logs sticking out at every edge. It's got a steep cone roof, and windows all around the top. "What is that?"

"My home. We call it a hogan."

There's a squat structure off to the side with braces showing through the canvas covering like the ribs of a skinny horse. The canvas door covering flaps in the wind. There's a really old tractor at the edge of what looks like a field. Hard to tell in the dark, but there are troughs in the frosty dirt, and here and there, plant skeletons poke out of the snow.

He turns off the engine, and all I can hear is the wind and the ticking of the cooling engine. "I have one more thing to tell you."

I reach for my backpack. "Yeah?"

He looks out the windshield. "It's just an RV, but it belonged to my shí másání—my grandmother. She was a powerful woman in my tribe, and her home should be treated with respect."

He turns his head and his eyes are so intense, I'm caught—I can't look away. "I get it."

"All right then." He opens his door, slides out, and slams it.

"Don't need to get your buckskin in a wad," I mutter, trying to get my heart to slow down.

He leads the way. There's a long, low...I can't really call it a building, because it's like a tube, covered in plastic. I've seen something like that before on farms we passed. "Are you a farmer?"

"It's my biggest passion, after my heritage."

"A cook, a Navajo, a farmer...what else are you?"

"Patient."

A corner of his mouth lifts, but I don't see what's funny.

We come around the corner of the house, and there's the

RV. One of those fifth-wheel things, up on blocks. It has a little sunshade over the door, with wind chimes made of little shells and tiny bells. They make a happy sound that carries on the lonely wind.

He walks past me, working a key ring. He unlocks the trailer and hands me the key. "You now have the only key. The lights and thermostat are just inside the door. I cleaned out the fridge and cupboards, so there's nothing to eat. I'll bring you a sandwich."

"Don't. I'm good."

"Are you sure? It's no trouble."

No need to start racking up debts. "I'm sure." I'll eat when I get to work tomorrow. Past the trailer there's a flimsy fence made from woven branches. "Are those sheep in there?"

He follows the line of my vision. "Yep. Churro sheep. They were my grandmother's. I'll tell you about them some other day. For now, I need to feed them, then get inside before I freeze."

"Yeah, okay." I take the step up and flip on the light. There's no way I'm going to be able to sleep if I'm lying in a dead woman's bed. "One more thing."

He turns back to me. "Yeah?"

"Don't take this wrong. But did your grandmother die in here?"

"No." His eyes cut through me like the wind, and just as cold.

"I'm sorry," I whisper, but he's already walked away.

It's like a deep freeze in here. I close the door, drop my backpack by the door, and crank the thermostat. The heater comes on with a roar. I tuck my hands in my armpits and look around. One step across the floor to the left is the kitchen, everything kind of miniaturized. Straight across from me is a little table surrounded by a cushioned booth with a window above it. Taking two steps to the right, I'm in a tiny hall. A bathroom with a Barbie-size shower opens off to the right. Two more steps, and I'm in the bedroom. A huge bed fills the whole space; you'd have to walk sideways to get around it. I push on the mattress. Sweet.

By now, it's warm. Small space doesn't take long to heat.

I take off my jacket, toss it on the bed, and return to the kitchen. Well, Mr. Fishing Eagle is efficient; there's not even a crumb in the cabinets, nothing but a box of baking soda in the little fridge. But there are silverware, plates, and stuff to clean with under the sink.

The wind moans around the corners, rocking the trailer just a bit. It's snug, warm, and just my size. *If* I decide to stay. I go hunting and pull open a closest to find a stepladder. Granny must've been short. I walk it to the kitchen and prop it under the door handle. It wouldn't stop a full-grown man, but it'd make a lot of noise, and wake me.

Too early to go to bed. I'm antsy. I'm never good with spare time. Thoughts swirl in my mind. I pull open a drawer, and there's a couple of pads of paper in there. The top one is from a feed store, advertising Cow Chow. I take it out, pull a pen from my backpack, and drop into the window seat to write. Maybe the thoughts will settle if I get some of them out of me.

Ma,

I don't know why I'm writing this, since you won't read it. But it's weird not to talk to you, even if you mostly were too out of it to talk back. So I guess I'm really doing this for me, but I'm okay with that.

I need someone to talk to. I'm so scared all the time, and everyone here is a stranger. Maybe I could talk to Carly, but I can't put her in danger; she has a husband, a business and the cutest little baby you ever saw.

I'm sure Jovie's pissed that I knocked him out. I'd say I'm sorry, but I'm not, because there's more where he came from. Too many more. You've been going downhill, you know?

Cisco might have let me skate if I hadn't stolen the money, but I can't be sad about that, either. And the "product" is better down the toilet than in your arm.

Truth is, I'm all alone. As much as I try not to need people, it's hard to do. It'd be great if someone had my back, so I could sleep sound for a change.

But I'll deal, same as always.

I might write more later. If I have time. But maybe not.

I am sorry for hurting you.

Nevada

CHAPTER 3

Nevada

I slept in my clothes with my shoes beside the bed, just in case. Doesn't take long to put them on and shrug into my jacket. It's still mostly dark when I step out of the trailer into an icy wind. Man, is it always blowing in this godforsaken place? I pull up the hood on my sweatshirt and flip up the collar of my jacket, but it doesn't help much. The shells and bells wind chime twists wildly, making a desperate jangling sound I feel in my chest. Why would anyone settle here to begin with?

Joseph's truck is gone.

It's early yet—maybe he had to bury a prairie dog or something. Guilt slices as fast as the wind. I shouldn't be a bitch—he's been nicer than I could expect. But why?

Whatever. He doesn't matter.

There's shuffling and noises coming from behind the fence, so I walk over. About ten small shaggy, dirty sheep are clustered by a long trough. They look up at me, and as if they rehearsed it, they all *baaaaaaah* together.

"You guys a choir?"

"Baaaaah."

"You need some new songs."

They crowd the fence, trying to get to me.

Big animals make me nervous. Dogs and cats are cool, mostly. These guys are kinda in between. I think about petting them, but they look hungry. Do sheep bite?

The littlest one squeezes his head through the fence and nibbles at my jeans.

"Hey!" I pull my leg away, then squat down. "What do you say, little dude?"

"Baaaaah."

"I know that's right." I put my hand out, palm up, ready to snatch it back if he bites.

He makes a chuffing sound and nuzzles my hand.

It makes me smile. "Whatchoo say, will you lend me your coat? It's kinda dirty but—"

I turn at the sound of the truck pulling in the yard. Joseph steps out in sweats and a stained hoodie, a bandanna around his head.

He spots me and trots over. "See you met the posse."

I push to my feet. "Where were you?"

"Running."

I don't know what I expected him to say, but that's not it. "Oh."

"I've gotta get a shower, and we'll head to work."

"What about these guys? They look hungry."

"Okay, we can do that first. Come with me." He walks to a mostly falling-down shed the size of a one-car garage. When he opens the door, it's full of bales of hay. "In summer, I turn them out to graze, but in winter, it's the dried stuff." He puts on a pair of canvas gloves, hands me some scissors. He hefts a bale that's gotta weigh fifty pounds like it's nothing.

I follow him back to the gate. He opens it and lugs the hay in. "Don't worry, they won't get out. They know where the food is." He drops the bale, then turns to look for me.

I'm standing outside the gate.

"Come on in."

"No, I'll just..."

He tips his head like a confused dog. "You're not scared of sheep?"

I shrug. "Never been around them."

He walks to the gate and opens it. "Past time you did, then."

The sheep are clustered around the bale, trying to pull out little wisps.

"Hand me the scissors."

I slap them in his hand like a nurse in an operating room.

He cuts the twine holding the bale together and pulls it out, wraps it around his hand, then kicks the bale apart. "You have to be sure to get all the twine. If they eat it, it'll get twisted in their gut and could kill them."

The sheep dig in. They're dirty and runty, but kinda cute. "I could feed them to pay for my ride to and from work."

He turns and looks down on me.

"If you want." I shrug. "Gotta do something to pay you back."

"Of course you do," he says in a tone that could mean anything. "I've got to get a move on, or we'll be late to work."

"I'll wait in the truck."

"You didn't eat dinner last night. There's food at my house."

I take a step back, shaking my head.

I hear his sigh over the wind. "Look, I'll lay it out plain. First, I've never in my life taken something a woman didn't willingly give. And besides, you're not Navajo." He turns and holds the gate open for me. "You're safe with me."

After a few steps, I follow him, jogging to keep up. "What, white women not good enough for you?"

He shoots me a glare but doesn't slow. "Our ways are dying because the kids are leaving for the cities. I'm doing what I can to remind them what they're leaving behind. I'm not against white. I'm pro Navajo."

Maybe, but there's something else there. I know shame when I see it. I should, with my childhood. Guess I've got nothing to worry about. Unless he's lying. I don't think he is, but I'll keep an eye out just the same. He opens the unlocked door, and I step into his house-hogan-thingy, mostly because I really am starving.

The logs on the inside are all blond wood and glowing in the lamplight. The floor is wood, too, a little darker than the walls. The ceiling is high, and it's mostly one big five-sided room, the living area on my right with dark brown leather furniture, Navajo rugs on the floor. To the left, separated by a long counter with stools covered in an Indian blanket design, is the kitchen.

But what draws my eye are the baskets. Displayed on shelves, hanging from the walls, on every flat surface. Woven baskets, in cream and rust, brown, black and ivory, big, small, and everything between. "What's with these?"

"My grandmother was a basket weaver." He glances around at them, his eyes soft. "I'm going to get a shower. You know your way around a kitchen, so take whatever you want to eat." He walks to the wall and climbs a slanted natural wood ladder to what I guess is his bedroom.

My stomach growls. I walk to the kitchen and pull open the fridge door. Lots here, but I don't want to make anything. A cook's kitchen is very personal. It'd be like going through his underwear drawer. I'll just grab something to gnaw on until I get to work. I close the door and look around. There are glass jars on the counter: flour, sugar, coffee, and...I reach for the middle-size glass one and open the top. Looks like strips of dried meat, with seeds and some kind of spice sprinkled on. I pull out a piece and sniff it. My mouth waters. Surely he wouldn't have it in the kitchen if it weren't food, right? I mean, it couldn't be like a sheep treat, could it? I don't think sheep are carnivores. Besides, it smells like heaven.

It takes two hands to hold it and tear off some with my teeth. I chew. And chew. The more I work, the softer it gets, releasing a smoky, rich flavor that's only a little gamy. What is it? I know beef, pork, and lamb and this ain't that. I swallow and bite off another chunk.

He comes down in jeans, boots, and a denim shirt, his hair braided and dripping. The soft light makes his hair shine. Even wet, it's beautiful.

"Oh, you found the pemmican. Good, isn't it?"

I turn the last bit over in my hand. "It is. What kind of meat is this?"

"Buffalo."

"You're shi—kidding me."

He smiles. "I never kid other cooks." He grabs his keys. "Let's hit the road."

I put the last piece in my mouth. I haven't eaten much, but my stomach is happy, having something to do. "Did you make this?"

"Yes."

I'd like to ask him how. But where would I get buffalo meat anyway?

He's different from anybody I've ever met. He seems to really care about people. I mean, he offered me a place to stay, and he could've pushed me out into the cold—especially since I'm not in his crew. But then there's that shame I saw—what's that about? It'd be interesting to figure this guy out.

If I stay long enough.

* * *

Joseph

I pull onto the highway, Nevada sitting as far from me on the bench seat as possible, clutching her backpack, and holding the door handle as if she'll bail if I make a fast move.

She is an odd combination; equal parts swagger and fear. Once you realize the swagger is a mask, it's easy to see the fear beneath. She's obviously a city kid, but more than that, I think she doesn't have much education past a keen survival instinct. "Did you finish school?"

Her head whips to me. "Did you have a family?" It's a taunt; an invitation to fight.

"Sure. My mom lives on the rez. I have a dad, not that he hung around much after I was born. Last I heard, he was in Oklahoma, but he could be dead by now, for all I know." I shrug. "You can't offend me by asking questions. I'm kind of an open book."

"Really." Her raised eyebrow adds a question mark.

"Well, I'm not." Arms crossed, head tipped down, she looks like a petulant child.

"Apparently. I'm just trying to get to know you."

"We know each other enough already."

I keep my eyes on the road. "Okay."

The only sound on the twenty-minute drive is the hum of

the engine and the whine of the tires. Fine by me. Silence is an old friend of mine.

She's out of the cab as soon as I brake to a stop behind the café. I take my time shutting the truck down and getting out. I unlock the door of the café and she goes in ahead of me. Hanging her backpack on the hook by the door, she shucks her jacket and pulls the hoodie off over her head. Beneath is a T-shirt, turned inside out, but I can still read the backward lettering: *Who left the bag of idiots open?*

She glares as if daring me to say something. I put up my hands and back away. Not my job.

With a quick nod, she turns and strides across the kitchen to the swinging door and pushes her way into the dining room.

Days always go fast when you're busy. By the time I take a breath, it's one-thirty, and the waitresses are rotating in and out of the kitchen to eat lunch.

First is Sassy. "That new girl is a good worker, but she's got a crappy attitude. I asked where she was from and she about bit my head off." She takes a forkful of salad, lightly dipping it in fat-free dressing.

"Also, I think she's trying to take my job. She's always going on refill patrol."

I flip a burger, chuckling. "You're wrong. She wants my job."

When Sassy leaves, Nevada wanders in. "Can I make my lunch now? I could eat the as—back end of a running prairie dog."

Lorelei steps out of her office, hand on her hip. "Nevada."

Her shoulders rise, her hands go out, palms up. "What? I didn't swear. And besides, the customers can't hear me."

Lorelei walks over. "I wanted to talk to you about your attire. Again."

She looks down. "They can't read it."

Lorelei *tsks*. "I can."

Nevada's features turn down: eyelids, eyebrows, and lips. Red spreads up from her collar. A muscle in her cheek twitches.

Lorelei stands her ground and stares Nevada down.

Defeat doesn't come easy to this one. Slowly her face clears, her shoulders slump, and she looks at the floor. "I don't have any other clothes."

Lorelei's turn to go red. "Well, why didn't you say so? I'll just give you an advance on your first week's pay, and—"

"I'm not wasting money on clothes. I have enough."

Lorelei rolls her eyes. "Right. You came in here with a backpack, and I didn't see any other luggage."

"I travel light."

"Just run down to the Five & Dime. They sell T-shirts, socks, and stuff like that. You don't have to buy more than one or two."

"This is bull—" She glances up at Lorelei's face. Whatever she sees there tells her she's already lost. She heaves a sigh so big I can feel the breeze. "Joseph, would you make me a burger and a chocolate shake? I'll be right back."

"Coming right up."

Lorelei takes a step to the office. "I'll just get some petty cash."

"I. Don't. Need. Your. Money." Nevada stomps to the back door, grabs her jacket, lifts her backpack, and she's gone.

Lorelei looks after her, shaking her head. "That one is a handful."

"You should let her cook some."

She turns to me, and her gaze is assessing. "You want to trade jobs with her, *Joseph*?"

"I'm just saying, during the busy times, I could use an extra hand."

Her brows come together. "I know she's staying at your place. Why are you being nice to her? She's as rude to you as the rest of us."

"Worse, actually. But I can't help but feel sorry for her. You can see she's had a hard way to go." I point the spatula at my boss. "If you tell her I said that, she'll kill me, and you'll be out a cook."

Her expression softens, and she smiles. "You've got a soft spot for the strays, Fishing Eagle."

"Well, don't tell anyone that, either." But I know how she feels. I didn't want to fit in, on the rez when I was young, then I found out what being on the outside really meant, when I tried to fit into the world outside it. I turn back to the grill and prep a plate. Nevada is a stray, but she's also a strong, good-looking woman. How could I not admire her grit? Or her loyalty. She wouldn't go for a better job, because it might hurt Carly. Better person than I, obviously.

I have Nevada's lunch ready when she slams in the door ten minutes later. She's wearing a denim shirt buttoned over the T-shirt. When she turns to hang up the backpack, embroidered on the back is: *Unforgiven: Home of the Fightin' Billy Goats*.

I hand her the plate. "Nice shirt."

She rolls her eyes. "The least stupid in a display of stupidity."

"Hey, our track team made all-state last year."

"Yay goats." Her tone is droll. She nibbles a fry. "What's with you and running anyway?"

I flip the bacon on the grill, then move to the cutting board to slice tomatoes. "Running is a tradition with the Diné."

"Translation?"

"Diné? It's what we call ourselves; it means 'the people.'"

"Oh, okay."

"Running gives pride and self-discipline. It's a part of our cultural identity. Besides, it's fun."

She squints at me. "Are you one of those endorphin freaks?"

"Pushing your body, testing your limits, greeting the Gods with the sun...doesn't get much better than that. You should go with me one morning. You might like it."

She shakes her head.

By the time we lock up, it's dark. And cold.

"Good job today, guys." Lorelei pulls her ponytail out of her winter coat and shoulders her purse. "Nevada, thank you."

She takes her backpack from the hook. "You pay me to do a job, same as everybody."

"No, thank you for giving in on the shirt. I think you even scored points with the locals for wearing it."

She ducks her head. "Not a goal of mine."

Like anyone didn't know that.

Lorelei stops in the doorway. "Um, Fish, did you forget that you promised to come help me tonight?"

I did. And that's not like me. I turn to Nevada. "I need to swing by Lorelei's house on the way home. You can wait in the truck if you want."

* * *

Nevada

I shrug. "Whatever." It's not like there's anything to do out in the Great Empty anyway.

We drive the opposite way out of town, and in two blocks we leave civilization (such as it is) behind. "So, what's the deal?" In the dash light, his face is all hard ledges and dark hollows. It's a strong face. A handsome one, if you notice stuff like that.

So why am I noticing?

"A while back, Lorelei's mother had a stroke. She's been through rehab, and now that she's about as good as she's going to get, Lorelei realized her mom needs to be on the ground floor. I offered to help her move. It's just the two of them out there."

"Ugh. Poor Lorelei." I know what it's like to have to look out for your mom.

"It's not as bad as it could be. It was a right-sided stroke, so she can talk. And walk, after a fashion. It's mainly her mind that was affected."

"Does she drool?"

He glances at me. "You really have no filter, do you?"

"No, I don't mean it mean. I'm just preparing myself, so I don't say something dumb."

"It's not like that. She forgets words, and has a hard time following complex instructions. She's always been a sweet woman."

I wince inside. I'm cutting Lorelei some slack in the future.

He catches my eye in the dashboard light. He nods with a half smile of approval. Is it for me being nice? Or me in general?

And why am I noticing *that*, much less caring about it?

He turns in at a dirt drive leading to a clapboard farm-house with a deep porch across the front. We bounce over frozen ruts, and in the headlights I can tell the house used to be white, but now the flaky paint is more a dingy gray.

Joseph parks and turns off the ignition. "Do you want to wait out here?"

"Nah, I'll come in."

"Okay then, be nice."

"I can be when I try, you know."

"Well then, try." He steps out and slams the truck door.

"Jeez, you make me sound like an ingrate." I get out and follow him to the side door, lit by a yellow porch light.

"The muscle has arrived," he says through the screen door.

Lorelei opens it. "I know this is probably the last thing—"

Joseph's hand on her arm stops her. "We're both happy to help. Really. Now, show us what you want where."

I follow him in. I have to admit, he *is* a nice guy. No man I ever met would go out of his way to help somebody, after a full day's work.

Lorelei leads the way through a kitchen out of the '70s, down to the avocado fridge. The dented and scratched front says it's clearly not a throwback fashion statement, like at Carly's. Next is a living room with the old people smell of cough drops and dust. The worn carpet matches the fridge, and there's a floral couch and chair with doilies, no less. She stops in a doorway at the far end of the room. "This will be Mother's new room. It'll make our lives so much easier."

"I'm used to taking orders from being in the Army. Just tell me what to do," Joseph says.

There's a steep staircase to the left of the room, and Lorelei flips on the light and starts up. "Honest, this shouldn't take more than an hour."

At the top, she turns right, to a door at the end of the hall. There she hesitates for a moment, hand on the knob. She takes a deep breath, flips on a smile, and opens the door.

"Momma, you ready to move? This is Fish and Nevada. They're going to help us."

Lorelei looks older than me, but her mom is *way* older than mine. She's a tiny, wrinkly woman with fuzzy white hair and little eyes magnified by Coke-bottle glasses, sitting in a rocker with one of those crocheted blankets over her legs, fuzzy socks peeking out from underneath. She frowns. "How are a state and a fish going to help?"

Chuckling, Lorelei squats by her mother's chair and pats her hand. "I meant their names are Nevada and Fish. Guys, this is my momma, Mary West."

Joseph actually bows. "I've been here before, helping Lorelei, but I haven't had the pleasure, ma'am."

"You're an Indian."

"Mom, that's not—"

"Yes, ma'am, I am."

"Good." She nods and looks to me. "Your hair isn't naturally brown."

Lorelei shoots me an *I'm sorry* look.

Her mom may be impaired, but not about everything. "That's true, Mrs. West. I dyed my hair."

"You should fire your hairdresser."

"Okay, Mom, we're going to get started now." Lorelei pushes to her feet.

"Started with what?"

"Moving you downstairs, remember?"

"Why didn't you tell me about this?" Her voice gets high and shaky, and her lower lip wobbles like a baby's.

I could give a crap about regular people, but I can't stand to see old people or animals hurting. I step to her rocker, sink to the floor, and put my arms around my knees. "Y'all go do what you gotta do. Me and Mary are going to have a good chat." I look up at the wall and point to an old black-

and-white photo of a couple coming out of a church. "Who's that, Mary?"

Her face goes all soft, and her little brown eyes sparkle. "Why, bring that down, and let me see."

I stand, and when my back is to Mary, I make shooing waves with my hands.

Joseph picks up two boxes from the floor. I'd have to be blind not to see the V-shape of his back, or the jeans pulled tight across his lean rear end. Lorelei blows me a kiss, picks up another, and they walk out.

I retrieve the framed photo and hand it to Mary.

"Oh, now I can see it. That's me and..." Her sparse brows wrinkle. "Me and..." Her mouth moves, searching for files that she clearly doesn't have access to.

"Looks like you were getting married, right?"

"Bruce! That's my Bruce." She strokes the man's face. "We were married fifty-five years and raised two daughters together."

So, Lorelei has a sister. Footsteps echo on the stairs, and a worried look crosses Mary's face. "Who's there?"

"Tell me about those days. I'll bet Lorelei was a handful, huh?"

"I should say so. She was a wild one. We were afraid she'd come home pregnant in high school."

Lorelei walks in, Joseph on her heels. Her cheeks are pink. "Momma, that wasn't me. That was Patsy."

"That's what I said. And it's impolite to interrupt."

Lorelei just shakes her head and takes another box. Joseph takes a huge painting off the wall: a house like this one, only way newer.

"That's my family homestead. Where do you think you're going with that? I don't understand—"

Joseph freezes like a spotlighted deer.

"Hey, Mary, tell me about this." I take a jewelry box from the dresser, put it in her lap, and sit down again.

Her face clears to the delight of a little girl. "Oh, how pretty. I forgot all about this." She opens the simple wooden box with a cameo on the lid. "It's a treasure chest. See?" She lifts an old-fashioned locket necklace and opens it. The picture inside is sepia, of a stern-looking woman in a chair, and a stringy man standing behind her. "This is my momma. She was born in this house, as was I, and my two babies."

"Wow." I look around the room. I've always thought of rooms only as a way to keep out the rain. I'll bet every dent in the wall, every nick in the window frame, has a story for her. What would it be like to live in one place all your life, and to know that your mom had, too? I can't imagine.

Joseph pads in, lifts the last box, and tiptoes out.

"Yes. And this." She puts the locket down and picks up a scuffed gold cufflink. "This was my daddy's. He was a rail-road man."

"What did he do?"

Her face crumples. "I don't know."

"That's okay, Mary, it doesn't matter."

"But it does!" she wails. "Life is being stolen from me, one bit at a time. You don't know what it's like…" She gulps a breath.

"I'm sorry, Mary." I pat her hand, wishing I could either give her back her memories or take enough away that she doesn't remember the loss. The in-between part has to be a freaking nightmare. Especially since it sounds like she had such a good life.

But at least she had it. Even if she doesn't remember, she's got two kids, and all those memories to leave them, both hers, and her parents'. A legacy they'll pass down, through stories. I think most everybody does. Not me, of course, but most people.

What will I leave? Nothing. I don't have any stories from my parents' past, and there's none of mine fit to pass on. Besides, future generations would mean I'd have kids, and I'm not. No brothers and sisters, either. Guess the Sweet line dies with me. And that's flat pathetic. Course, I haven't had much time to build up memories yet. And if Cisco has his way, I won't get much more. But if I somehow manage to survive this, I'm going to live. One hundred percent, flat-out. At least I'll have that, whether it passes on to anyone else or not.

Lorelei walks in, and seeing her mother crying, her eyes fill. "Oh, Momma."

"It's okay. She's just sad." I pet Mary's arm.

"I know. She gets like that sometimes." She walks over and puts out her hand. "Come on, Momma, time to go."

"Where are we going?" She takes her daughter's hand and lets herself be pulled to her feet.

"Just downstairs. I've put on the kettle, and I'll make you a nice cup of tea. All right?" She puts her hand under her mother's forearm for support.

"That would be lovely. But my friend has to come, too."

She turns to me and pats my face. Her fingers are cool and papery, and emotion puts a knot in my throat. "I'm coming, Mary. Right behind you." She only likes me because she doesn't know me. And because she's kinda losing it. But that's okay. She's a nice old lady.

Lorelei smiles at me and leads her mother out. Mary's left leg drags a bit, making her limp, and I can see where the stairs would be dangerous for her. Especially alone.

Joseph comes in as I set the jewelry box in the seat of the rocker. He studies my face. "You okay?"

The way he studies me, I can tell he's seen behind my snark. Like he's thinking there might be a good person underneath. I scowl. "Why wouldn't I be? You worry about you. I got me."

He raises his hands in surrender, then crosses to open the closet door.

I lift the rocker. She'll want this in her new room, first thing.

* * *

Joseph

An hour later, Mary is settled in her new room, we've turned down an offer of dinner, and we're saying good-bye.

"Seriously, you guys, I don't know what I'd've done—"

"Quit thanking us already." Nevada steps to the door, looking like she's afraid someone will make her stay.

Lorelei seems a bit stunned but recovers fast. "See you guys on Monday,"

Nevada looks at me, brows raised.

"Café's closed on Sunday."

"Oh."

I step outside and head for the truck. "We'll stop at O'Grady's on the way home and get you some groceries."

She ducks her head. "I'm good."

The Nevada I saw with Mary is a different species from this one—caring and tender, and almost soft. How can those two people be in one compact package? "So, you're not eating on Sunday?" Independence is a good trait, but she seems determined to take up as little space in others' lives as humanly possible.

"Oh, all right."

I pull out to the road and turn back to town. "You called me Joseph today. How come?"

"I gotta call you something." She shrugs. "Fishing Eagle is a cool name, but it's too long. Fish is just plain stupid. You don't look like a 'Joe.' So that leaves 'Joseph.'"

"My mother is the only one who calls me that."

"You look like a Joseph." She glances at me. "You said you were in the Army?"

"I was."

"I'd never sign up for that. Somebody in your face all the time, telling you where to be, what to do. Did you hate it?"

"That's hard at first. But you get used to it. I kind of liked it by the end."

"Then why did you get out?"

"When I left here, I never planned to come back."

"So why did you?"

Because it was a better choice than jail. I scan the landscape visible in the headlights. "Going away gave me perspective. Before I left, all I saw was what was wrong with where I lived. But the more I saw of the world, the more I realized that it wasn't so bad here."

"Funny, I've found exactly the opposite."

"How so?"

"Never mind."

We ride in silence. Nevada reminds me of a prickly pear; barbs on the outside, but the inside is soft. I pull into the crowded parking lot of O'Grady's.

"Damn, I didn't know there were this many people in this burg."

"Probably most are stocking up since you can't buy liquor in Unforgiven on Sunday." I follow her to the door.

We both grab a little plastic basket with a handle, and head down the first aisle.

She drops two of those just-add-water soup cups in her basket. "I'm done."

"You've got to get more than that."

Her chin comes out. "Mind your own business."

"I'm just trying to—"

"Look, I've been on my own since I was fifteen. I don't need you telling me what I ought to do."

"Hey, girl." A big guy with a spare tire, a patchy beard, and a greasy parka walks up, a twelve-pack of beer in each hand. "This Indian bothering you?"

He aims bloodshot eyes at me, and I'm washed in a wave of beery halitosis. Adrenaline shoots into my blood.

Nevada straightens and frowns. "Buzz off, Yeti."

He rears back like she slapped him. "What kinda' way is that for a lady to talk?" He squints, trying to focus on her. "Unless you're *with* this Injun, which means you ain't no lady a'tall."

I take a step, but she steps up, into his face.

"How is it your business if I'm a lady? Do I ask you how you live with only a brain stem?" She squints, and her mouth peels back from her teeth in a sneer. "I'm just curious. How *do* you remember to breathe?"

It takes him a few seconds to process the insult. "Hey." He raises his dirty hand.

I step between them, ready to swing, but only if I have to.

"I was tryin' ta help. Why you wanna be mean?"

She leans around me. "Because you're breathing your stinky ignorance all over me. Go get arrested for DUI, Bubba, and leave us alone."

This is going to degenerate, and fast. I take hold of her arm and walk away. She has no choice but to follow. I hustle to the produce department, practically dragging her behind me.

"What's with you? I didn't even swear. Do you know how hard that is—hey, lemme go." She stops and rips her sleeve away. "I told you, nobody touches me."

I round on her. "Do you want to end up in jail tonight?"

"Jail? He started it. Stupid drunk. I should—"

"What, call the cops? It's our word against his. You want to take that chance?"

A flash of something like fear crosses her face. "No."

Me neither. "Then shop. And don't tell me that's all you're buying." My words are as cold as anything in the freezer section.

"Fine." She walks to a display of apples and puts a small one in her basket.

When we go through the check-out line a few minutes later, the drunk is mercifully nowhere to be seen. I don't even try to pay for hers; I know better.

I recognize the taut line of her shoulders as she walks ahead of me to the truck, her head swiveling. Her radar is up. The feisty little thing wants to protect *me*. A warm spot fires in my chest. "Thanks for sticking up for me back there; that was a kind thing to do. Misguided, but kind."

I'm on the road out of town before she relaxes, as much as she ever does. "Does that happen often?"

"What?" I keep my eye on the road, watching for black ice, but I can hear her sigh.

"Prejudiced jerks like that, giving you a hard time."

"Not often. He's probably just passing through. People from around here treat me like anyone else, most of the time."

"You say that like you're not."

I lift one shoulder. "I'm not."

"I'll say." She mutters, but I catch it. "I get being different."

"I thought you would." I hold in my smile.

"Do you like it—being different?"

"Yeah." I need to tread carefully. She's like trying to pet a wild bird—it can be done, but it takes time and patience. "Don't you?"

"Don't know any other way." She stares out the window. "I think it's harder, though."

"But you get the benefit of being unique in a world of sameness."

"Says you."

"Do you want to be like everyone else?"

"As if." She picks at a cuticle. "It's tiring, though. Like you're always going uphill, fighting a cold wind in your face. You know?"

From what I've seen, she's been on her own for a long time. It makes me want to wrap her up. Keep her safe. "That's because you haven't found your tribe."

She chuckles; a dry sound that has no humor in it. "I don't have a tribe."

"Everyone does. I was lucky; I was born into mine. You have to gather people to be in yours. Family shelters you against that cold wind." I take a breath. "But you have to take chances. You have to let people in."

She's silent for a half mile.

"That's how people hurt you. You let them in, and they claw you up inside." It's a whisper in the dark.

It's a start.

CHAPTER 4

Ma,

A lot has happened since I left Houston. I've got nothing to do at night, and I'll go crazy if I just sit and think, so I'll tell you.

After the mess at the apartment, I ran, but I didn't want to leave you, or the city. I was dumb and thought that running to Waco Street would be far enough. I slept in the park during the day, but it was scary at night. Sketchy. So when a kid told me about a place I could go, I checked it out. I thought Haven House would try to push God on me, or try to make me go home, but they didn't. When it got cold, I stayed there all the time, and to pay my way, I helped out in the kitchen. They taught me to cook.

I guess I should'a known Cisco would track me down. Luckily, I spotted his minion first. I ran farther, the next time.

Anyway, I gotta go. People in Unforgiven are mostly nice, but I'm keeping an eye out. Even the middle of nowhere is a place on the map, and I'm not kidding myself that Cisco has given up looking.

Maybe I'll write more later. It kinda helps to write to you. Makes me feel a connection, you know?

I hope you're somewhere safe now.

  Nevada

* * *

Nevada

I have no idea what I'll do with this whole day. I fed the sheep before dawn, and the lamb (I'm calling him Little Dude) follows me around like a shadow, *baah*-ing all over the place. It's nice to sink my hands into his coat and warm my fingers. I think he likes it, too. He's a good listener. I don't need to worry about him telling anybody.

I walk all around the place while the sun comes up. Not much to see, just dead grass, old snow, rocks, and brush, rolling away forever. At least the wind isn't so bad today. I'm about to go in and read the back of a soup box when Joseph steps out of his house, axe in his hand.

He hasn't seen me. I freeze, wondering what he's going to do.

He walks behind the scruffy tent thing, where a pile of long logs lays scattered in the dirt. He puts his foot on one, and the axe falls with a hollow *chunk!* He raises the axe again, and *chunk!* Wood chips fly. He speeds up, whaling on that log like it dissed him.

In minutes, dark sweat stains his T-shirt, under the arms, and a thin line down his back. I could stand and watch him all day. His body is beautiful. I can make out his features: focused and fierce.

My feet lead me closer.

His head comes up. "Hey!"

I jump. "What?"

He lowers the axe to the ground. "You want to go running with me?"

No. But there's all day to do nothing, so... I shrug. "I guess." I walk over.

He looks me up and down. "You want to go change?"

"There's a dress code for running, too?"

"No. But do you have any other shoes? Those Keds aren't exactly the best for running. You need some support."

I look down. "It's this or flip-flops."

"Then you're ready." He jogs to his house, and in five minutes, he steps out and pulls the door closed. His hair is in a braid down his back, and he's wearing sweats, a hoodie, and fancy running shoes. "Think you can do a mile?" He bends over, stretching and warming up.

I cram my hands in my jeans pockets. "Sure." Running may be a tradition for his people, but where I grew up, it was survival. Kind of hard to outrun a bullet, though. Cisco's cruel features flick though my mind, and I glance around, feeling watched.

Joseph has started a small wood fire behind the flimsy tent-like thing. "Is it okay to leave that?"

"Yep." He takes off at an easy lope.

I follow, taking two strides to his one. We each take a tire track, and head for the blacktop. The sun has barely cleared the horizon, making a rim of gold. Birds chirp and scree overhead. The only other sound is the thud of our feet, hitting the dirt.

My muscles warm, and I relax into a rhythm. The cold air feels good on my flushed cheeks. Most people feel like they need to fill up the air with talking. I'm glad Joseph isn't one of them.

By the time we reach the road, I'm breathing deep and heavy, and still feeling good.

He looks over at me. "We turn back now, it's a mile." He glances right, down the empty tarmac. "Or go a bit farther. Which?"

I turn right and take off.

When he catches up, he's smiling. "You're pretty good. I run with the Diné Wings twice a week."

"What is that?"

"There's an organization, Wings of America. I started the chapter here. It's to teach Native youth the tradition of running, and all the benefits that come from it."

"That's good." The slap of my feet on the pavement matches a beat inside me. I realize that I'm having fun. When was the last time that happened?

"Let's turn around."

"I can go more."

"That's enough for your first day. You don't have to prove anything."

"Like I need you to tell me that." But I've got to admit, I'm proud I'm able to keep up.

He spins, and we start back.

By the time we hit the cutoff to his place, the backs of my heels are throbbing from these shoes. I jump off into the dirt, jamming my toes into the thin canvas.

Sweat slides down the side of my face and slips down the knobs of my spine. I'm breathing like a buffalo.

Joseph slows his jog.

"I'm fine."

"Hey, I'm tired, okay?"

He's not breathing half as hard as I am, and I'm having to work not to limp. Blisters, for sure.

Finally, we pull up in the yard. I stand, hands on my knees, dreading limping my way to the trailer.

"Okay, I've got something to do for a bit, but come on over to my place for lunch."

"Nah, I'm okay."

"What, are you going to sit in the trailer all day?"

"None of your business, is it?"

He tips his head. "You still don't trust me."

"Don't take it personal. I don't trust anybody." I take a step. My muscles clamp like a vise, squeezing my bones. My heels are killing me.

"Nevada."

I look up at him.

"You can trust me."

A bead of sweat rolls down his long cheek, glistening in the sun. His eyes are black pools of—what? I feel the need to name it, because the emotion brings an echo in me. So faint and so old, I almost don't recognize it. *Inner strength.* Of course I can't trust that, but just the same, it relaxes my shoulders and loosens the long, taut muscle in my stomach.

Maybe I can learn that from him, because I'm so *tired* of being afraid. But that would mean getting close, to observe? The thought sends squirrels scurrying in my mind.

The silence that was good earlier is starting to feel uncomfortable. To me anyway. He looks like he could wait all day for an answer. Hell, it's just a meal. And if he pushes, I'm in the wind. "O-okay."

"I'll see you in a couple hours." He strides off to tend the fire.

I make sure my back is straight and I'm not limping (much) as I walk to the trailer. When I peel off my socks, there's blood. I hobble into my Barbie bathroom and take a long, hot shower. When I get out, I dry off and fall onto the bed.

I don't know how long later, I bolt upright in bed. Something woke me, but I'm so bleary with sleep, it takes me a second to realize where I am. I catch a whiff of smoke and tweak the curtains to look out, half expecting it to be night. It isn't.

There's smoke coming from the flimsy hut.

Fire!

I push off the bed, take a running step, and almost go down. The muscles in my legs have shrunk two sizes while I slept. I look down to realize all I'm wearing is underwear. My brain is muzzy, working half speed. "Get a grip, Sweet." Driven by the smell of smoke, I move as fast as I'm able. I pull on my jeans and a T-shirt, step into my flip flops, and hobble as fast as I can to the door. The step down almost takes my legs out, but I keep my eyes on the column of smoke. *Fire—hurry!*

Where is Joseph? At the corner of the house I see a coiled hose with a spray nozzle. I crank the spigot all the way and drag it to the hut. There's something like moaning coming from inside. Oh my God, is he in there?

I rip back the flap; my hand spasms to a fist on the nozzle. The spray is explosive.

"What the—"

Sun pours in the doorway along with the water. Joseph jumps to his feet.

"There's a—I thought there was a—" I force my fingers to relax, and the spray shuts off as abruptly as it started.

Joseph stands there, dripping, skin slick and shining…

naked. He reaches down and snatches a pair of running shorts, steps into them, and pulls them up.

But not before I see. He is a god. Long muscled legs, taut muscle at his hip, a broad, smooth chest with swimmer's lats, and of course, there's that long, crow's-wing-black hair...and a pissed look on his face.

"What are you *doing*?"

"I woke up and smelled smoke. It looked like there was a fire. What are *you* doing?"

He reaches up and squeezes water out of his hair. "A sweat. Or I was."

Humiliation explodes in my brain, splashing heat onto my face. Anger isn't far behind. "How was I supposed to know you didn't need saving?" Steam billows from a pit with rocks in the middle of the tiny space. "What's a sweat?"

He steps into flip-flops and, shaking his head, pushes past me. "It's part of our religion. We come here to pray, and be purified, mentally, emotionally, spiritually."

Oh God. I disrupted a sacred thing. "I'm sorry, Joseph." But I'm not sorry for the picture etched in my brain. His body is like a cat's, sleek, supple, sinuous. I want to gather his hair, testing its softness in my palms, to trace the rivulet of sweat down the long muscle of his back with my finger, then raise it to my mouth, to taste it.

"I guess you meant well." He glances to the house. "Give me a half hour. You're still coming for lunch, right?"

"Only if you let me cook. After this, I owe you."

He smiles for the first time. "You're on."

* * *

Joseph

I'm getting dressed when Nevada knocks. I throw a black denim shirt on over my jeans and pad barefoot to the door.

I was too embarrassed before to notice what she was wearing: jeans and a black T-shirt with white lettering: *I'll try being nicer, if you try being smarter*. I keep forgetting how small she is. Not petite, just short, athletic, and compact. The short hair makes her look even younger.

She slaps by me in flip-flops, limping. "You know your hair is dripping on the floor, right?"

I pull the towel from my shoulder and squeeze the rest of the water out, then pull the comb from my back pocket and run it through. "Sit at the bar. I'm going to get you something for those blisters."

"I'm good." She heads for the fridge, pulls it open, and peers inside. "What do you want for lunch?"

"Come, télii." I pat the back of the bar stool.

Her head appears around the door. "What did you call me?"

"Stubborn." *Donkey*.

She rolls her eyes, *tsks*, but slouches over and sits down. "I've had worse blisters."

If she's allowing me to do this, I'll bet that's not true. I pull a tin of salve from a kitchen drawer. "You'll need to give me permission to touch you." I wait.

Her eyes won't meet mine, but she nods.

I step to her and open the tin.

"What's that?"

I take a fingerful. "It's my grandmother's recipe, from the sap of the piñon pine. The Diné have used it for centuries. It's antibacterial, and soothing. Hold your foot out."

When she does, I hiss air through my teeth. The blisters broke hours ago and beneath the broken skin are weeping blood blisters. "Ouch. Why didn't you tell me? We could have stopped."

"Not a big deal." Her leg shakes, and she laces her fingers under her thigh to support it. Her muscles have to be tired.

"Here." She jerks a bit when I cup her ankle. "Relax." Her feet are pale and delicate—vulnerable—the only part of her I've found that is. My hair falls over my shoulder onto her skin, and she jumps.

"It's cold."

I release her ankle, gather my hair, and braid it. "Just be a second." My fingers fly.

"Is it an Indian thing to keep your hair long?"

"It is tradition."

"It's pretty."

I know if I acknowledge the first compliment I've heard her utter, she'll button up, so I just pull the elastic from my wrist and twist it around the end of the braid and throw it over my shoulder. I swipe the salve gently on her heel. "Okay, the other foot."

This time, she accepts my touch without flinching. "It's taking the sting out."

"Good." I swipe salve over the other heel and let her go. Enough progress with the wild bird for one day. It crosses my mind to wonder what made her so skittish, but it couldn't have been anything good. She needs to know that not everyone is out to hurt her. "When are you going to feed me? I'm starving."

She pushes off the stool and toes into her flip-flops. "What do you want?"

"Surprise me." I settle on the seat she vacated to watch her work.

She stands at the open fridge door for half a minute, hips moving, then starts piling condiments on the counter. "I'm going to make you the best sandwich you ever ate. You just have to tell me what you want in it." She pushes the door closed with a kick of her heel.

"If it's in my kitchen, I like it. You pick."

"That's what I'm talking about." She rubs her hands together; probably unaware she's smiling. She doesn't ask, just pulls open cupboards and drawers until she finds what she wants.

She looks so young. Too young for my interest. "How old are you?"

"Twenty-three, for another two weeks. How old are you?"

"Twenty-seven."

She whistles. "Ancient."

I put my elbows on the counter and rest my chin on a hand. She cuts tomatoes, leftover roast, peppers... "What're you doing? I thought—"

She steps in, blocking my view. "You just want to steal my recipe."

"You're on to me. I brought you here for just that."

She nods. "That's what I figured."

"Where are you from?"

When her head whips up, I know I've pushed too far. Her eyes narrow. "Nowhere. Everywhere. What's it to you?"

I shrug. "Just asking."

"Well, stop asking." She whisks whatever is in the bowl. "Were you raised on the reservation? Is that where you learned your language?"

"Yes. It's all we spoke at home, since my grandmother spoke no English."

"Is your mom still alive?"

"Yes. She's still there."

"You're close?"

From a distance. I nod. "Are you close to your family?"

She flinches and turns to the stove. "Never mind."

Ten minutes later, she slides a plateful of Monte Cristo sandwich in front of me. "This looks fantastic."

She puts her own plate on the counter with a smug smile. "Taste it."

I try a bite, a thread of cheese stretching from the plate. "Wow. That is amazing. What's in the batter that makes it crunch?"

"Normally, I'd have to kill you, but I owe you, so I'll tell you." She glares. "You have to take the secret to the grave."

I trace an X over my heart.

"Pancake batter."

"Seriously?"

"I never lie to Navajo cooks."

Her smile is as soft and easy as our conversation. I don't want the wild bird to flit away, so I don't push. "Yeah, and I'm sure I'm the only Navajo you've ever met."

She gives me a one-shoulder shrug. "Easy then, isn't it?" She comes around the counter with her plate.

I laugh. "You're a funny lady." I pull out the bar stool beside me for her to sit on.

She ducks her head, and the words slip out in a whisper. "No one's ever said that."

"Probably because you don't let people close enough to see it."

"That's the way I like it." She steps off the stool. "I need water. Want some?"

"Sure."

I'm absurdly proud that she's opened up a bit.

And glad she hasn't noticed that she has.

* * *

Houston, Texas

"How hard can it be to catch one little girl?" Cisco slams his fist on the table in the back of the Casa de Mamacita restaurant. "If I have to do everything, what do I need you for?"

Marta eases behind Miguel, out of the line of fire.

Miguel holds out his palms. "Marta had her at that rodeo, but that Sweet kid is slicker'n snot."

He knew it. He'd been waiting outside the gate when she got out of prison, and he'd still missed her.

"Let me go, boss." Jovie sits across from Cisco. "I owe her."

"If you hadn't been banging her mother in exchange for a hit, this never would'a happened. Now I'm out the drugs *and* the money." But worse than that—if it got out that a teenager ripped him off, he'd be a joke on the street.

Cisco pulled out his phone. "Surrounded by idiots. I'll take care of this myself." He hit speed dial. "Tomás. I have a girl for you. Young."

"Good looking?" The oily voice is eager.

"Yeah. A little blonde. Should bring good money in Central America."

"You got a picture?"

"I'll text it to you when I hang up. Last seen at the Fort Worth Stockyards, at a rodeo. And Tomás, I want her gone for good. You hear me?"

"I'm on it, jefe."

CHAPTER 5

Ma,

So, I'm living with a Navajo guy, out in the boonies. Well, not exactly. I'm living in an RV out back of his house. He's nice. And gorgeous. He's kind of helped me out since I got here. I'm trying to find out why. He took me running with him yesterday. It was pretty cool.

Anyway, about what happened after I left. When Cisco's man tracked me to Haven House, I stashed the cash in a locker at the bus station, bought a ticket, and ended up near the Astrodome. Figured they would never think to look for me on the good side of town. I tried to get a job as a cook, but nobody would trust somebody my age to be good at it, so I went to a nice hotel and got a job as a maid.

I rented a crummy room, and a week later, I met a girl, a runaway. She was trying to get away from her mom's latest *bad-news boyfriend, to get to her grandmother in Lafayette, but she ran out of money. I bought her a meal and let her sleep on my floor. I wanted to help more, but I couldn't get to the money—I was afraid Cisco was watching the bus terminal.*

So, one day I was cleaning this guy's room and found his wallet in the bathroom. It was stuffed with cash. I figured he wouldn't notice if I took a couple of bills—just enough to buy her a bus ticket to Louisiana and maybe a couple of candy bars for the ride. It was a worthy cause, after all. I stuffed a fifty and a twenty in my pocket, and was putting the wallet back when the guy walked in. He pressed charges, and they accused me of taking the whole $1500 in his wallet.

I did twelve months. You're probably pissed to hear that, but it is what it is. Jail was scary enough, but then a drug-runner's girl told me Cisco would be waiting for me when I got out.

I gotta get to work. I'll tell you more later. But I'm writing this, so you know I survived.

Nevada

* * *

Nevada

Indian medicine is no joke—when I put my shoes on this morning, my heels are almost all healed. I barely feel the blisters when I go out to feed the sheep. My legs are sore, but that's no big deal. I step out into the pre-dawn. Still need my jacket, but the wind doesn't cut through me like a cleaver through steak. I'm sweating by the time I lug the hay to the enclosure. I make sure I get all the cut twine, like Joseph showed me. Little Dude lips my jeans.

"How goes it, buddy?" I scrub his head. He likes that. The other sheep swarm, wanting some attention. "You guys are a kind of tribe, too, huh? Must be nice to be safe together when it's cold, and the coyotes howl." I squat on my heels, so I'm even with them. It's warmer down here. "I have a coyote after me. A really mean one. I've been running from him for a long time now. See, human coyotes have long memories and they don't give up." I tug Little Dude's ears. He likes that, too. "See, he has to show the other coyotes that people can't get away with stealing from him." I scrub my palms over my cheeks and stand. "I'll see you guys tonight, okay? Be good to each other today."

I'm in the truck waiting when Joseph comes out.

He climbs in. "You could have come to the door."

"Why? I knew you'd end up here eventually." I clip my seat belt. "What do sheep eat besides hay?"

The truck cranks a long time before the engine finally catches. "Grass."

"No, I mean like what do they eat for dessert?"

He smiles big. "Ah, the lamb."

I try to hold my mouth straight and manage—mostly. "I call him Little Dude."

"He's an early lamb. A ram got to his momma late in the season, but we'll have more babies soon." He turns the truck and heads down the tire tracks that lead to the road. "The sheep like fruit. And carrots."

Maybe I can stuff a couple in my pockets at work.

"Don't even think about it." He's watching the road.

"About what?"

"Taking carrots from the café. If you want them, we'll run by O'Grady's on the way home."

"Oh. Okay." I know my face didn't give me away. Most people don't notice me. I'm invisible on purpose; just some generic chick. But this guy pays attention. I'll have to remember that.

"How did you like running yesterday? Except for the blisters, of course."

"It was okay. The stuff you used on my heels helped. Thanks."

We're quiet for a mile after he pulls out on the blacktop.

"I run with the Wings on Tuesday and Thursday mornings."

"Why you telling me?"

He chews his lower lip a minute, then looks at me with that stare-into-me look. "You want to come running with us?"

"I thought that was an Indian thing."

"Well, there's no law against a bilagáana running with us."

"I don't know. They probably won't be happy about a paleface showing up."

"You afraid?"

I snort. "Yeah, right." If I can survive the gangs in Houston schools and in prison, a few Indians can't be that tough. "How far do you run?"

"Only a little farther than we did yesterday. But you'll need to get some running shoes."

Running was cool, and I slept good for a change. But use more of Cisco's money? I've only spent a little on essentials: my bus ticket, this stupid shirt, some soup. Which, when I think about it, is kind of dumb. If he catches me, I'm just as dead with the money as I am if I blow it all.

But it's not only drug money—it's stolen money. And I don't steal.

Mostly.

"If you don't want to—"

"I'll go."

When we get to the café, I hang up my backpack and jacket, tie on an apron, and get to work. Someone must've told people we're giving away free beer or something, because the line is out the door all morning.

Midmorning, I'm emptying the dishwasher when Carly pushes through the kitchen door, carrying the baby in her arms. "I come bearing paychecks."

Lorelei steps out of her office. "And Faith!" She holds out her arms. "Come here, little one."

Carly hands the baby over, and she grabs fistfuls of Lorelei's hair. "Ow, ow, ow."

"Yeah, meant to warn you about that."

"You and I are going to have a good talk, girlfriend," Lorelei says to the baby as she walks back into her office, holding her hair out of reach.

Carly looks at me. "You. Me. Outside." She holds the back door open.

"What'd I do?" I step outside, and she lets the door fall closed.

"Nothing. But we haven't talked since you started, and I wanted to check in with you."

I forgot about what a mother hen Carly is. I look down at my feet. "I'm okay. I'm in an RV, out at Joseph's place."

She rolls her eyes. "Hon, this is Unforgiven. I know that. Question is, do you want to stay there?"

"Yes." It's out before I can stop it. My heart bangs my ribs. I don't want her thinking that I want to stay with Joseph. Or more, *why* I want to stay. *I* don't even want to think about that. Him, naked, flashes in my mind.

"Nevada Sweet. Are you blushing?"

"No. Look. We've done this before. I can handle my own life. Don't you have enough to keep you busy?"

The corners of her mouth curl up, and she nods. "You

sure you don't want that apartment?" She says it in a singsong schoolgirl voice.

"No. Mind your own business, Davis."

She sobers. "Hey, just be careful, okay? Fishing Eagle is hard-core Navajo. He's never gone out with anyone non-Native. He's got a history, you know?"

No, I don't. "Tell me."

Curls bounce on the shake of her head. "Not my story to tell. You hang around long enough, I'm sure he'll tell you himself."

Yeah, that's the rub. I'm sure Cisco has people looking, even now.

She pulls a sheaf of envelopes from her back pocket and thumbs through them. "Anyway, here's your paycheck. It's not a full week, but I figured you could use it."

"I can. Thanks." I take it and shove it in my pocket. "Really. Thanks, Carly, for giving me a job."

The sun comes out in her smile. "Oh, Sweet, I like having you around. You keep things interesting."

Before I can stop her, she reaches over and hugs me around the neck.

I pull away. "Back up off me, Davis. You are the huggiest woman I ever met."

"Yeah, but you love me." She winks, pulls the door open, and is gone.

I'd never admit it to anyone, but I kinda do.

When I walk back in the dining room, it's busier than ever so, coffeepot in one hand, iced tea pitcher in the other, I go on refill patrol. I usually ignore people talking to me, but I've been thinking—I owe it to Carly to at least try, so today, I answer them.

"No, I'm not from around here. Nowhere you'd know." "Name is Nevada, like the state." "No, I don't know why my mom named me that." "Yeah, I guess your town is okay."

At the counter, a guy introduces himself as Moe Wrigley, the owner of the Unforgiven Barber Shop. He asks if I know how Unforgiven got its name.

"I heard a story about a guy hung for running over a dog."

"Yeah, well, don't believe most of what Manny Stipple tells you. See, there was this seven-year-old little girl, way back when, the daughter of settlers. She was playing down by Chestnut Creek. Now that's a calm stream, except when there's a flash storm in the mountains. Then a wall of water comes down the canyon and turns it into a churning death trap. The little girl was washed away. Her body was found in a tree, six miles downstream.

"Her momma went crazy, wailing and pulling out her hair. One day, a trapper heard a rifle go off and went to investigate. He found the mother's body lying on the grave. Under her was a note that said, 'May God forgive me, because I can't.'" Moe shrugs. "And that's how Unforgiven got its name."

That story sounds as full of bull...pucky as the first, but I smile and move on.

At booth number two, there's a bunch of ladies who, from their pinched faces, are wearing their underwear too tight. I know they're gossiping, because when I walk up, they stop.

The one with the horse face points at me with long, skinny, Wicked Witch of the West fingers. "You. New girl. What's your name?"

"Nevada," I say through gritted teeth.

"Nevada...what?"

"Sweet."

Her nose goes up and she sniffs. "I am Ann Miner, head

of the Historical Society, as well as a prize-winning columnist for the *Unforgiven Patriot*."

She says it like I'm supposed to be impressed. "Yes,
ma'am."

"Miss."

"What'd I miss?"

She has zero sense of humor. Her lips pucker. "No, I'm a
miss. As in, I'm not married."

Big shock. I refill another lady's iced tea glass.

"One of my jobs is to interview newcomers to town. Kind
of a 'get to know you' piece." She pulls a little book from
her old lady purse and writes down my name. "I'd like you
to set up an appointment—"

Seeing my name written on that paper, my knuckles go
white on the pitcher. "No."

"Well, not today, or course. I have an important meeting—"

"No. Not ever." The odds of Cisco seeing a blurb from
a local New Mexico rag is small, but the consequences are
huge. Deadly.

She rears back, her chin tucked into her neck. "It will not
serve you well to be rude, young lady."

"You'll have to live with disappointment then, because
I'm not doing it." There's a fine shake to my hand, so I fist it
and shove it behind my back.

She squints up at me. "I think you'll find this town an un-
friendly place if you continue this type of behavior."

I know her type: big fish in a toilet bowl, lording her made-
up status over people who don't know better. "Like I care."

"*What* did you say?" Her voice ratchets to a screech.

"What's going on?" Lorelei walks up. "Ann? What's
wrong?"

"This…this dishwasher of yours insulted me."

The woman across the table whispers, "She was rude. To *Ann*."

Lorelei takes the tea pitcher from me. "Nevada, why don't you take your lunch break?"

I start to say something, but she gives me a tiny head shake. Fine. I stomp for the kitchen. I've screwed things up. But what else can I do? There's no way I can have my name published in that paper.

* * *

Joseph

I jump at the hollow *boom* of the door and look up. Nevada barrels through with a full head of steam and a thundercloud expression.

"What happened?"

"I really tried to be nice. But that reporter lady is a mean old bi-witch."

"Ah, Ann Miner. What did she do now?"

"Aside from act like I was gum on her shoe?" She paces from the counter to the back door.

"She treats everyone that way. Besides that."

"She wanted to interview me for her stupid column."

"What's wrong with that?" Finally, we're getting somewhere.

Her brows come down and she crams her fists in the pockets of her jeans. "Never mind."

Lorelei bangs through the door next. "What the heck was that about?"

Nevada stands square, like she's ready to take a blow. "Nothing."

"Sure didn't seem like nothing. Ann Miner is about to have apoplexy."

Nevada stands, fists clenched, stiff and silent.

Lorelei's bangs fly up on her exhale. "Look, I know you have a problem with authority, and I can see how Ann would fluff your feathers. But she's an influential person in town, and people listen to what she has to say."

"I don't give a flying... I don't care what that old witch thinks of me."

"Not *you*. The Café."

Nevada freezes for a heartbeat. "You mean she'd talk bad about this place to get back at me?"

Lorelei crosses her arms. "You met her. Do you doubt it?"

The mad drains out of Nevada like she has a hole in her shoe. "Oh, crap."

"Now there's something we agree on."

"Can you talk her out of it?"

"I just tried. We'll see. In the meantime, eat your lunch and cool off."

"I really was trying to be nice. Right up 'til I met her."

Lorelei rolls her shoulders. "I know, I heard you." She walks to her office and closes the door.

Nevada stares at it. "Do you think she's going to fire me?"

I'm shocked to hear that she cares, but I'm not saying that. It seems the wild bird is settling a bit. "What do you want for lunch?"

She looks up at me, a little kid's hope in her eyes. "Can I cook for a while?"

She's had a bad morning. I hand her the spatula. "You can cook while I'm eating. Deal?"

The clouds clear in her eyes. "Deal." She steps to the order wheel and her lips move, reading the tickets. Then she turns and heads for the grill, her steps light. "What do you want to eat?"

"Fish sandwich?"

"I'm not going to say it—you make it too easy."

I lean against the counter and watch her work. "What is it you're afraid of?"

She carries on as if she didn't hear.

"Don't tell me you're not; I've seen trapped coyotes calmer. You shoot glances out the front window like you're looking for someone. You freak out about having your name in the paper, and you jump at loud noises like a stepped-on cat."

She drops my fish into the basket and drops a burger on the grill.

"If you'll tell me, I'll try to help."

She spins, holding the spatula like a weapon. "Did I ask for help? Do I look like I need help?"

No to the first, yes to the second. But I'm not saying either one. "You don't have to get all riled about it." I lean against the counter.

"What do you want?" Her eyes narrow. "Why are you being so nice to me?"

I doubt she wants the truth, but people who don't want to know shouldn't ask. "It makes me sad to see someone who's obviously never had someone care for them. About them."

"Don't you say that!" Fury flies from her mouth, and her face flushes crimson. "I have someone...had someone...I don't owe you an explanation." She heaves in a breath and turns back to the grill. "I don't owe you anything."

"Yes, God forbid you might take something you hadn't paid for. Maybe carrots for a lamb. But something for you? Never."

She nods and flips bacon. "Good. We understand each other."

I head for the door to the dining room. "You don't even know. Life is much richer when you let people in."

Before the door falls closed, I hear, "Maybe in your world."

What happened to her? There are so many facets to Nevada Sweet. Trying to figure her out is like working a Rubik's Cube. What combination will unlock her secrets?

I can no longer pretend my interest is as a casual observer. I admire her. I *like* her. But I made an oath to my grandmother and myself, to live our traditions, and to pass them on to the next generation. Nevada is about as far from Diné as I'm likely to find.

And yet, I invited her to run with the Wings. The girls probably won't be welcoming, but I think Nevada can hold her own.

It's me I worry about.

* * *

Nevada

Thursday morning I'm up way before the sun, have the sheep fed when Joseph comes out his door. He's wearing sweats and a hoodie, and his long legs eat up ground. He doesn't notice me in the sheep pen, just beelines for the greenhouse. Lights come on inside.

I head for the trailer, but halfway, I remember there's nothing to do there. And I have more than an hour to kill before we leave to run. Besides, my curiosity is up. I about-face and walk to the flimsy building. The plastic walls are intact, but they bulge and snap in the breeze.

The door opens quiet, and I peek in. Bare lightbulbs march down rows of warped wooden tables covered in pots, plastic flats, and dirt. Joseph stands at one, his back to me, filling more pots with dirt.

"Come on in, Nevada."

I jump, just a little. "Is that an Indian thing, knowing somebody is sneaking up behind you?"

"Hardly. The cold draft told me."

"Oh." Don't I feel dumb. I step in and close the door. "What'cha doing?" I take a few steps and slap a hand over my nose. "It smells like sheep sh—poop in here."

"Planting, and it is. Sheep manure is great fertilizer."

I step to the table. He's measured out the exact same amount of dirt in each of five little cardboard pots, and he's tucking two seeds into each. "Yuk. Is that sanitary? I mean, people eat the stuff, right?"

He chuckles. "Funny."

"No, really. That's gross."

"Are you serious? You never studied the carbon cycle in biology?"

Not telling him I didn't get that far in school. "Science wasn't my thing."

"Well then, get ready." He hands me a little miniature shovel.

"For what?"

"Farming is my favorite subject, and I never get to talk about it, because everyone around here already knows this stuff. All you need to do is fill the rest of the pots, and I'll plant, okay?"

"Got nothing else to do." I cram the shovel into a huge bag of dirt on the floor and sprinkle it into one of the pots. "What are you planting?"

"Tomatoes. I've already started lettuce, Brussels sprouts,

and onions over there"—he waves his hand at the tables on the left—"and broccoli, cabbage, and eggplant over there."

"Who's going to eat all that?"

"I sell a bit of it to the café, but most goes to my friends down the road, and to the reservation. These are only the crops that need to be started indoors. In April, I'll plant a bunch more outside."

"Like what?"

"Chilis, pinto beans, peas, peppers, watermelons. I'm thinking about putting in some quinoa this year."

"Wow." Though I have no idea what a quinoa is. "Why?"

"Because I love it. Spending all my days outdoors, working with the plants and the dirt, creating healthy organic food for my people. I'd be a full-time farmer if I could."

"Why can't you?"

"Because I give it all away."

I totally don't get the draw, but you gotta admire the effort. "I thought y'all were hunters, not farmers."

"Don't believe the Westerns. Almost every tribe in North America raised crops."

While he gives me a farmer lecture, including the carbon cycle, we finish planting and he shows me how to water with a garden hose hooked up to a sprayer. It's actually not bad in here, except for the smell. It's snug and warm, and a lot bigger than my dollhouse trailer.

After about an hour, he dusts his hands and tells me he'll meet me in the truck in a few minutes.

When I get to the RV, I wash my hands then change my shoes. My new runners feel like they were custom-made for my feet. Joseph was right: it's better to spend extra for some things.

Not a lot, though. Only what can fit in my backpack. I keep everything in it, all the time, in case I have to run. I carry it out and sit in the truck until Joseph comes out fifteen minutes later. In the light of the security lamp, I can see him shake his head as he walks around to the driver's side. The door squeals when he pulls it open.

"It's like a meat locker in here. Why didn't you come bang on my door?"

Holding my bored look, I avoid his laser eyes. "Might as well get used to the cold before the run."

The truck cranks long enough that I think it's not going to start. *Come on. Come on…*

Finally, the engine catches.

"I've got to spend some time Sunday working on that carburetor."

When we hit the road, he turns away from town. "You mean people live farther out than you?"

"Many. While you're running today, listen. You may hear the Gods speak, then you'll understand why we live out here."

"I thought I heard the missionaries came through here and converted y'all to the one-God thing."

He chuckles. "We take a broader view. We incorporated their God into the ones we had already."

"How many Gods do you have?"

"Oh, a bunch. But the one you're most likely to hear on the run is Haasch'ééHi'í, the God of dawn."

"Yeah, I don't think a god has anything to say to me."

He looks at me so long I'm afraid he's going to go off the road. "Gods talk to all of us. But most don't listen."

"What are you, some kind of preacher?"

"We don't need them. Every person communes with the gods through their daily lives and rituals."

"Must be nice to believe that there's a god or somebody, looking out for you." I clamp my mouth shut. *Idiot.*

I may not know much about him, but I know that he noticed. Luckily, he lets my comment slide.

In about five miles, we bump off the road and drive to a cluster of homes: single-wides, hogans, and prefab.

"Here we are." He stops in front of a group of about ten teen girls in sweats, bouncing around and stretching. They look through the windshield, spot me, and freeze.

Might as well get this part over with. I open the door and slide out.

The other door slams. "Everyone, this is Nevada. She's going to run with us this morning."

The oldest girl snarls, "She's bilagáana."

"Acute observation, Asdzáá. She is, indeed, white."

She crosses her arms and leans her weight to one hip. "Well, I'm not running with her."

At least I'm not the only one; he does that stare-through thing with the girl. "Then you won't run with us."

She *tsks* in irritation. "She doesn't belong here."

Like I need an Indian chick to tell me that. Been hearing it my whole life. I should'a stayed back at the trailer.

He looks from her to the other closed faces. "We know what it's like not to belong. Why do you want to wound an innocent person with that?"

She flips her braid over her shoulder, sneers, and turns away. "Then she'll have to keep up." She takes off running. The others follow.

Joseph looks at me, then trots after them.

I stand, torn. Lots of other places to be in the world than where I'm not wanted. But I was invited. And since when do I need Joseph to tell me it's okay? "Screw that." I sprint after them.

My new shoes are tight in all the right places and cushy in all the others. My feet feel lighter; like I'm barely touching the ground, almost flying. I catch up to Joseph and pass him. My jeans chafe a bit, but my hoodie is snug. Only my hands, cheeks, and ears are cold. I pass the littler girls, huffing too hard to do more than grunt at me.

The path is just a trail worn in the dirt, and I dodge plants with waving fingers and pads of cactus. The wind in my ears blocks outside sounds, making me aware of inside sounds: my heart pumping, strong and true; my own breathing, fast and shallow.

I pass a few more girls and leave their whispers behind. It's just me and the land. I hadn't noticed, but the shadows are retreating; the black landscape is turning brown, the gray lightening to tan and sage green. The air smells of wildness and cold, and as I pull it in my lungs, tension flows out. I look up as the first laser blast of dawn hits my eyes. Is this the God that Joseph was talking about? *Hello?*

My cheeks heat. What am I doing? One God or a squad of 'em; it's all BS.

My footsteps flush a small bird from a cactus. Its wings thrum and it flies straight up. Something in me rises with it. I recognize the feeling—I'm grateful to be alive, to be here, now, alone. I run on, grinning like a fool.

I follow the path that winds around and eventually leads me back to the truck. The older girls are standing around trying to look bored, like they've been here for hours.

Whatever. My elation is gone, replaced by snorts, strain, and sweat. I stop beside the truck and bend over, hands on knees to catch my breath.

"I heard that Fishing Eagle was renting to some white girl."

I look up to the ring four older girls standing around me, arms crossed. "Yeah, so?"

"You can want him forever. He's True Navajo—he's going to marry one of us."

I snort. "Good luck with that."

The tallest looks down her long nose at me. "Huh?"

"Look, you got me wrong. I don't want him, or any man. But you gotta admit, he's pretty old for you." I look from one to another. "And if he wanted to be married, why would he still be single?" I shrug. "Just saying."

The one with the buck teeth smiles. "Oh, I get it. She's gay."

"Wrong again."

Another with holes in the knees of her sweats shrugs. "Hey, we got nothing against gay."

"I don't like people, no matter what sex they are."

"Then why not rent a room in town? Why live with Fishing Eagle?"

"He offered." I toss her a witchy smile. "Eat your heart out."

Her eyes narrow and she grabs my bicep. "You're evil."

I snatch her hand and throw it off. "And don't you forget it." I grind the words in my molars and spit them at her.

Man, if I didn't know better, I'd think I sounded like a jealous girlfriend.

We're nose to nose when Joseph runs in. "Hey, hey, what's going on here?"

"Her, that's what." She whirls to face him. "Why are you, of all people, messing with a white girl?"

He straightens like she's just slapped him. "I'm not *messing with her*, and you should know better. I'm surprised at you, Asdzáá."

"I'm surprised at *you*, Fishing Eagle." Anger and embarrassment redden her face even more. "Anyone can see you want her. The way you look at her. It says everything." She spins on her heel and sprints for the farthest house.

Joseph looks after her, his expression shocked, like the girl hit him with a board instead of just words.

His shock burns me like iodine in a cut. Does he find even the *thought* of being interested in me horrifying?

And why do I *care*?

CHAPTER 6

Joseph

My thoughts are arrows, shooting in all directions. But I can't keep from noticing, the air in the truck on the way home is frosty, and not from the temperature outside. Nevada sits leaning into the door, arms crossed, fuming. "So who am I, Quasimodo?"

"Huh?" I squint over at her.

"Never mind." She huffs.

I shake my head to try to forget about what just happened and focus on her words. "What are you talking about?"

"Look." She turns to me, lips tight, an angry line between her eyes. "You don't see me as a person. I get that. But to diss me in front of—"

"Whoa up there. Where did you get that idea?"

Her cheeks redden, and she looks away. "You know what? I don't want to talk about this."

I rerun the post-run showdown through my mind, trying to see what...oh. Heat climbs my neck. "You think...that

I find you...not..." How did I manage to squeeze myself between a rock and a hard place without seeing I was doing it? And how do I extricate myself without losing skin? "Um. You don't understand."

"I'm not dense. I get it. And that's fine, because I couldn't care less. Except, can you try not to show your feelings about me to other people? Especially ones who hate me?"

She glares from across the seat.

"You're cute when you're mad." It pops out before I think. The heat in my neck rises to my face. "I don't mean—"

"Right. Don't lie and try to make it better."

Lie? "Do you really believe that no one could find you desirable?"

From her startled rabbit look, she's found that hard place, too. "Nope. Really don't want to talk about this." She turns to look out the window.

That makes two of us. I don't know what shocked me more—Asdzáá's words, or my surprise at finding some truth in them.

* * *

In the middle of the lunch rush, I'm so swamped that when Nevada asks to help, I let her.

But it's awkward, two in a space that I normally take up by myself. We reach for the same knife, at the same time, and our hands brush. She leans left as I lean right, and our hips bump. I lean away, but with a grin, she bumps me again.

Well, you can't retreat from a bully. Everyone knows that. I bump her hard enough to push her back a step.

We're both chuckling when a voice comes from behind.

"Well, she's getting along better with you than she ever did me."

We jump apart. Carly and Lorelei are standing at the door to the dining room, watching with interest. So is the baby. From her stroller, she laughs and claps her hands.

Nevada's humor vaporizes. Her brows come down; her gaze falls to her feet. "We were just—"

"Working," I say. Nevada acts like it's a crime to laugh.

Carly is fighting a smile. "Hope they wanted those burgers well done."

"Oh, crap!" Nevada lunges for the grill and slaps the burgers on the buns.

I pull up the basket of burnt fries. "This'll just take a minute." I dump frozen fries in the next basket and drop it.

"We're not on the clock."

Lorelei smiles. "You're not in trouble, Nevada. What, I'm going to yell at you for working on your lunch hour?"

Carly studies Nevada. "It's nice to see you having fun for a change. You are real pretty when you smile, you know. But I still can't get used to you as a brunette."

Nevada tucks hair behind her ear. Red climbs her neck. "Oh, shut up, Beauch—Davis."

She winks. "Looks like you're settling in fine."

Lorelei pushes the stroller to the door of her office. "Faith and I have some things to discuss." She tips her chin at me. "Carry on."

Carly walks over and whispers, "You know, I was talking to Cora the other day."

Nevada, who was slicing tomatoes, freezes.

If I weren't so close, I'd miss Carly's whisper. "She said you left her at the Fort Worth rodeo. Gave some lame excuse and lit outta there like your tail was on fire. You want to tell me what that was about?"

Nevada's shoulders retract toward her ears. "If I'd have wanted to, you'd'a known by now, right?"

Carly sighs. "Same old Nevada—best defense is an offense. Fine, keep your secrets. But if you need help, you know where to find me."

I pull up the fries, and when Nevada offers the plates I use tongs to drop some on each.

Carly watches as Nevada walks to the window, sets down the plates, and hits the bell for the waitress.

I go about my business as if I haven't heard, but they have to know that I have.

Nevada lifts a plastic tub we use to collect dirty dishes, puts her butt against the door, but then stops. "I really don't mean to come off as ungrateful." Her glance bounces between Carly and me. "It's just safer for everyone this way." She pushes against the door and is gone.

There are commas of concern between Carly's brows. "Safer?"

Through the serving window, I can see Nevada piling dishes at booth one. I shrug. "I'm working the puzzle that is Nevada Sweet."

"I just hope you figure it out in time. Because it sounds like there's a timer ticking down somewhere."

"Yeah, but ticking down to what?"

Carly watches her, too. "There's something about that girl...vulnerability she tries to cover with snark and orneriness that I find impossible to back away from, even though I probably should." She takes a step and touches my arm. "I know you're caught by her as much as I."

I snort a laugh. "Caught. Good word."

Deep worry clouds her green eyes, like a stirred-up surf. "Please keep trying, Fish. If you ignore what she says, and watch what she does, you'll see she's special." She walks to her old office, and when she opens the door, I hear baby talk before she steps in and closes the door.

Nevada bends over the table, her soft shoulders swaying as she wipes it down.

It's taken me all morning to shake off Asdzáá's comment. I know Nevada's thinking about it, too, because I catch her shooting me looks when she thinks I don't see. I'm going to have to deal with my feelings about her. Soon. Somehow.

* * *

Nevada

The clock over the sink in the tiny kitchen reads ten when I look up from the paperback someone left in a booth at the café today. It's about a girl with another weird name, Scout.

Something bumps the wall of the trailer. Blood pounds in my ears so loud I can't hear over it. Bugs of worry scurry over my skin. I shoot a glance to the window, half expecting to see the pale moon of a man's face, peering in.

They've found me. I've gotta get out of here.

I turn off the light and wait for my eyes to adjust to the darkness. I can't see anyone from any of the windows, but that doesn't mean no one is out there. I tiptoe to the kitchen, listening so hard, I'm like a bat, *feeling* for sound. I slide open the drawer and touch a steak knife. Not much, but better than nothing, even if it only gives me the guts to meet them in the open, not cowering in a tin box. I grab my jacket and slip out into the dark, stepping away from the door, watching for movement.

The wind chimes tinkle a lonely sound in the light breeze. I walk about fifty feet out and circle the trailer. Nothing. Even the sheep are quiet. Asleep, probably.

They'd wake up if there was danger, wouldn't they?

It's clear and cold, but since the wind has calmed a bit, it's not bitter. A full flashlight moon shines bright enough for me to see my way as I walk out into the sagebrush, knife in a death-grip at my side.

The last time I relaxed, I almost got caught by Cisco's people at the Fort Worth rodeo. If they'd found out I was working her food truck, it would have put Cora in danger. I'm getting too settled here. Too relaxed. There's something about this town, but I can't afford to get sucked in.

No matter what Joseph says about finding a "tribe," it's safest if I'm separate. Outside.

Otherwise, I'll get to feeling all safe, which won't last long, because then I'll be dead. Cisco will never give up looking for me.

"Hey."

I jump and crouch, knife held in front of me.

There's no mistaking the lanky silhouette striding toward me, shotgun cradled in the crook of his elbow. "What are you doing wandering around out here this time of night?"

I drop the knife, straighten, and cram my chilled fingers in the front pockets of my jeans. I'll come back for the knife in the morning. I don't want him wondering about it. "I could ask you the same."

"I always look around before I turn in, especially this time of year. Coyotes come in during lambing."

Let's just hope they're only the four-legged kind. "Did you knock the side of the RV?"

"I did, sorry. Didn't allow for the length of the barrel. Did I wake you?"

His shotgun should make me feel safer, but instead, I imagine Joseph in a shootout, his bloody body stretched out in the mesquite. A shiver runs through me, making my hands shake like a junkie's. He may not care about me, but from my reaction, I can't even pretend I don't care about him.

He waves a hand at my feet. "You going to tell me why you felt the need to bring a knife out here?"

"Well, duh. You scared the crap out of me. You try being a woman alone."

He cocks his head and looks down at me. "You're not alone anymore. I'm here." His voice is soft, like he really cares.

Warmth shoots through my veins, melting my muscles, making me want to melt into *him*, to set down my worry and take shelter there in his strong arms.

Then I remember. He's not interested, and I'm a fool. He was out tonight, protecting his flock, not me. I look for something else to talk about. "It's really bright out here away from city lights. I've always liked the moon."

He glances up. "Ah, tł'éé'honaa'éí. I'm not surprised, since the moon was created by the First Woman. Let's walk. I'll tell you the story."

He walks slow, head down. "When the First People came from the underworld, they brought four lights, which they scattered over the four sacred mountains. But the people were unhappy because the lights carried no warmth and they needed more light to work. So, First Woman had two slabs of quartz gathered and had the craftsman shape them into wheels, which she decorated with sacred stones with special powers: turquoise and coral, horn and feathers. They were hung in the sky for heat and light.

"But the wheels didn't move, so one side of the land was bright and hot, and the other in cold darkness. So two old wise men stepped forward, offering their spirits to be bound to the wheels to let them move across the sky. And that's how the sun and moon came to be."

"Makes as much sense as Bible stories I've sat through."

"Why do you like the moon?" He sounds like he really cares about my answer. Like he really cares about what I think. I have to chill the soft spot on my heart before it spreads.

I stop walking to stare up at the familiar white face. "Growing up, I'd crawl out the window onto the fire escape, to watch it go across the sky." The words slip out of the hollow place in me. "When you're alone, the moon can be a friendly face."

The shadow beside me says, "You were alone a lot."

"You can be alone, even when there are people in the next room. Know what I mean?"

"I do."

I turn back to the trailer; home, for now. "I'll see you in the morning."

I can feel his gaze on my back as I walk away, and for some stupid reason, I feel safer.

* * *

Nevada

Saturday, midmorning, Lorelei calls me into her office and closes the door behind me.

"What now? I've been nice to customers."

"It's not that. You're doing fine." She lifts an open section of newsprint from the desk. "I didn't want you to find out when someone asked you about this."

It can only be one thing. I force my fingers open to take the flimsy paper.

BURIED TRUTH
By Ann Miner, lead columnist

You may have met our town's newest resident, Nevada Sweet, the new dishwasher at the Chestnut Creek Café. I try to be a positive, up-beat person, but I'm also a reporter—it's my job to tell it like it is. I'm surprised that Carly Davis would hire such a crude, churlish person to work food service. Perhaps she didn't know.

Since Ms. Sweet declined an interview, I did some online research to get background for this article. Imagine my surprise when it revealed a criminal conviction for felony burglary.

I'm a magnanimous person. I believe in redemption, and second chances. But Unforgivians have a right to know who their neighbors are, so they can make up their own minds.

"I'm sorry, Nevada." Lorelei's eyes are pools of sympathy. "She had no right to tell the entire town, much less in such a nasty backhanded way."

Her lack of surprise tells me that Lorelei already knew about my prison time. I imagine Carly told her. I hand her the paper, which is rattling from my shakes. "She is a b-witch, but she only told the truth. I just hope it doesn't hurt business."

"People know Ann, and her ways. I don't think it will. Besides, where else would they go? The Lunch Box for a side order of grease with everything?"

The odds that this rag would be seen in Houston are small. Unless... "Do you know if this paper is online?"

Lorelei frowns. "I don't know. I guess it could be."

If it is, I'm dead. Cisco is bound to have a Google alert out on my name, and how many Nevada Sweets can there be?

"I gotta take a break, okay?" I jerk open the door. "I'll be back." I snatch my jacket and backpack from the peg and, ignoring Joseph's startled look, run out the back door. The air is a cold slap before the heat of my flush hits. I jog past the truck and Lorelei's ancient Smart Car, skittering when my tennies hit icy patches. At the edge of the building, I cut down the alley, splashing through slush. The deserted sidewalk has been salted, so I speed up.

I'm not only risking myself. If Cisco thought I cared about anyone in this town, he'd hurt them to get to me. I'll pack tonight and have Joseph drop me at the bus depot on I-40 in the morning. Note to self: look up the schedule. Destination doesn't matter; only the pickup time. I fly past the Five & Dime, and at the end of the block, I turn right and leave the town square behind. I know I saw it somewhere along here... Ah, there.

The Unforgiven Library is housed in a blond brick building, which, from the faded paint on the side, used to be a feed store. Bouncing on my toes, I hold the door open for a mother and her toddler, then rush in. My wet soles hit the waxed tiles and I slip, almost falling on my butt.

"Be careful!" A startled librarian rushes around the desk, reaching a hand to steady me.

I take a step back, breathing hard. "Do you know if the *Patriot* is online?"

"Sorry, it's not, yet. I understand that's in the works for next year. I do have past issues on microfiche, though. Were you looking for something in particular?"

I lean over, hands on knees, trying to catch my breath and not laugh my relief. "No, thanks, that's all I needed to know."

"Are you sure you're okay? You don't look so good."

"I am good." For now anyway. "Thanks."

I turn away from her worried look, pull open the door, and head back to the café.

It would be safer for everyone for me to stick to my plan and catch the bus. But dammit, I don't want to. I've got a job that pays for my needs, and a warm bed at night. I've been hanging out in the wind so long, those two small things don't seem so small to me. Who's to say I'd find that much at the next place? And would I really be any safer? There's something to be said for living miles from nowhere—and having a strong guy with a shotgun living only steps away.

Besides, I'd miss some things here. Lorelei, and some of the crazy-coot locals at the café. And Carly. She acts like she wants to be my friend. The last time I tried to have a friend was in elementary school. I even got invited to two birthday parties. But that was before their mothers found out my mom's "career."

But might as well not lie; I'd miss Joseph most. I've been here all of two weeks, but already he and I are falling into a routine. Like slipping into a comfortable pair of shoes: they wouldn't fit everyone, but they fit you just right. This is an odd feeling for me, fitting with someone. I try to ignore it, but it's growing, like a special kind of secret. I find myself taking it out and turning it over in my mind, lying in bed at night and odd times during the day. I guess it doesn't hurt if no one knows about it, and as long as I don't delude myself, thinking that this could go anywhere. Even if I wasn't leaving, he's not interested in not-Navajo women. I turn down the alley next to the café.

If I let him matter, I'm gonna get hurt.

* * *

Joseph

"I don't know when I'll get out to see you, Ma. I've been busy." I set the wrench on the fender of the tractor.

Her sigh rasps in my ear. "The last time you were here was your grandmother's funeral."

And she doesn't know what it took for me to be on the rez then.

"I don't understand why you don't just sell out there and come live here. There are more people who need you."

"I have land to farm."

"Oh, please. The rez is, what, seventeen thousand acres?"

"Besides, you know the tribal council and I don't get along." That's one way to put it. On the rez, shame follows me like a second shadow. "Besides, there are almost as many Navajo here as there."

"But your mother is *here*."

"Ma, why don't you come live here, with me?"

"You keep asking." She sighs in my ear. "Joseph, only you hold your past against you. You belong here. Why don't you just..."

I tune out the same lecture I've been hearing since I got back from the Army, two years ago. Always the same thing. Guilt is an acid that distills with time, eating through the holes you patch, hoping that this time it'll hold.

"...and I'd think that you, of all people, wouldn't do that."

"Wait, what? Do what?"

Another raspy sigh. She's got to quit smoking. "Take up with a white woman."

"Whoa, Ma. Who told you that?"

"If you've forgotten how gossip flies like smoke from signal fires here, you *have* been gone too long."

Yet another reason I didn't return to the rez after the Army. "Let me set the facts straight. I have not 'taken up' with any woman, and you, of all people, know me better than that."

"Oh, then you haven't rented the trailer to a white girl?"

I feel my molars grind and force my jaw to relax. "I have." I've said all I'm going to say. The silence stretches like a bow string. With just as much tension.

"So, tell me about her."

I choose my words carefully. "Her name is Nevada. She's a friend of Carly Davis's. Carly asked me to keep an eye out for her, so—"

"Why does this girl need looking after?"

"Because she's all alone in the world, and she's running from something."

"And this is your problem, why?"

"It's not, Mother." I try to soften the steel in my voice. "But she's bright and obstinate, and so clearly needs help, in spite of being determined not to take anything from anyone."

"Oh, son, you can't lie to me. I know every nuance in your voice, every shade of feeling. You can still be true to your people and be happy, you know. No one said—"

"For cripes' sake."

"I am not judging you. If this bilagáana makes you happy—"

"Ma, I've got to go. I'll try and get out to see you soon." I lift the wrench and tap it on the edge of the crank case.

"Bring your white girl with you when you come." *Click.*

"She's not *my* white girl."

Twack! I hit the fender with the wrench, the metal sending shock waves up my arm.

Dammit, focus. If this tractor isn't running soon, I'm not going to be able to break on time, and then...

Why is it that I'm surrounded by Diné, and yet it's Nevada who has caught my interest? Her spunk. Her bravery. Her...body. We're in the truck together an hour a day; breathing the same air, touching the same bench seat. I find myself wanting to reach across the gulf and take her blunt-fingered hand. Her face is world-weary, but her eyes are innocent. I want to dive into her secrets.

But I have other obligations.

I go back to work on the tractor.

I've got to find a way to reconcile my past and my present. Soon.

CHAPTER 7

Joseph

I know Nevada gets bored on Sundays, so I bang on her door at dawn.

"Who is it?"

Her timid voice stops me for a moment. That's not like her. Who else would it be but me? "Joseph. Do you want to go running with me?"

She pulls open the door and shrugs, but I see the sparkle she tries to hide. When I tell her I'm taking her somewhere special, and we'll go in the truck, she changes shoes, then lifts that backpack full of money and probably everything else she owns, and follows me to the truck.

Funny, in the time since Grandmother died, it never occurred to me that I was lonely, until Nevada showed up. I drive out to the road, and turn right, away from town. She's leaned back against the seat, relaxed; as much as she ever is anyway.

Much as I've tried to deny it, Asdzáá's comment the other

day was true. She saw the attraction I was hiding from myself. And now my mother has her too-keen nose in the wind, picking up scents from ninety miles away. That means I'm farther into dangerous territory than I realized. I need to turn away. Stop before I get far down this new path.

And yet, Nevada is a mystery to me. I want to know more about her. Maybe if I can understand her, I'll be free to put this down and walk away. "Did you graduate high school?"

She tenses, frowning out the dirty windshield. "Nope."

"Didn't you like it?"

"It was all right. I liked English and reading. History was okay, if they didn't make us memorize dates and other useless crap." She shrugs. "Like I'm gonna need algebra to cook?"

"Why did you quit?"

"Why do the chicks in the Wings hate me?"

Again, the subject change when I get too close. "They don't hate you; they feel threatened by you."

"I never threatened them. Well, I didn't start it anyway. Besides, they're bigger'n me."

"You are small, but your snark is big. And sharp." I glance over. "Most of their lives they've felt 'less than.' Now they have the Wings and running—something that celebrates their achievements and gives them pride. Then you come along, and they feel like their safe place is being invaded."

"Then why did you take me?"

"You need to get to know the people who live here." I keep my eyes on the road. "And they need to realize that their pride doesn't need affirmation."

"Oh." Her mouth twists.

"So, why did you leave school?"

She turns her head to the mesquite rolling by the window and crosses her arms over her chest.

"The high school has GED classes at night. You could—"

"Did I ask for advice?" She glares at me. "Stop poking at me all the time."

"Yes, ma'am."

"I'm not going to be here that long anyway."

"Okay." I keep my voice calm, so she'll notice that we're having a conversation instead of an argument. And it wouldn't do for her to know it bothers me that she's thinking about leaving. Even though it does. A lot.

"You piss me off."

"Maybe you should look at what's really bothering you."

"What are you, a shrink?" Her face reddens and she looks like she wants to throw something. "You don't get to judge me. *You* clean up hurl when your mom gets a bad hit, lay on the couch, listening to her with a john, or go to school hungry...Just leave me alone."

I knew her childhood had to be bad. She admitted as much the other night. But poor, alone, and...no wonder she doesn't trust, or expect anything from anyone. I swallow the pity she'd hate me for. It's bitter as powdered aspirin.

A fierce protectiveness rises in me like warm bread. I want to wrap her in my arms and promise life will be better. That I'll keep her safe and make her happy.

I'm a fool. I'd hoped to tame a wild bird. Instead, the door is swinging shut on me.

I pull the truck off the road and stop.

She looks around. "How's this different than the land at your place?"

I open my door and step out. "You'll see."

She glances at her backpack on the floorboard, then toes it under the seat. "You're gonna lock the truck, right?"

"Right." When she scrambles out, I lock it. "Let's go."

I jog into the desert-scape, her footfalls behind me. No trail here—we dodge bushes and jump small stream beds.

Flat-bottomed gray clouds cover the sky like a lid on the world, cutting off the tops of the mountains on the horizon. I take off, running away from the road. The wind picks up in small gusts, but unlike the past week, it doesn't cut through my sweats. My leg muscles warm, and when I pick up the pace, Nevada follows, breathing easily.

After a mile, the ground changes. The little trenches become arroyos we run down, and out of. At the deepest one, I turn, and run along the edge. I hope she's not afraid of heights.

When I stop, she slides, almost ramming into my back.

"Why are we—oh."

She steps around me. We are standing at the edge of the cliff, overlooking the rocky plain that stretches to the mountains. I wave my arm. "This was all once our land."

"I'd be pissed about it, if I were you."

"What makes you think I'm not?"

"You'd never know it to look at you."

I turn and look down at her. "Don't believe everything you see." I step to a path at the edge of the cliff. "Follow me."

"I don't know about this."

The ledge is about a foot and a half wide, steep and rocky. "It's safe. I've been coming here for years." A big drop of rain hits the top of my head with a splat. "Best get where we're going before Tó Neinilii lets loose."

She follows, hugging the rock wall, watching her feet. Rain patters down, each drop raising a puff of dust on the trail. About fifty feet down, I take the corner into what I call my "cave," though it isn't big enough to deserve the title. It's more a depression, but it's deep enough to keep us out of the rain.

Her pasty face appears around the bend.

"Come." I reach out a hand, and she takes it. That last turn scared me, too, in the beginning.

Then she's beside me and we stand staring out at the rain.

"This would make a good place to hide."

Before I can ask, she fires off a question.

"What do you think happens to you when you die?" Her voice is thin, like she's squeezing the words out.

"We have a story about how men came to die."

She has a ghost of a smile. "Y'all have stories about everything."

"Almost." The skies open, releasing sheets of rain that flow in pulses across the valley. The desert releases its thanks with a rich, damp scent. "Long ago, one of the early Navajo people placed an animal hide in water. If it floated, no one would ever die. When he turned away, Trickster Coyote threw some rocks on top, sending the hide to the bottom. Coyote knew that if no one ever died, the land would become too crowded. Coyote can cause problems, but he is wise, too."

Mist from the rain pouring off the overhang touches my sweaty face, beads on my arms. "Death is just another part of the cycle. The Afterlife is just another plane."

"So you believe that something of who you are goes on after you die?" She sounds like a little girl, hopeful that Santa is real.

"I do. What do you believe?"

"I don't know. I hope all the religions are right, and you get to walk in the sunshine in some beautiful place forever." I see the gooseflesh rise on her skin. She rubs her arms.

This is the vulnerable side of Nevada Sweet. I'm careful to hold still, to not scare off the wild bird.

"Do you think there's a Hell?"

"We don't believe in that." I look down to her worried eyes. "You're too young to be concerned for yourself."

"No, not me. But I think we can make our own Hell, right here." She heaves a sigh. "I guess you don't read the paper, or you'd have asked by now. I've been in prison."

When I see she's serious, the chuckle dies in my throat. "For real?"

"Trust me. There's nothing more real than prison."

Despite her hard edges, I know she has a good heart. I sit, lean my back against the stone, and pat the dirt beside me. There's not much room in my cave. "Come. Tell me."

She tells an awful story, about working as a maid, taking money to help a runaway, and serving twelve months for larceny. She glances up, then away, like she's afraid to see my reaction. I'm the last one to judge. At least when she did wrong, she was trying to do good. "My people have an old proverb. It's wrong to have more than you need. It means you're not taking care of your people."

"Yeah, like I said, I don't have any 'people.'"

"You did then. That runaway."

She frowns out at the plain. "I guess I kinda did."

We sit in silence a while, watching the rain. If she can open up to me, I owe her at least as much. I swallow. "I'd be a hypocrite for judging you, since I know the inside of a cell."

We're sitting, shoulder to shoulder, and she leans away, to see me better. "No way. You?"

"Me."

She doesn't prod, just waits.

My eyes follow the sheets of rain. It's easier than meeting her eyes. "I was born on the rez. My grandmother taught me our ways, and when I was little, I soaked it up. But as I got older, and I saw that there was a big world out there that didn't live like we did, I got curious. When I got to be a teenager, I was antsy; rebellious. My father was long gone, but I'm not making excuses. My uncles tried to step in, but I was a handful. I thought I was missing life and couldn't wait to get away from home."

"I get that." Her voice is full of soft edges and understanding.

But she hasn't heard it all yet. "I learned roping from my uncle when I was little. I spent most of my time with a rope in my hand, until I got good at it. I was on the rodeo team in high school and got better. I researched, and the summer after I graduated, I hit the road, entering every event I could get to. Even eating only one meal a day, I ran out of money fast. I did odd jobs around the rodeo, helping with stock, cleaning stalls, stuff like that. My grandmother sent me what money she could." Shame burns, and I have to stop a moment, to catch my breath.

"I was lonely, and alone. The cowboys steered clear of me. I was Native, different, and they all knew each other. But I hung around the fringes anyway. They seemed comfortable in their own skins, with each other, and this world. They were what *I* wanted to be."

"You were a teenager. That's what teenagers do."

I look her straight in the eyes for the first time. "Did you?"

She shrugs and looks away. "It's pretty well established that I'm not normal."

Lightning cracks the sky, followed close by a loud boom of thunder that rolls in my chest. "Then I started winning, and things started to change. The guys accepted me into their fold; I guess through proximity and success, I proved I was one of them. At least, I went on the whole summer that way, thinking I'd found friends, somewhere I fit. The State

Finals Rodeo was in Albuquerque, and I somehow scraped together enough money for the entrance fees. This was my chance.

"My family came, to surprise me. I looked up in the stands, saw them, and froze. My mom, my grandmother, my uncles and cousins, fifteen in all. I was..."

"Proud?"

"Ashamed." I shake my head. "They would be a reminder to my new friends that I was different. I didn't want them to see; to know I *had* a family on the rez."

She winces. "Ouch."

"God, I was a fool. But it gets worse. I was nervous, roping. I missed a calf, then two. All the time, in my head, I'm blaming my family. If they weren't there, I could focus. I could win. After my events, I walked to the pen behind the chutes where the cowboys were packing up their gear. My family caught up with me. My uncle tried to put his arm around my shoulders and I shrugged him off, mumbled something, and walked away. My young cousin...he has mental disabilities. I always played with him back home, and I knew that I was his hero. He ran after me, yelling, 'Fishing Eagle, it's me! Hey, Fishing Eagle! Father, doesn't he hear me?'" My voice cracks, and I have to stop.

Nevada reaches over and takes my hand, a silent offer of support that I realize I've longed for. I don't know that she understands all I want; but that she'd reach out from her own pain to try to help me through mine makes my want burrow deep and put down roots. But I can't think about that now. Not when she's looking up at me, waiting for me to finish.

"I thought about turning around, but it was too late. My pride wouldn't let me go back. I gritted my teeth, put my head down, and kept walking. The guys acted like they didn't notice. Acted like I wasn't there. I was mortified, disappointed, and *pissed*: at my family, the cowboys, the world. But mostly at myself. What kind of person does something like that to the people who love them? I gathered my things, cramming them into my bags, hardly looking. I just wanted away. Away from the rodeo, people, myself.

"There were whispers, then a guy I never liked said, loud enough for me to hear, 'Did you see that retarded Indian kid? What's with that?'

"I lost it. I tackled him and took all my emotion out on his face. By the time they pulled me off, he was unconscious." I sit up straight, take a deep breath. "They took him to the hospital, me to jail. I don't know why my family would bother after how I treated them, but they got the tribal council involved, and I was given a choice: enlist in the Army, or face charges.

"I took the Army."

We sit in silence for a moment.

"You were a dumb kid."

"Nope. I was eighteen. The Army considered me an adult."

"Yeah, but still. Your brain isn't fully cooked at that age. Your family forgave you."

"I know my mother and grandmother did."

"What about the others? Surely—"

"I haven't really spoken to them."

She leans away. "What?"

"When I got out of the Army, I bought this land, and my grandmother moved here with me. The first time I set foot on the rez was her funeral."

"But your uncles? Your cousins?"

I shake my head and climb to my feet. "You ready to go?"

She scrambles upright. "Wait, you—"

"I've had about all the 'sharing' I can handle for one day. Okay?"

She holds my gaze for a moment, then nods.

I turn away from the soft caring in her eyes—the first softness she's shown me—wishing I deserved it.

* * *

Nevada

We're soaked to the skin, and rain drums the roof of the truck on the way back. I'm glad that Joseph felt safe sharing his story with me. I hurt for him. I wish I could somehow make it better, but I know now isn't the time. You can only push on a bruise so long without doing more damage.

God, I'm an idiot. I mean, he'd find out soon enough about prison, and I didn't tell him about what happened in Houston, but still, it's dangerous. For me, but for him, too. When I wonder why I can't keep my mouth shut around him, my brain feeds me the answer: because I care what he thinks of me.

His scent is stronger, thanks to rain and cooling sweat trapped in the cab of the truck, reminding me of the day I saw him naked. Rain is beaded on his strong, dark arms, and drips from his shiny hair.

I force my gaze out the window. It's one thing to hold my caring about him as a tender little secret close inside. It's another to wish it to be true. It's a wonderful feeling, but this...thing unchecked can tear me up inside when I have to leave.

We're almost home when he says, "Why don't you come to my house at, say, five? I have a surprise for you."

"What kind of surprise?"

He just lifts a brow.

When we get back, I feed and pet the sheep, grab a shower. There's still an hour before I need to go to the hogan, so I sit and finish Scout's story. I've never been real big on reading for fun, but this story sure was good. I wonder what I'd need to do to get a library card. Better not. I might not be here long enough to finish, and taking a book with me when I leave would be stealing. Besides, I travel light. I'll leave the book, and my soft secrets, here when I go.

I make sure it's exactly five o'clock when I knock on his door. I have no idea what this is about, but after today, I trust him.

He opens the door with flour-dusted hands, a towel over his shoulder, and a warm smile. "Come in."

I look around, but the place looks the same. Except he's cooking; the air smells of hot oil and frying meat.

He strides to the kitchen. "I'm cooking you dinner. A Navajo meal."

"What did I do to deserve—"

"Happy birthday." When he turns, he has a small, home-made cake in his hands.

"I...you...how..." Shock takes all my words.

He laughs. "You told me when you first came that your birthday was in two weeks. How close did I come?"

"It's—no, was—yesterday. I forgot all about it." He picked up on that tiny detail and went to all this trouble, just for me. I know how to handle people being mean. People not seeing me. People trying to hurt me. But this makes me nervous, and embarrassed, and *special*.

It's so new, I have no idea what to say. What to think. What to do.

"Hang on, oil's burning." He slides the cake onto the counter and steps to the stove and turns off the heat.

I squint at him. "Why would you do this?"

He takes two steps back to where dough sits in a dusting of flour on the counter. He pinches off a small piece, and works it, flattening it into a circle. "Your birthday is an important day. It shouldn't go by unnoticed."

Always was before. Oh, once Mom brought me home a cupcake from the day-old section at the store, but that was back when she had room in her head for more than thinking about her next hit. "Okay, but why did *you* do it?"

He rolls his eyes. "You may not know it, but this is how the civilized world behaves, okay? You do things for your friends."

He catches my glance and I can't look away. I'm trying to hold on to my armor, but it's melting in a blast of heat. "Is that what we are?" I never realized that niceness could be dangerous.

"Aren't we?" His hands still, and he waits, his dark eyes studying me.

His look has lasers that seem to burst through to the me that's underneath my armor. And it scares the snark out of me. If I say yes, am I giving away how I feel? "I—I'm not sure."

"Good enough for now." He nods, then carries the three dough circles he's made to the cast iron fry pan, turns on the heat again, and puts them in.

"Can I help?"

"No."

I walk around the big room, studying the baskets on the walls, each highlighted by little pencil spotlights high in the ceiling. I make my way to a bookshelf on the wall next to the window. They're all Indian books: basket weaving, leather working, Native New Mexico. I pull one out. *The History of the Diné*. I thumb through the pages full of drawings of Indians dancing, women working around fires, and more modern photos of men with rifles and dancers. I read the back cover. "Hey, can I borrow this book?"

"You're welcome to any of them."

I pick up the only thing atop the bookcase, a black-and-white photo in a frame. It's of a smiling Indian woman in Navajo dress, her arms around the young boy in front of her who frowns at the camera. "Who is this?"

He looks up and smiles. "That's my grandmother and me, at a powwow when I was little."

"She was beautiful."

"Yes, she was."

"You look pissed here."

"That's my steely look. I was pretending I was Chief Manuelito. He was our war leader, before we were forced on the Long Walk."

I don't know what to say. Sorry? I don't even know if my ancestors were in America then. Mom wasn't big on genealogy. But I want him to know that I hurt for what his people went through. "All that sucked for y'all." Smooth, Sweet. Real smooth.

But when he looks up, he doesn't look offended. "Thank you."

I don't know how he knows what I meant, but I let go of the breath I was holding, turn, and set the frame gently on the bookcase.

"Okay, now you can help."

I carry the book to the counter. He puts me to work pulling bowls of multicolor corn, cheese, lettuce, and tomatoes from the fridge. By the time I've done that and set the plates on the bar, he brings over a big bowl of fried loose hamburger, pinto beans, and a plate of the bread he was making. It's a combination of crisp and soft, a light brown circle like a tortilla only fatter. "What is this?"

"Navajo fry bread. We're having Navajo tacos. Sit."

I pile on the ingredients, then wait, not sure how to eat it. He picks his up and takes a bite, so I do, too.

"Hmmmm." It's like a taco, only better. This bread is amazing. "I think you just spoiled me for tacos for the rest of my life."

"You can find these all over the state." He doesn't look up. "Are you going to stay in New Mexico?"

Like I said, dangerous. I take a bite. "Hmmph."

We talk about everyday stuff through dinner: the town, the café, Wings. The light shines soft off his hair and the bones of his face.

I know he doesn't know what I'm feeling, so it's okay to relax and enjoy this. It feels so rare and special, I want to stop time, and just savor it.

After, we have cake. I'm grateful he doesn't try to sing "Happy Birthday." I'm not sure what I'd do...and if I cried, I'd never be able to face him again.

With him sitting right next to me, I can't help but be aware. He has long bones and a kind of graceful slouch, like a jungle cat, resting. He smells of sage; I don't know if it's from the spice, or the plant that grows all over around here, but it's nice. Kinda deep-down sexy.

My first and only experiment with sex was in high school. It seemed every girl in my school was getting laid and I wanted to get that whole virgin thing over with. I picked a nerd that I figured would be so grateful, he wouldn't blab.

It was good for him, he said. Me? I don't get the draw. Awkward fumbling and grossness. Who needs it? I can do it better, all by myself.

I realize Joseph just asked me a question, and I have no idea what it was. Blood pounds in my face like it's trying to bust out. What am I thinking, imagining sex and Joseph in the same ten minutes? "Uh, sorry. I gotta go." I hop off the stool.

"It's only seven."

I just wave a hand on my way to the door. "Gotta get up early and feed the sheep." Like I don't do that every day. "Thanks for dinner. And the cake. It was really nice of you."

"Wait, you forgot this." He walks across the floor and hands me the book I picked out earlier.

His eyes ask questions, and I can't look at him, for fear he'll see the answers on my face.

"Thanks. See you in the morning." I scoot out the door as fast as I can. The dark feels good. So does the wind, cooling my hot face.

I'd die if he saw the feelings I'm hiding. I learned early to hold a tough look, so no one knew I was scared all the time. I'm terrified, feeling that face slipping, when I'm around him. But the weird thing is, I'm not worried what he'd do—I trust him not to take advantage of it. I'm more worried what I'll do. I think that's what they call a slippery slope.

I could be in the wind tomorrow. A coyote howls, far off, and I scan the dark that isn't as friendly as it was a second ago. I hustle to the trailer, and I feel better when the stepstool is back under the knob.

What is wrong with me? I might notice a guy has a nice body, or something, but this…This is more. Wanting isn't me. It scares me.

But he's so nice. And he's the first guy who seems to care in…ever. I find myself wanting to relax into him and tell him everything. Stories from growing up, and not just sad ones. What I think about things I've seen, traveling. About my feelings I hide down deep. Just about anything, to have those soft, caring eyes on me.

And that could get both of us killed.

CHAPTER 8

Nevada

The truck's cab feels smaller today, and Joseph's sagey scent is making it hard to ignore him.

He glances over. "What's up? You haven't said more than two words."

"It's getting warmer, did you notice?"

He just raises an eyebrow at me.

Even his eyebrows are masculine; heavy and dark. "Hey, you wanted me to say something. That's all I got." I lay in bed last night, thinking about this until way too late. I guess my body got first, what my brain missed, but I'm cutting myself some slack—when you're worried about someone coming to kill you, you tend to be a little distracted.

But now that I'm aware, I'm terrified he'll somehow *know*. I'm not even okay with knowing it myself; I'd freak if he knew.

"Sounds like somebody needs coffee."

Subject change. That's what I need. "Do you want help in the greenhouse?"

His eyebrows go up. "Why, what do you need?"

"Why do you assume I need something?" I rub at an oil stain on my jeans.

He stares at me long enough I'm worried we're going to run off the road.

"Okay, I need to do laundry, and I'll have to pay you back by doing chores."

"Oh, for cripes' sake. You've gone all this time? Why didn't you just ask?"

"I've been washing stuff in the sink."

He just shakes his head. "I've never met anyone like you."

"You say that like it's a bad thing." I try for a smile, but I don't get one. "And besides, I kinda like the greenhouse. It's warm, and it's cool to see the plants poke up through the dirt."

"Ah, a closet gardener."

There's that smile.

"Hardly. How can you ever afford to live, if you give the stuff away?"

"I'm applying for a government grant to start a CSA farm. It would be enough to get me started."

"What's a CSA?"

"Community Supported Agriculture. It's where people buy a share, and they get a portion of the produce. Carly's in; the café will buy some shares. I know lots of townspeople will support it, but I need money, so I can quit work for a season and get it started."

"Wow. Sounds risky."

He shrugs. "Farming is always a risk. But just think. Good, natural food, supporting the community, the community supporting it. The Diné kids would have jobs." He sighs. "It's a dream."

He rambles on, about compost and insects and sheep poop. I only half listen. I've never known anyone like him, either. He really cares about people, and is willing to put his back, his money, and everything he has, where his mouth is.

Which only makes me like him more. And that can't happen.

Part of the problem is that I'm stuck in this truck for an hour a day with him. I need wheels of my own. I can afford it. It's about time I spent some of the money. Cisco might as well fund my new life—it'd be the first good thing he ever did. If I'm going down, why not go down large? Besides, if I have my own wheels, if I've gotta blow outta here fast, I won't have to wait to find a ride. Another thing I should have thought of a long time ago.

When we step into the back door of the café, Carly walks out of her office in a half apron. "Hey, you two."

I hang my backpack. "I thought you moved up to accountant. What are you doing in an apron?"

"Sassy needed the day off, and Lorelei is closing, so I dropped Faith off at Nana's for the day." She pushes open the swinging door to the dining room. "I just hope Faith doesn't come home swearing."

I pull an apron and follow her. "Hey, I've got a question for you."

"Ask while we get ready." She walks over and pulls out the coffee and filters.

I dampen a rag at the sink and wipe down the counter. "You're not riding your motorcycle anymore, right?"

"Austin would have a hissy if I did."

"Can I buy it?"

She stops, mid-scoop. "You don't know how to ride, do you?"

"No. But I could learn. Can't be too hard—you did it." Crap. "I didn't mean it like that. I meant—"

She rolls her eyes. "This isn't my first day, Ms. Snark." She chews the corner of her mouth, like when she's thinking. "Austin would be more than happy to have it gone. I swear he thinks that some pretty day, I'm going to take off on it." She thinks for a bit more. "I'll tell you what. I'll lend it to you."

"I've got money."

"It's not about money. Riding a motorcycle is different than a car. You may not like it. Let's just say it's a loan, and if you still want it after a month of riding, we'll talk, okay?"

The odds of me being here in a month are slim, but..." Okay." I catch her eye. "Thank you." I rinse out the rag and head for the booths, to wipe down tables and open the blinds.

"Let me check something with Austin." She pulls out her phone and dials. "Hey, babe. What'cha doing?...Oh, poor you, riding fence on a warm, sunny day...Hey, I'm going to loan the motorcycle to Nevada for a while. Would you teach her to ride, like you did me?" A blush shoots up her neck to her face. "No, not like *that*. And you keep her away from Chestnut Creek, where it curves by that mossy bank, y'hear?" She listens for a bit. "That's a great idea. No wonder you're such a brilliant businessman. I've gotta open, I'll call later, okay? Love you, too."

"I didn't mean for you to bother him. I can teach myself." They're trying to start up a rough stock business. The last thing he needs to do is spend time with me.

She turns to me with a smile. "He had a great idea. You

and Fish come out to our place on Sunday. We'll slap some burgers on the grill, then Austin will show you how to ride."

"I don't know if Joseph will—"

"What time, Carly?" he yells from the kitchen. I forgot you can hear everything through the serving window. My face gets hot.

"Let's say eleven. We'll eat, then Nevada can have her lesson. Okay?"

"Sounds good," he says.

I rinse the rag and hang it under the counter. "I'm bringing the meat. And don't you argue with me, Davis." I point a finger at her. "You know I can take you down."

"I don't know. That time I dogpiled you in the Costco aisle…"

I've gotta laugh. "That's the only time I've ever seen you mad enough to swear."

"Well, if anyone can drive me to it, it's you, Sweet."

"Mission accomplished." I glance at the clock. Time to open. I walk to the door and unlock it, but there's no one waiting on the sidewalk. "What the—where is everybody?"

Carly glances up. "Oh, they'll be here." But a lightning flash of worry crosses her face, gone almost before I grasp it.

"This is because of that broad at the paper, with her article." I stand in the empty doorway as dread thunks down, mushing my heart. "This is because of me."

"Oh, don't be silly. People are just running late on a Monday, that's all. Help me lift this bucket of tea, will you?"

But by lunch, even Carly is out of excuses. There have been diners, but less than half the usual. I bring a tray with only a few dirty dishes through the door to the kitchen to see Lorelei and Carly, heads together, with identical worried frowns.

I drop the tray on the counter with a clang. "That's it. I'm going over and kicking that Miner chick's butt."

"Oh yeah, then we can see what she writes *this* week," Lorelei says.

"It's not your fault, Nevada," Joseph says, arms crossed, leaning against the counter. I've never seen him so relaxed at work. Probably because he never has the time.

Guilt stabs at my gut. Trouble has followed me since that horrible morning in Houston. Now it's rubbing off on people around me. I'm the kiss of death.

"It's probably just that danged Dusty Banks, lowering prices at the Lunch Box again." Lorelei looks like she just sucked a lemon.

I rub my hands together. "This calls for reconnaissance."

"Oh no, Nevada, don't," Carly says.

"Why not? I've gotta eat lunch anyway." Before they can argue, I've grabbed my backpack, and I'm out the back door.

I cut through the alley to the sidewalk out front. The buildings block the wind and the sun is warm on my back. There's a faint tinge of green on the trees in the town square, like they want to bud, but are afraid of one last cold snap. A couple of people are wandering along the sidewalk, ogling at the stuff in the few windows that aren't butcher-papered-over.

Two blocks down, at the very end of "town," is a white stucco building standing alone. The faded red sign on top reads, THE LUNCH BOX. When I get there, I cup my hands and peer in the window. The inside is all red and white, like it's going for a '50s theme, but instead of trendy, it just looks old. Fly-specked windows, with the corpses on the sills. I step in, and tired gray linoleum leads me to the empty counter.

Exactly two of the tall-backed booths are occupied. If

Dusty Banks lowered his prices, people haven't heard yet. Suddenly, I'm not hungry. People staying away from the café is my fault. I turn to leave, but a voice comes from behind me.

"The special today is chili."

I turn. A tall, rangy guy about my age stands behind the counter, bright blue eyes lasered on me. His shoulder-length hair is black, except for an inch of blond at the ends.

"What do you say? You hungry?" He flashes startling white teeth.

Might as well scope out the competition while I'm here. "Sure." I straddle the bar stool. "I'll have the chili."

He wipes his hands on his apron, turns, and ladles up a bowl of chili from the squat electric pot on the counter behind him, adds a package of saltines to the plate, and sets it in front of me.

He offers a skinny, long-fingered hand. "Dusty Banks."

I don't want to shake, but his hand is hanging there. "Nevada." His grip is strong, but his skin is cold. Damn. He's gonna know I'm a spy. Unless he doesn't read the local rag—

His face lights up. "You work at the Chestnut Creek Café, don't you?"

Busted. "Yeah." I look down at the bowl in front of me. It's got a nasty sheen of grease and I don't see much meat.

He rests his elbows on the counter. "You know Lorelei West then, right?"

"She's my boss."

His face goes slack in a goofy look. "What's she like?"

He doesn't suspect I'm a spy...he's hot for Lorelei! I shovel in a spoonful of chili to give me time to figure out what to say. He's gotta be ten years younger than my boss. Grease slicks the inside of my mouth; I got a lump of tomato, no meat, and…There's a volcano in my mouth. I wave a hand in front of my face. "What'd you do, put ghost peppers in it?"

He smiles and pours me a glass of milk. "Nah, just habañeros."

When he sets the glass in front of me, I guzzle half in one gulp. "Where did you learn to cook?"

His brows come down. "Why do you ask?"

"Never mind. I've gotta get back to work." No way I'm eating more of that crap. I slide off the stool.

"Wait, you're not going to tell me about Lorelei?"

I pull out a couple bills and tuck them under my plate. "What is this, junior high? You want me to pass her a note?" I walk out.

Things are going south. I really need to blow town, but the thought pulls at something in my chest.

Dammit, I *like* it here. Maybe I could stay. Tell the police.

Oh yeah, they're probably going to believe that an ex-felon didn't steal all that money. That defense that didn't work last time. Then, on my word, they'll go look for a drug dealer who doesn't even live in their state. Yeah, 'cuz that's how it works.

My mood is lower than a Houston sewer when I step in the back door of the café. Joseph is eating a patty melt and it looks like Carly and Lorelei haven't moved since I left. They pounce.

"Did he lower prices?"

"Was there a line out the door?"

"No and no." No excuses left, I study my tennies. "It's me."

Carly grabs my sleeve and shakes it. "Ah, they'll be back. Don't you worry."

"Maybe I should go work at the Lunch Box. With my

reputation, I could put him out of business. But I don't know why his food hasn't done that already. I took one for the team and ordered the chili."

Joseph chuckles. "Moss says that chili gave him the runs."

"Good thing I didn't eat more than a bite, then. Oh, hey, Lorelei. Did you know he's got a thing for you?"

"I know what he wants." She crosses her arms over her chest and sticks out her chin.

I smile for the first time all day. "Wild, go-all-night sex?"

"No!" Her cheeks go pink. "He wants to shut us down. He's tried to hire Fish twice. I'm surprised he didn't try to hire you."

I wince. "Back to that reputation thing."

"Stop it," Carly says. "What we need is something to bring them back in. Let's put our heads together."

Joseph says, "We could give away a free slice of pie with every meal."

I've probably done more to take down the café than Dusty Banks ever has, and still, these people are being nice to me. I look at Joseph, and he winks, trying to make me feel better. Nobody's ever stood behind me before. "I gotta get the gum off my shoe. Be right back." I duck out the back door before they can see that I'm all leaky. I'm a mess of sloppy emotions: happy, guilty . . . but mostly, crazy-grateful.

* * *

Houston, Texas

Cisco sits in the back of his new Caddy, tapping his fingers on the leather seat.

His driver's eyes in the rearview mirror are worried. "Where to, boss?"

"Don't bother me. I'm thinking." The only sound in the car is his tapping.

His phone rings. He checks the number before answering. "I was just about to call you. Have you got her?"

"Not yet. It's like she dropped into a black hole when she left Fort Worth. You got any leads?"

"I'm not looking, idiota. That's why I called you!"

"I'm doing my best, trust me. My client is waiting for her."

"Mierda. I should'a known, I want something done, I gotta do it myself." He looks out the window at the late afternoon traffic snarl on Waco Street. "But if I find her first, your client won't want what's left. So you'd better try harder."

"On it, jefe."

He clicks End. "I'm surrounded by fools."

His driver's eyes are still on him.

"What're you lookin' at? Drive, fool."

* * *

Nevada

Despite a poster in every window on the square advertising a free slice of pie with your meal at the Chestnut Creek Café, a whole week has gone by, and business is still slow. Employees all act as if nothing's out of the ordinary, but the empty booths are anything but.

And with every day that goes by, the responsibility

weighs heavier on me. Carly depends on this place to put food on her table. And her grandparents'. The employees need their jobs; they're not easy to come by in this almost-dead town. I want to go out and shake every townie I see on the sidewalk, tell him I'm a good person, and drag him in by the ear, but I doubt that would make the right impression.

It's up to me to make it right. But how?

It takes me a while to figure it out; after all, I can be a little stubborn, and this is uncharted territory for me. After the lunch non-rush, I pull off my apron, tell Joseph I'm taking a break, and march out the back door.

I looked up the address of the newspaper in the phone book earlier, and spend the whole walk to the library trying not to think. If I do, I'll chicken out. I walk around the back of the building to a glass door with the *Unforgiven Patriot* in black scrolly letters.

I don't know what I expected, but it's just an office, with a counter up front, file cabinets on every wall, and a couple of cubicles. There's a girl wearing a phone headset at the counter, reading a computer screen.

"Can I help you?"

"Is—" I croak and have to stop to clear my throat. Good thing I didn't eat lunch, because it would be sloshing in my jittery stomach. "Is Ms. Miner in?"

The Wicked Witch of the West's head pops from behind a fabric cubicle screen. "Oh." She looks as surprised as if Dorothy and Toto just dropped into her lap.

And I'm feeling more like the Cowardly Lion. "Can I talk to you?"

She sniffs. "I'm very busy."

I'm finishing this. I walk around the counter.

"Hey, you can't—"

My "talk to the hand" stops whatever else the receptionist was going to say.

Ann Miner's eyes widen.

"I'm not here to make trouble. I just want to talk to you for a minute." I cram my fists in the front pockets of my jeans. My muscles hum with the message from my brain: *Leave, leave, leave!*

Her face is a mask of unconcern, but her pressed lips and darting eyes give her away. She's scared.

At least I'm not the only one.

"Look, about the article..."

"You can't claim slander. Everything I said is truthful."

"I didn't say it wasn't."

Her eyes narrow. "Then why—"

"Look, you can say whatever you want about me." I swallow. I know I'm taking a chance. If she's stone-cold-heartless, and not just your run-of-the-mill bully, I could be making it worse. "This is about other people. Business is off at the café. It's hurting Carly, and everyone who works there. And they don't deserve it." I watch her eyes for clues as to how she's taking this. "I came to ask what it'll take for you to back off. To make it right."

Her penciled-on brows come down. She's looking for a trap "What do you mean?"

"I can't be clearer. What do you want?"

She tilts her head and gets a gleam in her eye.

If she were green, I'd be looking around for flying monkeys.

"You, quit the café. You ruin the ambience for me."

My stomach drops to the floor of my pelvis, but I nod. I knew this was a possibility "Okay. But you've gotta promise that you'll write something nice about the café to help business."

"That's what you came here to tell me?" Her eyes are doubting.

"Yeah. What did you think?"

She touches her sprayed hair helmet. "I—I didn't know." She gathers herself, unhunches her shoulders, and her face changes back into the pinched spinster look. She lifts her nose. "I'll have to think about it."

"Nope."

Her eyes fly to mine. "What?"

"You have to decide right now. That's the deal."

"You mean that you'd pack up and leave, just to help Carly and the café?"

I shrug to hide that I'm squirming inside. "Isn't that what I just said?"

She stands judging me for what seems like ten minutes.

I force my feet to stay planted, and my gaze to stay locked on hers. It's not easy.

She turns back to the desk. "All right."

I've got my backpack; I'll just have to bum a ride to the bus station.

"You are rude and irascible, but clearly care about Carly and the café. That has to count for something. You don't have to leave. I'll write something in next week's paper."

"Really?" My breath rushes out of me in a whoosh as my muscles relax. I didn't know until right this second how *bad* I want to stay. I'm grateful, but damned if I'm going to tell her that.

No, I owe her that much. She's no Glinda, but she could've been much worse. "Thank you." I turn and walk past the shocked receptionist and out the door. I feel lighter.

It feels good not to turn tail and run for once in my life. To take responsibility. To take a stand.

Too bad that won't work with Cisco.

CHAPTER 9

Nevada

I leave the newspaper office, feeling lighter. I smile at the warm sun on my face, melting the ice inside me.

A dark Lexus with blacked-out windows turns onto the square. *Cisco.* My heart stumbles a beat, then cranks to redline. I duck into the alley next to the dime store on jelly knees and watch it roll past, real slow. This is it. The day I've dreaded for years. It pulls up to the curb, and the passenger window comes down. I recognize the Hispanic dude from the bad side of Houston; he's one of Cisco's foot soldiers.

He asks a lady I don't know on the sidewalk something, and she shakes her head.

He says something else, and she shakes her head again, turns, and walks away, glancing over her shoulder with a worried look.

"We've been here hours. Let's head to Albuquerque. Makes more sense she'd try to hide in a big city anyway." The window slides up. The car idles there for a moment, then pulls away from the curb. I watch it until it turns off the square, heaving giant lungfuls of air until the spots stop dancing in front of my eyes.

Gotta go to plan B. Easy to relax, easy to die. Why do I keep forgetting that? I never used to.

I step in the back door of the café and into Lorelei's frown. "You can't just walk out whenever you want, Nevada. There are tables to bus, Carly needs help with coffee patrol, and—"

"I just talked to Ann Miner."

"You what?" Carly screeches from the other side of the serving window. A second later there's a boom, and she barrels through the swinging door.

I shrug. "I apologized."

"You. Apologized," Carly says.

I nod.

"To Ann Miner." She looks to Lorelei, who can't say anything with her jaw hanging like that.

"Yeah. She says she's going to write something nice about the café in the paper next week. So hopefully, we should get busy again soon."

Lorelei puts her fists on her hips. "You beat all, Nevada Sweet."

"I don't care what you like," Carly says. "Prepare to be hugged." She steps over and wraps her arms around me.

I just stand there, arms trapped at my sides. "Enough, already." I step back. "It's not like I'm a hero—it's my fault she wrote that stinking article to begin with."

Carly smiles. "Maybe, but I also know what it took for you to do that. Thank you, Nevada."

"Can I get back to work now?" Cheeks on fire, I duck away from Joseph's stare, pick up a platter for dirty dishes, and walk out. Their whispers follow me. I guess when nothing exciting happens in a Podunk town, you have to make a big deal out of everything.

The shock of that black Lexus creeping down Main Street is harder to get over. I'm leaving soon.

* * *

On the way home, Joseph gives me that x-ray stare. "Why do you want to buy Carly's motorcycle?"

I just shrug.

"All of a sudden you need wheels? We're going the same place every day; why wouldn't we ride together?"

"I didn't say we wouldn't. But I can't be asking you every time I need to go somewhere."

"Where do you need to go, Nevada?" I can tell he's not asking about carpooling. His eyes are soft. They soften me.

"Nowhere, I hope." *Shut up.* "Hey, I'm a grown woman. There are things I need to do."

"Like what?"

Get out of town fast. "I don't know."

We pull up beside his door. He shuts down the truck. "Follow me."

I snatch my backpack from the floorboard and follow. He leads me around to the far side of the hogan, where a corrugated plastic overhang shades a cement slab beside the house, plywood sides sheltering it from the wind. I've noticed it before, but never checked it out. Inside sit a washer and dryer.

"Cool." I'm already imagining the feel of really clean clothes. "I'll work in the greenhouse every day to make it up to you, okay?"

He rolls his eyes. "Oh, by all means."

I point to a shelf above the appliances where some big

rocks and an old-fashioned washboard sit beside the deter-
gent box. "What are those for?"

"Those are my grandmother's." His smile takes a sad tint.
"When my mother was small, her mother washed clothes at
the river by pounding them on those rocks. When I was little, Grandmother used the washboard."

"Damn, that must've been backbreaking work."

"I don't think she appreciated any modern convenience as
much as this." He pats the washer.

"I'm going to go get my clothes, okay?"

"I'll be in the house if you need anything."

I reach up and run my fingers over the rusty galvanized
washboard. How cool to have old stuff passed down from
your family, even if it's just a couple of rocks.

I'm starting to realize that I have a hole in me, where
good memories and soft things should be. I didn't know
it before. When you're little, you think everyone is like
you. You can only start to see the holes when you see
how other people live and where they came from. Then
you start to feel around inside; to find the edges of where
things aren't. I haven't gotten all the way around it yet,
but I know enough to understand that it's a deep-space-size
hole.

Mary is old, and probably dying, but she has all those
memory-tied mementos to pass down to Lorelei. Joseph has
his whole culture, which has been passed down all the way
back before white men came.

I don't even remember my grandmother. Mom said she
died just after I was born. We didn't have anything of hers;
when you move a lot, it gets in the way. I'd always thought
of it as heavy baggage, and I travel light.

But I do have one thing. I reach in my pocket and run my
fingers over Mom's NA welcome chip.

It's like Joseph's rocks. Things don't have to be expensive to be priceless.

* * *

Joseph

Sunday morning, I bang on Nevada's door. "It's Joseph. Do you want to help with the breaking?"

The door opens. She's fully dressed and there's no sleepy edges to her—she's been up for hours.

"What do you need me to break?"

"The ground."

She puts a hand on her hip. "Look, I know you're all into this farming thing, but I'm not shoveling dirt on my day off, okay?"

"No shovel required. Come on, city girl." I walk away, and she follows. I'm glad for the sun, and the still wind, making it feel warmer than it is. I feel spring rising in me, like sap in a tree, and my body quickens.

"Beats the hell out of the alternative anyway," she mutters.

When we reach the tractor at the edge of the field, I pat the seat. "Climb up."

"This thing runs? I thought it was yard art."

"Nah, this old Farmall has a bunch of years in her yet."

She clambers up. "*Brrr*, the seat is cold!"

I chuckle. "Metal tends to be that way, sitting out all night." I step to the engine compartment. "Do you know how to drive a stick?"

"I've done it once or twice."

"Good. So push in the clutch. No, that's the brake. The

clutch is on the left. Good, now turn the key and pray to whatever God you know."

"Better not. You don't want me to get hit by lightning, do you? Here goes."

The engine cranks...and cranks. "Okay, stop." I pull a small spray bottle of ether from my back pocket and squirt some into the air filter. "Try again."

The engine fires right up. Then stalls. "What'd you do?" I ask.

"Do I have to keep my foot on the clutch?"

I pull a rag from my back pocket and wipe my hands. "I thought you said you've driven a stick."

She throws up her hands. "This is no car. The stick is between my legs, and I don't know where the accelerator is."

"Okay, looks like she's going to start, so I'll show you. Scoot."

"Scoot where? There's only one seat."

"Stand behind it." When she moves, I haul myself up and settle. "Thanks for warming the seat for me."

"Ah, so that's why you brought me out here."

Her smile takes the bite out of her words. I check to be sure the throttle on the dash is inched up, depress the clutch, and turn the key. When it starts with only a little cranking, I pat the dash. "See? Told you the old girl can still get with it."

"What?" she yells over the engine.

I just shake my head and let the diesel engine warm for a few minutes, then yell, "Hang on." I raise the throttle, ease the clutch out, and we bump over the weeds that have grown up since last fall. We hit a dip and her hands clamp on to my shoulders. Her palms are warm and strong. And I shouldn't be noticing. "Hang on," I yell over my shoulder, and her hands are gone, moved to the back of the seat.

I explain how to shift, how to drop the breaking plow, and explain turn rows. She's a quick study, and before long, we've switched places, and she's laying down only slightly wavy rows.

"Hey, this is kinda okay," she yells.

Tell me. The smell of turned earth—it holds the potential for new life. I've spent hundreds of hours on this seat, daydreaming, sweating, getting rained on—and enjoyed them all. If only I could spend all my days doing this.

I've put my application for a grant in with the government; I meet all the requirements, but there's no way of telling my chances. It depends on so much out of my control: available money, politics…bullshit. I don't hold much hope—I mean, what promises has Washington ever lived up to when it comes to my people?

I'd love not to rely on careless bureaucrats, to do it on my own. But I've been saving since I got back from the Army, and that amount wouldn't see me through the initial startup, much less insurance, electricity, and fertilizer. Hell, gas for this old tractor, for that matter.

Over the sound of the engine, I hear her singing, but not loud enough that I can make out the song. I tap her shoulder. "What are you singing?"

She sings louder, "*Old MacDonald had a farm…*"

I have to laugh. "What a naal'eełí."

"Old Fishing Eagle had a nalehche!"

"You totally butchered that."

"Hell, I don't even know what it is."

"A goose." It's good to see she's comfortable enough to relax. We bounce over ruts and I put my hands on her waist to steady myself. I can feel the vibration of the engine through her slim bones. I like breaking, but I have to admit, it's never been this fun.

* * *

The whole drive to Carly's, Nevada sits, knees bouncing, a bundle of energy with a lapful of packaged meat. I pull up in the Davis yard, but before I can shut the truck down, she's got the door open. Carly meets her on the steps, waves a *come on* to me, and they walk in the house, chittering like manic squirrels.

Austin walks over as I step out, but his eyes follow Nevada and his wife. "God, women. Endlessly fascinating, aren't they?"

"That's one way to put it."

He laughs, claps me on the back, and leads me up the stairs, across the porch, and inside.

The front room has wood floors and throw rugs and over-sized furniture. Over the fireplace hangs an oil painting of a cowboy riding a bronc through a campfire, scattering plates, dogs, and other cowboys. "Wow. This is way different than last time I was here."

"Combination of a woman's touch and a whole lot of sweat…mine, not hers."

"I heard that, Austin," Carly calls. "I did my part."

We walk into the kitchen. "Yes, you did, darlin'." He captures his wife around the middle and nuzzles her neck to make her giggle.

Nevada meets my gaze. She blushes and turns to put the burgers in the fridge.

"Stop it, horn dog." Carly smacks her husband's shoulder and tucks stray hair behind her ear. "Why don't you guys fire up the grill? We women have things to do."

Half-made deviled eggs and potato salad makings are scattered on the butcher-block counter.

"You got it, Tig." Austin nabs a deviled egg on the way out the back door.

"Hey!"

There's a cooler on the back porch, and Austin pulls two Lone Stars from it on the way by, handing me one. "Help yourself from here on. Only one for me, until Nevada's lesson is over."

We walk out to the grill beside a raw log picnic table. I sit, enjoying the sun on my face and the breeze blowing through my hair. "You've done a great job with the place. How's C&A Rough Stock coming along?"

He turns on the propane, fires the burners, lowers the cover, and sits across from me. "Better than budget, thanks to a stock contractor I know cutting me a sweet deal on some bulls and a couple broodmares. We'll have babies on the ground here in a couple months."

"Are you hitting the circuit with bucking stock this summer?"

"Nah. I'll wait until I've got some two-year-olds to buck in futurities."

"You rough stock riders always were a risky bunch." I shake my head. "Never had the urge to try."

He cocks his head. "That's right. I forgot you were a roper. Do you miss it?"

The few swallows of beer I've drunk surge into my throat, and I taste the bitterness of the past. "Nope."

He glances at the house. "I thought I would miss it like an amputation, but I don't. What with the family . . . and I help out with youth rodeo when I need a fix."

"Glad everything worked out for you and Carly." I wash out my mouth with another swig of beer. "Everyone knew you two belonged together."

"Yeah, well, bull riders are known for their hard heads, right?"

I shake my head. "Don't kid yourself. Ropers aren't much smarter."

The screen door opens, and Nevada comes down the stairs, a platter of burgers in one hand, paper plates and plastic silverware in the other. Sun shines off her short, brown hair, and she's smiling. It's all the prettier for its rarity.

"Here are the burgers. Carly says to put them on now, because everything else is about ready."

"Yes'm." Austin stands and takes the platter.

Nevada walks back to the house, and when the door slaps behind her, Austin says, "She's a handful, that one."

"When you get past her thorns, she's a real good person." I feel a dumb smile pull at my lips.

The meat sizzles when he lays it on the grill. "I'll take your word for it. She doesn't seem comfortable around me."

"If I had to guess, I'd say she's a little jealous."

"Oh, that's a good one." He chuckles. "Like Nevada Sweet wants domestication."

"Not that way. It's just that you and Carly have a close-knit family. She has no one."

He squints down at me. "She has you."

"She doesn't." Suddenly the sun has turned hot on my face.

He turns back to the grill. "Didn't mean nothing by it, Fish. Only that she knows you have her back."

"True, I have her back. But that's all." It doesn't matter that I'd like more. I made a vow.

The women come out of the house, arms loaded with bowls, the baby dangling from Carly's arm. Austin walks over to take the baby. "Look who's up from her nap. It's the Bean."

The baby's face lights up, and she reaches for her dad. Austin tosses her in the air and she squeals.

"You're going to drop her one of these days, and she's not going to think you're Superman anymore, Daddy." Carly puts the rest of the bowls on the table and sits.

"Nah, I'm her hero. Isn't that right, Faith?"

She's a beauty, with her momma's red hair, dimples, and startling blue eyes that must have come from her father, whoever he was. "I think you'd better buy a gun, for when she grows up."

"You must'a missed the shottie behind the back door." He hands the baby to Carly. "Who wants cheese on their burger?"

When we're all served, we dig in.

Nevada takes a bite of her burger. "Hmmmm. This is great. What did you put in it?"

Carly spoons a deviled egg and cut-up hot dog onto Faith's plate. "Good Schit."

Nevada gapes. "I can't believe you just swore."

"I didn't. S-C-H-I-T. It's a spice, blended locally. They sell it at the dime store."

"Well, the name is dead on. It is good shit."

Carly laughs. "Remember the time on the lunch truck, when you grabbed the wrong shaker and put chili powder in the soup?"

"Don't remind me." She groans. "Had to dump the whole thing."

"That guy isn't going to forget your soup anytime soon—he spit it all over his wife. Man, she lit him up." Faith is waving a piece of hot dog in a plump fist and talking baby-talk. "I know that's right, Bean. Hey, Nevada, tell them about—"

Nevada's sitting across from me. She ducks her head. "These guys don't wanna hear old road stories."

"I do." She looks up into my eyes and I'm frozen for a moment by a tiny shock of awareness.

"Hey, tell Fish the rattlesnake story." Austin takes a swig of the beer he's been nursing.

I smile. "I heard it, but never from you two. Come on, Nevada."

Red shoots up her neck. "Oh no—"

"Oh yes." Carly winks at me. "We're in the mountains, on our way to Alamogordo to meet Cora, when the truck broke down five miles out of Cloudcroft. Nevada had to pee, and…"

* * *

Two hours later, everything has been put away and my cheeks hurt from smiling. I realize it's been too long since I've gotten out like this. We all took turns telling funny stories from our past—though I noticed that Nevada's didn't go farther back than last summer.

Faith is toddling around the side yard, clutching her mother's finger, and I'm out front, sipping a beer on the porch steps, watching Austin teach Nevada about the bike. It is a pretty one; a royal blue Honda Shadow, with lighter blue flames rippling down the tank. Nevada's helmeted head nods, and she squats beside the bike to point and ask a question that I'm too far away to hear.

Today she gave a glimpse of the woman she would be if she didn't ride such tight herd on herself. Most of the time, Nevada is like a prickly pear, but this afternoon, it was like the cactus's flower opened, rare, vibrant…beautiful. I felt pulled like a bee to the sweetness.

I know many good-hearted, good-looking Diné women. I need to date more.

Austin lowers the back pegs, throws his leg over, pulls the clutch, and fires it up, talking to Nevada the whole time. She gets on behind him, holds his waist, and puts her feet on the pegs. He lets out the clutch, and the bike eases forward. He stops and demonstrates again, with Nevada looking over his shoulder.

When he lets out the clutch this time, he gooses the throttle. Dirt spits from the back tire, and they roar out of the yard. I have to smile at Nevada's joyous whoop.

Carly climbs the porch steps and sets Faith on a blanket, asking if I'll watch her so Momma can clean up the kitchen. I help the baby put colored plastic rings on a white plastic spindle, then she plays with my keys, then she holds my fingers and we walk around the porch. I'd forgotten how short a little one's attention span is. But she's happy and inquisitive, and we're both having a good time when the bike rolls back into the yard.

Nevada's arms are around Austin, hands on his thighs, her legs snugged right up under his. You couldn't get a sheet of rice paper between them.

Something shifts in my chest, like a snake coiling.

Austin shuts the bike down and Nevada steps off the back. When she pulls off the helmet, she throws her head back laughing.

Nevada Sweet. Laughing. *Austin* made her laugh.

Helmet in one hand, she gives him a high five.

The snake constricts, crushing my lungs. Knowledge smacks my consciousness like a speeding car into a hapless pedestrian.

I am jealous.

It's impossible to comprehend, because Austin is a happily married man, and Nevada...is Nevada.

Yet at the same time it's impossible to deny the truth, because I want nothing more than to step off the porch and beat Austin to a bloody rag, just for the high treason of being the one to make her laugh.

Faith squeals, and I look down to see I'm clenching her

fingers in mine. She looks up at me and, sensing my anger, begins to wail.

Carly steps onto the porch and lifts her crying daughter into her arms. "They're back." She's watching the two and smiling, so I know that must be the correct response, but it's beyond me. I turn to the yard, so she can't see that there's something wrong with my face. I have no more control of it than I do the snake in my chest.

I watch her, head bent to Austin's, nodding as he explains something. *Interest.* That's how it began. Somehow in the weeks since, it's morphed into . . . my mind shies from naming it.

I've gotten used to her, beside me in the truck. I've gotten used to coming across her, talking to my sheep. Seeing her small, tight butt running ahead . . . gotten *too* used to her. I've allowed myself to wander from my true path. It's past time I got back on it.

"Carly, thank you for everything. We have to go now."

"Why?" She puts a hand on my arm and pulls me around. "There's pie for dess—what's wrong?"

I hear the scree of my molars grinding and force my jaw muscles to relax. I long for my woodpile. My hands itch to clutch the axe's shaft. My arms ache to heft its weight. The only thing to take my mind off this is punishing physical labor that leaves my muscles spent and my mind quieted. "I've got something to do at home. I just remembered. Thank you for dinner. This was nice, really." I turn and take the steps in one leap.

Carly doesn't call to me, but I can feel her questions poking my back.

"Hey, Austin, it's getting late. Will you help me get this beast in the back of the truck? We need to get on the road."

Nevada frowns. "But I wanted to—"

"Look, we've spent all day out here." My words are as sharp as splintered glass. "I have things to take care of."

Nevada goes from open and smiling to deadpan in the blink of an eye. "You're right. I've taken way too much of your time already." She turns to Austin to thank him.

The snake rears back and sinks its fangs into my heart. Nevada never takes anything from anyone, and now I've made her feel badly about taking a bit of my time. My target changes; now I want to pummel myself.

Austin looks between the two of us. "I'll get a board, and we'll run it up in the back. It'll take two minutes." He jogs away, around the corner of the house.

Nevada walks to the porch and tries to give Carly back the black helmet with the gaudy pink flower on the side.

She refuses, and they discuss it.

Twenty interminable minutes later, the bike loaded and strapped down in the back, we pull out of the yard.

I feel her glances on my face, but I keep my eyes on the road. I'm pulled between wanting to apologize and wanting to yell. I've got to find a way to extricate myself from this...situation.

She turns to me. "Who put a bug up your butt all of a sudden?"

"I don't owe you an explanation." The snake bites again, but I don't care. If she hates me, she'll keep her distance.

"Oh, I see. You can pick at all my secrets, but yours are off-limits."

"That's about right." I nod.

"Okay, that's fine by me." She crosses her arms and slumps in the seat.

That lasts for all of two minutes. She cocks her head at me. "This freeze-out is not like you. What happened?"

"If you care, you shouldn't. Can we just not talk?"

"Hey, I'm all good with that." She turns to the window.

But without the distraction of words, it's worse. It's just me, the snake, and my tangled thoughts.

And the pissed-off woman whose scent fills my head, impossible to ignore.

* * *

Nevada

Joseph and I unload the bike, and ignoring my protests, he backs it into the hay shed, then disappears into the hogan. I don't want any special favors from him. Did I do something to piss him off? He was fine at lunch. It can't be about the bike; he offered to take me to pick it up.

And they say women are hard to understand.

I feed the sheep and hang out awhile with Little Dude. Joseph says the ewes are pregnant, but they're too fluffy for me to tell. I read about these sheep in the book Joseph loaned me. Navajo raised Churro sheep for centuries, but the white man almost wiped them out, seeing them as inferior to theirs. I swear, people get older, but from what I've seen, most don't grow up past junior high, politicians included. Maybe especially them. The Churro are coming back now, because the weavers prefer their fleece. And because they're sacred to the Navajo.

"See, Dude? You're sacred. That means super-special. And loved. Don't you forget that."

I give him a last pat and head to the RV.

I make myself a spam sandwich for dinner and then clean my Barbie-size kitchen.

Thwock!

I know that sound. I step to the window and flick the curtain. Joseph is at the woodpile, in jeans and no shirt, a red bandanna around his forehead. The sun is going down, and the gold rays catch on the sweat tracks on his skin. He sets another piece of wood on the chopping block, lifts the axe in a measured rhythm, his long muscles bunching and flowing. Then he brings it down with an explosion of power.

Thwock!

There's anger in that power, and in the set of his head, the tightness around his mouth.

I step away from the window, pick up the book, but then set it down. I feel storm-tossed; my thoughts and mood unsettled. My daydreams of more aside, I thought he was my friend. I should know by now—you let people in, and they tear you up. Well, forget him and his on-again, off-again. I don't need him.

But once feelings start coming, they're hard to shove back down. I pull out the spiral notebook and a pen.

Ma,

I miss you. But if I'm honest, what I really miss is the mom from when I was little. I don't remember a lot from back then, but I know we lived in a house with the yellow kitchen. And that sleeveless white dress you had with the tiny red polka dots, remember? I thought you looked like a model. And I remember your smell. Do you know the name of that perfume? I'd like to buy some, to spray on my pillowcase. You used to do that to help me sleep. Sure could use that now. I don't sleep so good anymore.

I guess what I really want to know is, was the high more important than me? If I knew for sure it was just your

*problem, I could let it go. I'm a grown-up. I don't expect you
to be perfect.*

*But what if it's me? If your mother doesn't think much of
you, how could anyone else?*

I do miss you.

Your daughter,

Nevada

CHAPTER 10

Joseph

The next morning, the atmosphere in the cab of the truck hangs like the weight of the air before a storm.

Nevada sits across the great divide of the bench seat, clutching her ratty backpack like a life preserver. She's been gnawing on her lip since she climbed in. I just hope it helps her hold back whatever words she's chewing, because I'm not ready to hear them.

She looks over at me. "You going to tell me what's wrong?"

I drape my wrist over the steering wheel, like my stomach muscles didn't just snap tight. "Nothing's wrong."

"You're lying. You couldn't see the pissed look on your face while you were chopping wood last night, but I did." She turns to frown out of the windshield. Despite her backpack shield, she looks vulnerable. "You want me to leave, I'll leave."

The air pressure drops. "No."

"I'll rent one of those places over the stores downtown. I could be gone in—"

"Stop it." The machine gun words bounce off the windshield.

"Stop what? I mean it."

"I know you do. You don't need to go." I don't want the complications of having her near, but I want her close. Closer even than the vast expanse of the bench seat. My arm wants to pull her next to me. Pressure builds in the cab. Or maybe it's just the pressure inside me. "Just leave it."

"Yesterday, you were fine, then after my ride with Austin, you were a jerk. If it's something I did, then just tell me."

"It was nothing you did." *And everything you did.*

She turns to me. "Then what is it? You're different, What is your problem?"

I didn't sleep much last night, wrestling with wants and needs and promises. I need to turn away, but I can't.

Her eyes are calm, steady. "I don't know if you don't tell me."

Maybe it's better to finish this. Get it out in the open, so she understands why there can be nothing between us. It'll be my problem to figure out how to live with the aftermath. I pull off the road and throw the truck in Park. I can't do this and drive, too.

"I told you that I went in the Army. I didn't tell you about coming home."

"So? Tell me." Her tone softens.

"My grandmother had cancer. She insisted my mother not tell me while I was away. She didn't want me thinking of her, and not taking care of myself. That's the kind of woman my grandmother was." I look out at the blacktop, stretching to the horizon.

"Wish I could have met her."

There's a wistfulness to her tone that pinches my heart and makes it harder to go on.

"When I got back, I moved her here, with me, so I could get her the best care, in Albuquerque. At least, that was *my* reason. Looking back, I think she gave up the home of her entire life on the rez, to make sure I was okay." The words come out in hitches and starts, hobbled by emotion. "She didn't want the chemo that the doctors recommended. They said she only had a five percent chance of five more years, even with it, but...I wasn't ready to let her go. We argued. I wasted weeks, angry with her for being *selfish*." The anger at myself that always simmers in my chest boils and spits, singeing my heart with pricks of fire. "It takes a massive immature, egocentric *child* to worry about myself, when *she* was dying."

Nevada sits with her arms crossed, looking out the window. "One of the hardest things to watch is someone going down, and not be able to do anything about it."

"That doesn't excuse my behavior." I stop to catch my breath, and the courage to finish. "Near the end, she wanted my promise to go back to the rez. To make amends with my family, and the tribal council."

"You haven't."

"I promised her that I'd spend my life passing on what she taught me to the young ones. To do what I can to help the tribe. To raise my children in the Diné way."

She winces. "Not quite the same thing as what she asked, though, huh?"

"Two separate things entirely."

Nevada's eyes are shining, but steady on me. "I'm sorry."

I grit my teeth to keep the sharp retort in. It's not her I'm mad at. "You, of all people, should know the last thing I want is pity."

"This isn't pity, idiot, it's empathy."

"Now you know. Not only why this thing"—I point to her, then me—"between us can't be. And you also know why you shouldn't want it to."

"I thought it was just me." It comes out in a whisper.

I glance over. Her eyes are big, big enough for me to see the innocence and longing she hides so well. It touches me in places I walled off, long ago. She knows who I have been and wants me still. "Oh hell." I unsnap the seat belt, and it retracts with a clang. I slide across the seat and take her face in my hands. She doesn't draw back—doesn't shutter the want in her gaze. When I lower my head, my hair falls, curtaining us. Our lips touch, a tentative bird's-wing brush. *Sweet.* I trace her lips with my tongue and she rises and takes me in. I fall into her, taking what she gives, and trying to give back.

When I realize she's crushed in my arms, and our breathing is loud in the enclosed space, I loosen my hold and force myself to back up. "That shouldn't have happened. Sorry."

She gives me a Cheshire Cat smile. "I'm not."

The wild bird I met weeks ago would never have allowed this. I should have realized, when you tame a wild thing, you're responsible not to betray their trust.

My knuckles are white on the steering wheel on the turn into the square.

There's a line in front of the café, waiting for it to open.

"What's going on?" Nevada rubs her jacketed forearm over the windshield, as if that will wipe away the illusion. "The paper won't be out until later in the week. Why are they here?"

"I expect because they're hungry." I smile for the first time since dinner last night.

* * *

Nevada

I want to sit mooning like a junior high schooler, savoring Joseph's kiss. Suddenly, I get it. Is this why he's been moody lately? He's been fighting against wanting me? *Me.* Nobody's ever wanted me before. Not really.

Cisco's minions left, heading for Albuquerque. They figure they covered this territory; I don't see them coming back. Could I even think about staying? A cloud of hope blooms in my brain. Could I really?

I'd love to sit and think about the possibility, and what Joseph said this morning, but there's no time for anything but trying to keep up for the first three hours. Lorelei has no idea what's going on, either, so she calls Carly, but she's as clueless as the rest of us. Lorelei tells me not to ask the patrons; it could jinx it.

But I need to know. So around ten, I go on a reconnaissance refill patrol. Most people meet my eyes, and a few even offer tentative smiles. I can't ask just anybody, because my mouth could go off and I'd be back where I started.

There are four ladies with pressed clothes and wrinkly faces in booth two, chatting over tea and bran muffins. *Most* old ladies are nice, right? I beeline over with hot water and the box of tea bags. "Anyone need a refill?"

One takes the box and pokes through it like a bird scratching up worms. The littlest one extends her cup for more hot water. "We know you wouldn't have stolen money from that man without a good reason." She pats the back of my hand.

"Wait, what?" The pot of hot water is suddenly heavy. Afraid I'll drop it, I plop it on the table.

The lady with the sugar-spun blue hair smiles up at me. "I think it's romantic. A lady Robin Hood!"

"Where did you hear that?"

The one picking through the tea finally chooses one. "On Ann Miner's blog, silly. It's all over town how you helped that poor runaway girl."

Thoughts are pinging in my head so fast I can't grasp one before another zips by. "Ann Miner has a blog. Online."

They nod.

"Did she use my name in this blog?"

"How would we know she was talking about you, otherwise?" She squints up at me, like she just realized I'm not very bright.

There's a crash in my chest—things are falling in there. I'm going to have to leave Unforgiven for sure now. Today. Not that Cisco would read a-nobody-from-nowhere's gossip blog, but if he has a Google alert out on my name, he'll know exactly where I am. I don't have my motorcycle endorsement yet but screw it.

"We should have known that Carly, that sweet girl, wouldn't have hired a bad person." She shakes her head. "I'm ashamed of the lot of us."

"I—I've gotta go. Y'all enjoy your muffins." They may have said something else, but I can't hear over the sirens going off in my head. That reporter did exactly what she promised. Too well. Chest tight, I stand in the middle of the noisy café and look around.

To think, just a couple hours ago, I deluded myself into thinking I could stay. What an idiot. I know what I did, and I know Cisco... as long as he's alive, he's not going to stop looking for me.

There's no choice; I have to leave.

At least I'll leave knowing I didn't hurt the café, or anyone here. Or Joseph. My heart shrivels, but I have no time for that now. Plenty of time for pain later.

All I see ahead are endless empty days: no strings, no contacts, no purpose but to stay one step ahead of a bullet.

But for the first time it occurs to me—is that enough to live for?

The rest of the afternoon, I'm on autopilot, while I try to pull together a plan. I need to run farther this time, but it can't be north. It's warming here, but on a motorcycle, seventy degrees is the new fifty. I can't go south; Mexico would be walking into the cartel's den. That leaves west. Nevada, Arizona, California…what does it matter? The only thing I know for sure, I'm flying solo from here on out. It hurts too much to leave people you care about. Jeez, I even fell for a scruffy little lamb!

I'm getting soft. And soft doesn't survive in a hard world. I learned that before I learned my times tables.

I'm not even buckled in for the trip home when Joseph asks, "What's wrong?"

"Nothing."

"Really? You've been a nervous wreck all afternoon."

"Okay, so it's nothing you can help with. Look, I've gotta think." But instead of mapping a route in my head, I spend the rest of the way home imagining what might have happened if I could stay. But I know that's a fantasy. He's committed to his twisted promise, and there's no room for me in that tiny, closed-in world.

He pulls up next to the sheep pen. "Looks like we've got a new lamb on the ground."

"Oh!" I scramble out of the truck to the fence. A tiny lamb on wobbly legs is nursing at his momma's side, his tail flicking like a windshield wiper on high. "How sweet!"

The truck door slams and Joseph comes up beside me. "Going to be a long night."

"Why?"

"The coyotes are attracted to the blood from lambing and come in to take the babies. I sit up with a shotgun to be sure I don't lose any."

Little Dude comes up to the fence. "*Baaaaah.*"

I stretch my hand over to give him a scratch and, ignoring Joseph's stern look, pull a carrot from my pocket. Surely Cisco wouldn't see the post the very first day. I mean, he could, but odds are against it. Even if he did, it'd take him a day or so to get here from Houston, right?

Today is Monday...If I leave by Friday, Saturday at the latest, I *should* be safe. Goddammit, I deserve that much, don't I? Besides, hard to imagine how I'd be safer than sitting most of the night with a gun in my hands. I'm being selfish, but if I'm going to die, I'd rather it happened right here. "I never go to sleep before midnight anyway. I'll take the first shift."

Joseph turns to me. "They're my responsibility."

"And mine. Don't I haul hay to feed them every day? Clean out their pen?" I frown at him. "You never treated me like a girl before. Don't you dare start now."

"Do you know how to fire a gun? You might need to, you know."

"I never shot one, but that doesn't mean I can't."

"Are you sure you want to do this? It's still cold at night."

I stare him down.

"Okay, come with me." He turns and walks for the house. After one last scratch, I leave Little Dude and follow.

Joseph comes out of the hogan with his gun, and we walk away from the house about two hundred feet into the scrub. "The good thing about a shotgun is that you don't have to be a great shot; you just aim in the general direction. The bad part is, it isn't accurate more than forty yards or so—and the shot scatters, so be sure nothing else is close you don't want to kill." He cracks the breech, shows me how to load, where the safety is, and how to sight down the barrel. Then he hands it to me. His eyes are warm. Trusting.

I almost drop it. "Unh. It's heavy."

"Yep. You sure you can do this?" He stands, arms crossed.

I tighten my grip and my stance. "What do you want me to aim at?"

"See that big mesquite?" He points. "Take off a couple limbs."

I lift the gun.

"Wait." He pushes the stock into my shoulder. "Be sure it's snugged up. It's going to kick, and if you don't have it held to you, it can break bones."

I try to hold steady the shake in the barrel.

"Sight like I showed you, squeeze the trigger easy. Be ready for the recoil."

It feels like I'm stepping over a dividing line—before/after. Maybe that's the way it should be. Holding something that could end a life comes with a heavy responsibility. I take a deep breath.

Boom!

The shock of the explosion runs through me, and the kick pushes me back a step, my ears ringing. "Holy shi—wow."

"Powerful, huh?"

"I'd say." I remember the drive-by shooting I saw in front of our apartment building once. How could someone aim at another person after feeling that power, and knowing what it can do?

"You hit it."

The mesquite is shredded. "Oh yeah, I'm bad."

He smiles down at me. "Small, but mighty." The smile slips, and his eyes dull. He takes the gun. "Why don't you grab some dinner, and I'll meet you by the sheep pen around dark." He turns and walks for the house.

When my heart pinches, I realize I'd hoped for a dinner invitation. Screw it. I've got instant soup. It's always been enough. Better get used to living spare again.

* * *

I work alone in the greenhouse most of the afternoon, watering and weeding the tiny plants. I'm kinda getting the draw—nurturing new life is rewarding, even if it's just a dumb plant. After sundown, I change into two layers under my jean jacket, and the wool gloves I bought at the dime store, and head out to the pens. The security lamp on a pole lights up the sheep pen, but beyond it is unbroken darkness.

Joseph is outside the farthest pen, so I walk around the perimeter to him. He's standing next to a webbed lawn chair, a rolled-up sleeping bag in the seat, cradling the shotgun in his arm.

"Are you sure you want to do this? You don't have to."

"If you told me I had to, do you think I'd do it?" I hope some humor will melt the cold spot in my stomach. It's just occurred to me that I might have to kill a living, breathing being tonight.

"Good point." With only a shadow of a smile, he shakes his head. "Spread out the sleeping bag. It'll keep you warm."

I open it, wrap it around me, sit, and hold out my hands for the gun. "I'm ready."

"Come bang on my door at midnight. Do you have a watch?"

"No."

"And you don't own a phone." He unclips the heavy watch from his wrist and hands it to me. "Midnight. Okay?"

"Yeah, yeah. Go get some sleep."

"I really appreciate this, Nevada. I'm usually a zombie, lambing week. This will make my life easier. Thank you."

I wave him off. "Go to bed." I can feel the flush in my face, even as pride warms the cold spot in my chest. I'm glad to be able to give something back in thanks for him being so nice to me. Even though I know it's not personal; it's just how he is. I finger the heavy watch, then slide it over my hand, even though it's way too big. It's still warm from his skin, which feels intimate, reminding me of his kiss this morning. I've never had a kiss like that. Strong and sure. And flat-out *hot*. It tugged at my heart, making me want to open all the secret places in me. I won't do it, of course, but before today, I couldn't have imagined ever wanting to.

I move the chair closer to the pen. Little Dude wanders over. "You going to keep me company? That's good, because it'll get lonely out here pretty fast." I pull the sleeping bag tighter around me. It smells of old campfires, and Joseph's sagey scent. I take in a deep lungful and hold it, staring out into the dark.

The sky is bigger at night—a black bowl over the world, pricked with ice-chip stars. The ground holds the heat of the day, but the breeze blows cold, bringing the smell of dust and wildness. The only sounds are the stirring of the sheep and an occasional skittering in the dark; a ground squirrel maybe, or a jackrabbit.

The dark expands, reclaiming territory. Why do we think we're so important? In the dark, you realize that all the stuff we stay busy with during the day is about as important as ants running around an anthill. Joseph's people have it closer to right, I think. We just share the earth with everything else on it; no better, no worse.

Little Dude sniffs at my sleeve, and I reach my hand through the fence to pet him. How cool would it be to settle down in one place and just live a small life in a big land like this? I don't know where I'll go next, but wherever it is, it'll be in the country, with animals. I'm done with big cities. This is better. Cleaner, simpler.

* * *

Hours later, the sheep are restless. I check Joseph's watch: twelve-thirty. I don't ever get more than four hours' sleep anyway. I'm not waking him until I'm tired. I stand and stretch. One of the ewes is off by herself in the corner of the pen. She walks in circles, then lies down, only to get up again. She licks her lips and circles again.

Oh man, she's going to have her baby. Her back end is bulging, and she's pawing the ground with her front feet. I don't want to disturb her, so I stay where I am, watching the night, watching her.

The gun gets heavy, so I lean it against the chair. Soon the ewe lies down and stretches off and on. "Poor momma. That's gotta hurt." I speak in a calm, quiet voice. I want to help, but I'm a city kid; verbal support is about all I'm qualified for. "It'll be over soon, and you'll have a sweet baby to show for it."

Tiny feet appear. Is that the way it should be? What if it isn't? I glance to the darkened hogan. I'll give her another half hour. If she hasn't made progress, I'll go get reinforcements. "Come on, Momma, you can do this. Hang in there. You're not alone."

Yip-yip-yip!

The long howl of a hunting coyote sends ice-water chills down my back.

Another answers. Closer.

I snatch up the gun. Adrenaline makes it easy to lift. I glance to the pen. The baby is out to the knees, and I can see its nose, nestled between. The ewe stretches again and makes a noise deep in her throat.

"You're okay, Momma. I've got your back." I click off the safety.

The sheep are bleating and milling. They must smell the coyotes.

Who smell the blood.

My arms and my knees are shaky, so I sink into the chair, pull my feet up, hook my heels on the edge, and prop the gun on my knees. That stops the barrel's shaking. The next howl is even closer. I strain my eyes for movement in the black-ness, so alert that my senses feel bionic.

I want to check the ewe, but don't want to miss...*there!*

Shadows shift, and eyes flash gold in the light.

"Get outta here!" My hands are slick. I wipe them, one by one, on my jeans. "I'll shoot, dammit. Shoo! Get away."

Four of them, close enough that I can see them slink in and out of the shadows.

I don't want to do this. God, please don't make me do this.

One darts in, almost to the fence, then away. I flip off the safety with shaking fingers. *Do not hit the sheep.*

Another comes in close. The sheep squeal.

"Scat!" I sight down the barrel and stroke the trigger. "Don't make—"

The largest runs for the fence, and leaps.

My finger jerks on both triggers, and there's a flash.

Boom!

The recoil slams my shoulder, but I hardly notice.

The coyote drops, rolls in the dust, and is still.

Reload! But I'm a ball of ice, frozen in the chair.

The other coyotes scatter into the darkness.

I stand and the barrel of the shotgun sways all over. I can't hold it still. I walk to the body. There's blood everywhere, and a gaping hole in its side. It's dead. My knees let go and I fall in the dirt beside it, breathing heavy, the world spinning. "Oh. I'm sorry. I'm *so* sorry." I reach to touch it, but stop, hand hovering.

"Nevada!" Joseph is there, beside me. He grabs my upper arms and sets me on my feet.

How did he get here?

"Are you hurt?" He runs his hands over me, his breath coming in gasps.

"It's not me." I force my eyes to the carnage. "It's him."

He looks down, then puts his fingers under my chin and lifts my face to the light. "You had to do it." He wipes his thumbs over my wet cheeks.

"No. I didn't. Why didn't I just shoot into the air? It would have scared them away. Instead, that beautiful wild thing is dead. Because of me."

"Aw, come 'ere." He wraps me in his arms. He's got a nylon windbreaker on, but no shirt. He holds me and I try to get a grip.

"It wasn't his fault. He was just trying to make a living..." My chest is tight, trying to hold the sobs in. They come out in tiny hitches that I can't stop. I want to stay in the safety of those strong arms too bad. I make myself step back and swipe my nose on my sleeve. "I'm okay. Sorry."

"No need to be. Life is sacred. It shouldn't be taken easily." He drops an arm on my shoulder. "Now, come see why you did it." He leads me back to the light over the pen.

The baby is born. It's lying in the straw, covered in slime, and Momma is up and licking it.

"Ahhhhhhhh." It squeaks.

And I'm crying again. Jeez, what is it with me tonight?

It tries to stand, and Momma's licking knocks it over. "Ahhhh." It tries again and, this time, makes it up on wobbly stick legs.

"That's more than enough for you tonight." Joseph shakes my shoulder. "Why didn't you wake me earlier?"

I can't talk past the ball of tightness in my throat. I wipe my nose on my sleeve again.

"You go. I've got this. Get some good rest." He pushes the middle of my back to get me moving. "And Nevada."

I stop. I don't want to turn and have him see my blotchy face.

"You did what you needed to. There is nothing wrong in that. Thank you for keeping my grandmother's sheep safe."

I don't want to leave him. Now, or in a couple days.

I climb into bed tired, but still I lie, hands behind my head, staring at the ceiling, for a long time.

CHAPTER 11

Joseph

I wake from my doze in the lawn chair in the morning. When I lift my head, my neck pops. There's no sunrise; just a lightening of the pewter-colored cloud cover. The slow drizzle that began around 2 a.m. hasn't let up, and the damp has seeped into my bones. There will be no Wings run this morning. I throw off the wet sleeping bag I've been using as a hood, stand, and stretch.

The new lamb is nursing, and the rest of the sheep crowd the fence, looking for their breakfast. I'll feed them. Nevada needs whatever sleep she managed to get last night. I walk the perimeter of the pen to the hay shed. I was surprised by her reaction to killing the coyote. She plays tough so convincingly, it's easy to forget that's not who she is.

I heft a bale of alfalfa and throw it over my shoulder, thinking about the kiss. I need to keep my nose in my own problems, and my focus on my people, where it can do some good for others, with no harm to me. I'm trying to be a better man than that selfish, stupid kid. Though Nevada almost makes me wish I was still ignorant. But hard-won experience comes with damage. I'd best remember that.

After a hot shower I dress, and when I bang on the door of the RV, she appears in her usual jeans and jean jacket and ratty tennis shoes, clutching her ever-present backpack, rubbing puffy eyes. Her look is unguarded, trusting, and flat-out adorable.

"Didn't you sleep?"

She yawns so wide her jaw pops. "A bit."

"Come on. We can't be late for work."

She follows me through the drizzle, climbs in the truck, props her backpack between her shoulder and the door, twists and settles, and is asleep before we pull out onto the highway. Head thrown back, her pale neck exposed and vulnerable. Her thin lips puff with shallow breaths.

Focus, idiot. And not on her.

I've made do with casual hookups, friends who also enjoy the benefits. The arrangement soothed the itch and solved the problem. I haven't wanted more. But now, it seems shallow—a shadow of what I really want—more. More connection, more sharing...just more. I find myself consumed by milky skin and light brown eyes. It's as if giving in to the attraction has made it gain strength, and like a magnet, it pulls at my attention, pulls her into my dreams. Last night's was the best yet. I dreamed I was behind her on our run and seeing that tight butt ahead of me was finally too much. I grabbed her, and we ended up sweaty and naked, on the bench seat of my truck. I plunged into her, over and over, and I woke up bursting, but unsatisfied.

I shift, to make room for the rod in my pants. I'm going to have to control this. My thoughts, my wants, my dreams.

She wakes when I pull in behind the café. "Thanks for letting me sleep."

"Least I could do." I duck out into the drizzle. I'm glad to get out of the cab, away from the scent of her. Busy. I just need to stay busy.

Nevada gets the café ready while I prep the grill and fire up the fryer. I'm getting condiments out of the walk-in fridge when she walks into it. It's only a narrow space between the racks on the wall; not enough room for two. "What do you need?"

"Ketchup and mustard, to refill the bottles on the tables." She points to the gallon jars on the floor.

I bend at the same time she does, and the sound of our heads cracking together is loud in the tiny space.

"Ouch!" She puts a hand to her forehead.

My anger flares with the pain. "Why don't you just let someone else do something for a change? You cause more problems, trying to do it all."

Her brows draw together, and the pain in her eyes isn't from the head bump. "Well, excuse me. I was trying to help."

"Well, you're not."

Her head tips back. Her nostrils flare. "You know what? Screw you. I'm tired of you and your crappy moods. And don't think I've forgotten that you never told me what species of bug got up your butt at Carly's last weekend."

"I just—" Her palm in my face stops me.

"I don't want to know. I don't care. A couple days' practice on the bike, I'll get my license, and I'm in the wind. You can take out your issues on somebody else." She spins away and takes a step.

My heart squeezes. She's leaving? Me, or Unforgiven? She can't leave town. Not yet. "Wait." I put my hand on her shoulder. It's warm under my hand.

She shrugs it off and turns to me. "What?"

"What is it you're running from, Nevada? Don't you trust me by now?"

Before I finish, her head is shaking. "You're too nice one second, a jerk the next. That doesn't inspire trust, dude." She walks out, then turns back. "But don't take it personal. I don't trust anybody."

"Now there's a news flash," I mutter, and bend to lift the jug of mustard. That's okay—fighting is good. It keeps me from kissing her.

Around ten, I'm dropping an order at the window when Carly blows in the front door, the blanket-draped baby in her arms.

"It's a toad-strangler out there." She stomps mud off her cowgirl boots on the mat.

"Carly Sue, you bring that sweet baby over here, right now," Bonnie Carver calls from booth three.

The baby puts her hands in Carly's hair and pulls.

"Ow, ow, stop that, Faith!"

Austin's mother is in booth three. She stands and extricates the baby's fists from Carly's hair. "Give her to me. I'll make the rounds."

"Oh, thank you. I won't be long."

"Aw, lemme see 'er," Manny Stipple slurs from the counter.

Moss Jones smacks his friend on the arm. "You'll just blow fumes all over her. Give her brain damage."

Grandma Davis winks at Carly. "I think you'd better plan on at least twenty."

Carly heads for the back, and the door booms when her palms hit it. "Hi, guys. I come bearing paychecks and presents."

"Paychecks are always welcome." Lorelei takes the stack of envelopes from her.

"And this is for Nevada." She walks to where Nevada is unloading the dishwasher. "I stopped by and picked it up for you." She hands over a booklet with a flourish.

"The study guide for the DMV test." Nevada's face falls. "Um. Thanks."

"Have you been practicing? The road out by Fish's place is perfect; almost no traffic."

She sighs. "Wanted to, but it's lambing, so we've been staying up...anyway, if it stops raining, I'm planning on doing that tonight."

"Well, you'd better study up, because I'll be by one afternoon next week to take you to the DMV."

"You don't need to—"

"Nevada Sweet, shut up." Carly wags a finger. "You're going to be a biker-chick. Biker-chicks take care of each other, so you're just going to have to deal with it."

"I just wanted wheels, not to join a sorority."

I flip a burger. "I'd think you'd fit right in with the whole biker-chick thing." Why does she look so sad?

* * *

Nevada

Thursday morning, I wake from a nightmare; the one that comes to me almost every night. I'm running in the dark, stumbling over sagebrush and rocks. There's panting behind me; the coyote is gaining fast. I trip and fall headlong, small stones digging into my hands and knees. I flip over, to face the jaws coming at my throat...*Bang!* I feel the shotgun blast in my chest. The coyote falls and rolls, and even in the dark I can see the gaping hole in his side.

I'm safe, but he's dead, and it's all my fault.

I scrub my hands over my sweaty face, then roll out of bed to get ready for work.

A half hour later, the chores are done, I'm in my running clothes, and we're on our way. I look out the window of the truck. Odd moments during the week, I'd stop, look around, and blink—as if my eyelids are a camera shutter—trying to stop time and preserve the picture in my brain. Not of anything special. Nothing that would mean anything to anyone else: the crowded café, a sunset, the lambs.

Joseph.

I glance across the bench seat to the hard lines of his face, his black hair pulled into a long ponytail. He's dressed in nylon shorts that show off the runner's muscles in his legs. His T-shirt has the sleeves ripped off, exposing the biceps he got from chopping wood and hauling hay.

I blink.

"What?" He looks at me. Into me.

I cut my eyes to the windshield. "Today, I'm keeping up with the fast wenches."

"That's not nice."

"Hey, they haven't exactly been nice to me." Since that first day, the older girls have mostly been silent, but they watch me out of the corners of their eyes. Then they snicker and take off, and I haven't been able to catch them. Until now. This will be my last day running, and damned if I'm letting them win.

"Give them time; they'll come around."

Time is exactly what I don't have. I've been practicing on the motorcycle, and I'm ready to leave on Saturday. I glance down at my bulging backpack. Sooner, if I have to. It's nice of Carly to offer to take me to the DMV next week, but I won't be here then. I'll just have to be careful not to get stopped by the cops.

The truck bumps off the paved road, and within a minute, we're pulling up beside the odd houses that make up the Native 'hood. I step from the cab, and ignoring the group of "cool girls," I stretch, then jog in place to warm up. I'm coming in first today, and those girls can just get happy. I bounce and shake out my hands.

"Yá'át'ééh abiní, dilwo," Joseph greets them.

"Morning, Fish," says the meanest girl. "I see you brought the one who can't run."

"Asdzáá, let's just enjoy the day." He leans on the bumper of the truck and stretches his hamstring. He always stays back with the young ones, to herd them along and make sure no one gets left behind.

"Hmph," she says, gives a tiny nod to her buds, then takes off, legs and arms pumping.

I'm ready this time. I'm on their heels when they pound out of the yard to the path that winds through the scrub.

The wind has laid down overnight; the air is cool and fresh. Bracing, I think they call it. The land rolls away, seemingly forever, and I keep my eyes on the mountains that materialize out of the dark at the edge of the horizon. The only sound is the slap of shoes on dirt, and shallow mouth breathing. I can taste the dust raised by the girls ahead of me. I won't be eating it much longer.

A half mile out, we start up the hill. This is where I always fall behind. I push through the pain to keep up, and lungs on fire, we top the rise. The six legs ahead of me slow to a jog, as they always do, allowing the girls to catch their breath.

Look out, chicks, coming through. My heart gives my legs a spurt of adrenaline, and I speed up, grinning as I pass.

"Hey!"

"No. Friggin'. Way."

The pounding behind me is close at first, then recedes as I pull away. A surge of triumph fills my chest, making me lighter until I'm flying over the land. I may be a pale-faced city girl, but they can never again say I can't run. After slinking and hiding for over a year, being on offense feels *so* good.

A half mile farther and my legs are about done. The girls are gaining ground—I can hear them behind me—but I'm not giving up the lead. Let them eat *my* dust for a change.

Sweat stings my eyes, and I run into the clearing on a wave of endorphins. I raise my fists like Rocky, just as the sun tips over the horizon, blinding me.

"Iiiiiieeeeeee!" A piercing shriek hits my ears.

Panic spurts into my bloodstream.

A dark figure barrels out of the brush, right at me. *Cisco! I'm dead.*

My ankle wobbles, then gives way, and I tumble to the dirt, my heart exploding in my chest.

I skid over the gravel, sharp pinpoints of pain flaring. The edges of the world go gray. Sounds dull.

It can't have been more than a few seconds when color bleeds back into the world. The mean girl, Asdzáá, is standing above me, yelling at a pudgy teenage boy. "Ashkii, you fool, what do you think you're doing?"

I'm not dead?

"Jeez, is she okay? I just wanted to scare you…"

"God, you're such a bisóodi. Get out of here." She pushes him.

He ambles off, head down.

My heart is banging my ribs hard and I can't get enough air. They're staring down at me like I'm some zoo animal.

My head throbs with an adrenaline hangover. It's like the fear has scraped off all my skin, leaving my nerves exposed. Pressure builds in my chest. I should get up, but I'm shaking so bad I don't think my legs will hold me.

It suddenly seems so hopeless. Is this going to be my life? Running from place to place, living in a bubble I create to separate me from people? No purpose, except to keep breathing. Living scared all the time, just waiting for the day that Cisco finds me?

"Are you okay?" the littlest of the faces asks.

"No." I cough out dust, dirt, and despair. "I'm so tired. So very, very tired." I hear the deadness in my voice, but I can't summon anything else; it's all I have. "Tired of running, tired of being afraid. Tired of being all alone." *Shut. Up.* These are the last people I should tell. This is like stripping naked and asking their opinion. I try to hold in the words, but I can't stop them any more than I can stop the tears falling in the dust. "I don't know what to do. I don't know what's right anymore. I just want to *stop.*" I sink my teeth into my forearm to hold in the words. My skin tastes of sweat and fear.

It's quiet, except for a bird with tiny chirps, somewhere nearby. I try to focus on that and pull myself together.

The littlest face above me whispers, "My brother is hiding out from the tribal police on the rez. I'm afraid for him."

The bird chirps for a bit.

"My dad hits my mom," another says. "I lie in bed with my little brother and sister and try not to hear his fists hit." A single tear tracks down her dusty face to join mine in the dirt.

Asdzáá's face is in shadow, curtained by her hair. "My little sister fell down an abandoned well last year. She can't walk anymore."

We just look at each other, suddenly recognizing: we're sisters in survival. We're the ones who knew long ago that fairy tales don't come true and bad things happen to people through no fault of their own, and all you can do is hunker down and wait out the tornado. They get it—there are some things you don't talk about. Not because they're awful—of course they're awful. But because there aren't words to describe how you feel about them. Or if there are, I don't know them.

Asdzáá reaches a hand down. "Come on. Get it together. Fishing Eagle will be here in a minute."

I take her hand.

I'm brushing off dust and embedded gravel when Joseph jogs up, his eyes wild. "What's going on? Asdzáá, did you—"

"Leave them alone." I squeeze her hand, let go, and swipe at my wet face. "They didn't do anything."

He puts his hands on my shoulders and bends a bit to look into my face. "Are you hurt?"

"Just leave her be, Fish. She's okay," Asdzáá says. "Right, Nevada?" Her face is deadpan, but her lips are thin and tight. She's telling me to put away my crazy.

I straighten. "Yeah, I'm good." I take a step and almost go down again.

Joseph grabs my elbow. "You're hurt."

"Nah. Just twisted my ankle." I shrug off his hand and limp to the truck.

The girls wave, then walk off to their own individual houses and their own problems.

Joseph fires up the truck and pulls out. I lay my head against the seat back, drained. I've cried more in the past week than I have in my whole life. Is it something in the water here?

"When we get home, I'm dressing that ankle. No arguments."

I'm all out of arguments, along with just about everything else. "Okay."

"Do you want to tell me what happened back there?"

Eyes closed, I smile. "I came in first, that's what." May not count for much in the world, but it means a lot to me. As well as what happened after, but that's between me and the Wings.

I sit trying to gather everything back into a pile: my energy, my thoughts, my dignity.

He pulls out his phone and hits speed dial. "Lorelei? Fish here. I hate to do this on a Monday, but Nevada and I are going to be a little late. She had an accident this morning." He listens. "No, no, she's fine, just a twisted ankle, but it needs some attention. We shouldn't be later than twenty minutes or so. Yeah, see you there."

I sit up. "Why'd you do that? I can be ready in—"

"Nevada Sweet." He points a finger at me, his face all stern. "You have to take care of your body if you want it to be there for you when you need it. No arguments."

He has a point. I've got to be ready to leave in two days. Wouldn't hurt to let him do his Indian magic on my ankle. "Okay, you don't have to get all bossy about it."

He mumbles something under his breath, and that's all the talking we do until he pulls in the yard and shuts down the truck. "Stay where you are." His stern voice warns me not to argue. He jogs around to my door, opens it, and tries to scoop me up in his arms.

"What? No." I slap at his hands. "Get away. I can do this myself."

"Really? Let's see…" He backs up enough for me to slide out.

When my feet hit the ground, there's an ice pick stab in my ankle, and my legs try to give out.

He grabs my arms. "Told you."

I lock my knees. "It's because my legs are trashed from the run."

"Here." He shoulders my backpack and slips his hand around my waist. "Okay?"

I could get to the RV under my own power, but it would hurt. I put my hand on his shoulder. "Okay."

He leads me at an awkward hobble toward the door of the hogan.

I tip my head. "Um. The RV is that way."

"You can take a shower at my place. I want to be sure you're close. If you need me, I mean."

He's sweated through his T-shirt, and the skin at the back of his neck is slick under my hand. His hip bumps me with every step. I'm sure I smell like a warthog, but he smells divine, like the sage has distilled, coming through his skin. I'm awkward, embarrassed, and uncomfortable... and I wish I could stay like this for a long time.

He opens the door and we hobble in across the floor, past the kitchen and living area to the bathroom that's too small for two people. I shoot a glance at the mirror. His skin is so pretty, muscles bunching underneath. He leans me against the sink, and I release my grip on his neck, but can't resist letting my hand slide down his arm. God, he's beautiful.

His eyes shoot to mine. Too late for me to cover up what I'm sure he sees there.

His eyebrows go up. Then come down. So do the edges of his mouth. "Gotta get you towels." He turns to walk out.

"Wait."

He freezes.

I pull at my backpack, hanging on his shoulder. "My clothes are in there."

He releases it, and walks out, closing the door behind him.

At least I'm not the only awkward one. I finger my short, sweaty hair. I wish I could let it grow out. Dishwater blond isn't great, but it's mine, and it bugs me to have to change it—like I'm not me. But that's the point, isn't it? I tip my head. Maybe black next? It'd make me look all goth, but it might throw them off. Maybe—

There's a knock and the door opens a crack, just enough for a rust-colored towel to fit through. "I'll mix up some salve. Come on out when you're done."

I know I'm making us even later, but showering in a place you can turn around without bumping body parts is so luxurious, I take my time. My muscles appreciate the hot spray, and I step out pink, my skin tingling. I dry off, limp to the sink, and pull on my "uniform": jeans, the stupid denim shirt, and the T-shirt that says *If you're happy and you know it, it's your meds* (worn inside-out, of course). I run a comb through my hair, and I'm done.

Socks and tennies in hand, I hobble out to the bar stools at the kitchen counter and sit. Joseph is waiting with his fingers in the jar of magic stuff. "This should help, but you're going to be sore for a week or so. No running for you."

Oh, I'll be running, just not the way he means. He sets my foot on his thigh and rolls up my pant leg. He rubs his hands together, and when he puts them around my ankle, an electric current shoots up my leg to my crotch. I shift my butt in the seat to stop the humming. His hands move slow, massaging the salve in. He moves in smooth circles, and I'm *hot*.

"Does this hurt?"

I moan, "If you stop, I'll punch you out."

He smiles and looks down again.

When the massage gentles to more of a caress, I allow myself a fantasy, one that's shown up the past week: *what it would be like if I could stay*. I know I could wear him down eventually—there's a tender look he gets sometimes, which makes me think that maybe I'd have a chance, given enough time.

But in a few days I'll be gone. A small sigh escapes. I'll ride away, and always wonder, what if?

"That's it." He pats my ankle and straightens. "Don't put your socks on. When I get out of the shower, I'll tape it. That should give you some support."

He's looking into me again. Just standing there, looking. Screw it. I have to try.

I wrap my hands into the fabric of his T-shirt, open my knees, and pull him to me.

Off-balance, he stumbles forward, catching himself with his hands on the counter and the seat of my chair. "What—"

I tilt my head and catch his mouth. If I'm going to make a fool of myself, I'm going for a ten. His lips are still at first, probably with shock, but when I press my tongue against them, he opens to me. I take him in like air, just as needed, just as sweet, like wind off the desert.

But it's not enough. I let go of his shirt and put my hands on the sides of his face, to pull him closer.

Safe.

I feel it when his defenses let go. Things change fast, and he becomes the aggressor, his tongue stalking mine, exploring my mouth, his breathing, fast in my ear.

My legs go around him without my say-so, and he lifts me, his strong arms holding me snug against his chest, hands roaming my back. My hips are plastered to his waist, and it sends bolts of wanting to my brain. I moan into his mouth.

It's as if the sound wakes him. He rears back, the look of a startled deer in his eyes. His arms loosen, and I slide back to the bar stool. He heaves a deep, shaky breath, runs a hand through his long hair, and steps back. His face gives me his answer: no.

Then he turns and, still breathing heavy, bolts up the ladder to his bedroom.

CHAPTER 12

Joseph

I hit the top of the ladder and strip, heading for the shower. No other way to say it; I ran away. Which would be embarrassing if my brain wasn't still trying to absorb the rock-solid fact that Nevada kissed *me*. Knowing she wants me makes me want to drag her up here and spend the day exploring her. Exploring each other.

Make that a cold shower—I'm hard as petrified wood.

I used to think I was on top of things. Maybe it's easy to do that from an impersonal distance; things get fuzzier the closer they get to *you*. I can run all the way across the state, chop all the wood in New Mexico. It's not helping. I'm out of control. And I cannot live through another bout of blowing up my world. I can hear the gossip on the rez now: *Fish? He's a dime store Indian. Ran around like he was the savior of the Diné, and now he's sleeping with a white woman.*

The cold water slaps some sense into me.

I climb down the ladder, still not knowing what I'm going

to say to Nevada. She's sitting on the stool where I left her, but her face is a thundercloud of anger.

"It'll just take a minute to wrap that, then we've got to get—"

"It's because I'm white, right?"

I don't look at her, just walk to the kitchen and open a cabinet door. "No, it's because you're not Navajo. I made a promise, and I—"

"You made a promise no one asked you to make. The one she asked you to make, you haven't done yet."

I find the Ace wrap and round the counter. My face burns. I trusted her with my secrets. I didn't do it to have it thrown back in my face. I kneel in front of her. "Hold your foot out."

She does. "So you can't be happy, because of some twisted logic you made up? Are you like those medieval guys, who wore hair shirts to pay for their sins?"

I glare up at her.

"Hey, I may not have graduated, but I did learn some things in school."

I look down, and start wrapping. "It's really none of your business, now, is it?"

"Maybe, but from what you told me of your grandmother, I don't think she'd be too happy with what you're doing, would she?"

I jerk the wrap too tight and have to start over. "Who are you to tell me about my grandmother?"

"Nobody. I wouldn't know, because I never had somebody love me like that. But I'd like to think if I did, I'd honor her last wishes."

I finish the last wrap, and hook the metal closures in. "Come on, we need to go."

"Joseph." My name is soft, and it pulls my head up. "My mom used to play old music, almost twenty-four/

seven. The words to one song stuck with me: *the truth you might be running from is so small.* See, when something lives inside your head for a long time, it gets bigger than it really is. You need to go to the rez. Talk to your family. I'll bet you anything that they forgave you long ago." She reaches out, strokes my hair. "We're all idiots when we're young. I know I was, and trust me, my sin was a lot bigger than yours."

I want to ask, but she pulls her foot away, slides out of the chair, and slips on her tennis shoe. "I gotta go."

"I know; we'll talk on the way in."

"Nah, I'm riding the bike. I need the practice." She walks for the door.

"Nevada."

She doesn't even slow.

"You know it isn't you, right? I'd love nothing more than to—"

The door clicks shut behind her.

She thinks I don't care. I guess it's better that way. I walk for the truck, trying to ignore the arrow lodged in my heart.

* * *

Nevada

"Jeez, Nevada, what's wrong with you today? That's the second plate you've dropped, and the high school principal had to go home to change after you spilled iced tea on him." Lorelei stands waiting for an answer.

I shoot a look at Joseph, but he's busy at the grill. "I didn't break anything. And that dude is a pompous jerk and a bad tipper besides."

"And here I thought you were evolving."

"Nope. Your Cro-Magnon busboy, that's me." I bend to lift more glasses from the dishwasher. Why did I ever think this job was fun? Scut work, that's all it is. Cleaning up people's leavings.

Might as well get used to it. I can't work as a cook again, since Cisco will know to look for me in a restaurant. Maybe I could find a job working with animals down the road. Wonder what kind of experience you need to work in a vet's office? Even if I'd just be cleaning out cages, it'd be better than this.

Oh, that's not true. I'm sulking. I glance at the back of Joseph's neck, where my hands were, just a few hours ago. He's acted like I'm invisible all morning. That's okay. *I* know what happened. And it wasn't just me in that kiss. He was *all* in.

I feel my lips curve in a smile. The memory will last me a long time, when I'm all alone on the road. I have him to thank for that.

Not that I will actually thank him.

Joseph unties his apron and pulls it over his head. "Lorelei, I'm off." He shoots me a soft look and a small smile as he walks to the back door.

"Okay, Fish, we'll see you tomorrow. Nevada, you're up."

"Up for what?" Where is Joseph going?

The door shuts behind him.

"Did he say where he was going?"

She tips her head and squints at me. "I didn't ask him. Why would I?" She waves a hand. "Anyway, you up for cooking?"

"Cooking?" I hate the little kid hope in my voice, but the words are out.

Lorelei throws a dishtowel over her shoulder. "Well, if I

do it, it'll drive away customers, so I guess that leaves the Cro-Magnon."

A huge grin stretches my lips. "Hey, cavemen were good with meat."

"Okay, let's do this." Lorelei steps to the swinging door.

"Wait."

"What?"

"I can't cook without music. Do you have a radio somewhere?"

She reverses and heads for her office. "I think I saw one in here once." There's banging of metal and grunting, but she returns with a radio that's way pre-boombox. "Here. It must have been Carly's nana's. If it doesn't work, you're SOL."

"Thanks." I plug it in. God, I hope they have more than pork futures and Bible-banging stations around here. Halfway down the dial I luck onto a metal station out of Albuquerque. *Sweet.*

I check the orders on the wheel, then get to work. You get a bunch of orders going, and it's like dancing, getting everything done at the exact right time. God, I've missed this.

Megadeth is halfway through "Countdown to Extinction" when I drop the first order (a brat with fries) at the serving window. Before I can ding the bell, Lorelei skids up.

"You've got to turn down that music. Three people have complained already."

I roll my eyes. "I'm not sure it's possible to listen to metal below an eight on the volume dial. These people should get some taste."

Moss is at his usual spot at the bar and says through the serving window, "Hey, is that Slayer?"

It takes me a second to process that this old guy with crumbs in his beard knows headbanger bands. "No, but you're close. Megadeth."

"Oh, of course," Moss says.

"Got any of Ol' Blue Eyes?" Manny Stipple slurs.

When he sways on the stool like a drunken sailor, Moss shores up his friend with a push. I'm not sure of the sailor part, but he's got the drunk part *down*.

"We are *not* taking requests." The look on Lorelei's face tells me I'm about to lose the radio.

"Okay, you win. Unbunch the panties." I dial it back and put more burgers on the grill. It'd be nice to buy one of those MP3 players. Then I could put the buds in, and not catch flak from the uninformed. But it doesn't matter, since I'm not going to be cooking wherever I go next anyway.

Which reminds me to enjoy yet one more "last"—cooking.

* * *

Six hours later, I leave work exhausted but smiling despite the emotional whiplash. After all, the day was more good than bad, and I'll take that anytime. I shrug into my backpack and put on the gaudy flower-splashed helmet. I may only have couple more days here, but there is no food in the RV. Gotta stop at O'Grady's on the way home.

Home. Yeah, in my dreams.

I wonder where Joseph went this afternoon. Not that it's any of my business. I ease out of the alley and cruise around the square nice and slow. Partly because I'm freaked about a car pulling out, partly because I'm not exactly legal.

O'Grady's is one of those metal barn-type buildings. I pull up near the front, shut the bike down, pull off the helmet, and limp in. Whatever I get, it's got to be small; not much will fit in my backpack. I stroll down the canned goods aisle to check out the chili.

Carly stands at the end of the aisle, hands on an almost-empty shopping cart. "Hey, nice helmet, Sweet!" She strolls toward me, looking like a country fashionista (if there is such a thing) in heeled cowgirl boots and a swingy floral-print dress.

"You up for rodeo queen again?"

"Hardly. Thursday is my day out. Nana takes Faith to Bingo, and I get to catch up on chores. I know, it's pathetic that I dress up for a trip to O'Grady's, but such is the life of a mom."

But her face is lit up and her smile looks permanent.

"Yeah, you look totally bummed about it."

She glances up and down the aisle, but there's no one. "Don't tell anyone, because if Jess finds out I didn't tell her first, she'll claw my eyes out." She leans in and whispers, "I'm pregnant."

My heart gives a skip, and before I can stop myself, I'm smiling. "Oh, Davis, you're such a breeder."

"I know. Isn't it great?" She grabs my hands and giggles.

"I'm happy for you. Now, lemme go."

"Sweet, you are not anywhere near as mean as you try to act. I lived with you for three weeks. I know." She shakes my hands, then lets go.

"Shut up. I am too mean."

She grabs the sleeve of my jean jacket. "Come on, we're celebrating. I'll buy you a hot fudge sundae at the Stop & Shop."

"I gotta get going."

"To an empty RV? Fish went to the rez, so you won't even have his company. Come on."

So that's where he is. I pushed him to it, but I'm not sorry. The way he's talked about his family, I know they won't be anywhere near as hard on him as he has been on himself.

I'm so glad for him. I let Carly drag me to the corner of the store where a couple of plastic tables and chairs stand before a deli case.

She parks her cart. "Sit. I'm buying. Chocolate or vanilla?"

"Vanilla, thanks." Amazing how easily that word slips out of my mouth. It used to cut, but it's like the days here have worn off the sharp edges. I put my little plastic basket and my helmet on the bench seat and sit.

Carly's back in minutes with two cups. "I admit, I'm using you as an excuse. I'll have to watch my weight soon, so this could be my last splurge." She sits and tastes a spoonful. "Hmmmmmm."

"You have cravings already?"

"Nah, I just love ice cream."

"Can't argue with that." I don't give myself treats often, and this is awesome.

"So, why are you riding before we go to the DMV and get you legal?"

She looks so much like a ditsy diva, it's easy to forget that Carly Davis is no dumb bunny. I focus on my sundae. "Gotta practice. Besides, Joseph took the truck—"

"Okay, Sweet, we'll do this again." She heaves an exasperated sigh. "People who open up to you—tell you a secret about themselves, they are showing you they trust you. If you want to be friends, or deepen the relationship, you have to open up to *them*." She pauses, spoon in the air, and waits.

I weigh my options. It's a risk, but she's going to sit there dripping ice cream, until I tell her something. She's been good to me. I don't want to hurt her feelings. I have two secrets, and I want to keep them both. But she won't buy an excuse, or a wimpy reveal. I think a few seconds, then choose the one that's less likely to put her in danger. I focus on my ice cream. "I kissed Joseph this morning." There's a choking sound, and I look up.

She's coughing into her napkin. "When you start flinging, you really let lose!" She leans forward, a glint in her eye. "Spill."

I stir the goop in the bottom of the cup. "No big deal. We went running this morning, and I turned my ankle." Funny, how I've hardly noticed it today. "Joseph put salve on it, and…well, he was rubbing my foot, and for some reason it turned really sexy." I shrug. "Couldn't help myself."

"Oh. My. God. I never thought I'd see the day."

At her smug smile, my put-down radar pings. "I'll have you know, he kissed me back. You think I can't have feelings? Or did you think I was gay?"

"No, of course not. Don't go all starchy on me; I'm just surprised, since, after his grandmother died, he only dates—"

"I know."

"He *told* you? Wow. That says something." Her eyes narrow. "So, what did you share with him, after *he* told *you*?"

"N-nothing."

She raises one auburn eyebrow. "Then you haven't told him you're leaving?"

"What?" Shock flash-freezes my bones.

"This isn't my first rodeo. You told me once that ex-con wasn't spelled s-t-u-p-i-d. Well, country girl isn't spelled that way, either." She reaches across the table and grabs my hand. "Don't go. Your beginning was a bit rocky, I know, but people are starting to see through to the real you. You could have a *home* here, Nevada."

Her sad green eyes make my heart heavy. She really is a friend. "Don't you think I would if I could?"

She tips her head. "This couldn't have anything to do with a guy in a fancy Lexus, could it?"

Adrenaline kicks in, and I'm on my feet before I know it. "What?"

"Moss told me some guy asked him about you."

"At the café?" I can't help it. I shoot a look around.

"No, out at his place."

"What did he tell him?" I've got to get out of town. Now.

"Nothing, of course. You're a city girl, so you may not know. We may gossip about each other, but no one's going to tell anything to a stranger." She frowns. "What is it, hon? You know I'll help if I can."

And put her and her little family in danger? Nuh-uh. No way. "Thanks for that. But all you can do is keep quiet about all this."

"Your secret is safe with me. Though if you care for Fish, it's only fair you tell him—especially after this morning. Your leaving will hurt him."

Not as much as a bullet. If I told him, he'd go all protective, and...it wouldn't end well. "You don't understand."

"How could I? You're as stubborn as a New Mexico mule. You're going to have to trust someone, sometime."

The back of my neck stiffens. "Look, I know you need all this 'sharing' crap, but I don't." I can hardly hear over the thoughts in my head. At the very least, I've got to get a plan together for leaving. Tonight.

"I'm not talking about *you*, Nevada. I'm talking about the guy you supposedly care about." Her lips thin and she puts her hands together on the table. "I know the damage that keeping secrets can do to a relationship. Heck, you were there for part of it. You saw how it almost destroyed us. Save yourself some heartache and tell him."

When I realize the words waiting to come out are about my drug cartel problem, I close my mouth. I can't tell her. I can't tell Joseph. I can't tell anyone.

"Does it help you to know that I want to tell you?" This is as close as I dare come to spilling the truth.

She smiles the saddest smile I ever saw. "It does. I know it's the best you can do right now." She pats my hand. "I'm going to pray that whatever it is you're afraid of, resolves itself soon."

* * *

Joseph

I survey the dusty roads of the rez from my rooftop vantage point. I'm grateful Ma put me to work as soon as I got here, because it gives me something to do to calm the twitchiness that hit the minute I pulled onto Diné land. I've fixed a leak in the kitchen sink, got the generator working again, and—

Bang.

—the roof is now watertight. Though the whole thing needs to be replaced soon, or it'll be leaking again. I'll do that before the harvest this fall. I tuck the hammer in my pocket and wipe my face with my bandanna. Ma does better than many here, thanks to her job at the trading post and the money I give her. At least she has electricity, though water still has to be hauled from the tank at the windmill.

The sun is cooking my bare back, but the heat has baked out my body's memory of cold winter winds. I'd like to stay up here all afternoon, but I've put off the reason I came long enough. I scoot to the edge of the roof and down the ladder.

I go straight to the kitchen area, dunk my bandanna in the water bucket, and rinse off.

Ma doesn't look up from the spinning wheel, her foot pushing the treadle, her fingers flying. "You're done?"

"Yes. I'll bring in water before I go."

"You're not leaving already?"

Knowing what I need to do doesn't mean I have to hurry to it. I cross to sit in the butt-sprung sofa. "No, not yet."

"Are you shearing soon? I'm almost out of wool."

"Probably next week. I think we're done with the cold weather." She cards, spins, and dyes the wool from Grandmother's sheep, then sells it to yarn shops throughout the state. She argued against the spinning wheel at first, claiming it wasn't traditional, but when she saw what a time-saver it was, she put away her spindles. It's yet one more reason she's able to afford luxuries, like a car. "We've got four new lambs on the ground."

She glances up with a sad smile. "Your grandmother would be so happy. She loved those sheep. You must be exhausted, staying up for the lambings."

"I had help this year."

"You did?" The eyebrow I can see in her profile rises.

"My renter, Nevada, helped. A lot. She killed a coyote the first night."

"Well. Sounds like she's handy to have around anyway."

"What's that supposed to mean?"

The treadle stops, and she meets my gaze.

"She's a friend." Except, that's a lie. She's more than that. And if this conversation goes on too long, Ma will sniff it out. She knows me too well.

She spears me with a look. "What are you going to say to people who think that you're turning your back on your culture?"

Bull's-eye. Ma always was a good shot. "You think I'm—"

"I'm asking what you'll say when *others* say that."

I launch off the couch. "It's none of their damned business what I do. I'm as committed to the tribe as I ever was.

Does that mean that I'm not allowed to date? I didn't sign up to be a priest, for cripes' sake." I pace the five steps across the living room. "Look, I don't want to talk about this, okay? I'm going to go get water, then I need to get back."

"You remind me of your grandmother. Down this trail lies heartache, Fishing Eagle."

I know my mother as well as she knows me. There's something she's not saying. "What about my grandmother?"

"Didn't you ever wonder why, when your grandmother was so respected, she was never on the tribal council?" She nods. "I wish she were still alive. She could give you wisdom about...never mind."

"Never mind? Really, Ma? You drop a bomb like that and expect me to walk away?"

"It is not my story to tell. I only know what I heard from others. Your grandmother never discussed a word about it."

I love my mother. But at times like this she tries my patience. "Ma, you obviously know something."

"You might want to talk to Ben Tsosie."

I know that look. She'll say no more on the subject. I sigh. "I'll haul in your water." I grab the two buckets by the back door and start the hike to the tank. The thought of living in the long shadow of the council is part of the reason I bought land outside Unforgiven when I got out of the Army. I wanted to go where people didn't know me; who would judge me by who I am now, not for the mistakes I made as a teen. The rez is both small town and family, with the best and worst aspects of both. I dip the buckets in the well. It's hard to stay where everyone knows your shame.

But Nevada opened my squeezed-tight eyes. Not only because of what she said this morning, but who she is. She has no family, no home. No one to fall back on when things go bad. Seeing her grit and courage makes me feel ashamed *and* cowardly. My family is a part of me. The rez was my home. I want them both back. I lift the buckets. I'm going to do what I should have done long ago.

I walk back in the house. Ma is where I left her, but the wheel is still. She looks up at me.

"Are you leaving?"

"I'm going to see Uncle Sani and Atsa."

She stands and, bottom lip quivering, walks over to wrap her arms around me, burying her face in my shoulder. We stay like that a long time.

"I know I should have done this long ago."

She looks up at me, her eyes shiny with tears. "Your grandmother would be so proud."

I wish I could be sure of that. In my dreams she doesn't speak, but her face has a pinched look of disappointment.

"You have been wandering a long time, son. Welcome home." She gives me one last squeeze and steps back. "I want you to be happy, most of all. I want you to know, if a bilagáana makes you happy, she will be welcome in my home."

Whoa. That is not what I was expecting. I study her face. It's a face that has seen many troubles, and many changes. I've underestimated my mother. I drop a kiss on the top of her head. "You know I love you, right?"

Her lips curl in a satisfied smile. "And I love you."

I walk to the truck and sit for a moment, deciding which long-put-off job to tackle first. Family. Family comes first. The truck starts, first try, and I put it in gear to begin the long road back.

The road isn't long enough. A few minutes later, I step out of the truck in front of my uncle's modular home. Atsa is listlessly swinging on a tire swing he's too big for, his tennis shoes dragging in the dust. He's gotten big. Hell, it's been six years; what did I expect? He must be...fifteen, this last January.

He looks up, squinting into the sun. Then his mouth opens in an O of surprise, and he jumps off the swing to run to the truck. "Fish!" He barrels into me and my back slams against the truck cab. "I'm so happy to see you!" He hugs me hard enough that I can't get a breath.

I pat his back. "Hey, Atsa. How you doing?" My voice cracks with emotion. In avoiding dealing with my past, I'd blocked out how much I *love* this kid.

"Oh, I missed you so bad." He backs up enough to see my face. "I asked Papa where you were, and he just said, 'Gone.' Where did you go?"

I extricate myself and throw an arm across his broadened shoulders. So strange to see the changes: he's tall as I am, and his face has hardened into a man's. But his sweet mind will always stay nine years old. "I missed you, too, bud. More than you know. I had to go away. To the Army."

"You were a soldier?" he says in an awe-inspired whisper. "Did you shoot the bad guys?"

"Nah. I mostly kept the heroes' Humvees running."

"Cool."

"No, hot. It was in the desert."

He smiles his all-in smile at me, and I kick myself again for missing all those years.

"You wanna play catch with me? I have a glove and everything. They let me be in the outfield at the baseball games. I'm good."

"I'll bet you are." I scruff the top of his head. "We will before I leave, okay? Is your dad around?"

* * *

Two hours later, I drive off, waving to Atsa and his father in the rearview. Turns out, my uncle forgave me years ago, and was giving me time to figure this all out for myself. My uncle also knew without my telling him how sorry I was, but he allowed me to say it anyway... because I needed to. We talked about old times, now times, and what's really important.

In the rearview mirror, dust kicked up by my tires obscures the road. "You were right, Grandmother."

Nevada was right, too. The truth I was running from *was* small. I invited Atsa to come out one weekend soon, to help me plow. I remember how sweet Nevada was with Lorelei's mother; I bet she'll love my cousin.

I feel like I've been through my mother's old wringer washer, but I have one more stop to make, and the outcome of this meeting is even less certain than the last. Ben Tsosie is a few years older than my grandmother. He retired from the tribal council a decade ago.

It's suddenly too hot. I crank the ignition and turn the fan on high. Gotta get the AC fixed soon, or I'm going to cook on my way to work, too.

I'm half afraid to hear what Ben will tell me. What if it's something bad about my grandmother? Something that makes me see her differently? Missing her is a badger in my chest, clawing to get out. No, if she has something to tell me, I'm going to listen.

I turn right at the crossroads, driving deeper into the rez. My grandmother's face floats before my eyes. "I wish we could talk, bił hinishnáanii. My heart is troubled, my mind confused." No answer, which all told is probably a good thing. I don't need to add delusions to my list of problems. "You were my compass. I know what I want, but not what is right."

And what I want is the feisty, stubborn, independent ball of energy that is Nevada Sweet—even if I shouldn't. The truck bumps over the washboard road, and I raise the windows to block billowing dust.

What if I just told everyone to go hang, grabbed her with both hands, and held on? What is the worst that can happen? My people turn away from me? My mother won't. I'm not saying it won't be awkward, introducing the two, but she loves me, and wants me happy. But the rest?

My head tells me they won't care. People are far more worried about their own lives than mine.

No, all that matters is what *I* think. And that's the pinch point, right there.

I look out at the stark landscape I was born to. I am Diné in much more than genetics. Our ways, our language, our beliefs are so much a part of me, I could no more rip them out than I could my DNA. Our ancestral home may be smaller now, but this land was ours long before Unforgiven, or New Mexico, for that matter.

I tried to fit in where I didn't, first in the rodeo, then in the Army. *This* is where I fit.

CHAPTER 13

Houston, Texas

Cisco sits in his restaurant, red-faced, listening on the phone.

"I have feelers out everywhere, Cisco. Airports, train, and bus stations. I've circulated the photo you sent to all my people. It's only a matter of time—"

"Time? We got no time. I want this girl gone. She should'a been gone three months ago."

"Believe me, I'm motivated."

"Then why, with all this 'motivation,' have you still not found her?"

Jovie flinches at the volume and glances around the restaurant.

But Cisco has nothing to worry about. This is his place. A guy owns it, but Cisco owns *him*.

"She's gone to ground, jefe. I'll dig her up, don't worry. I'll—"

He clicks End. "Useless. Well, you want something done, you gotta do it yourself. I don't know why I've wasted so much time with idiots."

Jovie's trying to be cool, but his eyes are worried "Do you want me to—"

"Get me a cerveza. It's all you're good for."

When he's gone, Cisco pulls up the Internet on his phone. He checks every couple of days, but so far, nothing. "Wherever she's holed up, it's—wait. What?" A blog. Some broad, running her mouth about some small-town garbage, but halfway down:

Oh, and I have some good news to report. I'm sure you read my article in the *Patriot* about Nevada Sweet, the new busboy down at the Chestnut Creek Café. As you know, I'm a fair-minded person, so I did some research. My facts were correct; she was in prison, but upon further study, it appears we have our own female Robin Hood, right here in Unforgiven!

"Here you go, boss." Jovie sets a Dos Equis in front of Cisco.

"Shut up." He scans the rest. How many Nevada Sweets can there be? He's got a thing or two to take care of here, but he should be able to take a road trip in a couple days. She thinks she's safe, so she's not going anywhere.

This time, *he'd* be taking care of business. He chuckles, "That chick is as good as gone."

* * *

Joseph

When I pull up and climb out of the truck, Ben Tsosie is sitting in a chair under a mesquite bush. "Well, Fishing Eagle. I expected to see you someday, but I didn't expect it to be today." He slowly pushes himself out of his chair onto his bowed legs and offers me his hand.

By reflex, I shake it. "I'd like to talk to you, if you have a minute."

"I have nothing but minutes these days, and most of them pass too slow." He points to another webbed lawn chair against the trailer. "Pull that in the shade, and we'll catch up."

I drag the chair across from him and force my knees to unlock. I'm caught between wanting to know and not. Between wanting to sit and wanting to run. Between the two forks in the road before me, and what I sense is going to be the push in the back that decides me.

His face is round and wrinkled as a dried apple. His eyes glitter from beneath fallen brows. Gray laces his long braids. "What do you want to know?"

"About my grandmother."

"One of my best friends, growing up. A wonderful woman."

"She was. My mother hinted at . . . something in her past. She said that you could give me details."

"Ah, you come right to the point. I remember that about you from when you were a boy."

Past history is the last thing I want to talk about. I swallow and keep my eyes trained on him, hoping he'll pick up the hint.

"Excuse an old man for wanting to keep you longer. I've

found that when you get older, you drop to the edges of the community. You swirl in the eddies and watch the younger ones in the river, rushing by. They respect you but have no time for you."

I have empathy for him. Of course I do. But old wounds leave scars. And scars don't bend much.

"You wanted the story. Will you hear it?" Ben's gaze holds censure, and I feel like I'm back in school, twitching under the teacher's withering stare.

"Sorry."

He sighs. "Doli has gone on before me, so I suppose there is no reason to hold her confidences any longer." He squints up at me. "Besides, if you've been sent to me, you must need the story."

I see my grandmother's nod in my mind. "I think I do."

He puts his elbows on the arms of the chair and tents his fingers in front of his mouth. Filtering words, maybe?

"Part of this I know because she told me, parts I witnessed myself. Doli married young, and after your grandfather died in the war, she had a long, lean time. Your mother was just a baby, and Doli had no family left. She'd been a basket weaver since high school, and she sold her baskets at any store that would take them. She lived, as many did then, on the edge of starvation."

I wince. I'd known about those times, but as a black-and-white history lesson. History becomes Technicolor when you realize someone dear to you suffered. She never even hinted at those times with me.

"Well, one day, a big black Crown Imperial drove onto the reservation. A white man rolled down the window and asked directions to Doli's. He was a New York art dealer on vacation and had seen her baskets. I'm sure he was shocked to see how she lived, but to his credit, he didn't show it. He asked if he could show her work in his gallery in New York. She was thrilled, of course."

"He took her for a good meal, then bought her groceries, and paid her an 'advance' on her sales. She came to tell me after, glowing with the attention, the food, and the good fortune. I assumed he was offering charity, but I was wrong. Her baskets did sell, and for good money. It seems that city people were interested in 'Primitive' Art.

"The man returned, many more times than needed, and for longer stays. Days. People began to talk. He was young and blond and rich, and infatuated with Doli." He looks over at me. "You may not know it, but your grandmother was a very handsome woman."

"I've seen photos. She was beautiful." My heart kicks. It's a revelation, seeing your grandmother as a person your age; facing much worse things than you. I wish I could talk to my shí másání.

"It was a different world back then. A white man and a Navajo woman? They would be swimming upstream into a waterfall of abuse. And it would be much worse, off the rez." He shakes his head. "He asked her to come with him to New York. For a showing, supposedly, but she knew he meant for much more."

"She came to me for advice." For the first time, he pauses. His hands drop to his lap and he studies them. They're gnarled, scarred, traversed by twisting blue veins, and I'm not sure he sees them. "He loved her. She loved him. It shone from her eyes, leaving me no doubt. I killed that light by telling her everything she already knew. She was being ostracized on the rez, by friends and neighbors. How much worse would it be in New York? She'd be an oddity; a relic of a Wild West Show. What chance did their love have in the face of that?" He looks up at me. "It was all true. Every bit of what I told her."

His tone is more defensive than his words warrant. There's a "but" in there somewhere. He turns his unfocused gaze to the dry landscape over my shoulder.

"I've thought about that conversation more times than there have been years since, but still, I'm not sure of my motives. See, I was half in love with her myself, even knowing she'd never think of me as more than a friend. She took my advice. The white man only came back once, to give her a present; a gold filigree hair comb with—"

"With mother-of-pearl insets." My blood is whooshing in my ears. She wore that hair comb every day of her life. It was as much a part of her as her smile. The last time I saw her, she was beyond speaking; but she took the comb from her hair and pressed it into my hand. I knew then, I would soon lose her. "I have it." I clear my throat, to try to ease the tightness. That comb is all the more precious, knowing what it represents. My heart hurts for that young woman.

"That is as it should be." He nods. "She turned him away. He continued selling her baskets, but she never spoke with him again; communication was through an employee. But the price she paid. She never remarried. Never had another man. I know she took the pain of missing him with her to the next world.

"Where would the other path have taken her? Heartbreak? Happiness? Both? I'll never know."

His gaze returns to me. "But I do know one thing. If I could go back, I'd tell her to reach out and hold on to him and never let go. Because none of the reasons I gave her really matter. If it didn't work out, her heart would have been broken. But she ended up brokenhearted in the end anyway, and she missed out on all the love she could have had in the meantime.

"I am too soon old, and too late wise. But that time taught

me something important. There is enough pain and sadness in life, so if you have a choice, always choose the side with love."

My heart aches for the young woman who was my grandmother. At the same time, the knots in me ease with their unraveling. Ben is right. Love is hard to find in this life. When it finds you, who are you to turn it away?

It's true, I worried what my people would say about Nevada. But if I'm honest, it's worse than that. I was afraid of letting myself down. Of being untrue to my own vision of who I am. What arrogance. I'd forgotten that I'd made up that shiny perfect image of a modern-day Navajo warrior. I was ready to walk away from what could make me happy for a child's dream.

My grandmother faced true prejudice; the only thing holding me back is my own.

*   *   *

Ma,

I've got all the chores done, and I'm alone here, so I figured I'd write.

I wish I'da talked to you more. Asked you about stuff that I'm only now finding out I need to know. 'Course, if you'd had the answers, you probably wouldn't have been an addict, but it would have been nice to have your opinion anyway. When you can't talk to anyone, you have to learn the hard way, by making all the mistakes until you figure it out. It works, but it leaves dents. I'm tired of the time it takes. And the bruises.

For the first time, I have a couple people who would listen, but I can't tell them what happened that day in

Houston. Because they'd try to help. You know the cartel; you get it.

But how cool is it that they want to? That's a pretty amazing thing, when you think about it.

And, there's a guy. Joseph "Fishing Eagle" King. He's Navajo, good and kind, and he knows me, even though I haven't told him hardly anything. Oh, and he's brave. He manages to stay open to people and not hate, even when they've hurt him. I can't imagine that kind of courage. Just by being himself, he's showing me the kind of person I want to be. Even though I'll end up being it somewhere else.

I should have left already. I know that. But how do you walk away from something—someone that rare?

I guess what I'm trying to say is that he matters. He makes me happy. He makes me feel like I'm enough. He makes me feel clean.

I thought you'd want to know that.

I'll try to write more later, but I'll be on the road, trying to stay ahead of Cisco, so it might be a while.

Nevada

* * *

Joseph

"Thank you, Ben, for my grandmother's story, your time, and your wisdom." I lean forward to push myself out of the chair.

"Fishing Eagle."

My stomach tightens at the command in his voice. The chair's webbing creaks when I lean back into it.

"You still carry a heavy heart, from before. That's why you stay away." He holds up a hand. "Don't deny it; you don't need the weight of a lie, too."

I sigh. I owe it to him to listen.

"You were young, and fierce and lost. That is what youth *is*, son. It is a time of learning, and the hardest lessons come with the harshest sentences." His bright eyes catch mine. "But it wasn't meant to be a life sentence. No one here holds your past against you. Why do you hold it against yourself?"

"Forgiving others is much easier than forgiving yourself."

He nods. "You see that time through a haze of old pain. Let it go, and it will fall back to the past. You won't have to carry it anymore. The choice is yours."

Ben is right. It's time to let many things go.

I walk to the truck. I may thank him someday for that advice, but I can't process it now; my head is too full of his first story. My grandmother had to have a hand in today's events; the coincidence of our stories are too similar, and me finding my way to hers when I need it is too great.

I look up to the azure New Mexico sky. "Ahéhee', shí másání." Thank you.

CHAPTER 14

Nevada

I'm sitting at the table reading a book about some spoiled Southern chick during the Civil War when a fist hits my door.

I jump to my feet, my heart beating so hard I can't hear around it. I snatch a knife from the counter and point it at the door. Would Cisco bother to knock? I can't afford to take chances. Knees shaking, I dart a glance around. Why did it never occur to me that there's no back entrance? The window in the bedroom is big enough to squeeze out of, but it faces the front, and the windows at the back are too small to crawl through.

Think, Nevada. All I have is the knife, and the chance of surprise. But only if I move fast. I step to the door, then hesitate for a loud heartbeat. If he has a gun, it's all over. I jerk the door open, already flashing the blade.

Joseph's expression shoots to shock. His hands go up and he steps back, off the step, stumbles, and falls on his butt.

"Oh crap." I lower the knife, take a step down, and offer him a jittery hand up. "Why didn't you say it was you? You about gave me a heart attack."

"You?" He takes my hand and pulls himself to a stand. "I thought I was dead."

That makes two of us. "Sorry."

He slaps dust off his jeans. "We need to talk."

I'm not sure I want to hear what he has to say, but after that kiss this morning, we do need to clear the air. "I guess you'd better come in."

I step up into the trailer, and he follows.

"I don't have anything to drink but tap water—" I turn around and my nose almost brushes his shirt. This place is built for Single Barbie. No room for Ken. His scent fills my nose, bringing warm memories and heat—to my face, and much lower. When I step back, my heel hits the kitchen cabinet. Does he see what he's doing to me?

His eyes get big.

Oh man, let me die now.

"Um, I'm good, thanks." He lowers himself to the bench seat and levers his knees under the kitchen table. It's a tight fit.

I go to the sink and pour myself a glass of water. Not because I'm thirsty, but because it gives me a bit of distance and a second to calm down. "What did you want?" I go for nonchalant, but it comes out defensive.

"I came to tell you something. But why did you come at me with a knife?" He leans back and drapes an arm over the back of the booth like he's got all night.

Carly's words come back to me: You've gotta share if you want to let people in. But that means they're *inside* your armor. I realize I'm wringing my hands and make myself stop. "You tell me yours first." When he opens his mouth to argue,

I add, "Please?" I hate the whine in my voice, but I'm panicking here.

He gives me a small smile and pats the table. "Come, sit, and I'll tell you about my amazing day."

Now that, I can handle. I take the two steps, sit, and when I try to pull my legs in, my knees hit his. "Sorry." I lift my legs and fold them beneath me on the bench and put my hands on the table. "Carly told me you went to your mom's. What happened?"

"My grandmother happened."

"Huh?"

He tells me a story that, if I didn't know him, would convince me to call in mental health professionals. But his face is all glowy—like he just got saved. And maybe he did. After twenty minutes or so, he winds down. "I know it sounds crazy, but I know shí másání had a hand in this. It's like she showed me the other side and helped me make a decision." One side of his mouth lifts, and he puts his hand over mine. His is tanned, long-fingered, and strong. Mine is butt-white, stubby, and nail-bitten. As different as they are, they look kinda right together. But as amazing as this feels, I can't let this make a difference. I'm leaving, and—

"I should have figured this out way earlier—we've shared so much: working together, running together, the coyote...It took you kissing me this morning for me to get out of my own way. It's like I got this idea in my head, that to be dedicated to my tribe, I had to stay within my tribe. I carried it around for so long, that it became a deep-down fact. I didn't even think to question it, or test the validity, because, in my head, it's like the sun coming up tomorrow."

He's looking at our hands, too, and I'm wondering how he sees them.

"I don't care what people will say if we're together. It

only matters how *we* feel about it. I believe what Ben said. If you have a choice, always choose the side with love." He looks up, into me. "So that's what I'm doing. I'm choosing love, I'm choosing *you*."

Bubbles of happiness form in my stomach and rise to my brain. I tried some leftover champagne when I was cleaning up a room service tray once; it's like that—I'm off balance and a little giddy. Me. Giddy.

Then I run into my wall of reality.

"What is it?" Joseph's fingers tighten on mine. "Do you want to choose different?"

"No." That's one thing I know for sure. "But you need to know some things, before you choose me." I pull my hand away and clasp them both in my lap. "Stuff I've never told anyone. About Houston."

But his eyes won't let me go. "Tell me."

I know I have to, and not just because of what Carly said. I want to. Because I *need* to. It's time.

* * *

Joseph

Nevada looks at her lap. I'm sure she's traveling to her past, and I'm just as sure it's not somewhere she wants to go. I want to make it easier, but I know she wouldn't appreciate that—Nevada does things on her own.

"I don't know when my mom started using drugs, because as far as I remember, she was always doing them. We were living in Vegas, and in the beginning, she worked as a night cocktail waitress at a casino and did pills to stay awake. It escalated from there. I was a kid. I thought everybody's mom was jittery and exhausted all the time. I thought everyone lived like we did."

She puts her forearms on the table and picks at her cuticles. They're not model's hands. They're like her: blunt and scarred and strong. I respect them.

"When the casino realized she had a problem, they fired her. She got another job, off the Strip, but for less money."

Her shoulders are shifting in small increments from a slump, drawing in, and rising toward her ears. The pads of her fingers are white when they press on the table. I want to reach out, to hold her hand, and let her know I'm here. That she's not alone. But I'm afraid it'll stop her words. And she needs to say them as much as I need to hear them.

"Then the money ran out, and her dealer was practically living with us. I begged her. We could pack up, move away, and start over, somewhere it didn't smell like trash and pee—somewhere clean. She really saw me that time. I know she did. She said she was sorry for being such a bad mom. That she'd always meant to be better."

She takes a deep breath that comes out in a sigh.

"I had hope when she went to a Narcotics Anonymous meeting. But that was it—one. Then things went back to 'normal.' I didn't want to quit school, but something had to change. She didn't eat much, but I needed to, and somebody had to pay the rent. So, I went out and got a job."

She looks up, her brows drawn together. "I'm not telling you this for a 'poor me,' only to explain so you can see how I got to where I did."

She may not be telling me for my sympathy, but she has it. My childhood may not have been idyllic—we didn't have much—but I had a dependable mom, and a grandmother who was my champion. Nevada had to grow up way too soon. No wonder she only depends on herself; she's never had anyone dependable around. And the fact that she's trusting me with this means more than it would for anyone else. This woman doesn't lean. She's trusting *me* to be dependable.

"I worked the night shift at the Stop 'n Go. One morning I came home, and the house was dead quiet. It was always quiet but somehow the quiet sounded different this time. I opened her door and stuck my head in the bedroom..."

She's looking at the wall over my head, hands in her lap, and she's rocking; tiny movements, rocking back and forth. I want to pull her into my lap. Watching her pain hurts me more than my own. But I know she doesn't want that. The only thing she needs right now is for me to listen. To hear.

"It was a picture I'd seen before. Mom and her dealer in bed, naked, dead to the world. Mom had been going downhill. And there was the reason for it, lying there like a blood-sucking leech, even when she had nothing else to give but her body."

She lowers her head to stare at the table, and her rocking speeds up. I don't know what to do, but I don't think it matters. I couldn't stop her until she gets through with this, even if I tried.

"I was standing by the bed looking down, when he woke up. He sat up and leered at me, said it was about time for him to 'break me in,' since my mom was used up."

She looks up, straight into my eyes, and her chin comes out, though her lower lip is wobbling. "Then he lunged at me. Got his hands around my thigh and pulled. I snatched an empty vodka bottle from the nightstand and smacked him in the face with it. He fell back on the bed—I thought I'd killed him. Hoped I had. I flushed his stash down the toilet, took his wad of cash, and ran out." She takes a breath, and her shoulders straighten. "I'm not proud of it. But that's what happened." Her shoulders fall to a defeated droop. "The dealer's boss has been after me ever since. It's about the money and the drugs for sure, but more than that, it's about his reputation. Word on the street is that he let a girl get away with dissing him. The cartel has no use for narcotraficantes who don't get respect." She takes a breath, and her shoulders straighten.

"I'm a fool. I knew better. But I just lost it..." Her jaw is clamped, her eyes flash with anger. And tears. "And now, I found you. For once, I have someplace I want to stay, and..." She pulls in a hitching breath. "I can't!" The storm she's been fighting breaks.

I knew this woman was strong, but I had no idea how heavy the burden she carried.

I'm around the table and pulling her up, into my arms, in one smooth motion. I wrap myself around her while she sobs. "It's okay. You have me now. You're safe."

I'll see to it.

* * *

Nevada

I should pull myself together and figure out how to fix this. I didn't mean to blurt that last part, and now Joseph's going to want to go all superhero on me. But being wrapped up in his arms feels too damned good to move.

Letting out the secret has opened a space in my chest, giving my lungs room to expand. I hadn't realized how long it's been since I've been able to take a deep breath.

Rain starts up, pattering onto the roof.

"Shhhhhh." His chin scrapes over my hair as he rocks

from one foot to another, a rhythm that quiets the panic in me. Even though I know I should, I'm too heartsore to step away from his comfort. His *caring*.

I'm not stupid; I know it's an illusion, this safety. I still have to leave. More now than ever, because I can't put him in the line of fire—this man who has seen beyond my disguise to who I am, deep down—and likes me anyway.

I back up only enough to be able to see his face. "Joseph, will you take me to bed?"

His arms tighten, and his mouth comes down on mine, but it's only a warm brush when I'm aching for *fire*. A cleansing fire, to burn away the real world, if only for an hour or two.

"Come." He lets me go, except for my hand, and takes the one step to the door.

"Where're we going?"

"My bed. It's big and comfortable. I've had enough of this dollhouse."

When I step out of the trailer, I realize the patter of rain has turned to a downpour. Joseph's T-shirt is darkening in streaks. He tightens his grip on my hand and takes off at a run for the house. I'm taking two steps to his one, and we're splashing through widening puddles, laughing like fools.

We're soaked through by the time we make it to his uncovered porch. Thunder booms overhead and my chest vibrates with it. He reaches to open the door, but I pull him back. The air is charged with electricity that gathers in my body—a ball of static that builds, pushing out, wanting release. My hands snake around his neck and I pull him down to me.

The kiss is wild and hot. His skin is warm and slick, and I want more of it. I pull up the bottom of his T-shirt, breaking the kiss just long enough to peel it off him. He stands with watchful eyes, water running off his long, beautiful muscles. God, I could eat this man for dessert. I lick his chest, and he pulls me to him and kisses me with all the fire I wished for earlier.

Lightning cracks the horizon and thunder hits with a boom that echoes through me, then rolls away across the land.

He tugs at my shirt and I peel it over my head. There's no one to see us out here, and I don't care anyway. I twist my front-clasp bra, and it falls away. My boobs are small, and I suddenly care too much about what *he* thinks.

But his eyes are soft and hungry, his mouth slack with want. He pulls me to him, and our wet, hot skin meets, hitting me like a shock of static. He twists against me, and my nipples zing an electric current between my legs. When he catches my mouth, I moan into his.

I pull away to toe out of my shoes while I undo my jeans.

"What—"

"Don't want wet clothes on your wood floor." I turn and peel my jeans down my legs.

I hear the hiss of his indrawn breath and it makes me glad I don't often wear underwear.

When I turn back, he's unbuttoning his Levi's, revealing a line of dark hair like an arrow, leading where I want to be. When he pulls them down, he springs out, hard, large, and long, and I realize that I used the wrong criteria when I chose that dorky *little* guy to take my virginity.

I reach to touch, but he grabs my hand. "My bed is—"

"Later." I pull my hand free and cup him; he puts his head back and moans. Rain runs down his face, his body. A body that deserves to be worshipped. I kneel and take him in my mouth. His skin is velvet on steel. But he only allows me a few strokes before he hauls me up, lifting me like I weigh nothing. I wrap my arms around his neck, my legs around his waist. I try to lower myself onto him, but his fingers find me, through the swollen flesh to the center of my heat, and everything in me turns liquid. He strokes me in a long, gentle abrasion. Once, twice, and I'm there, my muscles clenching in a spasm of ecstasy so intense, the world goes colorless for a few spastic heartbeats.

He catches my mouth and plunges into me, filling me, and my orgasm goes on, one long, shuddering explosion, carrying me places I've never been. Chest heaving, muscles straining, he pumps into me, then with a guttural cry he comes, buried in my wetness.

I cling to him as we fall back into reality. Random thoughts ping through my mind: water is cascading from the roof on us, running off his hair, and damn, I've got to be heavy. I kiss him on the nose, and when I unlock my legs, he slips out of me. He holds me tight as I slide down to stand on trembling legs.

I'm not sure what to say. I just stand there, trying to gather words. With the internal heat cooling, the rain no longer feels warm. A shiver rips down my spine, and I wrap my arms around my waist.

"Hey." He lifts my chin. "You okay?" He stands like a god, as comfortable in his nakedness as he is in his skin. The side of his mouth lifts. "Okay if we move this inside where it's warm and dry?"

"Um. Yeah." I look down at my pale feet and tuck wet hair behind my ear.

He takes my hand. "We need sustenance and showers. But don't you even think I'm done with you yet."

A smile skirts the tenseness in my chest. "I can get behind that."

He turns the knob and pushes open the door.

I tiptoe by him, and he smacks my butt on the way by. "We'll throw the clothes in the dryer later. I'm freezing, and starving, and we're not done talking."

I hoped the hormone surge made him forget. "*I'm* done talking."

He raises a brow. "Let's grab a shower first. I'd invite you in mine, but then we wouldn't eat, and I plan to need all the energy I can get tonight." He winks. "You know where everything is, right?"

"Go. I'll meet you back here. Oh, and I call dibs on cooking."

"You got it."

He looks like a jungle cat, climbing the ladder; all sleek muscle and grace. I can't turn away until his toes disappear, then I head to the bathroom on this floor for a hot shower. I go through the routine on autopilot, while my brain tries to work out how I got from there—in the trailer, wanting—to here, trying to recover from sex so wild it's like a scene from a movie.

Multilayered emotions pour over me like the hot water: fear, of leaving myself open, dread, of having to leave, regret, for the hurt I'm going to leave him with. But above all that, delight. A stupid, girly word, but it's what this feels like.

Joseph "Fishing Eagle" King wants *me*. He's got his pick of women—the Wings are practically cat-fighting over him. I see how women's eyes follow him, how they turn to check out his butt as he walks away. They react to him sensing, I think, his sense of self, his caring nature, his kindness.

And this incredible man chose me— a city stray with bad manners, no education, and a criminal conviction. How unbelievably amazing is that?

I step out and dry off. My smile in the mirror makes

me look even more like someone else. I towel-dry my hair, wishing it was blond again. Me again.

I realize I have no clothes. Screw it. I wrap the towel around me and head for the kitchen, happy to live in the "now." I've never cooked naked before. I pull open the fridge to see what there is to work with. It's gotta be something fast; my stomach is about to eat a hole in me.

I'm digging through cupboards when Joseph climbs down the ladder in his running outfit: shorts and a sleeveless T-shirt. I love the stark whiteness against his skin. His hair is unbound and still wet.

"Here." He tosses me a T-shirt.

I hold it up. It's red, faded to almost pink, and has *Gathering of the Nations—2006* across the front. "Oh, way cool. Just so you know, you will not be getting this back." I pull it over my head. It comes down to mid-thigh, so I pull off the damp towel. "I'm making doctored soup, okay?"

"You make it, I'll eat it."

"Now there's an endorsement if I ever heard one." I pull down two cans of generic soup from the shelf, and his arms come around me from behind.

"I love it when you cook." He nips my earlobe. "Both kinds."

My face gets hot, and I push him away. "Out of the kitchen. You're distracting me."

"Hey, how's the ankle? I never even asked about it."

"Almost good as new. Don't even need the wrap anymore. That salve of your grandmother's is amazing."

He sits in a chair at the bar. "Now, let's talk about how we get you out of this mess."

I'm pouring soup into a saucepan, and some spills over my fingers. "*We* aren't doing anything. This isn't your problem. Stay out of it." Fear makes my voice louder than I meant.

"Bull. Did you think that when I told you I wanted you, I meant for one night?"

A little zing of happiness vibrates in my chest before I squash it. "Doesn't matter what you want. I'm handling this."

"Really? How? By running for the rest of your life?"

"For as long as I can, yeah." I turn on the gas, pull out a frying pan, and root in the fridge again. "You don't know this guy."

"Nevada, listen to me. I can help. We can go to the police, and—"

"And what?" I whirl on him. "Tell them that I stole a guy's money? Me? The girl who did twelve months for larceny?"

"But we can—"

"Oh, and this crime took place in a different *state*." I'm nodding, forking butter into the pan. "They should jump right on that."

"They can protect you. Send out patrols."

"Hello, what part of 'head of the cartel' didn't you get? Do you think he's going to come into town with guns blazing?" I try to butter the bread, but all I'm doing is ripping holes in it. I drop it and turn to him. "It'll be a bullet fired from a silencer. Probably before I even know he's there."

"But we have to do something. The cops can look it up. Get in contact—"

"Look, I know you're trying to help. It means so much that you want to. But can we drop it now?" I turn back and finish buttering the bread, drop it into the sizzling pan, then put on sharp cheddar and Swiss slices, and the other buttered piece on top. "I'm not putting anyone else in danger. I'm leaving. End of the discussion."

* * *

Joseph

When Nevada sets her feet, it's time to quit pulling—that donkey's going nowhere. Doesn't mean I'm giving up. She's not the only one with donkey in her bloodline. Tomorrow, I'll break through her stubbornness. But I'll have to go slow, or she'll light out of here before the soup is cold.

We finish eating her rich, crunchy, grilled cheese sandwiches with soup that's way too good to have come from a can. My stomach is full, but I'm still hungry. She's adorable with my T-shirt falling off her shoulder, hair rumpled from finger-combing, her bare feet one on top of the other on the rung of the bar stool. I touch her hair. "Will you stay with me tonight?"

She looks up, and there's war being waged in her eyes. There's want, but reluctance, and . . . fear? Not of me, surely, after that crazy-hot sex in the rain. Every time I think I've figured out Nevada Sweet, I find another layer. I run a finger down her bare arm, loving her shiver. "I've dreamed of you, in my bed."

She tips her head to the side, and her cheeks redden. "You have?"

"Yes. And I want to see if reality could possibly be as good."

"Ah, that settles it then. I'm always up for a challenge."

"I'll clean the kitchen."

"I'll go throw our clothes in the dryer. I need my jeans for work tomorrow."

I've just turned off the kitchen lights when she steps back in the front door. I can't wait to peel my shirt off her.

I don't need to. She walks to the middle of the room, holds my gaze, and pulls it over her head.

We were so frenzied earlier, I got to feel her, but not look at her. I make up for it now, starting at her delicate feet, up her soft muscled legs, the blond thatch that proves her hair color a lie, her narrow waist, just-right breasts. The lamplight loves her creamy skin.

My cock strains the front of my shorts with a throbbing demand. It's going to have to wait, because I plan to take my time. I step to her and cup her face in my hands. "You are so beautiful."

"No." There's laughter in her eyes. "You are."

I capture her mouth, and when she opens to me, I begin a slow assault with my tongue. I run my hands up under her hair, then down, to trace the muscles of her neck. I'm like a blind man, imprinting her body on my mind. The long, hard curve of her collarbone, the delicate knobs of her spine, the pebbled tautness of her nipples. My stomach muscles jerk in response to my cock's demand, tipping my hips forward. *Whoa there, easy. You have all night.*

And I plan to use every minute of it.

CHAPTER 15

Nevada

I come awake in layers, like the lightening of a coma. When I open my eyes, the unfamiliar wood ceiling brings yesterday back: the talk, the rain, the *sex*. We did things last night I've heard of, but never thought I'd do. I had no idea getting that intimate—allowing someone to put their mouth on you—is about more than mind-blowing pleasure. It's about letting go and trusting someone enough to get inside you, not only physically. I turn my head. Joseph is lying on his side, head propped in his hand, watching me with soft eyes, which tells me he's remembering, too. My face goes all hot. "Don't you know it's rude to watch someone while they sleep?" But I can't help it. I reach out and run my fingers through his long, soft hair. God, I love his hair.

"I want to wake up this way every day."

He runs a hand over my ribs. "I was just thinking how small my problems seem next to yours. Makes me ashamed for going on—"

I put a finger to his lips. "Shhhh."

He kisses it. "One thing, and I'll shut up, because I know it embarrasses you."

He puts his arms around me, and pulls me in. I love that, too. I know it's a false safety, but it's warm and caring, and I'll take it as long as I can get it.

"I so admire you. Your strength, your independence, your courage."

I duck my head into his chest. "There's no courage in saving yourself. That's just survival."

"I'm talking about a lot more than that—"

"Wait." The sky I can glimpse through the small window isn't black. "What time is it?"

"I don't know..." He rolls over and checks his phone. "Oh man, it's six. We've gotta get a move on, or we're going to be late for work."

Six? How can that be? But I slept sound, with not one bad dream. I roll out of bed. "Let me get in the shower first, and then I'll run and feed the sheep and water the plants in the greenhouse."

"Go." He rolls out of the other side. "I'll grab us something to eat on the way."

Fifteen minutes later I'm waiting by the truck when he barrels out the door. He hands me a warm breakfast burrito on his way by. I take a huge bite and climb in. All-night-sex must burn a ton of calories, because I'm starving.

"Okay, we're outta here." He shoves in the key and cranks it. Nothing. Not even a whine of the starter, making an effort. "Crap. Battery's dead."

She shrugs. "Don't look at me. I stink at mechanical things."

"I'll call Asdzáá's dad. Maybe they haven't left for school yet."

I inhale the burrito while he tries the key again, then pulls out his phone and dials.

"No answer. Double crap. Maybe I could—"

I hold up a finger while I swallow the last wad of tortilla and egg. "Hang on." I slide out and run for the motorcycle parked in the hay shed. I roll it out to the truck and unstrap the helmet from the sissy bar. "We've got wheels."

He steps out of the truck and tucks the phone in his back pocket. "But I don't know how to work that thing, and you don't have a license yet."

I give him the side-eye. "Every idiot on the road has a license. In your experience, is that a guarantee of proficiency?"

"You have a point. But you've never ridden anyone two-up before."

I use the bungees wrapped around the sissy bar to secure my backpack to it, so there's room for him on the passenger seat. "Hey, Carly never had either when she rode me down a twisty mountain road. This is just a straight shot to town." I stand in front of him, as tall as I can make myself, trying to look confident. "I can do it."

"Looks like we don't have a choice. I haven't even been able to get hold of Lorelei." But he doesn't look happy about it.

"Be brave, Buttercup." I pull on the helmet. "Go put on a jacket. Road rash is a real thing."

He swallows. "Do you have to be so truthful *all* the time?" He jogs for the door and is back by the time I put down the back pegs and straddle the bike.

"Okay, there's only three rules, but they're important, so listen up."

Frowning, he looks the bike over like it might grow fangs.

"First, stay right behind me. If I lean, you lean, exactly as much or little as I do. You're my shadow. Got it?"

He nods.

"Second, keep your feet on the pegs, even when I stop."

"Okay."

"Throw your leg over." When he sits, the bike's springs almost bottom out. It wasn't made to handle this much weight. It wobbles when he puts his feet up. Damn, it's *heavy*. My strained ankle complains, but I don't have time for that. I choke the throttle, give it some gas, hit the starter, and it roars to life.

"Wait. You said three things," he yells in my ear.

"Oh yeah, the third is to hang on." I dump the clutch and almost stall it.

His hands come around my waist, and he hooks his fingers in my belt loops.

I ease out the clutch, and we're off, bouncing over ruts in the sandy trail. I knew it'd be hard to handle at low speeds, but damn. I swerve to miss a huge rock, and Joseph jerks. "Feet up and stay behind me!"

I white-knuckle it the whole way, until the highway comes in view. There's a hill up to the road and a lip at the top. I don't want to slow but have to look both ways for traffic. I stop at the bottom of the hill and we almost unbalance. I catch the bike before it leans beyond the point of no return. "Watch for traffic to the right and hang on. This may not be pretty."

"You've got this." But his hands lock at my belly button. "Clear right."

The bike is moving fast enough to stay up, but not so fast we shoot into traffic. If I stall, or lose balance on the hill, we're going over. I grit my teeth, rev it, and ease out the clutch, a millimeter at a time. And we're off.

Two feet from the top, the back tire squirms. Shit-shit-shit!

"Clear both ways!" Joseph yells.

I crank the throttle, and the bike shoots forward. I keep my feet out, just in case. When the back tire hits asphalt, it grabs, but by then, we're halfway across the road. "Lean!" I pull it over and barely skirt the right side of the pavement before straightening up. Crap, that was close! My heart is lodged in my throat, beating like a scared rabbit's. I wind the throttle to the point the bike wants to stay upright, and I make a jerky shift to second. The next shift is smoother.

"Good job," Joseph yells in my ear.

The bike is more stable at speed. We're flying down the highway. I take a deep breath of morning air. Joseph's long torso is molded to my back; his legs are snugged around mine. This part doesn't suck. But I'm flicking glances at the mirrors, the road, the scrub brush at the side, for animals. I'm carrying precious cargo, and he doesn't have a helmet.

When Joseph raises his arms, spreads them to the horizon, then pulls them in, I know he's greeting the sun.

"Hang on, idiot!" But I'm proud that I know that much. I'd love to know more: about his people's language, their customs, and their beliefs. But there's no time. I'm in the wind in hours. I'm not sure how many, but I can feel a stopwatch in my chest, ticking the seconds away.

We roll into town and get a couple of odd stares from the people in line in front of the café. That makes me smile. I turn at the alley, and park next to Lorelei's roller-skate car.

Joseph apologizes to Lorelei as soon as we walk in, explaining why we're late while tying on an apron and firing up the grill.

I push through to the dining room, and when I unlock the front door, people file in.

"Dang, Nevada, where you been? We're starving here," Moss Jones says and heads for his stool at the counter.

"You're just lucky I don't have any important meetings today." Ann Miner leads the Historical Society ladies to booth one.

Jess, Carly's friend, pats me on the shoulder on the way by. "Deal, people. It's food you don't have to cook, dishes you don't have to wash, and it's unlikely that anyone is going to spit up on you."

While Lorelei takes orders, I brew coffee as fast as the machine will make it.

Moss is talking to Pat Stark, the owner of the local garage. "They were gonna name this town Paredes, but then Gregorio got caught puttin' his iron on cattle that weren't his and they strung him up."

"You know that's not right," Pat says around a mouthful of pancakes. "It was when Alan Brown lost a bet on a horse race—"

"Y'all are so full of it." I turn and fill Moss's coffee cup. "I've heard four different stories since I got here, and not one of 'em rings true."

"Well, what do you think happened?" Pat holds his mug out for a refill.

"Haven't got a clue. All I know is, it must'a been something really bad."

"Why?" they chorus.

"Look around. End of a shut-down railroad line, stuck on the abandoned part of Route 66, and your high school mascot is a goat." I shrug. "However it happened, I think Unforgiven is a perfect name."

Pat shakes his head. "You got a point, I have to give you that."

Moss snickers. "Aw, you ain't foolin' us none, missy. You like it here. Come on, admit it."

I head out to pour coffee, but drop them a wink on my

way by, and they fall out laughing. I'm going to miss this danged town.

* * *

Joseph

The breakfast rush is crazier than usual. I can't even look up until ten-thirty, when there's a little lull. The next time Lorelei comes to pick up an order, I tell her, "I'm going to duck out the back to make a phone call. Just be a minute."

Lorelei puts the plates on a tray. "Sure, Fish, you earned it after this morning."

The heat hits when I open the back door. Even in the building's shade, Tsonahoai, the Sun God, is strong. I lean against the building, put one foot up, pull out my phone, and dial. My first call is to Pat's Auto Repair, to buy a new battery. The kid who answers lives out by me, and I offer him ten bucks to drop it by my place on his way home. I can't even imagine trying to carry the damned thing on the bike.

My second call is for reinforcements. "Hok'ee, how you doing, man? Called you this morning to hitch a ride, but you didn't answer."

"I took Asdzáá to school, and halfway there, I realized I left my cell at the house. What happened to your truck?"

"Dead battery."

"How'd you get to work?"

"Nevada and her motorcycle."

"Oh man, I'da paid to see that. Something going on there you want to tell me about?"

"Yeah, there is."

All I hear on the other end is breathing.

"You and me going to have a problem about that?"

"Why would we? Love is hard to find in this world. Wherever you find it, brother, I say it's good."

One down, the rest of the tribe to go. Not to mention the town. But whether they accept this or not is going to have no effect on me and Nevada. I decided that way before the sex that meant more than sex, last night.

"Is that what you called me about? Because I think it's not—"

"No, man. I need a favor. A big one. Nevada's in danger. Long story, and it's not mine to tell, but know that we're talking bad dudes, guns and all."

"You have my attention."

Hok'ee is older than me but he was also a soldier; special ops in Desert Storm. "I was wondering if you and a couple others would keep an eye on my place, just for a couple nights, 'til I can work out a plan. She's safe with me, but I'd feel better if I knew I had backup."

"You got it. I'll talk to Yas and Sani and a couple others. We haven't had a good hunting party in a while. It'll be fun."

"You're a good man. Thank you."

"Asdzáá isn't going to be happy when I break the news to her that you're off the market."

"You know I've always thought of her as a little sister."

"Yeah, but teenagers..."

"Hormones are dangerous things, brother."

"Tell me about it. That's how I ended up with two teenagers to begin with."

I pull open the back door. "Gotta get back to work, but Ahéhee', Hok'ee."

"You're welcome, Fish."

I haven't figured out how to fix this long term but I hang up, grateful for my friends, and my tribe. I can't help but think about the contrast—how lonely an existence Nevada has lived up until now. If this works out, she won't feel that way again. When I walk into the kitchen, she's there, filling the dishwasher. I step over, put a hand on her hip, and lean down to whisper, "I have an idea."

She straightens. "Oh yeah? I have a few ideas myself." She shoots a look around, pulls me to the corner where we can't be seen through the order window, and kisses me.

Her eager mouth almost makes me forget where we are.

I run my fingers over her lips, and step back. "Tonight. You and I have a date."

"Yeah? Your bed or mine?"

"That may be the ultimate destination, but it will be a long journey to get there."

"Sounds like an adventure."

"Oh, it will be." I give her a quick kiss and turn away from her lips before I do something stupid. I'm not worried about Lorelei or the others knowing that Nevada and I are together, but it's so new, I want to hold it close—hold *her* close—like the best kind of secret, for just a little longer. Good thing I'm wearing an apron to cover the bulge in my jeans.

Time stretches and the afternoon drags. Finally, I lock the door behind the last customer, say good night to Lorelei and Sassy, and jog for the back door, grabbing Nevada's hand on the way by.

"Wait, I've gotta get my backpack." She snatches it from the hook and lifts her helmet from the floor. "What's the huge rush?"

"We've got a date, and I don't want to wait."

"Oh, in that case, race you." She pushes past me and scoots the few steps to the bike.

In minutes, we're on the road out of town. The sun is

below the mountains, but the horizon is still glowing, and we chase the sunset home. The path off the road is easier downhill, or maybe we're just getting used to this. I'd like to get used to this—wind in my face, ripping through my hair, arms around her, my body molded to hers.

Oh yeah, she could stay on this road forever. I wouldn't complain.

When she pulls up in the yard, the new truck battery is sitting on my back step. She brakes to a stop, and I step off. "Go get into shorts. I'll get the battery in the truck, and we'll be ready to go in a half hour."

"I've gotta feed the sheep, too. Where are we going?" she yells over the engine, and through the full-faced helmet.

"It's a surprise."

* * *

Nevada

It takes me two minutes to change into my running shorts. I dig through my backpack, wishing I had something besides snarky T-shirts to wear. Wait, what? Me, in some girly summer blouse? Does sex make your brain chemistry change or something? But I want something special, to commemorate tonight. My snort is loud in my Barbie bedroom. "Next thing you know, I'll be borrowing clothes from Carly."

But remembering Carly gives me an idea. I unzip the side pocket of the backpack and dig to the very bottom. I pull out the makeup that Carly helped me pick out when we were on the road together. I spread it out on the bed: mascara, foundation, blush, lipstick. Do I even remember how to do this?

More important—do I want to?

I always thought of makeup as a small lie. Something a girl does to try to be someone she's not, to impress some guy. I figured if the dude didn't like who I was already, why would I want to be around him? And that theory worked, right up 'til now. Probably because I never found a guy who really liked who I was *without* makeup.

I carry the war paint into the bathroom and flip on the fluorescent light, the one that makes me look kinda green.

I think I get the makeup thing now. I don't want to be someone else. I want to be *more* me. I want to look good for him. I study my plain-as-oatmeal face in the mirror.

This is gonna take some work.

* * *

Joseph

I don't have much time. I jog to the house, get together the meal I planned in my head all day, run upstairs to change, and then race back out to the truck. I install the battery in record time, and I'm waiting when Nevada comes out of the trailer and saunters across the yard.

She's wearing makeup. Long lashes make her eyes bigger, she has a healthy glow, and there's an honest-to-God pink tint to her lips. "Wow. What'd you do with Nevada?"

Her cheeks redden even more. "Shut. Up."

"Don't get me wrong. I approve of this version."

"Quit." She punches me in the shoulder. "Now tell me, where are we going?"

I pull open the truck door. "Get in, I'll show you."

It's full dark by the time we get to Chestnut Creek, but it doesn't matter. I know this area like the contours of my own face. We bump off the road into tracks made by the countless trucks before mine. The headlights spotlight the piñon pines that huddle around the creek like old women around a well.

"Okay, we're here. But where is here?"

"Grab the blanket behind your seat and come on." I reach for the flashlight, step out, and pull my grandmother's basket from the bed of the truck.

I lead Nevada down the path to the open area at the bend of the river.

"Oh, cool. Is this the Chestnut Creek the café is named after?" Nevada takes the flashlight from me and walks to the edge.

"Yes. Be careful, that bank gets undercut with the spring runoff. Lifesaving is not in the plan for the evening." I spread the blanket just behind her, set the basket on it, and join her at the edge.

"Too bad we're not here in the daytime; I bet it's really pretty."

"It is. But I like it at night, too. Here, I'll show you." I take the flashlight and flip it off. "Sit."

She sits on the blanket, and I settle beside her. "Close your eyes."

The night sounds come alive. Water burbles over the rocks, speaking in a language I can almost understand. There's a lone frog somewhere close, croaking a ballad, hoping to get lucky on a Saturday night. A coyote yips somewhere in the hills. Another joins him. Crickets start up a chorus. Smells come alive, too, the plants releasing the breath that they held through the hot hours of daylight. The creek smells of dank, cold places.

"Now, tip your head back and open your eyes."

This far out of town, there's no light to dim the show. The Milky Way is splashed above us, like a bucket of diamonds thrown across the sky.

"Wow, you don't see that in Houston." She breathes. "In school, you study about outer space, but I didn't realize you can actually see it, three-dimensionally."

"Back in the beginning, holy people placed crystals on a buckskin robe, a plan, to show the Diné how to live. Then a coyote came, and—"

"That coyote sure gets around."

"He's a problem. Anyway, he grabbed the robe and flung it, messing up the order the People had planned. That's where the stars came from."

"I love your stories." She reaches behind me, pulls the tie off my braid, and unravels it. "I love your hair, too."

The soft tugs feel good. I reach for her, but she scoots away.

"Is there food in that basket? I'm starving."

I lay out the sandwiches, fruit, and brownies and we eat in companionable silence, serenaded by the night's song.

* * *

Nevada

I would never have thought hanging out in the desert at night would be interesting, but it is. The sound of the river calms my jitters, and it's like the dark closed around us and we're the only two people on earth.

I wish.

"Where do you see yourself in a year, Nevada?" Joseph's voice is deep and calm.

My heart taps a woodpecker's warning on my breastbone. "What are you smoking? A drug cartel is after me. I'm hardly planning what dish pattern I'll buy."

"Okay, but humor me." I can't see his expression, even though he's turned my way. "What if that was all resolved? What would you want then?"

"Why would I waste brainpower on that?" Thinking about what I don't have doesn't get me any closer to having it. I learned that before I learned to read.

"Are you telling me you don't have any dreams for the future?"

"Not past staying alive." It comes out pissy, but I don't care. Pissy is how I feel.

"That's just sad. Don't worry, we'll find a way. I've been thinking about it, and I—"

"Don't." The word cuts the night like a guillotine blade.

"Don't what?"

I force my shoulders down and take a deep breath. No reason to get all spun up. I'm leaving Monday. Tomorrow would be better, but he'll be home, and he'd try to stop me. "This isn't your problem."

"What are you talking about? Of course it is." He sounds a lot calmer than me.

Okay, he's not going to drop it; so the best way to distract him is to tell him what he wants to hear. I can dream with the best of them. I just don't very often allow myself to. "If I were free, I'd steal your job and stay in this dumpy town forever."

"With me?"

I can't see his expression, but the hope in his tone makes my heart bound like a deer in hunting season. "I don't know. Depends on how often you piss me off. I don't need—"

"Oh, really?" He moves fast, bowling me over and straddling me, holding my hands over my head. "I'm the one who should be complaining. You're snarky, prickly, and you have no filter."

"And you love it. Admit it." I'm laughing. I love how his hair hangs around us like a curtain, sealing us in.

"I think I love *you*."

The word pierces my armor. The armor I've spent all my life building up, layer by layer. It shatters, falling away in chunks. Without it, I'm more naked than I've been in my life. Panic pushes through my veins. I have no fight against those words; I have only flight. I push against his chest, but he lowers himself, so we're pressed together from toes to chest. His hands cradle my head and he leans in to kiss me.

The sweetest, softest kiss in the history of the world. My world anyway. Tears prick the corners of my eyes. God, I wish...this. I hook a leg around his and roll until he's under me.

"I'm—"

I push a finger to his lips. "Shhhh." I peel my T-shirt over my head, then unhook my bra and toss it away. I run my hands up under his T-shirt, to sample all that smooth skin, as I lower myself to kiss him. His hard length pulses against me and my tongue rehearses what will happen in just a few minutes. Sooner, if I have my way.

He rolls my nipples between his long fingers. It winds up my need. I feel a rush of wetness in my shorts. I sit back, and run my hands down his hard abs, to where his hips jut.

A wisp of a breeze flows over my hot skin, and I shiver.

"You're so beautiful in the moonlight," he whispers.

I've never been beautiful. But there's a naked honesty in his voice that makes me know *he* thinks so. And that's all I care about. I'd planned to take my time, to tease him, but I was kidding myself; I want him too bad to wait. I slip out of my shorts, then peel down the top of his until he springs free. He sucks in a breath and holds it as I guide myself over him. I might not last long, but I'm not messing up this part. I lower myself slow, and he slides into my slick heat. It seems forever until I'm resting on his hipbones. I'm panting, my body straining, but I hold still.

His hands come up, but I grab them, and lace my fingers in his. *Hold, hold, hold.* Then I start to rock, slow and easy. His fingers tighten to fists, and I feel the vibration of his taut muscles in my hands. I move forward in long, delicious strokes for me, back in short, hard thrusts for him.

Things speed up. He's moving beneath me, and I'm grinding into him, my muscles pulling, releasing, pulling... He rises to meet me and I throw my head back, riding his buck, both of us straining to get us where we want to be. Then, suddenly, we're there. I collapse on him, biting his pec muscle to anchor me from shattering in tiny, scattering pieces, like the blanket of stars flung by the coyote.

I'm sprawled on top of him, my muscles liquid, his chest rising and falling beneath my cheek, settling into a more normal rhythm, when I realize that leaving him is going to do more than hurt. It's going to flat tear me up.

I listen to his strong heart, beating under my ear. Taking what we've both wanted will come with a price that we'll both pay. I'm not sorry for me. I wouldn't have missed this for anything. But Joseph...

I'm torn between two emotions you shouldn't be able to feel at the same time: thankfulness and regret.

CHAPTER 16

Nevada

Sex indoors is civilized and focused, but sex outdoors blows my mind. It's like your awareness expands and the night takes you in, making you a part of it. Lying there afterward, staring up at the sky, thinking about all the other species, out in the dark, doing what comes natural. Maybe this is what Joseph was saying; that we're all just a tiny part of a huge plan.

Kinda nice to think that. Takes some of the responsibility off you.

I make a trip to the creek to clean up, then come back to help. He's turned on the truck lights, so we can see to pack everything up. I can't believe this beautiful man is mine, at least for another day. I'm so grateful for the warm spot in my chest—he's given me a break from my aloneness and, even more, proved that someone *could* want me, if things were different. "This was the best date ever, Joseph; thank you."

"The pleasure was all mine." His warm smile offsets the eyebrow waggle. "Well, maybe not *all* of it..."

I toss the blanket at him. "So now you're gonna brag?"

"Never."

We climb in the truck, and when I roll the window down, night-scented air flows in. I rest my arm on the windowsill and watch the gray shadows fly by. The whirlwind inside me has calmed, and for once, I'm thinking about nothing. Is this how most people are? Carefree and relaxed? I can't seem to achieve it for more than a few snatched minutes at a time.

"Nevada?"

"Yeah?"

"Will you come out to the rez with me, to meet my mom...and everyone?"

I whip my head up, but he's focused on the road ahead. In another girl's world, I'd be ecstatic. But that's not my world. I squirm inside, and to buy time, I take a swig from my water bottle.

"Hey, it's not like it's a marriage proposal."

Water goes down the wrong pipe, and I choke, coughing water out the window. "Jeez, you trying to kill me?"

He just smiles.

The truth slams into me, popping the little bubble I've been living in the past two days. What was I thinking? This could never work. Even if a miracle happened, and I could stay, I'm never getting married. I'm not having kids ever. I had no role model for motherhood, and I'm not screwing up some poor innocent kid.

That may not be what Joseph's talking about right now, but I'm not stupid—it's a turn down that road.

I'm not the only one living in a bubble of denial. I could learn his language, his customs, his Gods, but a bilagáana is never going to fit his dream.

And he's the guy who dreams.

Easier for me, because I don't.

His head is turned toward me, but I'm glad I can't read his expression in the dash light. "I promise, you might get some odd looks, but no one's going to bite you out there."

I try to smile, but what comes out feels like a piss-poor imitation. "Sure, okay."

So, a lie of omission. Sue me. I'm leaving Monday. No way I can put it off longer; I can almost *feel* Cisco getting closer.

Maybe someday I can come back. Say a miracle happens, and Cisco drops dead of a heart attack or something. Hey, it could happen. The whole operation would fall apart without him. He only hires flunkies, brainless chumps who will follow orders without question; no competition who could take over the business. I'm sure the cartel would put someone in his place, but he'd have no reason to come after me—odds are, I'd be free.

Bitterness fills me, overflowing into my throat. Even if somehow a miracle happened, it'd be better that I leave Joseph alone, to marry someone of his tribe. He'll be happier in the long run.

* * *

Joseph

It's strange. Since I went to the rez, all the worry and uncertainty I was carrying inside are as gone as last winter. It's like I was fighting my true path, and since I stopped, the road ahead has opened before me. I know what I want.

Nevada told me she wants the same.

I know I'm pushing her. I'm getting way ahead of ourselves. But when her problem is solved, I want to be ready to move forward. Because I have no doubt; the woman on the other side of the cab is meant to be mine. My grandmother knew it and led me to the answer. Now that I know it, I'm not letting her go. Ever.

There's just one obstacle in our road. And it's a big one. The thought of Nevada facing that monster makes my blood chill in my veins. I want to keep her safe, but she's so fierce and independent, if I tried to cage her, she'd be gone.

One of the things I love most about her could drive her away from me. So I have to walk a very narrow line. I've spent every spare second trying to find an answer. I've thought about hunting this wolf down, but I'd be on his turf, with his people around him.

I'm going to talk to her about us moving to the rez. If he's determined to find her, he will. Better he come onto *my* turf, where strangers are noticed, and remarked upon.

But if I told her tonight, she'd run. I'll find a way tomorrow. She won't be so spooky in the daylight.

In the meantime, I'm on guard. Like when I was small, I am Manuelito, War Chief. This is a battle I can't afford to lose.

*   *   *

Nevada

I spend the drive home trying to make plans, even though I can't think beyond turning onto the road that leads away from him. But for the first time in my life, a whiny voice inside is wailing, *It's not fair!*

But when has life been fair? I'd better build up my armor again, if I hope to have the strength to leave.

When the truck bumps into the yard, movement flashes in the headlights. "Shut it down!"

"What?"

I reach over, turn off the key. "Turn off the lights!"

"Nevada, it's—"

"Shhhhh. Get the shotgun." I reach up, flip the switch on the overhead light, so it won't come on when I open the door, crack it as quietly as I can, and slip into the inky blackness, glad I wore a black T-shirt.

The safety light illuminates the sheep's pen, and they're shifting around in there, bleating a warning. I jog around the house and lean against it, letting my eyes adjust to the darkness, trying to hear over my panting and the drumming of the pulse in my ears.

"Nevada." Joseph steps up beside me and lays his hand on my shoulder.

"Shhhh." I jerk away, straining every sense I have.

Joseph's arm snakes around my chest, holding me back.

A shape materializes out of the shadows, white splashes... God, it's huge.

"Fishing Eagle." The sound comes from high—above my head, high.

Joseph turns on the flashlight, aiming it at the ground. "Hok'ee."

A tall black-and-white horse steps into the light, ridden by a dark-skinned man about Joseph's age.

Joseph steps forward to touch the horse's neck. "Everything okay?"

"All is quiet, shik'is."

I'm so busy trying to stiffen my wobbling knees and not pee myself, it takes a few seconds to sink in. I turn to Joseph. "What is going on?"

"Hok'ee is a friend. Asdzáá's father, as a matter of fact. You know her from the Wings. She's the one—"

"I know who she is. Why is *he* here?" Though I already know. Joseph's gone all Superman on me, just like I thought he would. My guts slick with ice at the thought of him anywhere near the line of fire. His friends, too.

The guy eyes me. "I didn't sign up for this part. I'll be on the perimeter. Later, dude." He turns the horse's head and trots away.

"He's just keeping an eye on the place, that's all."

Joseph tries to take my hand, and I rip it away. "Did I ask for your help?"

"We are not arguing about this."

"You're right. We're done." I turn and walk toward the trailer.

"I'm not going anywhere." He follows. "Nevada, I didn't tell you because I knew you'd be like this."

"So you diss me by going behind my back. Yeah, that works. If you don't know me better than that by now, we never had anything to begin with."

"When are you going to learn?" He stands, shaking his head.

I whirl and plant a fist on my hip. "Tell me, wise one, what do I have to learn?"

"I'm not leaving you. You don't have to do everything alone. When you let people in, you have to let them in all the way. People who care about you—people who would love you if you give them a chance—they want to help."

"Well. They. Can't." I practically spit the words in his face.

"Hey." His hand clamps on my forearm. "Your temper tantrum doesn't scare me. A drug lord with a gun to your head. *That* scares me. Listen. I have a plan. I was going to wait to tell you, but... We'll pack up tonight and move to the rez."

My head is shaking before he finishes talking. "Oh no." Bring danger to *all* his people? That's the only thing I can think of that would be worse.

"No, you don't understand. We look out for our own. Strangers couldn't just come on our land and—"

"This is not your problem, dude." I want to hurt him. Make him turn away from me before it's too late. I can handle my pain. I can't handle seeing his.

"How can you say that after the past few days? You think this has just been some kind of hookup? Because it isn't. Not for me. Not by a long shot. I thought you understood that."

God, I screwed this up so bad. Any way I turn, he's going to get hurt. I never meant for this... I never meant for any of it. My throat goes tight and watery, and I try to pull away, but his hand is like a vise.

"This is my fault. I thought my actions were as good as words. Let me be plain, so you understand. I've wasted time, being all tangled up in my own head. I'm not wasting any more. I want you, Nevada Sweet. Not just your body. I want your mind. Your spirit. You heal parts of me that I'd hidden away. I want—"

"I *can't*." I say it to him, but also to squash the butterflies careering around my chest like happy little drunks. "Let *me* be clear. You're only temporary. Sorry, but that's the way it is."

Surprise loosens his grip, and I pull my arm away. "I told you, I don't like people touching me." I stomp for the trailer, glad that he doesn't follow. I want to look back, but I can't handle what I'd see. That I've destroyed him.

I close the door and look out the curtained window. My vision is all wavy, and I can't see his face for the shadows, but he's just standing where I left him. Then he turns and, head down, walks to the house.

* * *

Ma,

I've never told you I was sorry, and I guess it's time I did. People would say that I was a kid; that it wasn't my job to save you. But they weren't there. I'd been taking care of you since I was . . . hell, I don't even remember when I realized that someone needed to, and I was the only one around who cared.

Seems like all I ever do is run. I'm going to run again, but this time, it isn't so much to save me, as other people. Friends. A . . . love. See, I found there's worse things than dying—being responsible for people you care about being hurt—that's worse.

The only excuse I have is that I didn't know. I didn't know I'd come to this crazy town and find people. My people. Joseph says that everyone has a tribe, and I guess that's true, because I found mine.

But I can't stay here. I couldn't save you, but hopefully I can save them.

I am sorry, Ma.

   Nevada

* * *

Nevada

It's early when I give up trying to sleep. The coyote dream again. It's full of darkness, and blood. Not mine—the blood of people I care about.

I slept in my clothes, so all I have to put on is my shoes. I cleaned the trailer last night and I'm packed. All that's left to do is feed the sheep, grab my backpack, walk the motorcycle to the road to start it. It'd be easier if I could leave without saying good-bye to Little Dude and his tribe, but it's not fair that he misses breakfast because I'm sad and weak.

I step out into a warm breeze, making the wind chimes dance. Their sound is off somehow—a melancholy jangle that grates my nerves. I glance at the hogan. It's dark. I pray it stays that way. Walking into the shed, I pull in a deep breath of the smell of dusty hay and animals, trying to imprint the smell onto my memory. I schlep the bale to the pen, put it down, and open the gate. The sheep swarm me, bumping my knees, singing their *bahhhhh* song. The new lambs are growing fast. Joseph says he's going to shear the flock next weekend. I'd love to see what they look like with buzzcuts. I cut the twine, cram it and the jackknife in the pocket of my jeans, then shake out the flakes.

They all push forward to eat, except Little Dude, who head-butts my leg. It hurts. He's getting nubs of horns. I squat down to rub his head. "Now I'm trusting you to watch out for your tribe, you hear? You're old enough now." My damned voice wobbles. "And watch out for Joseph, too. Give him lots of head-butts, okay? He's gonna need them, because...well, just do it, okay?"

He sniffs me, and I put my arms around his neck and bury my face in his fleece. "I love you, Little Dude." Funny how it's easier to say things to an animal than to people. I stand, wipe my eyes on the sleeve of my jean jacket, and walk out without looking back.

The nagging hum of danger I felt in my sleep last night amps, rattling down my nerves, speeding my feet to the bike in the shed. Leaving today is better than tomorrow, but yesterday would have been even better. Cisco is coming; I feel him like a gathering storm on the horizon. I feel him *in* me.

I lift the helmet from the seat and settle it on my head. I left money and a note for Carly on the table in the trailer. I wanted to write a note to Joseph—I started one enough times to fill the trash can under the sink—but I ended up just writing *Sorry* and signing my name.

Grabbing the handlebars, I push up the kickstand and roll the bike out of the garage. It's heavy and awkward, but I can't risk waking him by starting it. When I outdistance the safety light and my eyes adjust, it's easy to see the tire tracks in the sandy soil.

I know it's stupid, but I hold my breath the whole way by the hogan. Once past it, I feel tingling at the back of my neck, like someone's watching, but I know it's just my guilty conscience. I've never seen anything good coming from saying good-bye. I can't say any of the things I'd like to say to him, and what I can say, I said last night.

That last hill to the road looks impossible. I get a running start, but momentum peters out before the top. Ugh! I clamp on the brake, and almost lose my balance and go over. That would be bad. I stand, panting, waiting for my heart to stop trying to bang its way out of my chest. The last three feet are going to be the worst.

I take a deep breath, count to three, and push, making it two steps before I have to brake again. My arms are shaking, but thanks to running, my legs are strong. One—two—three...*push*. One—two—three...*puuush*.

Finally, there's only the lip of the asphalt to overcome, and with one more heave, I'm standing in the empty road. While I catch my breath, I look back toward Unforgiven, then right, to the dark ribbon of road that's going to take me to whatever's next. I may not know where the name of the town came from, but I'll carry the name with me: Unforgiven. People here have been nice, when I've been mean. They've thought the best of me, when I didn't deserve it. One loved me, even though I didn't know how to handle that. Now I know what the town name should be: Forgiven.

I throw my leg over the bike, sadness burning a hole through me. Good-bye...Good-bye...

A few hundred yards behind me headlights flip on, hitting me like a spotlighted deer. I freeze. A high-performance engine growls to life, and the car rolls forward.

Even if I were naive enough to believe in coincidence, the loathing skittering over my skin on spider feet would make it a lie. That's Cisco, or his minions, in that car. Or both.

I flip the key, hit the starter, and crank the throttle.

Easy on the clutch. You stall it, you're dead.

Despite my brain screaming, *Go*, I let out the clutch, slow and easy. The engine wallows, but when I back off the throttle a bit, the bike shoots forward.

Heart redlining, I'm flying down the highway. If an animal decides to cross the road now, it's all over. When I risk a glance in the mirror, my heart almost stops. The black caddy is ten feet off my taillight.

I eye the edge of the road. The bike can go where he can't...but can I keep it up in the dirt? A flick to the rearview mirror tells me I have no choice. Before I can chicken out, I cut the throttle and lean. I bump off the road, and the back tire squirms in the gravel. I'm in and out of the bar ditch before I have time to think.

Too fast, too fast, too fast!

I cut the power, but I'm still too fast, slamming over brush and rocks, the headlight bouncing crazily like in a slasher movie.

Up on the road, brakes squeal. This might slow Cisco down, but I know better than to think it'll stop him.

Rock! Before I can swerve, I hit it. The bike tips, the wheels slide out, and I'm down, rolling in the dirt. The bike's engine dies, and in the silence, I try to gather my scattered chickens.

Ping!

Dirt flies a foot from my face. I'm on my feet and running before I fully comprehend—that was a bullet!

Think, think, think.

Thank God dawn isn't far away; I can see to avoid rocks, brush, and holes. Pretty sure I can outrun a fat drug dealer. Not his bullets, though.

I'm breathing harder than I ever did on a Wings run. Wait...that wind-twisted tree. I know that tree. My brain streams info too fast to make sense of it. What?

The cave. The cave where Joseph brought me before it rained. It's near here. I'm sure of it. The path to it is crazy-steep, but if I can stay far enough ahead to get down it, at least I'll have the element of surprise, in case he makes it around that last corner. I'll push him off. My gut clenches at the picture, but I have no choice.

My foot turns in a hole and I'm down again, skidding on my hands and knees. Gravel bites into my palms, but I'm up and running again.

There's another *pop* from behind, and dust kicks up ahead of me.

Terror gives me another spurt of adrenaline, but my legs are responding slower. I'm tiring.

The first rays of the sun hit the mountains, lighting them up. I skid to a stop. The edge of the cliff is ten feet ahead. His thudding footsteps get louder, but I make myself walk to the edge and look one way, then the other. Where *is* that damned path? Did I dream the whole thing? I know it was here some—

"The junkie's daughter. Finally."

At the wheezing voice, I turn to face the man from my nightmares.

CHAPTER 17

Joseph

Something wakes me from an uneasy sleep. All's quiet, but there's an echo of sound in my brain. What was it? There's a breeze blowing in the open window. Dawn is breaking. I toss off the covers and pull on a pair of running shorts. Something's wrong. Something besides the emotional hangover from last night. While tying my shoes, I glance at the clock. I get a jolt that stills my fingers.

Grandmother's hair comb is sitting on the nightstand. It's been in a drawer since the day I brought it home. I thought to give it to my bride one day.

The top drawer of the dresser is open. I pick it up and get a shock of static. "Shí másání?"

If I hadn't been listening hard, I'd have missed the sound of brakes squealing in the distance.

Nevada.

I'm down the ladder and out the door in seconds. The

truck is where I left it; the yard is empty. Maybe I'm just being paranoid. But still, my feet carry me to the trailer at a run. "Nevada?" I hammer on the door, but deep in my gut I already know—the trailer is empty.

The knob turns in my hand and I step into the smell of cleaning products. Everything is neat, except there's a stack of cash on the table and two notes I don't stop to read. I'm running for the shed, awareness spreading like a bruise in my brain. She couldn't actually believe that I bought her flimsy attempt to push me away last night, could she?

The answer is in the shed that holds only hay.

She's in trouble. I feel it in the electricity shooting down my nerves. In the voice, yelling in my brain, *Hurry!* I know it like I know that it wasn't me that left the comb on the nightstand.

I stop at the house only long enough to grab the shotgun, praying to the Gods I'm not wasting valuable time by doing it. I lay the gun on the floorboard of the truck, put the key in, and say one more prayer before turning the key. It starts right up. I glance up at the cloudless sky. "Thank you, Grandmother."

I take the dirt track to the road too fast, and dust roils in the windows. Before I pull onto the road, I look left. If she's leaving, she wouldn't go back through town. That would hurt too bad. I turn right, and when I slam my right foot down, the old gal actually manages to patch out.

I'm barely up to speed when I hit the brakes. A black Caddy sits at the end of a long trail of rubber, half on, half off the road, nose pointing to the desert. The edges of my vision go charcoal gray, and my gut is full of bees. This has to do with Nevada, and it's bad, bad news.

I grab the shotgun, turn off the key, and am out of the truck before the engine dies. I follow the motorcycle's tire tracks for five hundred feet, and when I find it on its side in the dirt, the bees in my gut start stinging. *Hurry!* Scanning the ground, I find two sets of tracks, heading toward the bluff.

The cave. Smart girl. I blank out the vision of her slipping on the trail, flip off the safety on the shotgun, and follow the tracks at a run.

* * *

Nevada

There! The edge of the path I'd been too panicked to see a minute ago. I take a running step toward it.

"I wouldn't."

I turn. Cisco raises the gun.

My feet stutter to a stop, and my heart about follows suit. Of course he has a gun. I raise my hands and use the only weapon I have: my mouth. "What'd'ya know? If it isn't the pathetic little man who hides behind minions and bodyguards. The one who can't manage to catch a mouthy little chica."

"Do you see bodyguards?" He spreads his arms, then trains the gun on me again. "And it seems to me you're caught." He smiles and waves the gun. "Let's go. There's a rich man waiting for you in Albuquerque."

I'm relieved for the tenth of a second it takes to process that death would be preferable to what he has planned. Then my guts flash-freeze to a twisted tunnel of ice. I flick a glance to the path—not an option. It's too steep to take at a run, and all he'd have to do is step to the edge and shoot. I've got to come up with a plan B. I need to buy some time.

"I haven't been in Houston in a while. What's the word on the street? That a girl outsmarted Mr. Big Man of the cartel?" Now, if I can piss him off bad enough to get mad, it might buy me some time. "They must be laughing pretty hard, huh? I'll bet your bosses don't—"

He runs at me and shoves the gun under my chin. "Shut. Your. Mouth."

He forces my head back until I'm looking up at the sky. Though my body is stiff with panic, at least he's closer, which is good when your only weapon is a jackknife. All I need is a little distraction…

"Move. I've wasted enough time on you."

He eases the gun off me, but now it's aimed at my back. We're only a step or two from the edge, but he's not directly behind me. I don't think I can…

"Hey!" Joseph runs up, shotgun in his right hand.

"No, *stop*." My voice is high and crackling with fear.

Cisco swings the gun to Joseph. "You dumb broad. You're supposed to call in the cavalry, not the Indians."

"U.S. Army, 1st Cavalry Division, Third Platoon." Joseph raises the shotgun to his shoulder and trains it on Cisco. "Let her go."

I put my hands out, as if I could push Joseph away.

Cisco steps behind me and a hand clamps onto my shoulder. Before I can move, the gun's muzzle is a cold circle at my temple. "You don't want her dead, put down the escopeta. We're walking out of here."

Joseph sights down the barrel. "Not happening. See, I told her I'd never leave, and I never break a promise."

"Do it, Joseph." I put all the pleading I have into my voice, and my gaze, and pray that he listens. "I'll go with him. It'll be okay."

"You know I'm not doing that."

Yeah, I knew, but I hoped. This is a standoff, and it's up to me to fix it. Think, Nevada, *think!*

"Come on, chica. Walk. He's not going to take a chance of spraying you with buckshot."

Damned jeans, he'll shoot before I can get to the knife. "I'm sorry, Joseph. I never meant for this to—" I take one step and let my knees buckle, kicking out like a mule as I fall.

There's a crack as my foot connects with Cisco's kneecap. I feel the leg give way, bending a way a leg can't.

He bellows in pain, and the momentum pushes him back a step.

I crouch and turn. The gun goes off an inch from my ear—the bang a physical hit, concussing the inside of my skull. I fall on my back in the dirt and all the air whooshes out of my lungs. There's a blinding flash of pain when my teeth slam down on my tongue.

On one leg, Cisco wobbles at the ledge, pinwheeling his arms, trying to catch his balance.

His heel teeters at the crumbling edge, his mouth opens in an O of horror. He leans...and leans...and he's gone.

My brain strips gears, trying to process what my eyes just saw.

"Nevada!" Joseph is here, kneeling beside me in the dirt, his hands running over me. "Are you hit? Talk to me!"

Warm hands. Hands I never expected to touch me again. I'm so grateful, but I'm too busy trying to suck air to push words out.

"You're bleeding!" His hands cup my cheeks.

"Back-*wheeze*-up-*wheeze*-off me." I slap at him until I have enough room to roll over. A high-pitched tuning fork sound zings through my head. I spit blood into the dirt, so grateful it's *my* blood. My lungs decide to unlock, and I pull in air, each gulp deeper than the last, until the black dots stop dancing at the edge of my vision.

"Please. Talk to me." The fear in his tight words bring me back to the present.

"Ah hit my hongue." I sit up, and glance at the empty edge of the world.

He stands, pulls me to my feet, and into his arms. He holds me like I'm made of glass. "I thought I was going to lose you. I have never felt as powerless..." When he pulls my head to his shoulder, my blood smears over his white T-shirt. Chest heaving, he holds me for a few seconds before pushing me away, to look down into my face. "You have done some stupid things since I've known you, but this is..."

"Dumb to the third power?" I spit blood. Damn, that hurts.

"Worse, but that'll have to do for now."

I step to the edge of the cliff, even though I don't want to. If I kill a being, I have to take responsibility. Even if it's a bloodsucking leech who deserved it. Cisco is, thankfully, facedown, a leg and an arm bent the wrong way. He's not moving. My guts heave, and I swallow bile. A surprise sob hiccups up from my chest. My perspective tilts, and I clutch Joseph's arm, and sink back to the ground.

He settles beside me. "Are you going to be okay about this?" He tips his head to the mess at the bottom of the cliff.

He knows me; I'm the one who cried over killing a coyote. A human is dead, and I'm responsible. Maybe it'll hit me later, but right now, all I feel is black-hole empty. "I felt worse about the coyote."

He touches his head to mine and gives me a one-armed hug. "I won't remind you later that you're crying."

"Shut up."

"Okay." He stares out at the mountains, looking like one of those guys carved in rock.

"You came." My voice comes out small, like a little girl's.

"I will always come for you. Always." He turns and looks down at me. "The question is, are you done running? I just need to know if I have to put alarms on the door or tie you to the bed."

That's not funny. It must be hysterics that make a laugh push up from my chest. Or relief. "I gotta tell you, I'll try anything once, but I don't think I'm into bondage."

His look-through-me stare dries up the hilarity.

"You want me to stay? Even now? Even after all this?"

"I—"

"Because I'm talking for good. You don't get to come back later and tell me you can't put up with me." I drop my chin, so I can't read his eyes. "'Cuz I know I'm a pain. I'm rude, I swear, and I don't know hardly anything..." I'm trying to talk past the ball in my throat.

He waits, like he always waits for me.

"And I wear rude T-shirts!" I'm full-out bawling now, and I can't stop it any more than I could stop this day from happening.

His arms come around me and he rocks me.

When the worst of the emotion passes, he lifts my chin. "I will want you always, Nevada. You have a home forever. With me."

His lips come down on mine, and for the first time in my life, I hold nothing back; my tears, my love...myself.

I know we're going to have to call someone about all this. Soon. But just for now, I'm content to sit with Joseph, watch the sun peek over the mountains, and begin to dream.

* * *

Nevada

One week later

When Carly suggested she could dye my hair back to its natural blond, I gave her a knee-jerk no. But when she argued that I couldn't go out to meet Joseph's mom with a skunk's stripe of blond roots, I gave in. Now she's standing over me in rubber gloves and an apron, pulling glop through my hair.

"Ow, dammit!"

"Oh, quit being a baby. Anybody who can face down a cartel can handle a little pain. Don't you know it hurts to be beautiful?"

"Can I just do it until I'm pretty?"

She puts her hands on her hips, which outlines her baby bump. "Hey, you don't want me telling everyone in town the hero of Unforgiven is afraid of a few chemicals, do you?"

"Oh, okay, but once this is done, you're not coming near my head again."

"See, you're assuming I want to be near your cement head." She goes back to her torture.

My eyes are watering from the stink. "I know, you're right. I'm being ungrateful. Sorry."

"Holy McMoly. Nevada Sweet, apologizing. Did the earth just move?"

"Oh, shut up, Red."

Her face appears in front of me. "How are you feeling, really? I know you've been all tough for the townsfolk, but this is just me asking."

I'm not sure there are words for the way I've felt the past week, but this is Carly. I owe her. "I'll wake up in the middle of the night, frantic, that I somehow forgot that Cisco was coming for me. That I've relaxed and now I'm going to pay…Joseph holds me and talks to me until he convinces me that it's over."

"That's what a good man does." She gives a smug little nod. "I'm so happy for you, I could wag my own tail."

"I wouldn't. That's what got you preggers to begin with."

"Oh, stop." She smacks me on the shoulder and starts pulling again.

Once the cops checked out my story, I was cleared of all charges. It helped that, when they caught Jovie, he caved like a trailer park in a tornado. He gave them the name of the guy Cisco was going to give me to in exchange for a solitary cell 24/7. Seems he was worried about his longevity in prison. Maybe he's not as dumb as I thought.

So, me and the cops are square, but the cartel? I only gave up Jovie (and if they're smart, they know that's no loss), so I'm hoping the vendetta died with Cisco and I'm in the rearview. But I have no way of knowing for sure.

All I know is that I'm alive today, and I'm sucking the marrow out of every minute. Well, except for the last thirty or so. "Ouch! What good is blond gonna be if I don't have any hair left?"

"Stop being such a wimp. How do you think I got to be rodeo queen? It took a lot more pain than this, let me tell you."

"Then you're tougher than I thought."

"And don't you forget it, Sweet."

* * *

Nevada

Two weeks later

Thanks to the rains, the high country is dressed for spring. Scrub is blooming in the landscape rushing by the truck's window. You have to look close to see it, but nowadays, I look.

Joseph raises his arm from my shoulder, takes a piece of my hair, and rubs it between his fingers. "It's so weird. You're the same Nevada on the inside but you look so different outside."

"For me, it's the other way. I feel like I finally look like the old Nevada, but inside, I'm way different." It was worth all the torture at Carly's, to see his face when he saw my hair. She made it even better than normal, with highlights and lowlights, whatever they are. I might be getting into this girly stuff, just a bit. I even put on makeup this morning. But today is a big deal.

"It doesn't matter, because I'm in love with the whole package." Joseph takes my hand, lifts it, and kisses my fingers.

Warmth floods my chest, melting the jitters. He loves me. That's all that matters. That's all I'll *let* matter. His arm drops back on my shoulder. It feels right there.

"Are you nervous?"

I snort. "A bilagáana meeting both your mother and your entire tribe for the first time? What's to worry?"

"It won't be bad. What with the rodeo and art show, the focus won't be on you."

I roll my eyes. "Oh yeah, probably." I tuck my now-long-enough-to-tuck hair behind my ear and drop my hand back on his leg.

"Everyone already knows about you, and no one has been ugly about it, promise." He glances down at me. "You won over the Wings. If you can do that, this will be a breeze."

"Dóola bichąą́."

"I should have known when you wanted to learn Diné, you'd learn to curse first."

"Hey, I can only say what I know."

"Well then, we've got fifty miles to improve your vocabulary."

An hour later, we pull onto the Pine Hill Fairgrounds. At least I'll be comfortable with the venue. It looks a lot like the rodeos I traveled to on the food truck last year, only miniaturized. It's mostly an open field, covered in kiddie rides, booths selling food and stuff. Farther out is an arena with three-step bleachers around it. Tons of people mill around the booths. My stomach turns into a butterfly zoo. I'm the only white person I can see, and a blonde to boot. "I should blend right in."

Joseph turns off the ignition. He turns, grabs my face, and kisses me, and I forget everything else.

I'm still not easy with saying it out loud, but I love this man. It never occurred to me that he wouldn't buy me trying to drive him away that awful night. Though, looking back, I should have known. Joseph *sees*. It used to make me nervous, but now, it's so nice that someone *gets* me, down to the soles of my shoes.

And likes me anyway, holes and all. I get it more now, about holes. I heard somewhere that nature hates a vacuum, so it tries to fill it. Maybe that's why I ended up here—nature, trying to fill a hole. Joseph thinks his grandmother had something to do with it. Hey, who am I to argue?

We're both breathing hard by the time he backs up, takes my hand, opens the truck door, and pulls me out. "Come on. It's going to be fine. You'll see."

I push my shoulders back and tip up my chin. I may feel like the albino horse in a herd of beautiful chestnuts, but I'm not going to act like it. The only thing is, I've changed. Since I let people in—people can hurt me now. But even if it goes bad, I'll still have Joseph. How can I lose?

I follow Joseph's braid and fine, tight butt across the grass.

"Yá'át'ééh!" Asdzáá and the other girls from the Wings run down the booth-lined corridor toward us.

"Yá'át'ééh!" I say back.

They stop. One says, "Not too bad for a white girl."

"I'm working on it."

An older man calls out to Joseph, and he walks the few steps to the guy, leaving me alone with the Wings.

Asdzáá punches a fist in her hip, and if her frown had sound, it would be thunder. "I still think Joseph should be with someone in the tribe."

I push out my chin. "If you think—"

"But I guess we could'a done worse."

I take a small breath.

"I mean, he could've picked an 'Oh My God, Brittany!'" Her voice goes all emo teenie-bopper and she flips her braid over her shoulder.

Another says, "Or a Jenn-i-fer!" She simpers and bats her eyelashes.

Asdzáá punches me lightly in the arm. "If I can't have him, I guess you're okay."

"Just okay? I can outrun you, ya tsisteeł."

She shakes her head. "I really gotta look up what that means. Come on, you have to see my mother's jewelry and all the other stuff. And the rodeo starts in an hour."

Joseph walks back to hear the last.

I plant my feet. "Thanks. We'll do that later, but first..."

"I have people for her to meet," Joseph says in a dooms-day voice.

"She's meeting your mother?" When he nods, Asdzáá's eyes get big. "Oh, poor you. She's yíiyáh!"

My fingers in my pocket tighten on Mom's NA chip, and the butterflies take shelter. "Scary? Did she say scary?"

The girls giggle.

"She's teasing you. Come on, let's get you over there before you have a meltdown. Girls, we'll see you at the rodeo. Save us seats."

I stick my nose higher in the air. "I do *not* have meltdowns."

"I know a rattlesnake that might dispute that." He walks me over to the first booth, where the tables are covered in hanks of wool and dyed yarn. Joseph's mother is sitting behind the table. I know, because Joseph's face is a male version of hers. She's beautiful. Her eyes flick to me and down to where my hand ends in Joseph's.

He steps up, but I step in front of him and put out a hand to her. "Yá'át'ééh. Shí éí Nevada yinishyé." God, I hope I didn't butcher that.

She ignores my hand; her steady gaze takes me in. "I know who you are."

I told Joseph this was a bad idea. *It doesn't matter. It doesn't mat—*

Her tight expression loosens. "You are not who I would have chosen, but you are the one who put stars in my son's eyes." Her face softens when she looks at Joseph. "You shamed him into facing his old shadows, and helped him put them behind him."

"But I didn't. I wouldn't shame—"

"Not on purpose." Her eyes stay soft when she looks back to me. "By example. He must have felt small to be running from his fears when you faced yours."

I look down, and sink my fingers into the clean, soft wool. "It's not like I had much choice."

"I know also what I see. Is it true that you want to learn our ways?"

"Yes, ma'am."

In the silence, I have to look up.

She reaches across the table and takes my hand. Hers are calloused, probably from the spinning. "I will call you Es-ta-yeshi." She drops my hand.

I look up at Joseph.

He has a smile in his eyes. "Es-ta-yeshi was the only Diné warrior woman."

"I'm floored, uh, honored. But I don't want you to think I'm brave, when—"

She raises an eyebrow. "You don't want to begin by arguing with me, do you?"

"No. No, I do not."

A customer steps up to the table.

His mother's smile is dazzling, like the sun coming out on a gloomy day. "Good. You two go see the fair. We'll talk later."

Joseph's hand tightens on mine. "Ayóó anííníshni, Má."

"And I love you, son."

We walk on to the next booth, but I couldn't tell you what's in it. Even my eyes are jittering. Did that really happen?

"Told you it wouldn't be bad." He smiles down at me.

"One down, a whole tribe to go." I blow a sigh of relief. "Your mother is beautiful."

"She looks a lot like my grandmother."

"Then you do, too."

"Let's wander. Then we'll get something to eat and head over to the arena."

My mood lifts from doom to hope. "You lead, I'll follow."

"Like I believe that."

"Are you gonna feed me now? I could eat the butt end of a running—"

"We're going, Es-ta-yeshi." He drops an arm on my shoulder and leads me down the midway.

Grinning like a fool, I put my arm around his waist as something like peace seeps into my soul.

* * *

Joseph

Six months later

"Atsa, dude, whatcha' doing? The pumpkins go over here," Nevada shouts from beside the road, and points to the ground. "We've gotta pile them high, so people will notice the sign."

"Oh, okay," Atsa yells out the window and backs the truck up the incline to the road.

Turns out, he's as good with the truck as he is with the tractor, laying perfect rows.

I walk up from the field that fronts the road, and pull sun-screen from my back pocket. "If you're going to insist on wearing that baseball cap backward, you need this."

Nevada smiles up at me, and my heart tugs. I wrap my arms around her and drop a kiss on her lips. As always, a small thing turns into a big thing, and by the time she steps away, I'm hard, and she's blushing.

She reaches out and tugs my finger. "Ayóó anííníshni, Joseph."

"And I love you." I squeeze her hand. This bird is settled in my nest, happily tamed; well, at least as much as a wild thing will ever be tamed. She keeps my days interesting, my nights hot, and my life full to overflowing.

Atsa walks by, carrying a massive pumpkin. "Why are we wasting pumpkins? People won't buy them out here by the road."

"That's called marketing, dude." Nevada carries a small pumpkin for the top of the stack. "It'll sell lots more than it costs us, promise."

This whole scheme was Nevada's idea. I read the whimsical lettering on the sign:

UNFORGIVEN PUNKIN PATCH & CORN MAZE
GET A PUMPKIN, THEN GET LOST!

Our first harvest. The government came through; we're an official CSA farm as of three months ago, and we're expanding. I was able to hire the local Diné to build a new barn and add an extension to the greenhouse. Next year, I'll have jobs for any of the tribe who wants one. Asdzáá and the oldest of the Wings will have licenses by then and are already making a calendar of what days each of them will haul produce to the rez.

Nevada calls Atsa over and slathers sunscreen on his nose.

All my dreams have come true. And a few of Nevada's have as well. When I quit the café, Lorelei gave Nevada the job she wanted from the first day she walked in. She's learning our language and our customs, all while studying for the GED. Says she doesn't need it, but that she's doing it for herself. My uncle allowed Atsa to move into Grandmother's RV to help me out in the fields, and he and Nevada study together at the kitchen counter every night.

"What now, Fishing Eagle?" Atsa looks up at me.

The hero worship in his eyes no longer hurts my guts. Probably because I'm trying so hard to earn it. "Lunch, that's what."

"Whoop! What're we having?"

"Navajo tacos, of course." Nevada smiles at his backside, running for the truck. "Hey, you leave the cook behind, you get no tacos, you know."

"Well then, quit kissing and hurry up, you tsisteeł; I'm starving!"

I put my arms around my woman's shoulder. She puts hers around my waist, and we walk for the truck.

"You know, I was thinking," Nevada begins, but falters, as if she's not sure how to proceed.

"Uh-oh," I tease her, knowing that's still the best way to get her to open up.

"No, really." She tugs my waist. "What do you think about having an old-fashioned barn dance after Halloween? You know, to kind of break it in."

"Hmmmm. Who would you invite?" Not that I'd say no to just about anything she asks; she wants so little.

"Oh, I don't know...the whole town?"

I laugh, remembering the tough, withdrawn chick who blew into town not so long ago. "I think that sounds just right."

EPILOGUE

Ma,

This is the last letter I'll write, and when I finish this, I'll burn them all. I know it's a little crazy to write a bunch of letters to a dead woman, but I was so lonesome and scared, I needed somebody to talk to, you know? And, it was my way of hanging on, trying to stay with you, I guess.

I'm writing this last time just to let you know I'm happy. Way happy. Joseph loves me, I love him, and every day is better than the last. We're not getting crazy and talking about marriage, but maybe someday down the road…never say never, right?

The whole Cisco thing is over. He's gone. But I don't want to talk about it. I'm still here. That's the important thing.

It's been six months, and I'd think if the cartel was com-

ing after me, they'd have been here by now, so I guess I'm in the clear. Hard to believe that I can plan a future now, just like anybody. Oh, and Jovie's money went for good; I donated it to the school on the rez.

That day I stepped into the bedroom, touched your cold hand, and realized you were gone, I lost it. What I did next set all this in motion, but I can't be sad about it, because it started me on the road to where I am.

The Navajo aren't big on what happens after you die, but who's to say you're not reading over my shoulder?

In case you are, I want you to know, I'll always miss you, Ma. I know you did the best you could. I'm hoping you're in a better place, and finally at peace.

Hágoónee,' Má. Which is a beautiful way to say, I love you.

Your daughter,

Nevada

ACKNOWLEDGMENTS

First, thank you to Laurelle Sheppard, my Diné sensitivity expert, for reading and your patience with my questions, making sure I got it right.

And as always, a huge thank you to my 'critters,' Fae Rowen and Kimberly Belle, and to my lay editor, Donna Hopson.

And to the Superwomen in my life, who always find time for me in spite of having enough to do to keep five women busy: the one who first took a chance on me—my agent, Nalini Akolekar, and my ever-patient editor, Amy Pierpont, who was brave enough to take a chance on this book.

DON'T MISS THE NEXT BOOK IN LAURA DRAKE'S
CHESTNUT CREEK SERIES!

CHAPTER 1

Lorelei

It's been the normal crazy-hectic twelve-hour day at the Chestnut Creek Diner, and I'm beat.

Nevada, our cook, ducks her head into my office. "See you on Monday, Lorelei."

"Enjoy your day off. Say 'hey' to Fish for me."

"Will do." She waves her fingers and the door falls closed. I'm glad Nevada's happy. Of course I am. She and Joseph "Fishing Eagle" King may come from different cultures, and be total opposites, but they fit together like layers of a Kit Kat bar.

My sister Patsy has her pick of cowboys on the rodeo circuit, Carly has Austin and her baby (soon to be babies), Nevada has Fish, and I...I'm just blue tonight, I guess. I shut down the computer, pull my saddlebag-sized purse from the drawer. I'm proud that our railroad-station-turned-café is the social hub of Unforgiven. I'm proud to be the manager, feeding hungry people. It's a good, clean, honest job. I just wish sometimes that I weren't so...invisible.

I am a human golden retriever: loving, loyal, dependable. But in my experience, humans with those traits tend to go unnoticed. The dogs, on the other hand, people find adorable.

I walk through the pristine kitchen and push through the swinging door into the diner. The streetlight outside makes little inroads in the room's deep shadows. I check to be sure there's plenty of coffee setups for morning.

In the quiet, the earworm that's floated through my head all night cranks up. An old melancholy song of yearning and broken hearts. I hold up my arms and waltz with a shadow-partner across the floor. I try to imagine his face, but of course, a shadow man has none. I remind myself that it's better that way. Happily-ever-afters happen for stray golden retrievers, not their human counterparts. My feet slow to a stop and I drop my arms.

I have friends. But the last time I had a date, we had a different president. I have so little time for whatever single people do for fun that I sometimes feel like I'm watching life from behind a pane of glass.

But I'm the one who installed the glass. When you put your young heart into the hands of a casual liar the first time, you scrutinize men's hands after that.

"Stop it, Lorelei, you sound whiny; you're not a whiner." I take the few steps to the door, unlock it. "Besides, Momma's waiting." I step out and lock it behind me.

Unforgiven doesn't literally roll up the sidewalks after dark, but if they did, no one would notice. Everyone is home with their families. I drive from the light of one streetlamp to the next, past dark stores, and too many windows dressed in butcher paper. The square and its dingy gazebo look tired and a bit spooky this time of night. Unforgiven has struggled since the railroad shut down years ago and we are miles off the interstate. Sure, some tourists come through, but fewer every year. "Route 66" means nothing to Millennials.

I turn off the town square and head for home. No streetlights out here to break the vast blackness of a New Mexico summer night. The only beacons are safety lights on poles and outbuildings. Three miles out, I stop at the mailbox with "West" on the side, and the little yellow tube below for the *Unforgiven Patriot*. Just the usual flyers and bills. I'm silly to think Patsy would write when she doesn't answer calls or texts, but still there's that little let-down sigh every time I open the box.

Patsy's off living an exciting rodeo-road life. That life isn't for me, but it would be nice to get a glimpse of it now and again—from a safe distance. Living vicariously would suit me just fine.

The headlights of my old Smart Car sweep the house, highlighting that it needs a coat of paint—or three. But I have no time, and there's no money to pay for someone to do it. Besides, if I had the money, it'd go for a new roof. The warm light from the kitchen spills onto the porch, drenching my smile. That light has welcomed me home every one of my thirty-seven years. Well, since I was old enough to leave it, anyway.

The screen door shushes over the lintel, and home wraps around me with the smell of meat loaf and the sound of laughter.

"That piece doesn't go there, Mary."

"Yes it does, see?"

"No, you can't force it. You know better than that."

I cross the worn linoleum to the living room. Mom and

Mrs. Wheelwright are at the card table, putting together their latest jigsaw puzzle.

"What's up, ladies?"

Mom's small, dried-apple face comes up, wreathed in smiles. "Oh, Patsy's home!" She stands, and ignoring her walker, shambles over and throws her arms around me. I hug her back, inhaling her dusting powder scent, choking back the sticky wad of disappointment in my throat. "It's Lorelei, Momma."

She backs up enough to look into my face, a wrinkle of worry between her brows. "When is Patsy coming home?"

"Don't know, Momma."

"Mary, I need help. Can you find where this piece goes?"

Momma totters off, Patsy forgotten. For now.

Mrs. Wheelwright gives me a small, sad smile. She is a godsend, staying days with Momma for next to nothing. She's only a few years younger than my mother, but she's a former nurse and says she's happy to help out. I think she wants to escape her too-quiet house, since her husband passed last year. I blow her a kiss and wander back to the kitchen to get dinner finished and on the table.

Momma mistaking me for Patsy usually doesn't bother me, but tonight it does. I have been the constant in Momma's life even before her stroke two years ago. I've stayed in Unforgiven, kept up the house, worked to pay the bills, keep her company.

Still, she longs for Patsy.

Not that I blame her. My younger sister got all the charm, looks, and the glitter; she was always everyone's favorite. I don't begrudge her that—I'm right there in her pack of admirers. You can't not like Patsy. She's so full of herself, and confidence, and ... life. She lights up the room when she walks in, and when her focus is on you, you feel special, smart, important.

I pull on the worn oven mitts and take the meat loaf pan from the oven, setting it on the back of the stove to cool. I cross to the pantry by the back door, reach behind the gingham curtain, and pull out the Potato Buds without looking. They've been on the same shelf, always.

But it sure would be great if Patsy could make it home sometime. The last time she was here was after Momma's stroke. But she was antsy and made more work than she helped. My sister is many great things, but caregiver isn't one of them. Within the week, she was gone, back on the road with her latest cowboy-boyfriend. And except for a sporadic text or two checking on Momma, nothing since. But we love each other in this family—it's our only superpower.

I pour the tea, finish whipping the potatoes, and move everything to the table. "Dinner's ready!" Mrs. Wheelwright starts dinner, I finish it—that's the deal. When they're seated, we hold hands, I say a quick prayer over the food, then pass the plates.

After dinner when Mrs. Wheelwright has left and I've gotten Momma into her nightgown and in bed, I sit in her rocker and pick up the book we've been waiting to start. Reading is beyond Momma now, but she loves to be read to. I enjoy it, too: it calms, helping me put the day down, relaxing my mind for sleep.

Momma loves all romance, but when I happened on a sci-fi romance last year, she's been hooked ever since. I picked up this one by Fae Rowen at the library. "You ready, Momma?"

She fists her hands on the sheet and nods, her eyes bright. Her stroke mostly affected her mind, making her childlike and apt to forgetting. Her face is as full of delight as a ten-year-old's—in bad need of ironing. I lean over and kiss her forehead. "Do you know how much I love you?"

"I love you too, dear." She pats my face. "Where would I be without you?"

"Well, you'll never have to find out, so you settle in." I turn to the first page. "O'Neill never expected a glorious red and purple sunset to be her enemy..."

* * *

Lorelei

I love summer for a lot of reasons, but especially because I can drive to work on a Monday with the sun coming up over the Sandia mountains.

George Strait sings "Amarillo by Morning" from my phone. If this is our high school busboy calling in sick, I swear— "Hello?"

"Is this Lorelei West?"

"Yes. Who is this?"

"Officer Beaumont, New Mexico State Police. Do you know a Patsy Lynn West?"

"What?" My hand jerks and the car makes a sharp swerve. My heart beats timpani in my ears; my blood swirls in a dizzying storm surge. I pull off the road, skid to a stop in the gravel, and throw it in park. "She's my sister. What—"

"Ma'am. I'm sorry to do this over the phone, but I need to inform you there was a vehicular accident last night—"

"Where?"

"Out on Highway 10—"

"No, where are you calling from? What *city*?"

"Oh, Las Cruces. Ma'am, I'm so sorry to inform you, but your sister died on the way to the hospital last night."

I'm dreaming. I'm in my bed, and this is just a nightmare, probably from the chilis in the meat loaf—

"Ma'am? Are you there?"

"Yes," the word comes out on an emphysemic wheeze.

"I'm very sorry for your loss, ma'am, but I need to know—"

"You're sorry?" The word spirals up as pounding blood spreads over my vision in a red-tinged haze. "Where do you get off, calling at"—I check the clock on the dash, like the time of day could make the least bit of difference—"five a.m. to tell me you're sorry?" My shout echoing off the windshield slaps me, making me realize I could be a tad hysterical.

"Ma'am."

I heave in a lungful of air and come back to myself. "No, *I'm* sorry. Give me a second here." My arm loses function, and the phone drops to my lap. I rest my forehead on the steering wheel. I'm not dreaming. Patsy is...gone. A picture flashes, of the last time I saw her. She gave me a hug and a dazzling smile, told me she loved me to pieces. Then she hopped in her truck, threw me a kiss in the rearview, and, dust billowing, rode into the sunset.

If I'd had any inkling of the future, I'd still be holding on to her. Even though she'd be kicking and screaming; she loved the excitement of the next rodeo down the road. How could she be gone for good? Forever? I feel like I've fallen into an alternate universe. Because *this* world has my baby sister in it.

"Ma'am? Ms. West?"

When I become aware of the tinny sound, I realize I've been hearing it for a while. The phone weighs a ton when I lift it to my ear. "I'm here."

"I am truly sorry, ma'am. I just need to know what you

plan to do about the baby, since neither the mother nor the father survived the accident."

I pull the phone from my ear and stare at it. Either I *am* sleeping, or he's crazy. Or maybe, both. "What are you talking about?"

"Your sister's baby."

"You're telling me Patsy had a baby." I dig my nails into my palm hard enough to draw blood. Funny, I never felt pain in a dream bef—

"Yes, ma'am. A"—papers shuffle—"Sybil Renfrow was apparently babysitting and called us when Ms. West didn't return." For the first time, his voice shifts from administrative to human. "I know this is a shock, but if you don't plan to come for the baby, I need to let Social Services know. Are you aware of any other—"

"Stop! Stop right there!" My brain does a slow, sluggish turn. "I'll be there, okay? I'm on my way." I check the clock again. "I'll be there by lunchtime. I'll take the baby. Text your address to my phone. You called me, so you have the number."

"I do."

"And, sir?" I take a breath. "How old is the baby? Do you know its name?"

More rustling. "Six months old, ma'am. Her name is Sawyer. Sawyer West."

Somehow, knowing her name makes her real. *Oh, Patsy.*

ABOUT THE AUTHOR

Laura Drake grew up in the suburbs of Detroit. A tomboy, she's always loved the outdoors and adventure. In 1980, she and her sister packed everything they owned into Pintos and moved to California. There she met and married a motorcycling, bleed-maroon Texas Aggie, and her love affair with the West began. Her debut Western romance, *The Sweet Spot*, won the coveted RITA Award for Best First Book.

In 2014, Laura realized a lifelong dream of becoming a Texan and is currently working on her accent. She gave up the corporate CFO gig to write full-time. She's a wife, grandmother, and motorcycle chick in the remaining waking hours.

You can learn more at:
LauraDrakeBooks.com
Twitter @PBRWriter
Facebook.com/LauraDrakeBooks

For a bonus story from another author that
you'll love, please turn the page to read
Wild Cowboy Ways by Carolyn Brown.

Blake Dawson hopes he can make Lucky Penny
Ranch finally live up to its name, but the property
needs a ton of work. Allie Logan and her carpentry
skills are his best shot at getting things in order.
Besides, her brown eyes and dangerous curves have
him roped and tied. Now Blake only needs to convince her that a wild cowboy *can* be tamed by
love—and she's just the one to do it...

CHAPTER ONE

The Lucky Penny had never lived up to its name and everyone in Texas knew it. Owners had come and gone so often in the past hundred years that if the deeds were stacked up, they'd put the old Sears catalog to shame. Maybe the two sections of land should have been called Bad Luck Ranch instead of the Lucky Penny, but Blake Dawson couldn't complain—not for the price he, his brother, and cousin had paid for the place.

A cold north wind cut through Blake's fleece-lined denim jacket that January morning as he hammered the bottom porch step into place. The wind was a bitch, but then it was winter, the first Monday in January to be exact. And that damn robin out there pecking around in the dead grass sure didn't mean spring was on the way. No, sir, there would be a couple of months of cold weather. If they were lucky, they wouldn't have to deal with snow and ice. But Blake wouldn't hold his breath wishing for that. After all, when had anything in this place been lucky? Besides, in this part of Texas weather could change from sunny and seventy to blustery and brutal with a foot of snow within twenty-four hours.

He finished hammering down the last nail, stood up straight, and stretched. Done. It was the first job of too many to count, but he sure didn't need someone falling through that rotted step and getting hurt. His dog, Shooter, had watched from the top of the four steps, his eyes blinking with every stroke of the hammer.

Shooter's ears shot straight up and he growled down deep in his throat. Blake looked around for a pesky squirrel taunting him, but there was nothing but the north wind rattling through the dormant tree branches. Blake gathered his tools and headed back into the house for another cup of hot coffee before he started his first day of dozing mesquite from the ranch.

Clear the land. Plow it. Rake it. Plant it and hope for a good crop of hay so they wouldn't have to buy feed all winter. His brother Toby would bring in the first round of cattle in early June. Blake had promised to have pastures ready and fences tightened up by then. Meanwhile, Toby would be finishing his contract for a big rancher. His cousin, Jud, would be joining them, too. But he was committed to an oil company out in the panhandle until Thanksgiving. So it was up to Blake to get the groundwork laid for their dream cattle ranch.

He shucked out of his coat and hung it on the rack inside the front door and went straight to the kitchen. Sitting at the table, he wrapped his big hands around the warm mug. He was deep in thoughts about clearing acres and acres of mesquite when he heard the rusty hinge squeak as the front door eased open. He pushed back the chair, making enough noise to let anyone know that the house was no longer empty, when he heard the shrill, muffled giggle.

Surely folks in Dry Creek knocked before they plowed right into a person's home. Maybe it was a prank, kind of like an initiation into the town or a bunch of wild kids who had no idea that the ranch had been sold. Whatever was going on, his instincts had failed him or else his neck was still too damn cold to get that prickly feeling when someone was close by.

Shooter, who had been lying under the table at his feet, now stood erect and staring at the doorway. Blake would give the joker one more chance before he let him know he was messing with the wrong cowboy.

"Who's there?" he called out.

"Don't play games with me, Walter." The voice was thin and tinny and definitely not a teenager.

"And who are you?" he asked.

"Don't be silly. You know who I am, Walter." The voice got closer and closer.

What the hell was going on?

Back in the summer when the Lucky Penny went on the market, Blake, Toby, and Jud decided that they didn't believe in all that folderol about bad luck. The Lucky Penny's previous owners clearly just hadn't put enough blood, sweat, and tears into the land, or it would have been a productive ranch. They hadn't understood what it took to get a place that size up and running and/or didn't have the patience and perseverance to stick it out until there was a profit. But now Blake was beginning to question whether the bad luck had something to do with the supernatural.

He scooted his chair back and stood, Shooter close at his side, hackles up and his head lowered. Blake laid a hand on the dog's head. "Sit, boy, and don't move unless I give you the command." Shooter obeyed, but he quivered with anticipation.

"Walter, darlin', where is she?" If it wasn't a ghost, then whatever mortal it was with that voice should audition for a part in a zombie movie.

Before Blake could call out a response, a gray-haired woman shuffled into the kitchen. The old girl was flesh and blood because no self-respecting ghost or apparition would be caught anywhere looking like that. She wore a long, hot-pink chenille robe belted at the waist with a wide leather belt, yellow rubber boots printed with hot pink flamingos, and her thin hair looked like she'd stuck her finger in an electrical outlet. The wild look in her eyes gave testimony that the hair wasn't the only thing that got fried when she tested the electricity that morning. He felt a sneeze coming on as the scent of her heavy perfume filled the room.

"Aaaaachoo." He grabbed a paper napkin from the middle of the table in time to cover his mouth, when it burst from him like a bomb.

"I hope you're not getting sick, Walter," she said as she marched across the room, grabbed his cheeks with her cold hands, and pulled his face down to kiss him on the cheek. "Katy's wedding is coming up, and I don't want a red nose and puffy eyes."

"Of course not. Just a tickle in my nose, that's all." Best thing he could think to do was play along until he was able to find who the hell the old girl was talking about.

The woman hung her cane on the edge of the table and plopped into a chair. When she sat down the tail of her robe fell back to show that she was wearing jeans underneath it. She must have escaped from an institution, but Blake couldn't remember anything resembling a nursing home closer than Throckmorton or Wichita Falls, and the old gal would have frozen to death if she'd walked that far.

She laid an icy hand on his forearm. "Is she out feeding the chickens? Are we safe?"

"I'm not sure." Blake eyed her closely as he sat back down.

She squeezed his arm pretty damn tight for such bony fingers. "Aren't you even going to offer me coffee? I walked the whole way over here to see you, Walter, and it is cold as a witch's tit out there."

Holy smokin' shit! Would the real Walter please stand up and do it in a hurry?

Blake opened his mouth to tell her that he was not Walter, but then clamped it shut. If he made her mad, he'd never find out her name and without that, he wouldn't be able to get her back where she belonged. He could call the police, but Dry Creek depended on the sheriff's department out of Throckmorton for emergencies and he didn't have that number.

"Yes, let's get you warmed up. You take cream and sugar, sweetheart?" he drawled.

"Oh, sweetheart now, is it? You know very well I take it black, Walter."

"Should I call you baby? Sugar bun? Hot lips?"

"Irene will do just fine," she harrumphed, but Blake could see a smile tilting her lips.

He patted her hand as he pulled his arm away and got up from the table to retrieve a second coffee mug. "How about a toaster pastry to go with that?" he asked. Maybe if he got some food in her, she'd snap out of it and figure out he wasn't Walter.

"What in the hell is a toaster pastry? Your mama usually makes gravy and biscuits." The smile faded and her eyes darted around the room.

"Not this morning, darlin'." So the woman who put even

more craziness in the old gal's eyes wasn't Walter's wife but his mother.

"I keep telling you to move out on your own," Irene continued as he placed a steaming mug of coffee in front of her. She wrapped her hands around it like a lifeline. "If you had your own place, I'd leave my husband and we could be together all the time." She pursed her mouth so tight that her long, thin face had hollows below the high cheekbones. "A man who's almost forty years old has no business living with his mother, especially one who won't make you a decent breakfast."

"But what if she can't get along without me to help her?" Blake asked.

She shook her fist at him. "You've got four brothers. Let them take a turn. It's time for you to own up to the fact that this ranch is bad luck—always has been, always will be. You aren't going to make it here, but we could do good out in California. We'll both get a job pickin' fruit and get us a little house in town. I always wanted to live in town." She took his hand, hope shining in her eyes. The old girl just about broke Blake's heart.

"Let me make a call and see what I can do," he said gently.

The only phone number he had for anyone in Dry Creek was right there in bold print on the bottom of a 1999 feed store calendar hanging on the wall beside the refrigerator. Strange but January 4 was on a Monday that year, too. Blake wouldn't even need to get a new calendar.

Maybe the folks from the feed store would know who to call. He hoped to hell that phone number hadn't changed in the past seventeen years.

"Well, what in the hell are you waiting for?" she yelled, all the piss and vinegar coming back in a hurry. "Call one of them. Call them all. I don't really care but it's time for you to cut the apron strings and get on with your life, Walter." She picked up the coffee and sipped it. "And put that dog outside where he belongs."

"Yes, ma'am," he said.

The wild look in her eyes got even worse. "Don't you ma'am me! I'm not an old lady, by damn. I'm a woman in her prime and don't you ever ma'am me again."

He had to bite his cheek to keep from laughing out loud. Whoever this woman was, she wasn't about to let anyone steamroll her.

"And after you've called and we've had our coffee, we can fool around until *she* gets back in the house." Irene smiled up at him.

As if Shooter understood he wasn't welcome, he circled around the table, keeping a wary eye on the newcomer until he got to the back door where he whined. Glad to have an excuse to leave the table, Blake went to open the door and let the old boy out, wishing the whole time that he could escape with him.

Just exactly what did she mean by "fool around"? Did it mean the same in her demented mind that it did in today's world. If so he'd have to make that cup of coffee last until someone could come get this woman or else learn a whole new level of bullshitting his way out of a messy ordeal.

He eased the cell phone out of his pocket and poked in the numbers from the calendar. Irene seemed very content to sip her coffee and mumble about a damn dog being in the kitchen where womenfolk made food. Dog hairs, according to her, were covered with deadly diseases that could kill a person if they got into their fried potatoes.

"Dry Creek Feed and Seed. May I help you?" a feminine voice answered on the third ring.

"Ma'am, I'm the new owner of the Lucky Penny, and an elderly woman named Irene showed up at my door this morning. It's starting to rain and…" He didn't get another word out.

"Oh, no! Just hang on to her and I'll send someone for her in the next few minutes. Don't let her leave," the woman said, and the call ended.

CHAPTER TWO

Allie hated two things: cleaning and cooking. But every third week it was her turn to clean the big two-story house known as Audrey's Place.

Back during the Depression, Audrey's had been a rather notorious not-exactly-legal brothel. Miz Audrey, the lady who owned the place, had seen an opportunity where everyone else around Dry Creek saw defeat. She'd hired six girls at a time when everyone needed jobs. She was one of the few folks who hung on to her land, her business, and came out on the other side of the Depression with more money than she knew what to do with. Her girls, too. The hundred-year-old house had withstood tornadoes, winds, and all the other crazy weather that Texas could throw at it.

But Allie wasn't appreciating her family home's rich history as she trudged through each of the six bedrooms on the second floor to vacuum, dust, and tidy up. She would far rather be the one creating mess. Give her the glorious smells of wood shavings, plaster dust, or varnish during a home remodel and she'd be much happier than breathing in pine-scented cleaners.

She paused on the bottom step, made sure that Granny was arguing with the characters of *Golden Girls* on the television in the living room, before she toted the bucket of cleaning supplies up the stairs. Allie had put in the new railing the previous spring and still liked to run her hand over the new wood, taking a moment to admire the intricate spindles she'd turned on her lathe. Her father had given her the tools, the knowledge, and the love for carpentry. Some days she missed him even more than others, like when she opened the bathroom door and there was the lovely vanity they'd worked on together the year before he died.

She was about to return downstairs, when her phone buzzed in the side pocket of her cargo pants. She pulled it out and without even checking the caller ID she answered, "Hello."

"Alora Raine Logan," her mother said.

"Why are you double-naming me? I couldn't possibly get into trouble while cleaning the house!"

"You let your grandmother get away from you." Katy's voice was so shrill it hurt Allie's ears.

"Impossible, Mama. The doors are locked with those new baby guards that she can't open. Besides, not fifteen minutes ago, I checked on her. She was sitting on the sofa watching *Golden Girls*."

Granny had shaken her fist at the television with a string of cuss words. Even in her moments of confusion, she never lost her spirit.

"Well, she's at the Lucky Penny now," Katy said.

A gust of cold wind hit her in the face when Allie reached

the foyer. The door was thrown wide open, and Lizzy's yellow boots were gone from the lineup beside the hall tree.

"You're right. She's gone! But why the Lucky Penny?" Allie was already cramming her feet down into a pair of boots.

"She must've heard us talking about a new cowboy buying that place. I can't leave the store so you'll have to go get her," Katy said. "It's going to rain so take a vehicle. I hope she at least put on a jacket or else she'll catch pneumonia, frail as she is."

"Lizzy's rubber boots are missing from the foyer and I dressed her in jeans and a sweatshirt this morning." Allie stuck her free arm into a stained mustard-colored work coat.

"Thank goodness she's at least got something on her feet. Last time she went over there, she was wearing nothing but a nightgown when I went to get her. There she sat on the porch flirting with someone in her head because the only living thing on the whole ranch was an old gray tom cat," Katy said.

Allie picked up her van keys from the foyer table and headed out the door. "I'm on the way, Mama. She's probably sitting on the porch like last time. I don't think anyone has moved in yet."

"Lizzy said that Herman Hudson came in for a load of feed this morning and that at least one cowboy moved in on Saturday," Katy said.

"How'd you find out where she is?" Allie asked.

"The crazy cowboy who bought the place called the feed store. The number was on the bottom of one of those calendars we used to give out at Christmas. Lizzy answered and then called me."

"I'll call you when I've got her back in the house." Allie jogged out to her work van and hopped inside. She shivered as she shoved the key into the ignition. They'd had a mild winter up until now, but January was going to make up for it for sure if this was a taste of what was to come. She didn't give the engine time to warm up but shoved the truck into gear, hit the gas, and headed down the lane toward the road where she made a right-hand turn. The steering wheel was as cold as icicles, but in her hurry she'd left her gloves on the foyer table. Half a mile farther she made another right and whipped into the winding lane at the Lucky Penny.

Had she gone by foot, Allie would have walked a few hundred yards, crawled over or under a broken-down barbed wire fence, and gone another hundred yards to the old house. That's most likely the way that Granny had gone, and it took less than ten minutes to get there. Allie came to a screeching halt outside the house and with a carpenter's eye saw how much more dilapidated it had gotten since she was last on the ranch.

How long had it been? At least eight years because she'd been divorced more than seven, and the last time she'd been there was back when she and Riley, like all the other kids in that day and age, parked there to make out. Looking back, the smartest thing she did when she and Riley split ways was take her maiden name back.

A big yellow dog met her halfway across the yard. His head was down and his tail wagging, which meant he wasn't going to take a chunk out of her butt. But the sight of him did slow her down.

She held out a hand. "Hey, feller, what's your name?"

The dog nosed her hand in a friendly gesture, so she rubbed his ears. "You got my granny in that house, or is she hiding in one of the barns this time?"

The first big raindrop hit her on the cheek and rolled down her neck. It was as cold as ice water, and more quickly followed before she made it to the porch. Shivers chased down her spine as the water hit her bra and kept moving to the waistband of her underpants.

She knocked on the door and waited.

"Walter, don't open that door," her granny called out loud and clear.

"Are you Walter?" she asked the dog, who'd followed her to the porch, just as the front door swung open.

"No, he's Shooter. Are you Katy?"

Allie looked up into the greenest eyes she'd ever seen rimmed by dark lashes. Her gaze traveled to his wide shoulders, the Henley shirt stretched over bulging abs, and the big belt buckle with a bull rider on it. She had to force herself to look back up, only to find him smiling, his arms now crossed over his chest.

Lord, have mercy! Crazy cowboys who bought a bad luck ranch were definitely not supposed to be that sexy.

She wanted to crawl under her work van because there she stood wearing cargo pants, a faded thermal-knit shirt frayed out at the wrists, black rubber boots, and the old coat she wore on the job site. She smelled like pine oil and ammonia and didn't have even a smidgen of makeup on her face.

Granny shuffled across the floor. "Don't be silly, Walter. This is Katy, my daughter. You've seen her lots of times at church for the past six months. Don't you have enough sense to get in out of the rain, girl? Why haven't you invited her inside, Walter? Where are your manners?"

"Granny, I am not Katy. I'm Allie, your granddaughter. You know better than to sneak out of the house like this. You scared all of us," Allie fussed.

"Maybe we can sort this out inside where it's warm and dry," Blake offered. He stuck out his hand. "I'm Blake

Dawson. C'mon in." His eyes were so green that she would have sworn he was wearing colored contact lenses.

She put her hand in his. "I'm Allie Logan, your neighbor. I'm so sorry about this."

Her hand tingled and the feeling lingered as she followed him into the house and through to the kitchen, tugging Granny after her. Maybe it was the weather, or the fact that he was one sexy piece of baggage. Most likely it was the fact that she hadn't had sex in so long that she might have to get out the how-to booklet to even remember what body part went where.

"I'm ready to go home now." Irene's head tilted to one side and she shoved her hands into the pockets of the chenille robe. "I came over here to welcome this young man to Dry Creek. You should have come with me."

"You live nearby?" Blake asked.

"Yeah, the big house called Audrey's Place. It's just past your east field and over the fence."

"Audrey's Place? Is this Audrey? She told me her name was Irene." Blake shoved his thumbs into his hip pockets.

Irene's face went into that mode that reminded Allie of a dried apple doll; all wrinkles with deep-set eyes and a puckered-up mouth, hollowed cheeks and a sharp little chin. She poked Blake in the chest with a bony finger and raised her voice as high as it would go. "Hell, no! Audrey was a whore. I'm a fine, upstanding churchgoin' woman. I'm not a hooker like my great-great grandma. I am Irene Miller, young man, and don't you forget it."

She held her hand up to catch a drop of water when it fell from the ceiling. "Don't know why we're wasting our time with makin' casseroles to welcome him. He won't be here more'n a year. The good-lookin' ones never stay. Couple of ugly ones made it two years, but the cold winter will put this one on the run."

"Granny!" Allie said as soon as she could get a word in edgewise.

Irene shrugged. "Better get a pan and put it under that leak, young man, or you're going to be mopping all day. Now take me home, Allie."

"Granny, you're being rude."

Blake chuckled. "She does manage to keep things lively."

"You have no idea." Allie glanced at the drip coming from the ceiling. "It's been leaking a while from the size of that brown ring. You're lucky someone put down linoleum flooring because it could ruin carpet or hardwood."

Blake nodded. "Damn. I hoped that the water marks on the ceiling were from a long time ago and the leak had been fixed. I'll just have to add it to the list of the million other repairs."

"Allie's great at repairs," Irene piped in. "We have a construction business, and we're damn good at what we do."

"Really?" Blake's eyes lit up. "Could I hire you to put on a new roof?"

Allie threw an arm around her grandmother, wishing she had a muzzle. "We'll have to check our workload and get back to you."

"You was complainin' last week that you needed a job and things were slower," Irene fussed. "But I'm not doing one damn thing to help anyone on this ranch after the way Walter acted. You didn't know him like I did, Allie. What in the hell are we doing here, anyway? Take me home right now."

"Let me get your things, Miz Miller," Blake said.

Allie's eyes followed him as he walked away. He filled out those jeans really well and she could imagine what that tight butt would look like with nothing on it at all. Good lord, she had to get a grip.

"Who's Walter?" Allie asked.

Irene's lips tightened and she shook her head. "You just stay away from this ranch. It don't bring nothing but heartache and pain to anyone who comes around it because no one ever stays. It should be called Hard Luck not Lucky Penny."

Allie folded Irene's hand in hers. "Tell me more about Walter and his family. When did they live on this ranch?"

Before Allie could get any more information, Blake came back with Irene's flamingo boots and her cane, plus an empty trash can to put under the leak. "So, can you ask the carpenter in your family if he'd be interested in a job?"

Irene waggled a finger at him. "No and that is final. We ain't interested in your leaky roof and I'm not talking about Walter even if you put me in my room and give me nothing but bread and water for a month." She pulled free from Allie's hand and stormed out of the house into the rain.

Allie watched as she marched straight to the van, stomping right through the mud puddles. The bottom of her robe was soaked by the time she slung the passenger's door open and crawled inside.

Blake chuckled. "And to think thirty minutes ago she was trying to talk me into running away to California with her to pick fruit. Someone named Walter must have lived on this ranch and she loved him at one time."

"Sorry that you had to be Walter, whoever he is, today," Allie said.

"I wasn't going to argue with her. Besides I got to meet you. Like Mama says, dark clouds can have silver linings." He shot her a wicked grin that zinged right through her. "You will check that calendar and have your carpenter give me a call. I'll get you my number." He hurried over to the sofa, wrote the number on the bottom edge of a magazine page, and handed it to her.

His fingertips grazed hers and there was definitely a tingle. Sweet Jesus! She had to remind herself that this was the Lucky Penny. Folks came and went on it and no one ever lasted, especially not any sexier than hell cowboys. She straightened herself and put some steel in her spine.

"I'll call when I check the calendar. And I'll keep a better eye on Granny. Thanks for calling the feed store."

"You could call about other things, too . . . if you wanted," he drawled.

The glint in his eyes promised some temptation beyond imagining, and the gravel in his voice had an underlying tone of making all her dreams come true. She came close to promising to build him a brand-new house for free from the ground up. Lord, have mercy! He was flirting. Flirting with Allie when she looked like shit in her work clothes with her hair up in a messy ponytail. He was a player for sure, one of those wicked, wild cowboys who got what they wanted with a slow drawl and a sexy strut. He flirted, not because he was interested in Allie, but because it was a way to get a roof on his house.

"I should be going. She's going to be a handful the rest of the day. Her mind is like a dozen jigsaw puzzles in one box. Who knows what pieces go with what time frame? It's all a muddle. Thanks again for taking care of her." Allie opened the screen door and took a step out onto the porch.

Blake leaned against the doorjamb, his arms crossed— the perfect pose to show off those long legs and broad shoulders. Just the sight had her almost forgetting about her grandmother altogether.

"Well, you're both welcome here anytime. Pleased to meet you, Allie," he said.

"Good-bye, Blake." She jogged through the rain to the van but she could feel the heat of his eyes on her back the whole way.

CHAPTER THREE

Shooter gave Blake a wistful look with his big brown eyes and wagged his tail.

"What?" Blake said. "She has pretty brown eyes, and I need a roof on the house."

Shooter yipped as if arguing with him.

His mama said that good looks and hard work would get a cowboy far in life but charm would get him anything he wanted. So far she'd been one hundred percent right. Hopefully, the charm would work one more time and then he'd settle down to being a stable rancher.

Shooter growled and gazed at the window.

"What is it, boy? That poor old lady back to yell at me some more?" Blake rushed to the window to memorize the phone number on the side of the van. The first six numbers were the same as the one on the calendar, which meant Logan Construction was a local company. The last four were 2200. His birthday plus two zeroes. He went straight to the kitchen and wrote it on the bottom of the old calendar right below the feed store number. He wasn't going to take any chances on not being able to reach Allie again.

His phone rang and he grabbed it from the cabinet beside the sink, checked the ID, and said, "Hey, Toby."

"How are things going down there? Are you getting unpacked?" his brother asked.

"It's raining and there's a leak in the living room ceiling, but I've got a trash can under it. Just found out there's a carpenter next door, so if he's not busy..." Blake went on to tell his brother what had happened that morning, conveniently leaving out any mention of the old lady's offer to fool around.

"What a welcoming committee!" Toby laughed. "I wish I'd been there to see that. You say she even put old Shooter out?"

"I opened the door but he didn't waste any time scootin' his butt outside. At the time, I wished I could follow him. Even that cold wind and rain would've been better than having coffee with our neighbor."

"Good you're getting to know the neighbors—even if they are crazy. Most small towns are alike. Friendly folks who make newcomers pretty welcome. I saw a church when we moved you down there. Did you go yesterday?"

"No, I was too busy just trying to make the place habitable. It's a mess, bro. And now we need a whole new roof on top of everything else." Blake leaned his head back and stared at the rusty rings on the ceiling. "I've cleared land, plowed land, worked with cattle, even ridden a few bulls in the rodeo, but redoing a whole roof by myself is beyond me. I just hope that the neighbor has a slot on the calendar with enough time to fix it."

"Oh, come on, now," Toby said seriously. "Surely you

can sweet talk that woman into getting her family to work for you."

"It's against my rules to play in a sandbox that close to home. It'll get you in trouble every time. And I'm trying to leave that player reputation behind me and start a new life here," Blake said.

"I'll believe it when I see it," Toby said. "I'll drive up in a week or so for the weekend to see what I can do to help out—even if it's sweet-talking the neighbor myself."

Blake tensed at the thought of his brother trying to charm Allie. He practically had to restrain the growl that rose in his throat. "I'll take care of it," he said curtly, rolling his neck to get the kinks out.

Toby just laughed. "I'll see you either this weekend or the next. Soon as I can get away."

"From what? Your ranch or the bars?" Blake asked.

"Both. Got to get these new folks comfortable with the place before I leave them with it and I'll get my time at the bars while I can, especially since the Lucky Penny is in a dry county."

"Yeah, you keep playing while I do all the dirty work," Blake grumbled.

"Just remember the end game," Toby said. "I'll be there in the spring and Jud before the end of the year. In five years we'll have the Lucky Penny solidly established, maybe even with a decent barn built to have our own cattle sale if we work hard at it. Suck it up, brother. This is only the first week."

Blake inhaled deeply and let it out slowly. "Think you and Jud will be able to survive with no bars in the whole county?"

"If you can, I can. I'm tougher than you and now I've got to go." The call ended before Blake could reply.

He went to the kitchen, poured another cup of coffee, and stared at all those boxes stacked everywhere. Saturday seemed like years ago. The excitement of finally moving onto the ranch had been replaced with doubts as big as Longhorn bulls' horns.

"My first challenge after getting this damn roof fixed is to work my way into the community." He looked up again at the dripping ceiling. "Look on the bright side, Shooter. At least it's dripping in the hallway and not right on top of my bed or on your lazy old hide. And I'll be damned if I let Toby and Jud think I can't manage my end of this bargain."

The dog answered with a couple of tail thumps but he didn't open his eyes.

Blake picked up a notepad from the end table where he'd started a grocery list and carried it with him through the house. Roof first and then if there was money left in the repair budget for the house he'd see how far he could stretch it. He started in the living room, checking everything and writing down what needed to be fixed, putting a star beside the things that were most important in each room. Two hallways split off from the living room. The one to the north led to three bedrooms with a bathroom at the end. A huge country kitchen and a dining room opened up from the southern hall. The small table with four chairs around it looked even tinier in the huge kitchen, surrounded on three sides with cabinet space. An archway on the other end led into the dining room, which was every bit as big as the kitchen but empty except for boxes.

Whoever built the house either had or intended to have a huge family. Lots of room in the huge living room for children to play, in the dining room for an enormous table to seat lots of people, and the kitchen for family to gather around at mealtimes. He shut his eyes and imagined a day in the future when there would be laughter as well as arguments in the old ramshackle house. It would look different then because it would be a home filled with love, not a house where one lonesome old wild cowboy lived with his dog.

As he went from one room to the next, writing what it would take to restore the house to some kind of livable conditions, his mood sunk. The place hadn't seemed nearly so dilapidated back when they came to Dry Creek and looked at the ranch. But then back in the summer, they'd been a whole lot more interested in the ranching part of the deal and not the house.

"I will make this work," he mumbled.

Shooter's tail thumped against the worn leather sofa.

Blake gulped down the last of the coffee and set the cup on the coffee table. "Are you agreeing with me or telling me I'm an idiot?"

Shooter's eyes snapped shut and he snored.

Since it was raining and he couldn't do any outside work, Blake decided to tackle everything his mama had marked "kitchen" when she helped pack boxes. He ripped the tape from a box and started the job. Dishes in the upper cabinets. Food in the pantry right off the utility room. Pots and pans in the lower cabinets. During the whole process, he thought about Allie.

She was a pretty girl and he could sink into her dark brown eyes and drown—not exactly his usual type, but there was something about her he couldn't get out of his head. He and Toby tended to go for the tall willowy blondes with blue eyes. It was Jud who liked petite brunettes. Blake didn't like the thought of befriending Allie just to have Jud swoop in and steal her heart.

When the rain finally stopped, he carried an armload of flattened boxes out to his truck and threw them into the back.

Later, when he figured out where his burn pile would be, he'd take care of them. He heard a vehicle coming down the lane and parking in the front yard and hoped that Allie had returned to tell him that the Logan Construction Company would fix the roof. He jogged through the kitchen and dining room, and threw open the door the minute she knocked.

A tall blonde holding a casserole dish smiled at him from the other side of the screen door. "Welcome to Dry Creek. I'm Sharlene Tucker." She batted long lashes and tilted her head to one side.

He picked up on all the take-me-home-tonight signs and instinctively moved in to close the deal. "Come right in, darlin'. It's shapin' up to be a fine day when a pretty woman brings food to my door."

A brighter smile and a definite extra wiggle under those skintight pants said that she was there for more than food and talk.

"Let me take that for you and then I'll help you with your coat." He lowered his voice an octave and whispered softly.

"I'll just come in and put this in the refrigerator for you and be on my way. I work at the bank in Olney and I'm already a little late, but thank you for the offer. Maybe I'll take a rain check." That deliberate brush of her breasts across his chest as she walked by said that she'd be glad to come back around anytime.

"The church ladies will be coming around in a day or two with food, but I wanted to welcome you personally, Mr. Dawson." She bent over to put the casserole on the bottom shelf of the fridge, giving him a perfect view of a rounded butt stretching the seams of her black pants.

She straightened, turned around, and tipped her head up, moistening her lips seductively. "Don't you tell that I came a little early." She tapped a manicured nail against his chin.

"This is just to hold you over until they get here. Got to run. Call me if you need anything, Mr. Dawson." A pen appeared out of her jacket pocket and she wrote her name and number on the outdated calendar. "We'll have to see about getting you a new calendar. Bye now and enjoy the casserole."

He followed her to the door and opened it for her. "Thank you so much for the food and I'm Blake, not Mr. Dawson."

"Right nice to meet you, Blake. I'll be waiting for you to call."

Katy Logan popped her hands on her hips. That gesture usually brought her three girls to attention, but since Fiona was in Houston, only Lizzy and Allie sat up straighter in their chairs. "I heard the new cowboy next door is pretty damn handsome. Sure you're not planning to do any more than fix his roof?"

Allie took down four plates from the cabinet, put the silverware in the top one, and started setting the table for breakfast. "For God's sake, Mama. I'm not going to marry the man. I'm going to put a roof on his house and that's it."

Katy pushed her dark hair, with streaks of white starting to show, behind her ears. "Your grandmother said he looked at you like he could eat you up yesterday when you were over there."

"Hell's bells, Mama. Granny was so busy talking about Walter that she didn't know who she was or where she was. And I smelled like pine oil and ammonia. I don't think he wanted to bite into that. He just wanted to get me to say yes to helping him out. His kind isn't interested in women like me."

Her youngest sister, Lizzy, whipped her dishwater-blond hair up into a ponytail and went to the pantry to get several bottles of syrup. "This new guy sounds like a player. Why can't you find a good decent man like my Mitch? He wouldn't have to be a preacher but he needs to be a godly man."

Allie rolled her eyes. "Yes, we all know Mitch is a paragon of men. But I had a man. A husband! I gave him my heart and he broke it. So no, thank you, not just to godly men but to any man. I'm going to the Lucky Penny to put a roof on the house, not have a fling," Allie said.

Lizzy plopped the syrup on the table and went to the refrigerator for the butter dish. "If you go over to the Lucky Penny, you can bet you'll be in the gossip spotlight even worse than when you left Riley. Besides every unmarried woman in Throckmorton County probably is layin' out plans to get to know Brian. I heard that Sharlene was making a Mexican casserole to take to him. You know what that means."

Allie popped Lizzy on the arm. "His name is Blake and I did not leave Riley. He left me and that was seven years ago. And yes, I know that Sharlene expects something hot in return for her hot Mexican casserole."

"Mama, she hit me," Lizzy said.

"I barely touched you," Allie protested. Sisters might grow up in body but in spirit they stayed children. Some habits weren't breakable, like Allie's instinct to slap Lizzy for being a smartass.

"Don't get all pissy with me," Lizzy said. "I'm trying to make you see that this is a bad idea. You can't stop gossip and it's been a long dry spell in town for good rumors."

Allie brought out butter and a bowl of fruit. "A roofing job will only last a week. What can happen in a week?"

"Stop your bickering. You know it upsets your grandmother." Katy piled the pancakes on a platter, slathering each layer with the butter she had melted earlier. "Who did you say she kept calling the new guy? Walter? I remember some folks who lived there years ago and tried to make a go of that place. An elderly woman and her son. I think his name was Walter, but that was about the time I married your father so I didn't pay a lot of attention in those days."

"Maybe she knew him but was married to Grandpa at that time. I can't see her falling in love with a man when she'd been married more than twenty years," Allie said.

"She's got it all mixed up. I bet she liked some guy from over there back when she was a young girl and her mama refused to let her get mixed up with him because she knew no one ever lasted over there," Lizzy said.

Allie peeled paper towels off the roll to use for napkins. "I'm going to take this job. I don't give a shit what people say. We're lucky that the weather is going to be decent the next few days."

"You'll call Deke?" Katy sighed. "Promise me you'll call Deke. At least you'll have a chaperone as well as someone to help you. Maybe folks won't talk so much that way."

"I don't need a chaperone, Mama. But I called Deke this morning and he's free the rest of this week." Allie nodded. "One of you will have to take Granny to work with you today so I can make a trip to Wichita Falls for supplies. If the weather holds we can get started today and have the job done by Friday."

Lizzy pushed a strand of wayward hair behind her ears. "Mitch is supposed to come by today. You know how Granny hates him so you'd best take her today, Mama, and I'll babysit tomorrow."

"I still don't like it," Katy said. "That new man didn't even come to church on Sunday. If he wanted to fit in with the community, he'd come to church."

"He was settling in on Sunday, Mama, and his name is Blake," Allie said.

"I hear Granny rustlin' up the hallway. Best stop talkin' about the Lucky Penny. Seems like that sets her off into a tizz." Lizzy put a finger to her lips. "And, Allie, there ain't no need to remember his name anyway. He won't be here past spring. Besides, Brian could have come to church for one hour just to show the community that he is a God-fearin' man."

"Blake as in Blake Shelton, your favorite country singer," Allie said.

"Okay, okay! I'll remember. Why is it so damn important to you anyway? You said you weren't going to marry him. Is he handsome?" Lizzy slapped a hand over her mouth. "He is, isn't he? Mama, he's sexy and she's going to make a fool out of herself again."

"You cussed! Not very fitting for the future wife of a preacher. Mama, did you hear that?"

Katy gave her daughter a hard stare and sighed. "Really? What are you girls, five years old again?"

Lizzy shrugged. "Quit trying to change the subject and just answer my question. Is he sexy?"

Allie took a step closer to her sister. "You answer mine first. Why should he come to church?"

"Because that's the first thing a respectable person should do when he moves to a new town. For all we know he's going to run a brothel over there," Lizzy answered.

Laughter exploded out of Allie. It bounced off the walls and echoed all the way through the two-story house. "That's the pot calling the kettle black for sure. And darlin', he is so damn sexy that my underpants crawled all the way to my ankles."

Lizzy pulled out a chair and loaded her plate with

pancakes. "Mama, she's takin' up for him and talkin' dirty, too."

"Don't you worry none about Allie," Katy said. "She's learned her lesson."

Lizzy smiled smugly. "At least I've got more sense than that. My Mitch is a man of God."

"Well, bless your little heart," Allie smarted off. "I'm happy for you, but even men of God have faults."

"Not my Mitch," Lizzy declared.

Irene poked her head around the corner and giggled. "I've been eavesdropping for a long time. In my opinion, it's a bad idea for Allie to go to the Lucky Penny. That man is plumb deadly to women, and she can't afford another broken heart. And, Lizzy, crawl down off that high horse. The Good Book is full of men who couldn't keep it in their pants. Even David, the man after God's own heart, had a problem along those lines." She crossed the room and pulled out the fourth chair. "Pancakes. I do love pancakes."

CHAPTER FOUR

Blake's and Shooter's breathing fogged up the cab window of the bulldozer that morning before the heater finally kicked in. The machinery was far from new and the heater worked sporadically, running a while and then shutting down until it was damn good and ready to start up again.

Shooter sat straight and tall in the passenger's seat and listened to the music coming from the radio. At least the speakers worked better than the heater.

Blake hummed along to a Josh Turner song.

Shooter kept his eyes straight ahead, watching every mesquite tree that the dozer blade ripped out of the cold ground by the roots.

"You lookin' for rabbits or squirrels to come out from those thickets?"

Shooter's ears shot straight up.

Blake's phone vibrated against his chest and he unzipped his coveralls enough to reach inside and fetch it. He glanced down and took a deep breath. This was it. Either Allie was calling to tell him that Logan Construction was taking the job or else he would have to learn how to shingle a roof.

He touched the screen and put the phone to his ear. "Hello."

"Mr. Dawson, this is Allie Logan. We have decided that we can fix your roof. We're going for supplies this morning after we run by and measure it. And we will probably start removing the old shingles this afternoon. Do you have a preference of shingle color? White is what you've got on there, but before we agree on a price, you have to understand that if I'm needed at home to take care of my grandmother, then I'll have to work around that."

"Whew! Slow down, Miz Logan! That pretty little mouth of yours was made for something other than talking too fast."

"Flattery won't get you anywhere with me. Do you still want me to fix that roof?"

"Yes, I do," he said. "And I was stating a fact, not flattering you. Your lips are perfect and made for kissing."

"I want to get supplies today and get to work so it can be done by the time the bad weather rolls in that the weatherman is calling for."

He chuckled. "Thank you for that."

"Now, shingles or metal roof?"

"Which is cheaper? I'm on a budget." She was a tough nut to crack for sure. Usually those lines had a woman in his pocket for at least a night and maybe a whole weekend.

"Shingles." One word. Her tone said business.

"Then that's the route to take and I'm not particular about color. What would you suggest?" Blake asked.

"Are you going to repaint the outside in the spring when it's warm enough?" she asked.

"Of course. The way the paint is peeling, it's a wonder some of the boards aren't rotted out," Blake answered. "Thank goodness the lower half of the place is fieldstone."

"What color?" Allie asked.

"The color of your eyes when the sun makes them sparkle."

"Get serious, Blake Dawson!"

"Okay then. Light gray with white porch railings and trim work." He wasn't sure where the idea came from, maybe from that big two-story house painted gray with white trim he noticed as he drove through Throckmorton on his way to Dry Creek. "How do you see it?"

"That would be beautiful. How about a charcoal gray roof?" Allie asked.

Blake turned down the volume on the radio. "Sounds good to me."

"Do you want to see samples? I could send pictures by phone."

"Couldn't you bring them by? We could decide together over a cup of coffee or a bowl of ice cream." His voice went into its most seductive mode.

"Maybe you need to consult with your girlfriend?"

She was all business. Nothing was working. Holy smokin' shit! Did the bad luck on this ranch turn his good luck with women upside down?

"That's not necessary. Don't have a girlfriend and don't imagine my two partners give a damn what color the house is. Just pick out what you think would look good with light gray and bring it back with you. Do you need a check before you send your men after the supplies?"

"No, but I will want half this afternoon when we get there and the other half when the job is done, maybe by Friday evening, definitely by Saturday," she answered.

"That sounds great." Blake gave Shooter the thumbs-up sign.

"I'll be over there by noon and we'll get started removing those old white shingles and seeing how much damage control we need to do to the decking. Good-bye, Mr. Dawson," Allie said stiffly.

He caught his smile in the rearview mirror. "Call me Blake. We *are* neighbors."

"Thank you. You can call me Allie and is it convenient for me to drop by in an hour to do some measuring? You don't have to be there. It's all outside work," Allie said.

"Whatever you need to do is fine and the back door is unlocked if you need to go inside the house." Blake tucked the phone inside his denim jacket pocket and whistled through his teeth.

By noon there were two enormous piles of mesquite in the pasture ready to be cut up into firewood and/or burned. Blake felt like his butt had calluses on it from bouncing around in the dozer seat all morning. When he stepped down onto steady ground he did several stretches to get the kinks out of his back.

Shooter raced past him, put his nose to the ground, and flushed three rabbits before Blake could take two steps away from the machinery. Then the old dog was off and running, barking happily until the rabbits took refuge in a pile of dead mesquite and Shooter couldn't figure out a way to get inside the tangled brush at them.

Blake caught up and scratched the old boy's ears. "Don't worry. They'll have to come out sometime. Would you look at all that beautiful firewood? We'll bring the chainsaw out here real soon and tear up their hiding places."

The wind had gotten colder since he'd started work that

morning. It was so cold that it burned his lungs when he took a breath so he pulled his coat collar up over his mouth and nose. Shooter backed his ears and took off for the house in a dead run. Blake did a fast trot right behind him, cleared the steps, and landed on the porch. He did not envy Allie and whoever she had working with her one bit. Working on a roof with that cold wind whipping around them would be a real task.

He hadn't even hung up his coat, when someone knocked on the door. He turned around, opened the door, and there on the other side was a curvy brunette with streaks of blue in her shoulder-length hair. It looked like someone had cut it with a chainsaw. Maybe that's what happened and it had terrified her so badly that it turned part of her hair blue.

"You must be Blake Dawson. I'm Mary Jo Clark and I brought over some chili and a chocolate pie to welcome you to Dry Creek," she said in a gravelly voice that matched her skinny jeans and form-fitting sweater.

"Well, thank you, Mary Jo Clark. I was about to fix myself a sandwich but chili does sound so much better," he drawled in his most seductive voice.

"If you'll bring those big strong arms and help me carry it in from the van, I would appreciate it." She batted her eyes at him like a seasoned bar bunny.

He followed her to the van and she raised the back hatch. "You carry that slow cooker, darlin', and I'll get this box. My phone number is right here." She pointed to the end of the cardboard box and there it was, written in three-inch numbers. "If you need anything at all, honey, you just give me a call and I'll be here in five minutes."

"You want to stick around and eat some of this with me?" he asked.

"Oh, darlin', I would love to but I've got to be in Wichita

Falls by one thirty. I work at the hair salon in Walmart and I've got the late shift today. But maybe on my next day off we can plan something."

Yep, a seasoned bar bunny. He could spot one from a hundred yards and reel them in like a catfish out of the river. And by damn, Mary Jo was proof that he hadn't lost all his luck with women. It was Allie Logan who couldn't be swayed with his pickup lines, not the whole damn female population of Throckmorton County.

He wiped his brow and then remembered that he really wanted to leave the wild cowboy ways behind him. *Get thee behind me, Lucifer! You are not going to make this change in my life easy are you? Already you're throwing up temptations that are pretty damn hard to avoid.*

When they'd unloaded the food on the kitchen cabinet he followed her back out to the porch. That was the polite thing to do. After all, she'd brought enough chili to last until spring thaw, a chocolate meringue pie, and that sure enough looked like jalapeño cornbread in the box with the pie.

When they reached the yard gate, he stuck out his hand and said, "Thank you again, Mary Jo. That was real sweet of you to welcome me to Dry Creek."

She bypassed the hand, ran her hands up under his jacket, and pressed her body close to his. She rolled up slightly on her toes and kissed him on the chin. "Put that hand away, Blake. I believe in hugs to welcome a person, not a handshake. And the second time I see you, I'll expect a hug and a real kiss."

He didn't even hear the truck coming up the driveway until it stopped beside her van, and there was Allie staring right at him from the passenger window. Mary Jo winked at Allie and hugged Blake one more time.

The window of the truck rolled down slowly. "Didn't take you long to find a girlfriend."

Blake propped one forearm over the other against the truck, his face only a few inches from Allie's. "Just met her ten minutes ago. Don't think we've got far enough to call it a relationship."

"Hello." A big man reached across Allie with an open hand. "I'm Deke and I'll be helping Allie put a roof on your house."

Blake's arm grazed Allie's shoulder when he stuck his hand through the window. He blamed the sparks on the cold weather and a little static electricity.

Deke had a firm handshake and a friendly smile, but it was too cold to stand outside and talk when a warm fire and a pot of chili waited in the house.

"Let's take this conversation inside," he said.

Deke nodded.

Blake was careful not to touch Allie again as he pulled his hand back and then jogged to the house. The second the door was open, Shooter raced inside and curled up in front of the fireplace on a worn rug. Blake laid a couple of logs on the embers and the old dog sighed.

He went to the kitchen and lifted the lid from the slow cooker. The spicy aroma of chili filled the whole room. He'd be eating it for a week or else divvying it up into plastic containers and freezing it. The crunch of tires pulling the trailer around back filtered through the kitchen window, but it wasn't until someone knocked on the back door that Shooter's head popped up.

Blake slung the door open and Deke, taller than Blake's six feet by at least four inches, stood behind Allie. He had curly brown hair that covered his ears and poked out around a well-worn cowboy hat. His hazel eyes studied Blake like he was a bug under a microscope. Allie's husband, maybe? He couldn't help the twinge that ran through him at the thought.

"Come in." Blake motioned them out of the cold weather. "I put a couple of logs on the fire so it's getting nice and warm in here."

Allie handed him a bill. "This is for the total job. Gray shingles were on sale this week so I got a little better deal than we talked about on the phone. It's five hundred less than the estimate I gave you. You can pay half now and half when the job is done or pay all now."

Deke sniffed the air. "Is that chili? Don't mind Allie's rudeness. She's worried about this bad weather and she wants to get this roof done before it hits. And she talks too much when she's nervous."

"I was not being rude," Allie countered with a shove to the tall man.

"Yes, you were," Deke said. "You didn't even say hello before you threw that bill on the counter. That's rude. Loosen up, woman. We'll get the job done."

"Sorry if I was rude," she said. "I'll start all over. Hello, Blake. How are you today? Can we talk about this bill, now? How do you want to pay?"

Blake glanced at the bill and reached for the checkbook on the top of the refrigerator. "Might as well take care of it all right now. Glad that y'all could take care of it for me this quick. Y'all want to have dinner with me? Mary Jo brought enough chili to feed an army."

"I love Mary Jo's chili. Got dessert?" Deke asked.

"Talk about rude," Allie said.

"Well, I've got a sweet tooth that will not be denied," Deke admitted.

Blake made out the check and handed it to Allie. "Man's

got to speak his mind and if he's got a sweet tooth, then he doesn't just want dessert, he needs it."

His gaze went from Allie's work boots, past those luscious curves, to her eyes. That line should have worked on anyone, but her eyes said that he bored her.

"That's right and I will eat with you. Besides I see a chocolate pie and jalapeño cornbread in that box over there on the counter." Deke removed his coat and hung it over the back of a kitchen chair. "Where's the bowls? I'll get them down. I got a six-pack of beer in the truck I can contribute."

"Deke!" Allie hissed.

"Hey, it's a hot meal with dessert in a good warm house. I ain't turnin' it down for a bologna and cheese sandwich in a cold truck." He opened the cabinet door that Blake pointed toward. "You stayin' with us or goin' out to the truck?"

"I've got my dinner in the truck. I'm not eating here. This is a job, not a social visit," she said.

"It can just be a meal, not a social visit. You can eat without talking and then leave without even cleaning up," Blake said.

Her hesitation said that she considered it, but then she shook her head. "No, thank you."

"Good! That leaves more for me. I can't believe you are turnin' down a good bowl of chili when I know for a fact it's your favorite. Are you sick or have you started getting that shit that your granny has?" Deke asked.

"Hush. I'll meet you on the roof in thirty minutes." She marched out the back door, back straight and chin up.

So Allie wasn't married. She wasn't afraid of hard work. She liked chili better than anything in the world, and she had a temper to boot. His kind of woman if she'd been tall, blond, and had clear blue eyes.

"I've never been in this house. Looks like it needs more than a roof job," Deke said.

Blake removed a block of cheese from the refrigerator along with a jar of hot dill pickles. "Yes, it does. You reckon you and Allie could do some patch jobs in here to get us through until we can start showing a profit on the ranch? It needs new drywall on the ceiling and maybe some paint on the walls. Don't want to spend a lot until we start making money, but that shouldn't make me have to take out a mortgage on the place."

"If Allie's got time to do some work for you, I reckon I could help her. But come spring, I'll be busy with my own place and the rodeo rounds," Deke answered.

"We don't need three bowls, Deke. My dog, Shooter, he doesn't like chili."

Deke chuckled. "Allie will be back. She don't turn down chili for nothing."

And they called the cowboys who bought the Lucky Penny crazy? Hadn't Deke seen the look on Allie's face when she marched out of the house?

"How long has it been since a real family lived here?" Blake kept an eye on the door and an ear tuned to the sound of boots on the wooden porch.

"Maybe four years. Last bunch didn't last a month. Moved in, came to church one time, and left. Guess they took one look at all that mesquite and cactus and threw up their hands in defeat before they even got started. Before that they came and went so fast the folks in Dry Creek didn't even get a chance to get to know them. Do you really think you can make this work?" Deke asked.

"Hope so," Blake said. "My brother and cousin and I've sunk a lot of money into the place. I was just wondering if the place had gone empty for seventeen years since the calendar on the wall is that old."

"Be damned if it ain't. Guess someone liked that picture of a barn on it," Deke said.

Allie bit into a cold bologna and cheese sandwich and got madder each time she chewed. Chili—damn fine chili—Mary Jo's chili, which was the best in the whole county, was in that house. What was wrong with this picture? She took her phone from her coat pocket and called her sister.

"I hope you are happy. Blake and Deke are eating chili and I'm sitting in a cold truck eating a soggy, cold sandwich, because I'm proving to you and Mama that this is just a job," she blurted out before Lizzy could even answer.

"You get one star in your eternal crown for such a sacrifice," Lizzy said sarcastically.

"I deserve two diamond stars because it's my favorite food and Mary Jo made it and it smelled so good."

"It's not a social call," Lizzy smarted off. "Eat your sandwich and do the job and forget about the chili. Folks are already gossiping. I'll be glad to report to the next one that comes in the store that you didn't succumb to the devil's wiles because he offered you chili. Got customers. See you later this evening," Lizzy said.

"Somebody's Knockin'" started playing on the radio and Allie groaned.

She remembered the lyrics so well that said someone was knockin' and she wondered if she should let him in; that she'd heard about the devil but who would have thought he'd be wearing blue jeans and have blue eyes when he came knocking on her door.

Allie squeezed the sandwich so hard that her fingers went

through it. She wanted a bowl of that chili so bad she could taste it. And she was meaner than the devil and one bowl of chili did not mean it was a social call. It was food that would provide warmth for her to work on the roof in the bitter cold all afternoon.

Lizzy could fuss at her later that night, but she was going back into that house and eating chili at a table and maybe even a piece of chocolate pie afterward. Besides, Deke loved Mary Jo's chili even more than she did and he'd tease her all afternoon about how good it was if she didn't eat with them.

The house smelled scrumptious when she knocked on the back door and entered without waiting for an invitation. "I changed my mind and I don't want to hear jack shit from you, Deke Sullivan."

"I ain't sayin' nothing. I was about to walk on back to my ranch if you hadn't come on back in here," Deke said.

"Why did you change your mind?" Blake asked.

"Because the day she turns down chili, then I figure she's gettin' that stuff that her granny has and I ain't workin' with a woman who's holdin' a nail gun if her mind ain't right. Why are you in a bad mood today anyway?" Deke asked.

Allie scowled at him. "I'm not in a mood. Where are the bowls?"

Blake pointed. "There's a bowl beside the slow cooker. Help yourself."

She removed her coat and hung it over the back of a chair.

Blake's eyes caught with hers and sparks flew. "Well, whatever the reason, I'm glad you changed your mind. A dinner table is always nicer with a lovely woman sitting at it."

Deke pushed back his chair and in a couple of long strides

he was beside Allie. "You best not skimp on your helping because I'm having seconds. Mary Jo hasn't made chili for me in more than a year."

Allie filled her bowl to the brim and carried it carefully to the table. She sat down and dipped her spoon deep into the chili, keeping her eyes on the food instead of looking at either Deke or Blake. "Mmm. Mary Jo's chili is the best in the world."

Deke set his second bowl on the table. "If you hadn't come back I really was going to give you hell about it."

Blake pushed back his chair and went to refill his bowl. "Sometime I'll make a pot of chili and let y'all be the judge if it's this good. My mama had four old ornery boys and she said that we had to learn our way around the kitchen. So every fourth day one of us had kitchen duty. We hated it but I can make a pretty good pot of chili and I know how to grill a steak. And sharing it with a pretty lady and a friend makes everything better."

"Allie still hates the kitchen. Only thing she hates worse than cooking is cleaning. She's pretty good at both but that don't mean she enjoys it," Deke said between bites.

"I'm sitting right here," Allie said bluntly. "You aren't supposed to talk about me when I'm close enough to smack the shit out of you." Allie reached for a piece of cheese and then cut it up in cubes on top of her chili. "I'm surprised you didn't buy this place, Deke."

"I started to. Went to the bank and asked for a loan and then changed my mind. It's not what I really want."

"And that would be?" Blake asked.

One of Deke's shoulders raised a couple of inches in a shrug. "I want the place my cousin has across the road from mine. He'll get tired of his bitchin' city wife within the year and put it up for sale. Besides, this place ain't nothing but mesquite and cow tongue cactus. Only thing it's got going for it is those three spring-fed ponds so you don't have to carry water to the cattle in the hot summertime."

"Mesquite can be removed right along with cactus, and the ranch was cheap." Blake changed the subject. "Got a wife and kids, Deke?"

Deke slapped his forehead. "I forgot the beer. Not that this sweet tea isn't good, but I said I'd contribute the beer to our dinner. Sorry about that."

"He doesn't have a wife or kids." Allie answered the question for him.

"And you, Allie? Got a husband or kids?" Blake asked.

"No." Her answer was tight and left no room for discussion.

Deke went on. "I got a little spread of about three hundred acres and I run some cattle, grow some hay, and do odd jobs with Allie when she needs a tough cowboy. It butts up to your place on the west side. Other than that, I'm a rodeo junkie. I ride a few bulls and broncs and even play at rodeo clown when they need me. No wife. No kids and ain't interested in neither one right now."

"That's because no sane woman could live with you. He's so set in his ways that you'd think he was eighty-five rather than twenty-five." Allie pushed back her chair and took her bowl to the cabinet for a refill. Lizzy could scream that she'd sold her soul but the chili was worth every bit of her sister's bitching.

When she returned she reached for a piece of cornbread at the same time Blake did, and a shiver ran from her fingers to her gut. Dammit! She was not giving in to her hormones. She had to keep things in perspective.

"You look like you are getting in that mood again," Deke said.

"She might be fighting with the voices in her head. My brother gets that look on his face when he is doing that," Blake said. "Most of the time it involves which woman he's taking home from a bar. You thinkin' about a fellow, Allie?"

"Hell, no! That's the last thing on my mind. Do you ever fight with yourself, Blake?" Allie asked.

One of Blake's shoulders hitched up a few inches. "I do it all the time."

Deke made circles with his forefinger up next to his ear. "I swear she'll be loony by the time she's thirty. Maybe I should leave the beer in the truck. She can't hold her liquor worth a damn."

"What are you talkin' about? Just because you are big and mean and tough don't mean I can't drink you under the table," she protested.

Deke held up a finger and swallowed. "They say that liquor kills brain cells and you've been talking to the voices in your head. I rest my case."

Allie shook her fist at Deke. "Enough. Eat your dinner and stop being a clown. We've got to get at least half the shingles kicked off today and new felt put down if there's not rotting boards."

"Y'all get in a bind, holler at me. I can leave what I'm doing and help any way I can," Blake said.

"We might do just that if it starts to get dark. Days don't last nearly as long in January as they do in July." Deke polished off the last of his chili. "Is it all right if I get the chocolate pie out and slice it up?"

Blake refilled his glass with sweet tea. "Help yourself to the pie. There's a Mexican casserole in the refrigerator and lots of leftover chili. Y'all might as well join me at noon while you're workin' on the roof. I hate to see good food go to waste."

Deke said. "Count me in. Is that Sharlene's Mexican casserole?"

Blake nodded.

"Thanks for the offer, but you don't have to feed us every day." Allie met Blake's steely gaze down the length of the table.

"It's no problem. The food is already here. We just have to heat it up and I sure like to have someone other than Shooter to talk to while I eat." He smiled and went back to eating.

Deke reached under the table and squeezed her knee. She jumped like she'd been hit with a stun gun and shifted her gaze to him. He was warning her that he could and would go home before the first shingle was removed if she didn't agree to Blake's offer.

"Okay, then," Allie said. "Thank you. It's very generous of you to invite us."

An hour later, Deke had unloaded shingles from the trailer onto a couple of pallets, and had repositioned the trailer to catch the old shingles as they threw them off the roof. The sound of the dozer tearing trees up by the roots could be heard in the distance as Deke set up a boom box on the roof and put in a Conway Twitty CD.

"I'm a pretty damn good judge of bulls, broncs, and cowboys," Deke said, climbing back down the ladder and then toting two shingle remover tools up to the roof.

"So?" Allie scrambled up the ladder right behind him.

"So Blake Dawson is a good man."

"And?" Allie picked up one of the bright orange tools

with a long handle and slid it under the shingles at the peak of the roof.

Deke started on the next row, sending shingles sliding down the roof to land on the trailer.

"He won't be our neighbor long. And besides I did my homework on this one."

Deke's eyes widened. "You investigated him?"

"Gossip works more than one way. I can find out things pretty easy, especially if it happened only a little more than a hundred miles from here. There are four of the Dawson boys. The older two are married and settled, but the younger ones have quite a reputation," she said.

"For ranchin'?" Deke asked. "Or with the ladies?"

She expertly popped off a shingle and moved down to the next one. "Both. Rumor has it that they're both cracker-jack ranchers and their cousin Jud, who's buying the Lucky Penny with them, is not only good with ranching but he can smell an oil well. How are you going to feel if they strike oil on the Lucky Penny and we've got all those trucks running through Dry Creek night and day?"

"Hell, Allie! That might be the kick start that Dry Creek needs to grow and maybe some of us other ranchers can talk Jud into sniffin' around our land. Now, tell me about the part about him being a wild cowboy."

Shingles started sliding down the slope of the roof and landing on the empty trailer. "Why? You afraid of the competition?"

"Hell, no! I'm the most eligible bachelor in the whole county. I can share. Come on, Allie. Tell me."

"They call Blake the wild Dawson and his brother, Toby, the hot cowboy. They say that they can talk women out of their underpants in less than two hours of the time they meet them."

Deke threw back his head and laughed. "So that is the reason you wouldn't look at him at the dinner table. Don't worry, darlin', you can super-glue your under britches to your butt and you'll be safe."

Allie moved on down the roofline. "Maybe I want him to sweet-talk me."

"What did you say?" Deke yelled.

"Nothing," Allie replied from the other end of the roof.

CHAPTER FIVE

The squeaky sounds of rusty hinges told Blake that he had to start making sure his doors were locked. If Irene had arrived five minutes earlier she would have walked in on him strip-stark naked standing in front of the fireplace. Thank goodness when she eased the door open he was wearing flannel pajama pants and a long-sleeved thermal knit shirt. Before the door closed he grabbed his phone from the end table and hit the numbers to call Allie.

While he waited, he picked up the remote control, put the television on mute, sighed, and threw back the throw he'd tossed over his legs. Shooter's ears popped up and he growled but he didn't move a muscle.

"Gettin' kind of slow there, old boy. I heard the hinges squeak before you did. And we thought that we were moving to a quiet place. Boy, were we wrong," Blake said.

"Walter, darlin'." Irene stopped and glared at Shooter. "When did you get a dog and what is it doing in the house?

They have fur to keep them warm outside. They don't belong in the house." Irene crossed her thin arms across her chest. That night she wore purple sweat pants and cowboy boots that didn't match on the wrong feet. Springs of gray hair poked out around her hot pink stocking hat. The stained work coat was three sizes too big and bright red lipstick had sunk into all the wrinkles around her mouth.

"Shhh! You'll hurt my dog's feelings, Miz Irene. Have a seat. I'm making a phone call," he said.

"I didn't come over here for you to shush me, Walter. Do you think it's easy getting out of that house? Well, it's not and besides it's cold out there. I swear to God on the Bible, it's going to snow before the end of the week."

Allie answered on the fifth ring. "Hello."

"Hi there. This is Walter," Blake said.

"I'm on my way as soon as I can get my boots and coat on," she said.

He returned the phone to the end table, flipped the lever on the side of his worn brown leather recliner, got to his feet, and dragged a wooden rocker up close to the fire. "Here, darlin', you must be freezing. Sit right here and warm your hands while I make you a cup of hot chocolate. Can I take your coat?"

She must have loved Walter a lot, not only to trudge through the snow, but to wear a coat that weighed half as much as she did. It's a wonder that the thing didn't fracture her frail shoulders.

"Yes, you can and I like my hot chocolate with lots of extra cream, but you know that, and why aren't you wearing your glasses tonight? You know you can't see anything without them."

"I got those newfangled contact lenses, remember?" he said.

Irene squinted up at him. "Those what?"

"Little tiny lenses that go right in my eyes," he said. "I don't have to wear glasses all the time now."

"That's crazy, Walter. I bet they were expensive if there is such a thing and your mama paid for them to make you feel guilty about wanting to move her in with your brothers, didn't she?" She eased down into the rocking chair and held her hands out to the blazing fire. "When did you get that fancy chair? Did she buy that for you, too? I'm not surprised since she let you bring that mangy mutt in the house. She'll do anything to guilt you into keeping her with you forever."

Once she was settled, he went to the kitchen and put a cup of milk into the microwave for a minute. While that heated, he searched in the cabinets and found a box of instant chocolate mix. When the milk was ready, he removed it and added the mix plus a heaping tablespoon of coffee creamer, stirred it well, and carried it to the living room.

"Did you put in the extra cream?" Irene asked.

He set the chocolate on the coffee table. "Of course I did, ma'am. I know exactly how you like your hot chocolate. Be careful now. The mug is hot."

"Don't you ma'am me. I'm not your mother or an old lady." She picked it up and wrapped her hands around the mug. "Ahh, nice and warm for my hands as well as my freezing insides. Well, crap! I hear a car coming down the lane. Who would be coming around this late? Don't folks have any manners at all? You don't go visiting after dark. It's not proper."

"Maybe someone lost their way and needs directions or maybe they're turning around in the driveway," he said.

Irene nodded and sipped her chocolate while she rocked back and forth in front of the fire. A gentle knock on the door brought the rocking chair to a stop, and Irene's expression changed. Blake turned on the porch light, opened the door, and motioned Allie inside.

Irene's old eyes narrowed into little more than slits. "What the hell are you doing here? You're supposed to be having a good time with your girlfriends because this is the last night before you get married tomorrow."

"Granny, I am Allie, not Katy, and it's time for us to go home, now," Allie said.

Irene's face went blank as she looked around the room. "Why did you bring me over here to this place? I told you to stay away from here. It don't bring nothing but heartache and yet here you are, flirting with this cowboy. It's a good thing I saw you sneaking out of the house and came to get you. I'll have to watch you closer or else you'll ruin your life like your mama almost did."

"You want a cup of hot chocolate or coffee?" Blake asked.

Allie shook her head. "What's this about Mama ruining her life?"

Irene popped up out of the rocking chair and pointed her finger at Allie. "I don't want to talk about that, Alora Raine Logan. I told Katy that she'd have to get over it and she did so we're not discussing it no more. Let's go home and I swear to God, if I catch you over here one more time, you're going to be in big trouble."

"Let me help you with your coat," Allie said.

"I'm a grown woman. I don't need any help," Irene protested.

Allie stood aside and let her grandmother get the heavy coat up on her shoulders, then watched as Irene slammed the screen door and stomped out to the van. "Thanks for calling. We thought she was asleep in her room. She crawled out a window. Guess I'll have to put locks on them so she can't get out."

"She must've loved Walter a lot," he said.

"I don't even know who Walter is. He might be a boyfriend she had in the fourth grade and she's got him mixed up with someone who lived over here at some time in her life. Who knows what triggers what these days." Allie sighed.

Shooter whined, yipped, and then opened his eyes wide. He jumped up and raced across the floor like he'd been poked with a red-hot brand. Blake barely had time to sling open the screen door before the yellow blur sped past him and Allie. Then, as if in slow motion, Allie was tumbling forward, grasping at nothing more than air to break her fall.

Blake quickly wrapped his big arms around her and pulled her to his chest. Her heart pounded against his as he tightened his arms around her and her arms snaked up around his neck.

"I am so sorry," she gasped, but she didn't push away from him.

"It's all right. I've got you," he whispered. "Sorry about Shooter. I've never seen him act like that and I've had him since the day he was born."

Her arms fell to her sides and her face turned scarlet. "I had visions of a broken arm and not being able to work."

Blake didn't know that women blushed in today's world, especially those who were tough enough to put a roof on a house and run a construction business.

Without thinking of anything other than comforting her, Blake kissed her on the forehead. "So did I, and all I could think was that the roof wasn't nearly finished."

She stiffened and took a step back. "I should be going. Thanks for not letting me fall."

In seconds she was outside and Blake wondered what in the hell just happened. It was a simple kiss, nothing passionate or demanding, and yet there was no denying that fear in her eyes. Was it just him or was she afraid of all men? And why?

With a racing pulse and feeling more than a little like a teenage girl who'd just gotten her first kiss, Allie crawled into the driver's seat of the van. She touched her forehead and was surprised to find that it was cold as ice and not on fire.

Granny had crossed her arms over her chest, which wasn't a good sign.

Allie started the engine and turned to face her grandmother. "Granny, you could have hurt yourself crawling out the window like that. Promise me right now that you won't do that again." She backed the van around to her left so she could straighten it up and drive down the lane. "You are going to fall and hurt yourself one of these days and then the doctor will make us put you in a nursing home."

"I did not crawl out a window. I drove over here to get you. Don't you be making me out to be the one who did wrong. It was you and I'm tellin' your mother what you've done. I told you to stay away from this place and I'm getting tired of having to get out in the cold and come get you," Irene said.

"Okay." Allie reached the end of the lane and turned left. "Who is Walter?"

Irene stuck her lip out in a pout. "I don't know why you keep asking me that. I don't know anyone by that name, but your mama fell in love with a boy from over there and he was bad news. The apple never falls far from the tree and you are going to fall for that sexy cowboy who wants to get into your pants."

"Was Walter the man Mama fell in love with?" Allie asked.

Irene stomped her foot against the floorboard. "Hell, no! And we're not talking about Walter. We're talking about you and that cowboy. You need to stay away from him. Nobody ever stays long on this place and you'll get your heart broken like lots of women have in this part of the state."

Allie parked in front of the house, but before she could get her seat belt unfastened, Irene was out of the van and marching toward the porch with purpose. When Allie reached the foyer and shut the door, her grandmother was tattling, pointing at Allie and her old eyes were flashing anger.

Dementia was a demon disease and nothing could explain the way it worked other than what the doctor told them about the jigsaw puzzles. It must have been frightening to grab a piece from this part of her past and a piece from that one, and try to create a world that made sense when she was losing control of everything.

Allie could not imagine living in such a constant state of turmoil and hoped that someday only one puzzle remained and her grandmother would have a few days of lucid peace before everything was completely gone.

"Alora Raine won't do what I say and she's got a boyfriend and you know those men at the Lucky Penny are drifters who never stay in one place. I'm going to get a cookie and go to my room," Irene said tersely.

Katy winked at Allie. "I'll see to it that she's punished real good. You get your cookie and go on to bed."

Allie hung her coat on the hall tree and kicked off her boots. "Mama, who is Walter? She keeps going over there and flirting with Blake because she thinks he's Walter. And tonight she talked about you being in love with a boy from the Lucky Penny."

Katy looped her arm through Allie's and led her to the kitchen. "I've got a pot of hot spiced tea made."

Allie poured two cups of tea. "Granny said that you got mixed up with some no-good man from the Lucky Penny, too. Is that true, or just another one of her crazy stories?"

"She's remembering Ray Jones. He was about eighteen when his mama and daddy bought the ranch. I was seventeen that year and we rode the school bus together." Katy busied herself cleaning an already spotless countertop.

"And did you love him?" Allie asked.

"It was a long time ago." Katy disappeared into the utility room and returned with half a basket of kitchen towels and washcloths. She set it on the counter and started folding them. "And yes, I loved him very much, but Mama threw a hissy fit because he was wild. He was damn good lookin' with that hair combed back in a duck's tail and those pretty blue eyes and Lord, have mercy, but he could kiss good. But trouble followed him around like a little puppy and he liked taking risks."

"What kinds of risks?"

Katy's mouth twisted up in a grin. "Like throwing stones at my window at midnight and talking me into sitting on the front porch and making out with him. Mama caught us one night and she almost sent me to a convent over it."

"We're not Catholic," Allie said.

"She would have kissed the pope's ring if it kept me away from that wild boy, and he was really pressuring me to do things I didn't want to do and that I'm not talking about now so I listened to her."

"So you broke up with him?"

Katy sighed. "Yes, I did and then I fell in love with your father and figured out what real, mature love was." Her hands shook as she folded the last towel in the basket.

Allie picked up a towel and folded it neatly. "Do I hear a *but*?"

Katy finished the last tea towel and sat down at the table. "There are always buts with every story, but that's all I'm saying tonight about Ray."

"Then who is Walter?" Allie sipped her lukewarm tea.

Katy opened the cookie jar in the middle of the table and removed a chocolate one with a chocolate cream center. "He and his mother moved in after Ray's family moved out west. They were only there a year and it was when I was all tied up with my engagement to your dad and planning my wedding. I was eighteen, but I do remember that Walter was a tall man with dark hair. But Daddy was still alive so I can't imagine Mama being in love with him. Want a cookie?"

Allie shook her head. "I think she was in love with Walter, and Blake has brought that memory to surface."

"Surely not! She'd been married to Daddy nineteen or twenty years that summer when I got married. I remember because she said that she could easily be a grandmother by the time she was forty, but we waited to have you and she was forty-one not long before you were born. I can't imagine her having an affair."

"Maybe they were only flirting." Allie laid a hand on her mother's arm. "And you don't have to worry, Mama. I'm not so sure there's a man out there that I could even learn to trust. I loved Riley with my whole heart and look what happened. If it hadn't been for hard work, I would have lost my mind that first year. I couldn't eat or sleep and my brain kept running in circles trying to figure out what I could have done to prevent it. I don't think I can ever take a chance on hurting like that again. It might never be all put back together enough to trust someone else."

Katy stood up and carried a stack of tea towels to the cabinet. "You deserve something better than a pocketful of bad luck if you ever do fall in love again. And like you've already heard dozens of times, no one stays on the Lucky Penny very long."

"Thank you, Mama, but you don't have anything to worry about."

Katy sighed. "It's late and we've got a full day ahead of us tomorrow. When you finish your day's work at the ranch, you need to figure out a way to lock those windows. It's a wonder Mama didn't break a hip or an arm crawling out. And that first love business. You'll know or you won't. No need to talk it to death."

"I'll get new locks put on the windows tomorrow and be sure they're the kind she can't work." She dropped a kiss on Katy's head as she passed by her and went straight to her room.

She eased down into an overstuffed rocking chair in the corner and looked up at the moon hanging in the top half of her bedroom window. Only a quarter of a mile across the pasture, Blake could be looking at that same moon.

Shaking her head did not erase the picture of him in those pajama pants and that tight knit shirt. And that kiss! His soft lips on her forehead, the heat it had fired up in her heart, the way it had made her knees go so weak that she had to stiffen her whole body—all of it combined to awaken emotions she thought she'd finally buried.

She'd known Riley her whole life. He'd loved her and they'd had a marriage and still he'd broken her heart. Besides, according to what she'd learned, Blake Dawson was as wild as a class-five tornado and Allie did not need that in her life.

But need and want are often two different things altogether, and Allie's heart was daring her to test the waters in a river that she had no business putting her toes into.

Blake was amazed at how much work Deke and Allie had gotten done in only half a day. The front part of the roof was without shingles and covered with black tar paper. Deke had said that tomorrow, they'd put on the new gray shingles and on Thursday they would repeat the process on the back side of the roof. With that in mind, they'd be done Friday, so Blake only had three more days to enjoy having someone to talk to at noon.

Suddenly, the loneliness of living so far from his family and friends hit him. He'd thought it would be easy because he'd work hard all day and be ready for bed come nightfall, but he hadn't figured in the fact that dark came so early in January. It wasn't even eight o'clock and he was bored out of his mind. It was five months until Toby would move to Dry Creek. That meant lots of lonely nights on his own if he didn't make friends.

Make friends, the voice in his head said loudly. *Go to church. Drop in the feed store and make friends with the lady who answered the phone. Go to the convenience store to buy a coke. Talk to Allie. You can ask about her grandmother.*

He started to poke the telephone numbers into the phone and made it to the last number before he stopped. That was the lamest excuse to call a woman that he'd ever used and besides after that impromptu kiss on her forehead, she might not even finish the roof. He could be up there trying to figure out how to get the final half of the roof done by himself come daylight.

He tried to watch a movie but it couldn't hold his attention. Then he picked up a book and read ten pages without knowing a single thing he'd read. He could call Toby but he'd only get a hat full of sarcasm out of him.

Yes, Blake had volunteered to live on the ranch alone for the first stretch, to get enough land cleared, to get enough fences repaired or built to hold a small herd by summertime. Then Toby would join him and then the house wouldn't seem so empty. Then in the fall, Jud would move in with them and he'd be wishing to hell he had some peace and quiet.

He paced the floor, went to the kitchen, and opened the refrigerator. Nothing looked good. He took a cookie from the jar but it didn't have any taste and he gave the last half to Shooter. He went to the window and pulled up the ratty blinds. The moon hung out there with a whole sky full of stars around it. They looked cold up there in the sky, as if they were aware that in a few days they'd be blotted out from sight.

What in the hell was wrong with him? He had called many women with less reason than to ask about her grandmother. Had this place robbed him of all his wild ways? No, sir! Nothing could tame a wild Dawson cowboy! And if Allie didn't want to talk, he could call Sharlene or Mary Jo.

He poked in the numbers again without pausing.

"Hi, Blake. Please don't tell me Granny is back over there," Allie answered.

He paced the floor again as he talked, moving from living room to the kitchen, around the table and back to the living room. "No, I wanted to be sure you got her home all right, though."

"She's fine," Allie said.

"You got time to talk?"

"About what?"

He hesitated, looking for something, anything, to keep her on the phone other than the job. "Did you figure out who Walter is or was?"

"Mama says he moved in over there more than thirty years ago."

"I wonder what it is that she remembers in bits and pieces." He could listen to her read the dictionary with that soft southern twang in her voice.

"Mama said it was the year she was planning her wedding and she got married when she was eighteen. I think Granny had her when she was about nineteen because Mama is fifty-one."

Shooter looked up from the end of the sofa and Blake stopped to scratch his ears. "And you are how old?"

"Twenty-nine in the spring, and you do know it's not polite to ask a woman how old she is or how much she weighs?" Allie said.

"One hundred twenty-five pounds but that's with your boots on." Did that slight lilt in her voice mean that she was enjoying talking to him?

A long pause made him check the phone to see if she was still there. Then Shooter went to the door and looked up at the doorknob.

"Just a minute, old boy," he whispered. The dog could cross his legs for a few minutes. Blake was just starting to get Allie to open up and he wasn't about to lose the opportunity to talk to her some more.

"What did you call me? Did you really say *old boy* to me? And I'm going to shoot Deke for telling you my weight," Allie said.

"Deke didn't tell me. I caught you when you fell and I'm a pretty good judge of how much dead weight I can hold."

Blake started for the door to let Shooter out, but the dog changed his mind and returned to his rug by the fire.

"So how old are you?" she asked.

"Twenty-nine last November and I weigh two hundred pounds without my boots." He searched his mind for something else to talk about so she wouldn't make an excuse to end the call. Church! He planned to go on Sunday to get to know more people in the area. That was a safe topic. "Do you go to that church down the road from the feed store?"

"It's the only church left in Dry Creek, so yes, that's where my family goes on Sunday."

She surely must not be nervous because she wasn't talking too fast or spitting out too many details like Deke said. Was she only being nice to him because for the next few days he was her employer?

Shooter went back to the door and he headed in that direction. "Do they make newcomers walk through hot coals?"

"Not last time a stranger attended. We tend to welcome them, not punish them. But we might kill a chicken and use the blood for war paint on your cheeks." She giggled.

He shivered at the visual that reply produced. "Is that initiation, or do you get your cheeks painted, too, since you invited me?"

"I didn't invite you. I just said that we have church and we welcome newcomers," she argued.

He opened the door but Shooter barely stuck his nose out. "So if I showed up in my best jeans and polished boots, they might not tar and feather me?"

"No, but they might make you eat the raw chicken, feathers and all, to prove you are tough enough to live in our part of Texas." She laughed.

Her laughter was like tinkling bells on a belly dancer's

costume. Matter of fact, the only time he saw a real belly dancer she had dark brown hair and brown eyes. Could Allie have secrets hiding somewhere in the pockets of those cargo pants?

"Sounds like I'd better sneak in late and sit on the back pew so I can make an escape if I hear clucking."

"You might as well sit on the front pew. Where's the fun in not taking risks?" she answered.

She was warming up. He could hear it in her voice. He closed his eyes and imagined her doing a seductive dance for him in a flowing costume with little bells sewn into the fabric around the hips. His breath caught in his chest and he gasped.

"So you don't take risks?" she asked.

"Shooter can't make up his mind whether to go out or stay in. Cold wind about took my breath away. And, honey, I do take risks. I bought the Lucky Penny, remember?" He closed the door but Shooter didn't go back to the rug.

"Point taken," she said. "Don't bother polishing your boots or they might take you for a city boy. We're pretty casual here in Dry Creek."

"Do you polish your boots?" he asked.

"Mama says that on Sunday I have to wear shoes and a dress. It's painful but I do it for her."

Blake sat down in his recliner. "Where do the strangers sit?"

"Anywhere there's an empty pew."

He would have liked it a lot more if she'd said that he could sit with her family, but then that could prove disastrous if Granny decided he was Walter halfway through the service.

"So are you thinkin' about coming to services on Sunday morning, then?" she asked.

Shooter came over to his side and he scratched the top of the dog's head. "Thought I might. You want to drive over to Olney and get a hamburger with me afterward?"

"Already got plans for Sunday dinner but thank you all the same," she said.

"Another time?"

"We'll see," she said. "I hear Shooter whining. Sounds like he's ready to brave the cold. Thanks for checking on Granny."

"I feel sorry for her, trying so hard to get things in order. Poor old girl doesn't need to be traipsing through the cold. See you tomorrow at noon. Hey, would you know anyone who'd like to have some firewood? I'll give away all the mesquite wood that anyone wants to haul off. It's already piled up so they can bring their chainsaws and help themselves."

"You could put up a sign in the feed store and Mama's place. Lots of folks around here use wood in the winter, and mesquite burns really well," she said.

"Good idea. Thanks, Allie. And thanks for visitin' with me. See you tomorrow."

"Good night, Blake," she said softly.

He hummed all the way to the door to let the dog out one more time that night and decided as he waited for Shooter to water a nearby bush that he didn't want to talk to Sharlene or to Mary Jo. Maybe he was making progress after all.

CHAPTER SIX

A blast of warm air and the familiar smell of a feed store hit Blake square in the face when he opened the door to the Dry Creek Feed and Supply store that cold Wednesday morning. He removed his sunglasses and tucked them into his coat pocket while he took stock of the store. Not too different from the one he and his folks used in Muenster but quite a bit smaller. Shelves of supplies to his right along with a small assortment of tools, three or four round racks of clothing to the left, with a few sacks of feed piled up at the back of the store. Most likely that door at the back led into a warehouse where folks who bought large quantities of feed backed their trucks up to load them.

"Can I help you?" A lady made her way to the front.

"I need to place an order for about three hundred steel fence posts, five feet tall should do it, and maybe ten rolls of barbed wire," he said. "I'm Blake Dawson and I'm new in town."

"I know who you are." She was pretty danged cute in those tight-fitting jeans and chambray shirt tucked in behind a cowgirl belt that cinched up to show off a small waistline.

"But I don't know you." He smiled.

She smiled. "I'm Lizzy, sister to the woman who is putting a roof on for you. Welcome to Dry Creek."

"I'm pleased to meet you, Lizzy," he said.

"I have what you need in the warehouse. It's twenty dollars extra to deliver it unless you spend five hundred dollars, and I can get it there tomorrow." She circled around behind the cash register and hit several buttons, then looked up and said, "Cash or credit card?"

"Credit card and I reckon that order mounts up to a lot more than five hundred dollars so I'd appreciate it if you'd deliver it to the Lucky Penny. Tomorrow is fine. You mind if I put a flier up there on your bulletin board with those others?"

"What are you selling? Surely you're not already leaving the ranch." Her dishwater-blond hair was pulled up in a ponytail, and those light brown eyes had more questions behind them than whether he was leaving Dry Creek before he'd even unpacked.

Blake headed toward the front of the store. "Not selling anything and, no, I'm determined to make that ranch profitable so I'm not even thinking about leaving. I'm giving away mesquite wood to anyone who wants to come get it. Folks are welcome to cut down however much they want for free." He used four thumbtacks stuck on the outside of the corkboard to attach the flier he'd made the night before on his computer. "How long have you been in business?" He handed her his business credit card.

"My whole life." She pulled it free from his fingers and ran it through the machine, then handed it back, waited a second for the tape to roll out of the cash register, and laid it in front of him. "Sign right there."

He scrawled his name on the bottom. "Are you the person I talked to when Irene showed up on my doorstep?"

She gave him his copy. "Yes, I am. Are you going to be home before noon today? I hear the church ladies are bringing more food."

"Yes, ma'am, I will definitely be there. How long have you worked here?" he asked.

"I own this place," she said.

She'd been coolly friendly but she hadn't flirted with him. Was he losing his touch? What if he was never able to entice a woman into his bed again?

Then he saw the engagement ring on her left hand and he could breathe again. "When are you getting married?"

She held up the ring and looked at it as if seeing it for the first time. A bright smile lit up her face. "In March. If you are still here, you are invited to the wedding. It will be held at the church with the reception in the fellowship hall."

"Thank you. I'll be there for sure because, Miz Lizzy, I will definitely still be around." He stopped at the door, settled his cowboy hat on his head, and turned around before he opened the door. "You own the store down the block, too?"

"No, that's still Mama's business but she won't mind if you put up a flyer," Lizzy answered. "Don't forget. Eleven o'clock. And act surprised. Don't tell them I told you. Don't want them to be disappointed if you weren't home. They've probably been cooking for two days."

He gave her the thumbs-up sign and stepped out into the harsh January wind. Oklahoma had its own song about the wind coming swooping down the plains, but they couldn't hold a candle that day to the Texas wind blowing dead leaves and dirt down the sidewalk between the feed store and the service station–slash–convenience store on the other corner of the block.

Four empty buildings with either dirty windows or newspaper covering the windows separated the feed store on one corner of the block and the convenience store on the other end. The faded signs said at one time there had been a beauty and barbershop combination, a clothing store, a café, and a bakery in Dry Creek. He glanced across the street at the empty places on that side with windows so dirty that he couldn't even see what kind of signs might have been written on them in past days.

He bypassed two gas pumps and crossed a wooden porch into the store that was set back from the rest of the empty buildings. The windows were sparkling clean and the inside of the store was neatly put together. He was met with the rich aroma of breakfast food, maybe sausage gravy and hot biscuits.

"Hello, what can I help you with?" It was easy to see that this was Allie's mother. They had the same brown eyes and although her hair had a few gray streaks, it was still mostly dark brown. Katy was taller than Allie by a couple of inches and a few pounds heavier. Crow's feet around her eyes said that she'd enjoyed life and laughed a lot.

The store was set up with the cashier's counter to the right inside the door and shelves of staples lined up neatly to the left with restroom signs in that corner. Tables were back there with chairs pushed up around them, and a meat counter with a stove behind it took up the room beside the counter.

He removed his cowboy hat. "I'm Blake Dawson and I'd like to put up a flyer to give away mesquite wood. So this is a gas station, convenience store, and a café all combined?" he asked.

"Not a real café. Since we don't have a place for folks to grab a bite of lunch on the run I put in a small deli counter and I make one thing at noon. Something simple like chili or soup or maybe tacos."

"Beer, bait, and ammo," he said with a smile.

"Something like that only it's gas, cokes, and tacos." She grinned back at him.

"Walter! What are you doing here this time of morning?" Irene pushed back a chair from one of the three old tables covered with yellow Formica with mismatched chairs around them. "You moved away and said you'd never come back to Dry Creek."

"Miz Irene, look at me closely. I'm Blake Dawson, not Walter," he said gently.

"That's right. You're that scoundrel who's trying to get Alora Raine into bed with you. Well, it won't work. I'll protect her." Irene stuck her nose in the air and disappeared behind a curtain separating the front of the store from the back.

"Sorry about that," Katy said.

"It's all right. If I tell her often enough that I'm not Walter maybe she'll forget about him. So I can run in at noon if I don't want to cook?"

"Or in the morning." She pointed to the chalkboard above the counter.

He took his gloves off and shoved them into the pockets of his coat. "Breakfast and dinner, both. I'll have to remember that."

"Breakfast is the same every morning. Sausage gravy and biscuits. Dinner is take it or leave it but I've got a lot of folks who are willing to take it. I do make deli sandwiches out of the meat market back there." She nodded toward the display of pork chops, steak, and lunch meats.

"And I thought this was only a convenience store," he said.

Katy handed him a roll of tape. "Go on and put your flyer in the window. But you might get more folks on your ranch than you want though. Mesquite makes for some good hot fire."

He laid two packages of chocolate chip cookies and a bag of chips on the counter. "I'd also like two pounds of bologna sliced thick and a pound of ham sliced real thin. My dog, Shooter, likes a piece of bologna every night before bed-time."

She headed for the back of the store. "And the ham?"

"That's for me," he said.

"I'll take care of it. Blake, you do know what they say about the Lucky Penny?"

"I'm hoping to change that," he said.

Allie was sitting on the roof waiting for Deke to bring up another roll of tar paper, when her phone rang. "Hey, Lizzy. Please tell me Granny hasn't run off again."

"Nope. But I did just meet your hot cowboy. No wonder you keep going over there every chance you get."

Allie wanted to chew up shingles and spit out bricks. "You're right, darlin'. I might seduce him soon as I crawl down off this ladder," she said, her voice laden with sarcasm.

"Alora Raine!" Lizzy gasped.

"For the last time, I'm only here to put on his damn roof. Now Deke has the paper ready to roll so we can get this job done. Was there something you needed, or were you just calling to annoy the crap out of me?" Icicles dripped from Allie's words.

"Well, for your information," Lizzy huffed, "Mitch's cousin Grady is coming for his tux fitting, and we've planned a dinner for the four of us in Wichita Falls on Friday night. He sounds really eager to see you again. Play your cards right, and I bet he could make you forget all about your cowboy."

Allie came close to dropping the nail gun at the thought. The way Grady looked at her made her skin crawl. "God almighty, Lizzy. I'm perfectly capable of taking care of my own love life, and I'm absolutely not going to dinner with Grady."

"Yes, you are. Be ready at seven and that means good jeans or a dress and makeup, too," Lizzy said.

"You'd better have a backup plan in your hip pocket because I'm not going," she said.

The phone went silent and she looked at it. Sure enough her sister had hung up on her. Deke had barely gotten the tar paper unrolled across the length of the roof, when her phone rang again. She fished it out of her pocket, hoping that it was Lizzy so she could give her a piece of her mind.

"I know you are busy so I won't talk but a minute," her mother said. "I really think you should go with Mitch and Lizzy on Friday night. You will be standing up there with her and he's the best man. It's not a date but an evening to discuss wedding plans."

"That damn tattletale! What makes you take her side in this? Why would you want me tangled up with Grady? He's even worse than Riley was," Allie fumed.

"She's your sister and she's worried about you and frankly so am I. Blake came in here today and the way he looks, he's got heartbreaker written all over him. Come on, Allie, listen to the voice of experience when it talks to you," Katy said tersely.

Allie took a deep breath and let it out slowly. "I'm not going to dinner with them." Allie heard Deke huffing and puffing as he climbed the ladder with a heavy roll of black roofing paper on his shoulder.

"Okay, then I'll invite them to Sunday dinner and you can discuss wedding plans then," Katy said.

Allie had never wanted to hit something so badly in her life. "Mama!"

"Friday or Sunday. Your choice?"

She thought about it a second. "I'm not going Friday."

"Then Sunday it is," Katy said. "Blake bought a few things and put up a flyer to give away mesquite for firewood. And Allie, the church ladies are coming at eleven this morning to welcome him to Dry Creek. You might want to be on the roof working instead of in the house with him. Even if y'all are only talking business, it wouldn't look good."

Allie motioned for Deke to drop the roll of black paper beside her. "Good way for Blake to get to know the people, ain't it? Give them something for free? And Mama, stop worryin' about me."

"I'm a mother. It's my job to worry. Men that good lookin' are out for a good time and all they leave in their wake are tears. Grady is a good man. Youth minister at the church up around Gainesville," Katy said.

"Whoopee for him. I've got to get to work. Deke is ready for me to start nailing. See you at supper." Allie pushed the END button.

"Who's giving away what for free?" Deke asked.

Blake poked his head up over the edge of the roof. "I am. News travels fast around here, don't it? I'm giving away all the mesquite wood anyone wants to cut up for firewood."

"You care if we sell it once we take it off your place?" Deke asked.

Blake chuckled. "You can boil it and make mesquite pie with it for all I care. I want it gone."

"You've got a fireplace." Allie looked up from her nail gun. "Why don't you use it?"

His gaze locked with hers, the heat melting the cold all around her. She'd never had a man look at her and create such an intense reaction. One part of her, the emotional side, wanted to dive into those green eyes and see what lay beneath that flirting nature—down deeper than his wild cowboy ways and into the very man. The other side, that sensible side, told her to run from him as fast as she could.

"I'm going to cut up as much as I can this afternoon and stack it up behind the house. I can probably save enough on my heating bill to pay for the ceiling and the paint that way," he said.

She looked down at her nail gun and snapped another shingle in place. "Price of fuel these days you just might."

"Thought I'd check on the progress before I take the chainsaw out to the brush pile. This roof is lookin' really good. I guess you really will get it done by the weekend." He took a step back down the ladder.

Allie looked up from the nail gun and nodded. "If the weather holds for us, we will. I told you in the beginning I thought we could get it done by quittin' time on Friday."

Now that her mother and sister kept going on about how sexy Blake was, it was all she could think about as she pulled the trigger on the gun and moved down the roof to the next spot.

Blake nodded. "See y'all at noon. I'll be in a little early today. Allie, you want me to heat up the leftover chili?"

"Yes and thank you," Allie said.

"Will do," Blake said.

"Now what's got your panties in a twist?" Deke asked as soon as Blake disappeared.

"That's not something a guy friend says." Allie snapped another nail in place. "You'd best get to unrolling the next length."

"Not until you tell me what Lizzy's done now. Only she can put a look on your face that would melt the North Pole." Deke expertly rolled a length of paper out and cut the end with a box cutter.

"Mama and Lizzy are trying to fix me up with Mitch's cousin Grady."

Deke went back to the other end of the roof and started rolling out more paper. "You don't want to get tangled up with that guy. I know him and believe me when I tell you his hat ain't coverin' up a halo but horns."

She snapped a couple of nails in the paper to hold it down so the wind wouldn't whip it off the roof before she answered. "Lizzy and Mama think he's a saint because he's a youth minister."

"Yep, but that don't make him any less of a devil when it comes to women. I've played poker with him and Mitch a few times and he ain't a bit better than your ex, so steer clear of him," Deke said.

"Talk, Deke. I want to know about Mitch." She flipped the safety on the gun and rolled back on her butt. "Is my sister making a big mistake?"

Deke positioned half a dozen more shingles, then sat down beside her. "Well, Mitch and Grady were really players, but in the last couple of years they've had a come to Jesus experience and now they're ready to get married. They've been bragging about how it's their biblical right to have someone cook and clean and do everything they say."

"Shit!" Allie hissed. "I knew that Mitch was a snake. You should tell Mama."

Deke reached for the nail gun. "Hell, no! She wouldn't believe me, and Lizzy would bury my body back in the mesquite so far that even the coyotes couldn't find me. I'm not sure where Katy stands where Grady is concerned, so I'm not sayin' a word. I damn sure don't want to be on either of their bad sides since I run a bill at both of their stores. But honey, you steer clear of Grady."

CHAPTER SEVEN

Blake brought a load of wood to the house just before eleven that morning but didn't take time to stack it. The steady sound of hammering up on the roof let him know Allie and Deke were hard at work as he hurried into the house. Blake threw a couple of logs on the fire so there would be a welcoming blaze, put on a pot of coffee, and slid the Mexican casserole in the freezer.

Several vehicles pulled up in front of his house at exactly eleven o'clock, but he waited until someone knocked on the door to open it.

"Welcome to Dry Creek!" one of the dozen ladies standing on his porch said cheerfully. "We brought food so you'd have something to eat until you can get settled in."

Sharlene winked from back behind the woman.

Mary Jo smiled at him from the sidelines.

"Thank you all so much," Blake said. "Please come right

in and excuse the mess. I'm not nearly unpacked yet. Can I get you ladies a cup of coffee?"

Sharlene ran her forefinger down his arm and locked it around his pinky. "I've been waiting for your call," she whispered.

Mary Jo pushed between Sharlene and Blake to hug him. "Welcome to Dry Creek. We're a friendly bunch and we hope you do better on this ranch than the other folks have."

"I'm Dora June. This is Lucy." The woman with three chins made so many introductions so fast that he'd never remember all their names. "And now for the food! You'll have to freeze some of it, but I reckon you'll want to have my fried chicken for dinner since it's still hot."

"Why, Miz Dora June, how did you know fried chicken was my favorite food in the whole wide world? My mouth is already watering," he said.

"All cowboys like fried chicken," she beamed.

In a few minutes his kitchen table was filled with food, his counter space was covered with desserts, and a couple gallon jugs of sweet tea had been set in his near empty refrigerator.

"I see my slow cooker in the 'fridge with leftover chili in it," Mary Jo whispered while the other women talked non-stop about how good it was to have someone living on the ranch. "All you have to do is call me when it's empty and I'll come get it, night or day."

Sharlene waited until Mary Jo moved to the side and looped her arm in Blake's. "And you've eaten my casserole already. I'll bring another one right over any ole time of the day...or night." She gave his right butt cheek a squeeze. "We might build up an appetite and then we could share it. I brought my pot roast today and if you like it better, give me a day's notice."

Blake had fallen into a wild cowboy's paradise. Hell, he didn't even have to go bar hopping on the weekend. All he had to do was make a phone call, but...

Dammit! Why did there always have to be a *but*?

But, the voice in his head said loud and clear, *what if these women are looking for more than a one-night stand or a weekend romp in the sheets? What if they want a long-term relationship? Then you'll be up shit creek without any sign of a paddle because the whole town will turn against you for hurting their feelings.*

Lucy clapped her hands. "Okay, ladies. This man has work to do if he's going to get this place whipped into shape. Let's go on now. We will see you in church on Sunday, won't we, Mr. Dawson?"

"You are all such sweethearts to take care of me like this and yes, ma'am, I will be in church Sunday. I might be twenty pounds heavier after eating all this good cookin', but I'll be there," he promised.

Lucy nodded. "You've got an open invitation to go home with me and my husband, Herman, for Sunday dinner anytime, honey. You might get lonely and Herman can talk the legs off a kitchen table when it comes to ranchin' and cows."

"Thank you again for everything." Blake followed the parade back through the living room.

"You don't need to come out to the porch, cold as it is," Ruby said. "Just get on in there and open up that fried chicken and my potato casserole. They go right well together. And I do believe that Nadine sent her famous apple pie."

"I can't thank y'all enough for making me welcome," Blake said.

"Honey, I'd like to show you just how welcome you are,"

Sharlene said softly just before she followed the rest of the crowd outside.

Blake was still shaking his head, wondering how in the hell he was ever going to deal with so much temptation on every corner, when Deke pushed into the back door.

"We're at a stopping place. Mind if we come in and get warm. Holy shit! What is all this? I saw them bringing in stuff but man, this looks like a buffet for an army."

"Take off your coats and get comfortable. Make yourselves at home. Most of this will go in the freezer. Thank goodness it is only half full and will hold everything, but I reckon we won't have to cook much for a few weeks around here. I understand that the fried chicken is still warm and there is a potato casserole somewhere," Blake answered.

Deke headed for the living room. "Sounds like heaven to me."

Allie pulled off her gloves, tucked them in her coat pocket, and then hung it on the back of a chair. "Okay if I wash up at the kitchen sink? The hot water will warm up my cold hands. And then I'll help you find the chicken and potatoes and after we eat, I could help you put the other stuff in the freezer."

"Help yourself and thank you," Blake said.

"Ahhh," she said as the water went from cold to warm and then hot. "I need to do inside jobs in the winter."

"Speaking of that. Do you have anything lined up right now? I could sure use some help on the ceilings where the roof leaked through. Any advice you can give would be appreciated," he said.

She turned off the water and looked around for a towel. "Well, it should just take some drywall and a paint job. Probably not too expensive."

Blake picked up the hand towel from the cabinet and held it out toward her. "Would you be able to do the job? I'd be glad to help."

She turned around quickly and ran right into his chest. "Oh, s-sorry," she stammered.

He ran the back of his hand down her cheek and looked deeply into those brown eyes. He tipped her chin up with his knuckles and slowly bent to brush a soft kiss across her lips.

Never had a first brief kiss affected him like that, not in all the years he'd perfected his wild ways with women. The feeling was so new that he wasn't sure what to do with it. Did he apologize for kissing her or kiss her again with more intensity?

She took a step to the side and her hand went to her lips. "I can work for you, Blake Dawson, but you cannot do that again."

"Are you seeing someone?" He handed her the towel.

She dried her hands and threw it over his shoulder. "No, and I'm not looking to be either. I was married at one time and I loved that man with my whole heart. When the marriage ended, my nerves were shot. It's a long story and it's sure nothing to do with you but..."

"Guess I got mixed signals. Can we at least be friends?"

"I don't know, but I..."

Two buts in less than a minute. Two women chasing him, ready and waiting for his call and the one that had *but*s at the end of every sentence was the one who turned him inside out with a simple kiss. God hated him!

"Hey, it smells good in here." Deke appeared in the doorway rubbing his hands together. "Blake, why don't you hire Allie to give this place a facelift while her business is slow?"

In a couple of long strides, Allie was behind her chair, her hands gripping the back where her coat hung.

"That's what we've just been talking about," she said.

Deke pulled out a chair and sat down. "Well, I'm going to be cutting wood if Blake was serious about the mesquite. I can make more at that than helping you, but I will miss the dinners."

"If you are willing to clear mesquite, I will gladly provide dinner. You can eat with me and Allie every day," Blake said.

Deke glanced over his shoulder toward Allie. "You okay with that since I'm not going to be helping you?"

"Yes, of course," Allie said. "It's Blake's house and his food, not mine. Besides, I'll look forward to seeing you every day."

Allie was surprised that her voice sounded completely normal. Every nerve was humming loudly in her body. She pulled out the chair and sat down, glad to be off her weak knees. What in the hell had she done?

You took another job and Deke won't be there and you kissed that cowboy just like I knew you would. It was Lizzy's voice, no doubt about it, fussing at her. Allie hoped that when Lizzy did something stupid that she heard Allie's voice in her head telling her all about it.

Suddenly Deke touched her on the shoulder. "Earth to Allie," he said.

She was amazed to see that a disposable pan of fried chicken and one of potato casserole had been set on the table. Both Deke and Blake were looking at her like they expected her to say grace or do something.

"What?"

"Blake is going to say the blessing. Bow your head," Deke said.

A cowboy who said grace?

Her chin went down and she peeked out of one eye. Blake's long lashes rested on his cheekbones and that slow drawl sounded sincere when he said a quick blessing over the food.

"Now, let's eat," he said.

Allie picked up the potato casserole, helped her plate, and sent it to Deke. "It smells really good. I'm sorry about awhile ago. I was thinking about the ceilings. Do you want drywall, or would you like a framework and panels? That way a panel could be removed and replaced if it got messed up and you wouldn't have to do the whole ceiling. They make the framework now to look like wood so it's not so modern looking." She was talking too fast and talking business when what she really wanted to do was curl up in the rocking chair in her room and think about that kiss.

"Bullshit! You weren't thinking about ceilings at all. Your eyes were all dreamy and soft so you were off in Cinderella land. Did the prince ask you to dance yet?" Deke laughed. "But if that's your story, I'm sure you'll stick with it. Besides you are talking too fast and about work too much so I know you aren't telling the truth. You want a chicken leg or a breast or a thigh?"

She nodded. "Leg is fine."

"Who won?" Deke asked.

"Won what?" Blake asked before Allie could answer.

"Allie was fighting with herself again." Deke forked out a wing and a breast to lay on his plate. "She does that a lot. Lizzy or you? Who won?"

Allie managed a weak smile. "It was a tie this time."

"What were they arguing about?" Blake asked.

"Friday night." She answered honestly but kept her eyes on her food.

Blake passed a container of marinated vegetables to her. "What about Friday night?"

It didn't help that his fingertips brushed hers in the transfer. Thank goodness there was food in her mouth, giving her a minute to think before answering.

"Her sister, Lizzy, the one you met at the feed store, is getting married this spring," Deke said. "Her boyfriend is Mitch and his cousin Grady is the best man. Lizzy is trying to fix Allie up with him while he's in town this weekend. Why were you thinking about that Allie? Did you change your mind?"

She shook her head. "Not in a million years."

"Good." Deke said. "I can get you out of that Sunday dinner real easy. I'll call and say that we have an emergency plumbing problem on Sunday right after church. Pipes could freeze right here at the Lucky Penny and we wouldn't have a choice but to fix them. Might take all the way to supper to get the job done. I'll bring the beer. Besides it could snow and if it does, Mitch might not be able to get down here to go to church with Lizzy."

"Don't even suggest such a thing or it might happen," Blake said. "And I thought y'all were talking about Friday, not Sunday."

"She has to put up with Grady on Sunday at her mama's house since she won't go out with him on Friday. I'm her best friend so I'm trying to help her out here," Deke explained.

Blake nodded. "So that's the reason you can't go get a burger with me?"

Deke chuckled.

Allie pointed her fork at him. "It's not funny."

"Yep, it is."

"Changing the subject here since my mama says it's not nice to make a lady blush," Blake said.

Allie could have planted a kiss right on those full sexy lips at that moment. She was sick of Lizzy's wedding plans, and she'd rather talk about busted sewer lines than those ugly orchid taffeta dresses Lizzy wanted her and Fiona to wear.

"Are you really going to start hauling wood off this place tomorrow?" Blake asked.

Deke refilled his plate. "Yeah, I am. And I got a feeling there'll be a lot more folks out there with chainsaws. I bet Herman Hudson is the first one out here with his crew of grandsons. What do you think, Allie? You think that anyone can beat Herman when there's free wood to be had?" Deke asked.

Allie took a sip of the tea. Not too sweet but with enough sugar and strength to know she was drinking southern tea and not murdered water. "He's got a big wood yard and we've got a lot of winter left, so he sure won't pass up a chance to get at this much mesquite for free."

She didn't want to talk about wood or anything else. She wanted to be back on the roof with her nail gun working on the job where she'd have lots of time to think. Maybe even with her earbuds in place and listening to George Strait, who had helped her through the most difficult time of her life with the lyrics to his fifty greatest hits. Back when she first found out that Riley had been cheating on her for years, she'd leaned on country music to get her through those sad, tough times.

She stole a sideways glance toward Blake and found him staring at her. Their gaze caught above the fried chicken and time stood still.

* * *

Those dark eyes mesmerized him and Blake wished that she'd let him in long enough to see into her heart. He knew women, could look into their eyes, see past the glitter and glam, and know what they wanted from him. If it was a good time, he provided it. If it was a relationship, he was gone in a hurry. But this was something different. Could he really be courting a woman for friendship? If so, he was damn sure in virgin territory.

Deke pushed back his chair, picked up his plate, and carried it to the sink. "I bet that's Nadine's apple pie, isn't it?"

"That's what the ladies said. Help yourself to all you want. I hate apple pie. Ice cream is in the freezer if you want to top it off," Blake said.

Allie pushed back her chair. "I'm too full for dessert, even Nadine's pie, which I do like. I'm going back up on the roof. See you when you get done. Thanks for dinner, Blake. We'll discuss the next job after we finish the roof."

Blake waited until she was out of the house to ask, "What's her story?"

"Lived here in Dry Creek all her life, most of it over at Audrey's Place. Crazy the way that name has stuck for more than a hundred years."

"House is almost a hundred years old?" Blake rinsed dirty dishes and set them aside.

"Pretty close to that. Before the Depression it was a small hotel but Audrey found out pretty quick that folks didn't have money for traveling. No one ever called it a brothel but she hired six girls, gave them a room and three meals a day and a big cut of what they made. At least, that's the story. Who knows what is true and what is rumor around here?"

Blake poured two cups of coffee and set one in front of Deke. "It looks like it held up good."

"Foundation is good and solid. Allie is afraid to knock out walls for fear the ceiling will sag. I told her that she couldn't knock them out because the studs are petrified by now," Deke answered.

Not caring that he was being nosy, he wandered into personal territory that went deeper than mere friendship. "Tell me more about Allie."

Deke dug into his pie. "She has two sisters. Lizzy that you met and Fiona who lives down in Houston. Works for some big crackerjack law firm and is married to one of the partners. Allie's daddy was a carpenter and she learned the trade from him. Married right out of high school. Divorced after two or three years. Can't remember exactly how long they were together, but he cheated on her. The rest you'll have to ask her. She's my best friend and I'm not getting into any more trouble."

"Sometimes her eyes look sad," Blake said.

Dozens of wrinkles creased Deke's forehead when he frowned. "Allie? Sad? Not that woman. She's the happiest woman I know. She likes what she does and she's the easiest woman in the world to work with and for."

"How long has she been a carpenter?"

Deke polished off his tea and refilled it one more time. "She started helping her dad when she was in middle school. I think she was about fifteen when she went on the payroll. She bought the cutest little pickup truck when she was sixteen. She's still got that truck somewhere over there at their place, but mostly she drives the business van these days."

Blake nodded, remembering his first crush on an older girl. "Gloria Anderson."

"Who?" Deke asked.

Blake grinned. "She was my Allie. I was about twelve and she was seventeen and in love with the football quarterback."

Deke piled ice cream on top of the apple pie and carried it to the table. "Seems like we all do that, don't it? When I was sixteen and she was twenty, she hired me to help her put the first roof on a house. It was her first solo job and she was so nervous and—damn you, Blake Dawson, you got more out of me than I should have told. You interested in her or what?"

"She's going to be working on my house. I wondered if something about this place makes her sad, like her ex-husband lived here at one time. Or if maybe she used to sneak off and meet him here?"

"Hell, no! Riley wasn't..." Deke shook his head. "All I'm sayin' is that this house does not make her sad and my lips are sealed past that. You want to know more about Allie, you go to talk to her. She'd fire me on the spot for shootin' off my mouth. Now I'm going to change the subject. Are you going to tear up some more mesquite after dinner or start fixin' fence?"

Blake cocked his head to one side. "Why would you ask that?"

"There's the feed store truck coming down the lane." Deke pointed out the window. "I reckon it's bringin' all that barbed wire and those fence posts you bought. There are no secrets in Dry Creek, especially when it comes to the Lucky Penny. You might as well live in a glass house."

"Why are folks so interested?" Blake's skin crawled at the idea of people watching him through the windows of a glass house.

"Because you are the new guy in town and they want to see if you'll last through the winter. They've probably already got bets on how long you'll stay. The ones who bet for you will be nice and the others, not so much. You'd better get out there and tell them where to unload that stuff or they'll drop it right in your front yard."

CHAPTER EIGHT

Allie hummed as she made her way to the kitchen that Friday morning. She was sure she and Deke could finish the roofing that day. Rays of sun poured into the foyer through the window in the door and the aroma of fresh coffee floated from the kitchen. The humming stopped when she saw Lizzy sitting at the table. Their kitchen wasn't as big as the one over at the Lucky Penny, but their dining room could match it for size. Most of their meals they took in the kitchen unless they had company and then Katy set the table in the dining room.

Allie liked the kitchen better with its bright yellow walls and white woodwork. It brought cheer into the house on the darkest mornings. But the dining room, with its paneled walls and heavy curtains, told a different story. It said to sit up straight and be nice, there was company in the house.

"It's your morning to make breakfast," Lizzy said coldly.

"I made coffee, but I'm not helping cook, not if you won't go with me and Mitch and Grady to dinner tonight."

Allie filled her father's favorite mug and sipped it, hoping that holding his old cup would give her the strength for yet another fight with her sister.

"Aren't you going to say a word? You know I'm right. That bad boy next door isn't for you, isn't interested in you other than maybe a quick romp in the sheets, so wake up and smell the bacon," Lizzy said.

"What makes him a bad boy?" Allie asked.

"Sharlene and Mary Jo have been over there already and he's been flirting with them. I heard he even called Dora June sweetheart and she's sour as rotten lemons. If she smiled more than twice in a year, she'd probably drop dead. Sharlene says that she intends to bed and wed him by the end of the year and you know how wild that girl is. Only a bad boy would take her eye," Lizzy answered.

"What I do or do not do with the cowboy next door is my business. I'm old enough to take care of myself." Allie sipped the steaming-hot coffee. "Besides, who died and made you God?"

"Don't blaspheme!" Lizzy raised her voice.

Irene shuffled into the room with Katy right behind her. "Don't yell in the house."

"Mama, talk some sense to your oldest daughter." Lizzy rolled her eyes.

"God is a hell of a lot farther away than the ceiling, so you might as well not be lookin' up there expecting him to leave important work to settle your fight." Irene went to the cabinet, poured a cup of coffee, and took it to the table. "Is Allie cooking this morning? If she is, I want pancakes."

Allie began to gather the ingredients from the refrigerator

and pantry. "I'm tired of this fight, Mama. And yes, Granny, we are having pancakes if that's what you want."

"We need to get this settled," Lizzy said.

"Sounds to me like it is settled," Irene said. "Lizzy, you need to stop your whining and carryin' on like a two-year-old. Allie don't like that rascal Grady and neither do I. He's got wandering eyes and probably hands that match."

"Granny, he's a youth minister!" Lizzy protested.

"That don't mean shit, girl. There have been men since the beginnin' of time that wasn't worth a damn and Grady is one of them. His ancestors probably spent a lot of time in this very house back when Audrey was doin' what she could to keep soul and body together," Irene declared with a frown. "And you can wipe that grin off your face, Allie. Ain't no good ever come from the Lucky Penny so you need to be careful, too."

Lizzy exhaled so loudly it bordered on a snort. "I thought you'd want her to be involved with a decent man rather than someone who'll just run off and break her heart again."

Irene scratched her temple. "If you two want to fight, then take two butcher knives to the backyard but remember, the one who comes back in the house had better have the strength to dig a six-foot hole because I'm not helping you. And remember, too, that the ground is cold and harder than a mother-in-law's heart."

Lizzy pushed her chair back. "I'm going to the store. I don't want pancakes."

Irene grabbed Lizzy's arm. "You are not going anywhere. You are going to sit down and behave yourself and when Allie has breakfast ready, you are going to ask the blessing on it this morning. God needs to soften up your spirit or you'll never make a preacher's wife." Irene blew on her coffee and then sipped it loudly. "And it wouldn't hurt you to learn how to make decent pancakes. Allie's are light and fluffy. Yours are like shoe leather. If your marriage depends on your pancakes, Mitch will throw your ass out in the cold within a week."

Lizzy threw up both palms defensively. "Hey, why is this pick-on-Lizzy Friday? I don't think Mitch is going to leave me because my pancakes aren't perfect."

Allie pulled a cast iron skillet down from the hooks in the utility room and set it on the stove to heat while she mixed up the batter. "I remember when you used to make pancakes for us girls at breakfast. And in the hot summer you let us pretend the big tub upstairs was our swimming pool and you let us take our Barbie dolls swimming."

Irene's thin mouth broke into a lovely smile. "Remember when you played beauty shop and cut all their hair off, Allie?"

Lizzy raised a hand. "I do. I hated her for weeks for making my dolls look like boys."

"Boys?" The light went out of Irene's eyes as suddenly as if someone had flipped a switch. "I hear there's a new boy over at the Lucky Penny."

Allie crossed the room and wrapped her arms around her grandmother. Maybe a hug would bring her back for a little while. "Yes, there is, Granny. His name is Blake Dawson. You've met him."

Irene shook her head. "His name is Walter, not Blake. That's not a first name. It's a last name."

"Let's talk about my wedding. I think you'd look lovely in a dark purple dress since the bridesmaids are all wearing orchid," Lizzy said.

Katy wore her robe and slippers to the kitchen that morning. She poured a cup of coffee and sat down at the head of the table. "I think you'd look lovely in a dark purple dress, Mama."

"I thought you picked out pink for your wedding. When did you change your mind to purple? I've already bought my dress. Now what are we going to do? Besides you know I hate purple. Always have," Irene said.

Katy patted her mother's shoulder. "Lizzy is mixed up. Of course she's using pink for her wedding."

"Good. I'm going to the bathroom to wash my hands. Will my pancakes be ready when I get back?"

"Yes, Granny," Allie answered.

"It was good to have her for a few minutes." Katy sighed.

Allie stacked three pancakes on the side of a plate and added as many sausage patties on the other side. "Mama, I've figured out the triggers that send her backward in time so fast these past few days. It's when we talk about Lizzy's wedding and the Lucky Penny. She keeps thinking about this Walter guy who lived there when you were planning your wedding and getting times all jumbled up in her mind."

"Makes sense," Lizzy said. "You shouldn't mention the Lucky Penny in front of her and you shouldn't take that job. Which is more important? Having the money from the job, which you don't even need, or having Granny lucid for a little bit each day?"

"Then you shouldn't get married to Mitch. Which is more important to you? Marrying a man who's going to expect you to be this little submissive wife who bows to his every command, or having Granny lucid?" Allie shot right back at her.

"I'm marryin' Mitch whether you like him or not." Lizzy tilted her head like she used to do when they were kids and she knew she was wrong but all the angels in heaven couldn't get her to admit it.

One of Allie's worst fears was realized in that moment. Lizzy was arguing too hard for Mitch. She had always been levelheaded when it came to business and relationships, seeing opportunities in business, knowing when a relationship was headed in the wrong direction. Her sister was marrying that snake-in-the-grass because she wanted to be married and any man would do—even a self-righteous prick who would make her life miserable in the end.

"And I'm going to work at the ranch next door," Allie said. "So I guess Granny is going to have lots of bad days."

Allie was on Blake's mind that Friday evening as dusk settled on the Lucky Penny. He was in one of the spare bedrooms gazing at more unopened boxes, when someone rapped hard on the front door. Hoping that Toby had decided to surprise him by showing up that weekend, he turned around so fast that he had to catch himself on the wall to keep from falling over Shooter.

Shooter raced him to the door but he wagged his tail when Blake threw it open to find Deke.

"Come right in. What's going on?"

Deke was dressed in creased jeans and a pearl snap plaid shirt, and his boots were shined. "Let's slip up over the county line and go have some barbecue." He winked.

"There's food in the house. We don't have to go out and buy more."

Deke chuckled. "Frankie's is way back in the woods and it's more than barbecue, but in order to get a drink, which is illegal as hell right there, you have to buy some food."

"A bar! Hot damn! How far is it from here?"

"Maybe nine miles. Got to warn you, it's not a country bar. How fast can you be ready?"

"Give me ten minutes. Does it serve beer?" Blake was

already on the move toward his bedroom at the end of the hallway.

"Yes, they serve beer but you'll want to try Frankie's special brew and have some barbecue before you start lookin' at the ladies." The crunch of tires on the gravel outside brought Shooter's hackles back up for the second time. "Go on. I'll get the door. It's most likely Herman asking how early he can be here tomorrow morning. He was up around Archer City all day cuttin' wood or he would have been around sooner. He's real interested in getting all the mesquite he can to sell at his wood yard."

"He could have called. I put my number on the flyer." Blake's excitement level jacked up from the bottom of the barrel to cloud level in the time it took him to find a decent pair of jeans, dust off his boots, and change shirts.

Blake was on his way to the living room when Deke opened the door and said, "Come on in here out of the cold. Blake and I are about to take a ride. Want to go with us?"

"No thanks," Allie answered. "I came to do some measuring for supplies if that's okay," she said. "I can do it tomorrow though if y'all are going out."

"You're running away from family." Deke chuckled.

"Maybe...But I do need to measure the rooms to get an idea of how much drywall to buy."

"You might as well go with us if you are running from family." Blake grinned.

"And maybe Grady and Lizzy will get the message if they figure out you'd rather be with us as with them." Deke chuckled.

"I didn't come over here to crash y'all's party," she said.

He'd always seen her in cargo pants and paint-splattered knit shirts, but tonight she wore skinny jeans, cowboy boots, and a knit top that stretched over her breasts and cinched in a tiny waist above well-rounded hips. Her hair, usually worn in two dark braids with a stocking hat stuffed down over them or a ponytail, hung to her shoulders in soft waves.

"I'm not taking no for an answer. You can measure tomorrow morning. We're going for a ride. Besides you're dressed up. Be a shame to waste all that beauty." Deke placed his hands on her shoulders and ushered her out onto the porch. "I'll drive, Blake, since I know the way."

In minutes Allie found herself wedged between two big cowboys in the front seat of Deke's truck, heading north out of town. The sun was dropping quickly behind the gently rolling hills and the moon had already made its appearance. Stars would be popping out soon, but right then that lazy part of the evening called dusk had settled in and she didn't care where they were going as long as it took her away from Grady.

Deke turned the radio on to the country music station but she couldn't concentrate on the songs that played one after the other. Not with Blake sitting so close that she could practically feel his pulse and especially not when they hit a bump in the road and it sent her sliding even closer to him.

She righted herself and listened to Lizzy's voice in her head lecturing her about how foolish she was to even go for a ride with those two bad boys. She pushed the voice away about the time they passed from Throckmorton County over into Baylor County, and her eyes widened, grew dry when she couldn't blink, and then she gasped.

"My God, Deke, are you headed for Frankie's?"

"I am." He grinned. "How do you know about Frankie's?"

"Everyone knows about it, but..." she stammered.

Deke patted her knee. "But no decent folks go there,

right? Matter of fact, if Frankie don't know you pretty good, then you don't get anything but barbecue. He'll tell you that the beer and the liquor is for his personal use and isn't for sale. Don't worry, darlin'. Frankie knows me and if I vouch for you two, he won't toss you out on your asses."

"What is this place, anyway?" Blake asked.

"Private barbecue club, but I have a membership since Frankie buys his beef from me. Don't know who he gets the pork from but they've probably got a membership card, too."

"Have you ever been there?" Blake asked Allie.

"Hell, no!"

Deke made a left turn and then a right before the road ended in a rutted trail that led another quarter of a mile through thick mesquite and scrub oak. Finally, he parked in front of a weathered old two-story house with dim lights showing through the downstairs window. "Well, y'all are going tonight. We're going to have some of the best ribs in the world and then we're going to have a few drinks and maybe dance to the jukebox."

"Sounds like a bar to me," Blake said. "But it doesn't look like a bar."

"It's not a bar because half of it is in Throckmorton County and that's a dry county. The other half of the house is in Baylor County, which is semi-dry. They can sell beer in some parts of it but no liquor by the drink. Truth is the living room is in Throckmorton County. Don't worry. Nobody messes with Frankie, not even the police. Come on. Let's go have some fun," Deke said.

Allie could sit in the truck all evening or she could crawl out and go into a place even more notorious than Audrey's Place. Frankie's had been the evil place that teenagers were afraid to say the name out loud for fear the wind would carry it back to their parents and they'd be put into solitary confinement until they were twenty-one years old.

Deke walked onto the porch with confidence, slung open the door, and held it for them to enter before him. "Hey, Frankie, these are my friends, Allie and Blake."

Allie had always pictured Frankie as someone as big as a refrigerator with a scowl on his face and a shotgun in his hand. She was surprised when a little guy who barely came up to Deke's shoulder nodded at her. His baby face was round and he wore little round wire-rimmed glasses. There were no wrinkles in his face and his size made it hard to guess his age. She squirmed beneath his dark eyes when they scanned her and Blake.

"Any friend of Deke's is a friend of Frankie's but the first three times you come through that door, he has to be with you. Understood?"

Allie nodded.

Blake stuck out a hand. "Pleased to meet you, Mr. Frankie. I hear you've got some of the best barbecue in the state."

"No, sir," Frankie smiled as he pumped Blake's hand a few times and then dropped it. "And I am Frankie, not Mr. Frankie. Mr. Frankie was my grandpa and my daddy was Little Frankie. I'm just Frankie. And son, my barbecue ain't some of the best. It is the very best. Now what can I get y'all?"

"Ribs," Deke said. "We'll all have ribs and French fries tonight and maybe a double shot each of your famous brew. After that we'd better settle with beer since none of us wants to be a designated driver."

Frankie leaned across the bar and said seriously, "You get wasted, I don't take your keys, you remember that. You get lost gettin' out of here, the coyotes can eat you for breakfast."

Allie's eyes adjusted to the dim light and she scanned the room. The bar ran the length of the side where Frankie could watch the front door. A dozen chairs surrounded a couple of mismatched tables pushed up on the other side. It was small for a bar and barbecue combination but large for a living room. She could smell a delicious aroma of smoked beef and pork somewhere at the back of the house.

Everything was spotless clean. She could see the reflection of the bottles of liquor in the top of the bar. The hardwood floor looked as if it had been freshly waxed and there wasn't a spot of dust anywhere. She'd always expected something a hell of a lot seedier when she thought of Frankie's, but then she'd painted a very different picture of the owner, too.

She propped a hip on a bar stool in between Blake and Deke. "Not what I expected."

"Me, either, first time I came here. I thought Frankie would be ten feet tall and bulletproof. I expect he's still bulletproof even if he isn't that tall. The place will come to life in about thirty minutes. That'll give us time to eat and then we can party. I'm taking home a woman tonight. How about you, Blake?"

"How?" Allie asked. "Y'all going to throw them in the back of the truck?"

"I'm just here for some beer and maybe a little dancing, not to take someone home," Blake answered.

"Why?" Allie asked.

"Lord, you sound like a newspaper reporter." Deke laughed.

Frankie carried three red plastic baskets to the bar, filled to the brim with ribs and steaming hot fries, and lined them up. "Y'all's the first customers tonight. Now what weight do you want that special brew, Deke?"

"Peach pie." Deke smiled.

"You got it." Frankie chuckled.

"Frankie has several famous brews, but I want you to taste his peach pie first. He manages to make moonshine taste like fresh peach pie right out of the oven. But don't let it fool you. It's got a hell of a lot more kick than pie," Deke explained.

Frankie reached under the counter and brought out a quart mason jar filled with an amber-colored liquid. Then he set three glasses on the bar and put a double shot in each. "Sip it. Don't throw it back. It's made to enjoy."

The door opened and a couple of women wearing short skintight skirts, high heels, and crop tops plopped up on bar stools. One of them winked at Deke and he smiled at her.

"How you doin', Prissy?" he asked.

"Right fine, darlin'. You?"

"Real good. You workin' or playin'?"

"Workin' tonight. You want to book some time?"

He held up his glass. "Naw, I'm just here for supper and some peach pie."

"Good stuff." She smiled, showing off a gold eyetooth. "How about your buddy?"

Deke shook his head.

"Y'all change your mind, I got room three booked and Lacy here has paid for room four."

It wasn't the bite of the peach moonshine that made Allie gasp but the fact that Deke had brought her to a whorehouse as well as an illegal bar. Lord, if the gossip hounds ever got a hold of that bit of news, she and Blake both would be ruined for life. And Blake didn't act like any of it fazed him one bit!

Lacy's butt looked like it was going to pop out of that skirt when she went from the bar to the jukebox and plugged several quarters into it. Then she and Prissy started doing a seductive dance as Etta James's soulful voice singing "At Last" filled the whole room.

Allie's eyes must've been the size of saucers because Deke poked her on the arm.

"I told you that it ain't a country bar," he said softly.

"I kind of gathered that," Allie said.

Blake held out a hand. "May I have this dance?"

"What about our food?" she asked.

"Deke won't let anyone get it."

Deke nudged her with his shoulder. "Go on. Have some fun."

She slid off the stool and Blake picked up her hands and wrapped them around his neck. His arms rested loosely around her waist as he began to move slowly and smoothly around the dance floor. The lyrics of the song said that he smiled and the spell was cast. God help her, but truer words had never been spoken.

Instead of taking her back to the bar he kept dancing when the first chords of guitar music started an old blues song, "Ain't No Sunshine."

"Do you listen to this music?" she asked.

"No, but my grandpa loves rhythm and blues so I'm no stranger to it," he answered.

The third song was something fast and furious with lots of horn music in the background. Blake mixed swing dancing with something that she'd never seen or done before. It took all her concentration to keep up with him, and when the song ended she was breathless.

"Time for a sip of peach pie?" Blake asked.

* * *

This whole business of settling down might not be so tough after all. He could withstand the temptations of the local women if he could have some time at Frankie's occasionally. Allie had said she wasn't interested in any kind of relationship, so they could have good times with no strings attached. By spring he might be completely weaned away from his wild cowboy ways.

When they'd finished their ribs and shots, the bar was full of people. They moved from their stools to dance in the corner where Deke ordered a round of beers. Prissy hugged up to a cowboy and pretty soon they disappeared back behind a beaded curtain as "When a Man Loves a Woman," played on the jukebox.

"You like this place?" Allie asked.

Blake leaned close to her ear so she could hear him. "It's different for sure and beats unpacking boxes. What about you?"

"I'm glad I'm not here alone." She smiled. "Is that Etta James again?"

Blake nodded. "She's singing 'Damn Your Eyes.' Anyone ever tell you that you've got gorgeous eyes?"

"Not lately and certainly not anyone I would believe."

"Something's Got a Hold on Me," another Etta James tune, started as soon as the first one ended. Blake hugged Allie tightly to his chest and moved slowly around the floor.

"Do I have a hold on you?" she asked.

"Oh, honey, you don't have a clue," he teased.

The music stopped and she hurried to the jukebox. She bent over it to see the song titles better and there was that cute little denim-covered butt just tempting him. His mouth went dry and his pulse jacked up a few notches. He laced his fingers together on top of the table to keep from taking a few steps forward and cupping her fine ass in his hands.

He would not seduce Allie. Not even if he could already feel her body next to his, under him, working with him, and satisfying the ache behind his zipper. He was trying hard to make her his friend and that did not include benefits. She was an important part of his strategy to get past his wild reputation. He really, really needed for the folks in Dry Creek to see him as a responsible rancher, not a bar-hopping cowboy with nothing but a good time on his mind. No one in Muenster would take him seriously, and that had always bothered him.

The jukebox spit out "Lean on Me." Was she telling him something? She returned to her chair and smiled. "I remember some of these songs from when I was..." She clamped a hand over her mouth. "Granny had some of these on vinyl. I wonder if she was ever here?"

Blake smiled. "Darlin', your granny has lots of secrets."

At midnight Deke handed Allie the keys to his truck and said, "Place closes at two. Frankie says y'all can stay long as you want. Leave the keys on the front seat, Blake. I've got a lady who says she can make a mean breakfast come daylight." He grinned and disappeared in a fog of smoke.

"One more dance?" Blake asked.

Allie stood up and moved out to the middle of the empty floor as Sam Cooke sang "Bring It on Home to Me." She wrapped her arms around Blake's neck and smiled up at him. "It's not hard to imagine my granny in her best dress out here on this very floor dancin' with my grandpa to this song."

"Who says she came here with your grandpa? Maybe it was with Walter," he teased.

"I don't want to think about that." She leaned back and looked up at him.

She'd said no more kisses but those dark brown eyes mesmerized him. He tipped up her chin and whispered, "Then let's think about this."

His lips closed over hers and his arms pulled her tighter against his chest, his tongue finding its way inside her mouth, tasting the peach pie moonshine. Finally, she put her hands on his chest and pushed.

"Blake, I told you about that," she said.

Her tone wasn't very convincing so he brushed another kiss across her lips. "I was just seeing if the peach pie tasted better on your lips than it did straight from the glass."

"Have you always been a charmer?" she asked with a smile.

"I can't help it when I'm around you. You don't have any idea how beautiful you are or how you affect a man, do you, darlin'?"

"On that note, I think it's time for you to take me home." She blushed, shrugged, and threw up her palms all at once. It was so damn cute he wanted to kiss her again. "I mean, take me to my home, so don't look at me like that."

The dance ended and he led her out to the truck. He wished the whole way back through the rutted road and to the county road leading home that she was sitting as close to him as she had been on the way to Frankie's, and cussing himself for wanting her for more than a friend.

CHAPTER NINE

Blake opened the door before she even knocked that Saturday afternoon. "Come right in out of the cold. Man, I'm glad y'all got the roof done. I believe the weatherman just might be right and we'll get that six inches of snow on Sunday."

"I won't take long. Just a few measurements and then I've got to get to Wichita Falls for supplies before the weather hits." She pulled a steel tape measure from one of the pockets on her cargo pants and headed down the hall.

Deke pushed in the back door without knocking and yelled. "Hey, Blake, do you mind if I use your chainsaw sharpener?"

"You sure can. I didn't think you'd be around today after last night."

"I'm energized and ready to work," Deke said. "I'm filling my travel mug with coffee. Once that snow gets here, the wood-cuttin' business will have to wait."

"Sharpener is in the barn," Blake said. "There's spaghetti sauce made from venison simmering in the slow cooker. One of the ladies brought it by when they delivered all that food. We'll have it for supper tonight? Y'all want to join me?"

"Sure, maybe we'll go back to Frankie's," Deke yelled, and the back door slammed.

"How about you?"

"How about me what?" Allie asked.

"You got a problem with venison?"

It was on the tip of her tongue to say that she'd eat anything he served but she'd prefer to do it in bed, after sex, and before the next round of sex. But she bit her lip and shook her head. "No, I don't mind it at all. Daddy hunted every year so I was raised on wild game. I also like fried rabbit and frog legs, but I don't like squirrel fixed any way. It's just a rat with a fluffy tail to me."

She took a step, tangled her foot on a wrinkle in the carpet, and plunged forward into his arms. "I'm so sorry," she stammered. "Okay, which room first?"

"My bedroom and excuse the mess. I'm still not unpacked."

"I'm not here to judge your housekeeping, Blake." She set about measuring the room and then pulled a notepad from her pocket to write down the measurements. "Color? And will it be for the whole house or different for every room?"

"What would you do if this was the bedroom you'd be sleeping in the rest of your life?" he asked.

Lord, have mercy! That question put a visual in her mind that practically made her pant. "Something neutral, like a soft ivory or maybe a really light tan with white trim and doors. It would lighten up the place. Whoever painted it this god-awful shade of pink should be shot. It's evident that the room has always been the master bedroom. No one paints a room where a man is going to sleep this color." No wonder she was talking so fast and furious.

Blake chuckled. "So you aren't into pink walls and lacy curtains?"

She thought carefully before she answered so she wouldn't go off on another tangent. "You should be able to tell that by looking at me. Pink and lace were my youngest sister's things. I was always the girl who'd rather be running around behind Daddy and playing in the sawdust."

Something about that king-size bed with the tangled gold sheets set her hormones into overdrive. Thank God she had a notepad because she couldn't remember a single, solitary number she'd written down on it. She did recall something about sand-colored paint with white woodwork but to be on the safe side, she probably needed to note that, too.

What was wrong with her? Hell, she couldn't even hang on to Riley and he wasn't a tenth as sexy as Blake. Deke appeared in the doorway and pointed toward the ceiling.

"Every joint has been affected by the leaks. Hall looks to be four feet wide and twenty feet long, so you'll need five sheets for the hall. Write that down. Living room is a twenty-foot square so figure that many sheets. I ran back by to say we can't go to Frankie's tonight. I promised my cousin and his wife I'd go to dinner with them."

She wrote down the numbers. "Thanks, Deke."

"Y'all decided what to do with the floors?" Deke asked.

Blake shrugged and looked at Allie. "What do you suggest we do with this ratty old carpet?"

Deke went to a corner and pulled up a corner. "Looks like oak hardwood under it. I'd pull the shit up and throw it out. Wood floors are easier to clean. I pulled it all out of my house a couple of years ago and ain't regretted it one time."

"Want me to rip it all up after I get through painting? If you do, then I won't have to cover the flooring to keep from getting paint on it," Allie said.

"That sounds good," Blake said. "How long do you think the whole job will take?"

"About a week if you will help me get the drywall up on the ceiling. Trim work takes longer because it's tedious, and the doors will have to be sanded. But I'd say a week for each room."

"So roughly a month unless you have to take a day now and then to help take care of Miz Irene?" he asked.

"That's right." She bit her tongue to keep from spitting out a monologue about woodwork, floors, carpet, and anything else to keep her mind off those sheets.

"Either of y'all want a cup of hot chocolate or coffee to warm your bones before you go back out in the cold?" Blake asked.

"Not me," Deke said. "I'm outta here. Got wood to get cut and ready to sell while the sun shines. Can't do much in that area if it's bad weather next week."

His boots didn't make a noise until he hit the kitchen floor, and then she heard the back door slam again. She tucked the notepad and tape back in her pocket. "I'll pass. I don't want to get caught in a rain storm with drywall on the trailer."

He raised his arms over his head and stretched, working the kinks out of his back by bending to each side. Allie's eyes were glued to that broad chest and the way his biceps stretched the arms of the T-shirt. How long would it take her to strip that thing up over his head? How would it feel to bury her face on his chest while afterglow settled around them?

Afterglow is not real! You know that, Allie Logan. It's

something that romance authors made up to make all women think there is something wonderful out there. Kind of like sex that lasts all night and isn't over in ten minutes with the man snoring on his side of the bed.

"What about fish?" he asked.

"What are you talking about?" Had she been so lost in her argument with herself or in the pictures she'd conjured up in her mind of him half-naked that she missed something about going fishing?

"You said you don't like squirrel. Do you eat fish?" he asked.

She nodded. "Any kind long as it's cooked. I'm like Granny when it comes to sushi."

"And that is?" He smiled.

She stood up and took a couple of steps toward the door. "Raw fish is called bait in our world."

Blake followed her. "Alora Raine? Where'd you get that name?"

"Is this twenty questions or something?" she asked.

He leaned a shoulder against the wall beside the coatrack. "It could be. I was trying to get you to stay longer."

"We'll have to play that game another time. I'll see you later. App weather forecast on my phone says no bad weather until tomorrow, so my stuff will be all right on the trailer until after church. I'll cover it with a tarp." There she went talking too much again.

Her arm brushed against his when she reached around him and picked her coat off the rack. The scent of his cologne mixed with a manly soap filled her nostrils every time she inhaled.

"Do you miss your family?" she asked as she slipped her arms into her coat and buttoned it up the front. One more layer of protection, not against him but herself.

"More than I thought I would. We went to my grand-parents' house every Sunday for dinner after church." He straightened her collar. "Cousins fought. Men sat on the porch with a beer and talked crops and cattle. Women gathered in the kitchen to talk about girl things. I wasn't interested in the kitchen, but I learned to love ranchin' out there listenin' to those old men talk about cows and hay and spring plantin'."

The warmth of his fingertips on her neck sent electricity bouncing all around her. Did he feel it, too, or was it just her?

"But you did learn to cook," she said.

Blake stepped back. "Only because I had to. Most of my expertise starts with a big stew pot. I can't fry chicken worth a damn and it's my favorite food. Deke says you hate to cook. Was he teasing?"

She slowly shook her head. "He was telling the truth. I hate to cook but that doesn't mean I can't cook. I can fry chicken that will melt in your mouth."

"Biscuits?" His eyes twinkled.

She nodded.

"Gravy? The good stuff with no lumps?" A grin tickled his sexier-than-the-devil mouth.

Another nod.

"Will you marry me?" he asked bluntly.

Had he seriously just proposed? "I might fry chicken for you to celebrate when we finish this house, but I'm never getting married again."

"I don't take rejection well." He laid a fist over his heart and dropped his head in a fake pout.

Allie took another step toward the door. "Sorry about that, cowboy. You'll have to get over it."

He sighed. "Will you attend my funeral on Sunday? I

promised my brother, Toby, if I ever found a woman who could fry chicken like my mama, I would ask her to marry me. It's going to kill me to tell him that the woman of my dreams has turned me down."

"You're full of horse shit." She laughed.

Allie deliberately stayed out late that evening, hoping to avoid Mitch and Grady. The Friday-night date with her sister and the two guys had been postponed at the last minute until tonight, so she didn't want to go home until she absolutely had to.

Instead, she decided a little retail therapy at the mall might be in order until she was sure they'd be out of the house. She meandered through three stores and bought a new pair of skinny jeans, a beautiful dark green sweater dress, and two shirts. Then she grabbed dinner on her own, wishing the whole time that Deke and Blake were sitting with her at the table.

It was a little after eight when she made it to Dry Creek and saw Mitch's truck right there in the driveway. Damn! She slapped the steering wheel but the truck did not disappear.

She tiptoed across the porch and eased the front door open, then closed it behind her so carefully that it didn't make a bit of noise. She didn't realize she was holding her breath until she reached the landing and it came out in a loud whoosh. Quickly peeking over the banister to make sure they hadn't heard her, she sucked in another lung full of air and hurried into her room. Without turning on the light, she slid down the backside of the door and wrapped her arms around her knees.

"Alora, let me in." A soft whisper on the other side of the door startled her. She hopped up and opened the door a crack to find Irene in her red flannel pajamas.

Her grandmother held up a package of chocolate chip cookies in one hand and a soda pop in the other. "I snuck in the kitchen and up the stairs and they didn't hear me."

"Who's down there?" Allie pulled her grandmother inside and flipped the light switch.

Irene crawled up in the middle of the bed and ripped open the cookie package. "Katy and Lizzy and those two men. Lizzy is dumber than a box of rocks."

Allie didn't care if her granny left her bed in a mess of crumbs or even if she spilled the can of soda pop. To have Irene there in her right mind might take her mind off Blake Dawson and that despicable Grady at the same time.

"I loved your grandpa. I really did," Irene said. "But there was a time..."

Allie waited for her granny to fall back into another time.

She finished a cookie and reached for another one. "I forget things, Allie, but I want you to know something while my mind isn't all jumbled. Your grandpa started it when he had that affair with that woman from Throckmorton. But we got past it and fell in love all over again. We had four wonderful years before he died."

Allie crawled up on the bed with her grandmother. "It's okay, Granny. It's in the past and Grandpa loved you."

"I know that and I loved him. I never did love Walter like I did him. I was getting even with him." She handed Allie a cookie. "But we need to talk about Lizzy. She is about to get into a mess. I never have thought that boy loves her like he should. She's marryin' just to be married. Leastways that's what I think, which ain't worth much these days the way my head is working. I'm afraid she will regret it and I can't tell her anything so you're going to have to stop that wedding. You owe me this much because you wouldn't listen to me when it came to Riley. He was a sorry bastard."

"I know, Granny." Allie nibbled on the cookie as she talked. "You were right. Riley thought he could change me and turn me into a little wife who stayed home and had dozens of babies for him. When I didn't get pregnant in those almost three years we were married he blamed it on the work I do."

"Stupid bastard. And then he left you. It wasn't your fault you didn't have them babies. It was probably his the way he poked his thing into anyone who'd lift their skirt tail for him. Most likely rotted any sperm he had up in there. Here have a drink of this soda pop and get the taste of his name out of your mouth." Irene passed the soda over to her.

Allie took a sip and handed it back. "Thank you, Granny."

"I wanted to kill him but I couldn't figure out a way to do it and not get caught and you needed me then. But now I'm a burden so I want you to kill that sumbitch that Lizzy is about to marry." Irene dropped cookie crumbs on the bedspread. "I'll say I did it and they might put me away but it's okay. I don't want another of my precious babies to hurt like you did."

Allie picked up the crumbs and tossed them in the trash can beside her bed. "You are not a burden, Granny. We all love you."

Irene clamped her bony hand over Allie's knee. "If you love me and your sister, then put a stop to her marryin' that man. Promise me you won't stop short of killin' him."

"I'll do my best, Granny," Allie said.

Irene's mouth set in a firm line. "Okay, you've given me your word. I'll be packed and ready to go to the nut house when you get it done. Just tell me how you do it so I don't flub up the story. I'm going back to my room now and we'll talk later."

She slid off the bed and tiptoed to the door, peeked out

and gave Allie the thumbs-up sign before she left. Allie threw herself back on the pillows and stared at the ceiling. Granny was worried about Lizzy but the true message from her ten minutes of being lucid seemed to be that Allie needed to put the past behind her...after she killed Mitch, of course.

CHAPTER TEN

Several people turned around in the church pews that Sunday morning and stared blatantly; some whipped back to whisper behind their hands to the person next to them. Without even turning around, Allie knew exactly who had just walked in. The extra beat in her heart and the way her pulse raced told her it was Blake.

Grady scooted close to her and put his arm around her, his hand resting on her shoulder. Allie gritted her teeth and tried to shrug his arm away, but he was a persistent son of a bitch. When the music director said that the congregation would sing, "Abide with Me," he held the hymnbook and pulled her even closer.

She didn't even try to sing. She didn't want God to abide with her that morning. She wanted him to strike Grady graveyard dead in the pew where he sat or maybe send a bolt of lightning through the roof to turn him into nothing but ashes. She didn't even mind getting a little bit of scorch on her new pretty sweater dress if God would grant her the desires of her heart.

Her granny sang a different song, loud and clear in her soprano voice. The folks in the church had long accepted that Irene Miller lived in many worlds each day and didn't pay a bit of attention to her that morning as she sang, "I'll Fly Away," while the rest of the congregation sang, "Abide with Me."

"You look really gorgeous this morning," Grady whispered when the song ended.

His breath was warm and it was supposed to be seductive, but Allie wanted to brush it away like a fly that had lit on her earlobe after visiting a fresh cow pile. If she inhaled deeply, she could even smell the cow shit.

"I'm looking forward to dinner," Grady said.

"Shhhh," Granny said. "No talkin' in church."

The preacher opened his Bible, cleared his throat, and said, "Good morning. We have a newcomer back there on the back row. Welcome to Dry Creek, Blake Dawson. We all know that you've bought the Lucky Penny and we welcome you to our church. Now, this morning my sermon is from the verses that say that God will not lay more upon a person than they can endure and he will always provide a way of escape."

Irene tapped Allie on the knee and said in a very loud whisper, "I've got to go to the bathroom and I don't know where it is." She frantically looked around everywhere, from the ceiling to the windows.

Allie laced her fingers in her grandmother's and they stood up together. The preacher read verses straight from the Bible to support his opening statement as the two ladies, one in fear of wetting herself and the other giving thanks that God had provided an escape, made their way to the back of the church.

The ladies' room was located off the nursery and two elderly ladies looked up from worn old rockers where they each held a baby in their arms.

"Good morning, Dorothy and Janet. Looks like you've got your hands full today," Allie said quickly so that her grandmother would know who the ladies were.

"We love babies. Hello, Irene. It's good to see you again," Dorothy said.

"I don't know you so how can you say that you ever saw me in the first place?" She leaned toward Allie and whispered in her ear, "You'll wait for me, right?"

"I'll be right here, Granny. I'm not going anywhere."

Irene closed the door behind her and Allie slumped down in a third rocking chair.

"She's not going to get any better, is she?" Dorothy said.

Allie shook her head. "The doctors say that this puzzle stage will get worse until she finally settles into one phase of her life. Probably when she was the happiest and that she might not know us most of the time, especially if she stops when she was a young girl and we weren't even in her life then. We keep hoping one of the medications they are trying will work."

"I'm so sorry," Janet said. "We used to love having her help us here in the nursery and we were all good friends. The three of us and Hilda, but Hilda's been gone now for years. Died with cancer back when she wasn't much more than forty."

Evidently Irene overheard the name *Hilda*, because when she came out of the bathroom with her skirt tail tucked up in the back of her white granny panties, the first words out of her mouth were, "Hilda, something ain't right with my clothes. Help me, please."

Allie didn't mind being Hilda if she didn't have to sit

beside Grady anymore that day. "You want to stay in here or go back out into the church?" She stood up and put her grandmother to rights. "The preacher has another twenty minutes at the least before he winds down."

"Are we having fried chicken? Is that mean man coming to dinner?" Irene asked.

"What mean man?" Allie asked.

She popped one hand on her hip. "You know who I'm talking about. I'm not sitting on the same pew with him. I hate him."

"Then you do want to stay in here? And Mama put a pot roast in the oven for dinner so we aren't having fried chicken." Allie sat back down in the rocking chair. The church was small with two sets of pews, a center aisle, and just enough room on the sides for folks to get out of church single file. She didn't want to follow Granny but then she didn't want to lead the way, either, because there was no telling what she'd do if Allie didn't keep a hand on her arm.

She shook her head. "I'm not a baby. We're both ten years old and we don't belong in the nursery anymore. I'm going to listen to the preacher but I'm not sitting on that pew." She marched out of the nursery like a little girl in a royal snit.

Allie jumped up and followed her right down the center aisle, which meant she'd have to skinny past Grady to get to the end of their pew. Irene made it to the back pew and stopped. She frowned as if trying to remember where in the hell she was and what she was supposed to do next and then cocked her head to one side.

"I'm sitting right here and if you don't talk in church, you can sit beside me, Hilda. And I think I will go home with you today for dinner. Your mama makes good fried chicken," Irene said loudly.

The preacher never missed a single beat, but Allie did

hear a few snickers in the crowd. That brought out her protective nature and she would have marched forward and sat on the altar with her grandmother if Irene had wanted to do that. But instead Irene pushed past Blake and sat on his left. "You can sit on the other side of Everett. If he pulls your hair, kick him in the shins."

Allie slid in beside Blake. He was freshly shaved and the smell of something woodsy, mixed with his soap, sent her senses reeling. She waited until Irene was settled and whispered softly, "Sorry, it's not a good day. It started off good but it's gone to hell in a handbasket."

Blake smiled. "I'm not a bit sorry. I may buy her an ice cream cone after church."

"And where would you get that?" Allie whispered.

"Shhh. Everett Dunlap, you know better than to talk in church." Irene popped him on the shoulder. "And don't you dare pull my hair."

It was downright crazy: one man's hand on her shoulder made her want to run; the other sitting a foot away almost made her hyperventilate right there in front of her grandmother, the preacher, and even God. Life and fate were both four letter words and both should be put on the naughty list with the other cuss words.

Allie breathed a sigh of relief when they made it through the benediction without her granny announcing to the whole place that it was about time the long-winded preacher shut his mouth so they could go eat dinner. Everyone was standing up and the noise level was rising by the second as folks talked about everything from the sermon to the weather and lined up in the pews to shake the preacher's hand at the door.

Blake extended a hand to Irene. "Thank you, ladies, for sitting with me."

She took it and nodded. "It was our pleasure, I'm sure. I don't believe we've met. Are you Hilda's uncle?"

"Isn't this Everett, Granny?"

Her grandmother's eyes went dark as she searched for a puzzle piece that would tell her who Everett was, then suddenly she clapped her hands. "Everett pulled my hair and I kicked him. He tattled on me but I didn't care. I think he likes me." Irene giggled. "But he didn't come to church today. I'm glad your uncle is here, though."

"I'm glad, too," Blake answered with a smile.

"Are you going to Hilda's for dinner, too? Her mama always makes fried chicken on Sunday and my mama made roast beef today so I don't want to go to my house," Irene asked.

"Your mama might want you to go home today since Lizzy has invited her boyfriend over for dinner," Allie said.

Irene looked up, waved at Katy, and shouted above the noise of dozens of conversations. "Mama, I am going home with Hilda and her uncle today. I don't like Lizzy's boyfriend or that mean man that runs around with him."

"Shhh, Granny," Allie said.

"We are all going home. You can ride with Allie," Katy said sternly.

Irene stopped in the middle of the aisle and glared at Katy. "When those two mean men go away I will come home. Besides I want fried chicken."

"I'd planned on driving over to Olney to a little restaurant that specializes in fried chicken on Sunday," Blake said quickly. "I'm sure my niece would enjoy her company and I could have her back at your place by mid-afternoon."

"Yes, yes!" Irene clapped her hands. "Please let me go. I don't get to go to a café hardly ever."

"You put her up to this. You put the idea in her head,"

Lizzy hissed at Allie. "I will never forgive you for ruining my entire weekend."

"I did not. Next Sunday you can sit beside her and take her to the bathroom," Allie said.

Katy slipped her hand around Allie's arm. "This does not mean any more than taking care of your grandmother, does it?"

"No, ma'am," Allie said. "She'll make a scene if you don't let her go with me and Blake. She thinks I'm her childhood friend, Hilda. They mentioned her name in the nursery and that's probably what set her off."

Herman Hudson stepped out from his pew and fell in behind Katy, separating her from Lizzy and the two guys. "Blake Dawson, I hear you've got wood to give away."

"Yes, sir, I do," Blake said.

Herman stuck out his hand. "I'll be glad to take all you can pile up for my wood yard. You got a problem with me selling it?"

"No, sir, not one bit. I'd just be glad to get it cleared away and not have to burn it all up," Blake said.

"Then me and my kin folks will be there soon as this snow stops. We don't mind workin' once it's on the ground but when it's fallin', it makes it tough. Thank you, son," Herman said.

Irene wiggled in the backseat like a little girl eager to get to her destination. "We'll be there in a little bit, won't we? Can I have ice cream if I eat all my chicken?"

"Yes, you can or whatever dessert you want," Blake answered.

"I like your uncle," Irene said.

The café had two empty tables when they arrived. The waitress waved them to one and said, "If you'll sit there, we'll save the bigger one for more folks. Be right with you."

The waitress finally got around to them, handing out menus, which consisted of one laminated page with the listings for breakfast on one side and lunch on the other. "What are y'all having to drink?"

"Sweet tea," Irene answered.

"Same here," Allie and Blake said in unison.

His leg touched hers under the table. That's all it took to flood her mind with pictures that she should not be entertaining after church or in a restaurant. Most of them did not involve clothing, menus, or even church music.

"We've got two specials today. Fried chicken tenders with hot biscuits, your choice of two sides, and pecan pie with or without ice cream for dessert. Second one is roast beef with all the same," she said.

"Fried chicken, mashed potatoes, macaroni and cheese, and I want ice cream on my pie for dessert," Irene said.

Blake handed her the menu. "Same only with okra instead of mac and cheese."

"Me, too, except I want corn casserole for my vegetable." Allie's arm brushed against Blake's when she gave the waitress her menu, and the pictures in her head became even more vivid.

"I'll have it right out." The waitress hurried off to seat a family of six at the larger table and clean off a small four-person table for another group just arriving.

"So what are you ladies going to do all next week?" Blake asked.

"School." Irene rolled her eyes. "I hope we don't have homework every night."

"Why is that?"

Allie had no doubts that Blake was a very good uncle to his nieces and nephew. He was a natural in the role.

Irene sighed dramatically. "If we have homework, then Hilda can't come and play with me after school. Her mama won't let her and my mama makes me sit at the kitchen table until it's all done, and it takes hours."

"Do you like Dry Creek?" Blake asked.

Irene shrugged. "It's where I live so I have to like it. Someday I'm going to move away to a big place, though. I'm going to live in a house in town so I can go to the movies and to a café and have coffee in the mornings."

Blake nodded seriously. "And do you like coffee, Miz Irene?"

"No, but I'll learn if I can move away from Dry Creek. Why are you asking me so many questions?" Irene asked.

"I want to get to know my niece's friend." He smiled.

Lord, have mercy! One more of those killer smiles and knee touches and Allie would need one of her mother's hot flash pills. Come to think of it, Blake should carry those little white pills in his shirt pocket and dole them out to the women he came in contact with. One if he smiled. Two if he strutted past them in tight jeans. Go ahead and fill up a coffee cup with them if he kissed a woman.

The waitress brought their food and drinks at the same time and Irene concentrated on her food. Allie was afraid to say anything at all because it could make her grandmother shift gears and suddenly not know either her or Blake.

"Allie." Irene touched her on the arm. "What are we doing here?"

Allie laid a hand over her grandmother's. "You had a forgetting moment, Granny. Deke's friend asked us to go to dinner with him and you said you'd love some fried chicken."

"This is Blake from the Lucky Penny. He's not Deke's friend," Irene argued.

"Yes, he is. He and Deke are really good friends. Our fried chicken is here. Let's eat it before it gets cold," Allie said.

"I do like fried chicken. Did Grady and Mitch go home with Lizzy?" Irene asked.

Allie nodded.

"Well, I'm glad I came with you and Blake because I really don't like either one of those guys." Irene dug into her dinner with gusto.

Blake bit into a piece of fried chicken. "Is your chicken this good?" he asked Allie.

Irene laughed. "Oh, honey. Her fried chicken is even better than my mama's was. And her biscuits would make the angels in heaven weep for joy."

"Now you have to marry me." Blake grinned.

Where were those hot flash pills? She needed a mug full to eat like candy corn.

"No, she's not going to marry you. We might go to dinner with you when fried chicken is involved, but the women of Audrey's Place do not marry the men from the Lucky Penny, and that's a fact." Irene's mind and body both shifted from little girl to grown woman in the blink of an eye. "If we had some fried green tomatoes, this would be the ideal Sunday dinner."

Without another word, she cleaned up her plate and pushed it back. "Now I want pecan pie with ice cream."

Allie caught the waitress's eye and the lady hurried right over to their table. "Ready for dessert? Three pecan pies with ice cream."

Irene giggled. "No, three slices of pecan pie with ice cream. I can't eat a whole pie."

"Yes, ma'am." The waitress patted her gently on the shoulder.

"Old people can say whatever they want and folks don't even mind," Irene said. "But I'm glad these people over here in Olney—we are in Olney, aren't we?"

Blake nodded. "Yes, ma'am, we are. I heard you liked fried chicken and that this place served up a good Sunday special."

"Well, I'm glad that we're here and not in Dry Creek. That café has been closed for years in Dry Creek, hasn't it?"

Allie's head bobbed. "Yes, Granny. You are remembering very well today."

"Some days are better than others," she said.

Floating from one time period to the next always exhausted her grandmother. The poor old dear curled up next to the window on the way home and went to sleep. What little Allie and Blake did say to each other was said in low tones so they wouldn't wake her. Twenty-five minutes from the time they'd left the restaurant, he drove past the church, the feed store, and the convenience store and on out to the lane that led back to Audrey's Place. He parked in front of the big two-story house and Allie saw the house through his eyes.

"Not what you were expecting?" she asked.

"I'm not sure. I don't see red lights or scantily clad women or even a sign that says Audrey's Place." He looked up at her through the rearview mirror.

"Well, it's not still a whorehouse! Truth is it was always referred to as a hotel. The porch is an add-on and I've redone a lot of the interior," she said.

Irene roused up and looked at the house as if seeing it for the first time in her life. "Where are we? Why did you bring me here?"

Allie touched her on the arm. "We're home. Are you ready to go on inside and get warm in your own bed?"

Irene blinked several times and skewered up one side of her face as she finally found a place that made sense. "I'm not going in there. Not until he leaves. He shouldn't have slept with that woman and I don't want to be married to him anymore."

"Who?"

Irene had settled on the time when her husband had cheated on her. "Your grandpa. He's in there trying to be nice to Mama so she'll make me stay with him. He's lower than a snake's belly and I will get even. I can still turn a man's head even if I am almost forty."

Blake started to back the truck out of the driveway. "Where do you want to go? You name the place, Miz Irene, and I will take you wherever you tell me to."

"Granny, that is Mitch's truck. Remember? He's engaged to Lizzy," Allie said.

Irene nodded slowly. "That's right. I get things mixed up sometimes, especially when I first wake up. It's like I'm in another world. Let's sneak inside. We can't go anywhere else with this snow coming down."

When they left church there was about a flake to the acre as her father used to say when it was barely spitting snow, but after they left Olney the skies turned a solid gray and it started to get serious about the business.

"Come on in with us, Blake, but you will have to be very quiet." Irene's eyes twinkled as she put a finger over her lips.

Blake shut off the engine. "I should be going."

She folded her hands over her chest and glared at him. "Nonsense. I'm not getting out of this truck if you don't go in with us."

Allie nodded ever so slightly when he caught her eye

in the mirror again. "I guess you'll have to do what she wants."

"Thank you," Irene said. "Now you can help me out and I'll hold on to your arm so I don't fall going up the porch steps. You do remind me of someone but I think he wore glasses."

Blake slung open his door and then opened hers. He looped her arm through his and held his hand over hers as he matched his step to hers.

Allie was on the other side and Irene grabbed her hand. "I think we had a good time today but I can't remember much about it. Is it Monday?"

"No, Granny, it's Sunday. We went to church this morning."

"That's right and we sang, 'Abide with Me,' didn't we? And now it's snowing like the weatherman said. Can we make snow ice cream tomorrow?"

"You had the prettiest voice in the whole church." Blake took the three porch steps one at a time, making sure her footing was steady before he went to the next one. "And I've got a real good recipe for snow ice cream. I'll make a big bowl full and bring it to you if Allie is too busy to make it for you."

"Thank you. I like that hymn. It was Mama's favorite. And I really like snow ice cream," Irene said. "You are a good man to help me inside, but now it's time to be quiet and not talk or we'll have to be nice to that sumbitch that Lizzy is engaged to marry. Some folks have to learn their lessons the hard way."

Allie opened the door and they slipped inside the foyer and all the way back to Irene's room without getting caught. When Audrey's Place was first built, the owners occupied the only bedroom on the first floor. Granny and Grandpa shared that room until he died, but now it was hers alone. She let go of Blake's arm and Allie's hand and eased the door shut. "They're in the kitchen. I'm safe now and I'm going to sleep a while so y'all can go on. Allie, don't you stay out late and Blake, you see to it she's home by ten. Decent women are in bed at ten. And it feels like I had a good time today so thank you for that."

"Yes, ma'am, I will see to it that she is," Blake said.

When they were in the foyer, Blake hugged her close to his side. "It has to be the scariest thing in the world for her. She's probably afraid to shut her eyes when her world is right because she's afraid she'll lose what control she has while she's asleep," he said. "Poor old darlin' is such a sweetheart when she's lucid. I would have loved to have known her before this disease started eating away at her mind."

Allie leaned into his shoulder and it felt so right. "We never know what will set her off. She doesn't like Mitch or Grady, so that might have made her regress to her childhood so she didn't have to think about them. The doctor says one day she simply won't remember any of us, so we take the good when we can get it."

"Well, look who made it home." Grady's shifty eyes darted from Blake to Allie and back again. "I told Lizzy I heard you out here."

Allie put a finger over her lips. "Shhh. She's settled down for a nap. If she hears voices it will upset her."

Grady's nose curled in disgust. "She needs to be put away in a place where they take care of people like her. It has to be draining on the whole family to put up with those tantrums when she goes back to being a child, if she does."

"What is that supposed to mean?" Allie asked coldly.

"She doesn't like me or Mitch. She's told him that she

hopes he dies before the wedding, so I figure that she's playing the whole bunch of you. I'd be willing to bet that she
wasn't a little kid at all this morning." Grady tilted his chin
up like the know-it-all he thought he was.

"You really think so?" Blake asked.

"I don't think so. I know it but right now I will speak for
the family and say thank you for playing along with her and
bringing Allie home early. I hear that you bought the Lucky
Penny? How long do you think you'll last before you give
up and go back to wherever you came from?" Grady asked
coldly.

"I don't give up easy. When I want something I work my
ass off for it and treat it right," Blake answered.

"And," Allie said, "you don't need to speak for the family
since you are definitely not a part of it."

Grady laid a hand on Allie's shoulder. "Now don't get all
huffy, darlin'. It's not becoming for a lady."

She shrugged it off and sucked in enough air to give him
an earful of what she thought of him, when Katy pushed past
Grady and hugged Allie. "You are home. I heard y'all talking and wanted to thank you, Blake, personally for what you
did today for my mother and daughter. We've been told to
play along with whatever time frame she's in and I'm very
glad that you helped us out today."

"You are very welcome," Blake said. "I suppose I really
should be going before the snow gets worse."

Snow!

God Bless Blake Dawson's soul!

It could be her salvation from that slimy Grady.

She hugged her mother and ignored Grady. "Granny
switched gears about the time we finished eating and she
wanted a nap. She's resting so it might be best if y'all took
your conversation back to the kitchen. I'm going to follow

Blake over to the Lucky Penny to unload all the supplies I bought yesterday. They're under a good strong tarp but if they get wet, it could be disastrous."

Blake nodded toward Grady and smiled at Katy. "It's been real nice meeting all y'all. I guess we'd best get going if we're to get things unloaded before the snow gets any deeper." He ushered her out of the house with his hand on the small of her back.

Allie could feel Grady's eyes boring holes into her but she didn't give a damn. If it wouldn't have wakened Granny, she would have liked to put a well-placed knee in his crotch when he made that remark about her grandmother. Watching him roll around on the floor holding on to his balls would have brought her so much satisfaction.

"Thank you. If I had to stay in that house I might really do what Granny asked me to," she said.

"Which is?"

"Kill Mitch. Only if I'm going to jail for a murder, I might as well make it two. When Grady looks at me, my skin crawls like it did..." she stopped.

"Go on," Blake said.

"Not today. I'm sorry we've ruined your whole Sunday and now you'll have to help me unload wallboard and lumber," she said.

"Do I make your skin crawl?" he asked.

"Hell, no!" she said quickly.

He chuckled. "Then I don't need to know any more. I'll follow your van and trailer to my ranch. That way if anything flies off, I can stop and get it. Don't look like this is going to slow down any."

"My van is parked around back. I'll...well, shit...I'm still wearing my Sunday clothes."

The north wind had picked up and blew Allie's hair

across her face, snowflakes as big as dimes sticking in it. Blake reached out and tucked the errant strands behind her ear. "And you look mighty lovely in that pretty dress. You drive over to my house and I'll give Deke a call. We'll unload the trailer for you if you'll keep that dress on so I can enjoy the view a little longer."

"Does that pickup line work for you?" She grinned.

He leaned on the hood of his truck and grinned down at her. "Don't know. You tell me." His eyes smoldered. "Is it worth writing down in my pickup line book?"

Allie giggled. "You've got a book?"

"That's classified information. See you at the ranch," he said with a wink.

As she drove from her place to his, she wondered how many names were in that book and how many pages were devoted to pickup lines. Could he tell by looking at a woman which lines he should use and which ones wouldn't work? Or did he fly by the seat of his pants, using whatever came to his mind in the moment?

Why did she care anyway? She slapped at the steering wheel, which seemed to be a regular thing these days. But dammit anyway! Blake infuriated her with his flirting. She wanted him to back off, but then she loved the excitement in his eyes, in his touch, and in his kisses. Her breath caught in her chest and her hands went clammy when she thought about that heat in his eyes just minutes before. It was one of those damn conundrums that drove her batshit crazy. She couldn't have it both ways. Either she had to make him step back or trust him, and how in the hell did she do either one?

Deke was already waiting in the yard when Allie arrived in the van. It took some fast work but everything was in the house before snow changed to big cold rain drops falling from the sky in buckets. He and Blake shucked out of their coats and hung them on the rack. Blake headed for the sofa and Deke headed toward the kitchen. "Anyone besides me want a beer?"

"Well, make yourself right at home," Allie scolded.

Deke landed a brotherly kiss across her cheek on his way to the kitchen. "Don't gripe at me like I was your little brother. If I can be called on to help a friend, then I can make myself at home, right, Blake?"

"That's right and so can you, Allie." He turned around and went back to help her out of her coat.

There it was again when his hands brushed against that soft spot on her neck. An intensified surge of emotions rattling through her body wanting more than a touch, more than a kiss. Then her brain kicked in quite loudly and reminded her that he was wild and wicked and not to be trusted. God Almighty! Which one did she listen to anyway?

"I hate Sunday nights," Deke said. "They are the most boring hours in the whole week."

"Why is that?" Allie asked, as breathless as if she'd had an actual argument with someone.

"The rest of the week we need forty hours in a day to get everything done. Friday we celebrate the week ending with a trip to Frankie's or a good cowboy bar and maybe Saturday night, too. But Sunday night is downright lonesome," Deke said.

"That's the gospel truth." Blake nodded in agreement. "At home at least there was family that stuck around until bedtime."

"We could make some popcorn and watch a movie and be bored together. It would keep Allie from havin' to go home." Deke sighed.

Allie would watch Shooter sleep if it would keep her from having to spend time playing Monopoly or watching the kind of movie Lizzy and Mitch picked out. She wished that Frankie's was open on Sunday evening. Listening to Etta James and Ray Charles, dancing with Blake, maybe indulging in just one more of those steamy kisses, watching Deke flirt with the women—now that sounded exciting.

"I haven't got cable yet, but there are a few western movies that I brought along with me and it would be good to have some company," Blake said. "Y'all want to follow me and we'll pick one out together."

"How many did you bring?" Deke asked.

"A boot box full," Blake answered.

"Y'all choose. I'm going to the restroom," Allie said. "Meet you back in the living room."

"Allie is quite a woman," Blake said. "Beautiful, talented, and smart."

"Yep." Deke nodded. "I like this one." He held up *Quigley Down Under* starring Tom Selleck.

"That'll do fine. Between me and you I'd rather be at Frankie's than doing this."

"Me, too, but Frankie is religious. He's closed on Sunday."

"You've got to be kiddin' me! Moonshine, hookers, and he's religious?" Blake drawled.

"There's layers to everyone, my friend. Frankie attends church over there in his community and leads the singin'."

Blake shook his head all the way up the hall to the kitchen. "So tell me about Allie's layers." He found a box of instant hot chocolate in the second place he looked and set three oversized mugs on the counter.

Deke put a bag of popcorn into the microwave. "She is a woman underneath those work clothes. She has a heart as big as Texas. She is a good sister even though she and Lizzy argue all the time. She's a damn fine granddaughter and the best friend a man could have."

"I've never had a woman for a friend," Blake said.

"Then start with Allie. She's the best."

"Who is the best?" Allie's big brown eyes looked from one cowboy to the other.

"You are," Deke said.

"At what?" she asked.

"Being a man's friend. Hell, you're even better than my dog, and I really love that dog." Deke grinned.

She poked him on the arm. "Aww, now ain't that the sweetest thing a woman can hear. What are we watching?"

"I picked out *Quigley Down Under*."

"Never have seen it. Can I help do anything?"

"Not a thing. It's about ready to take to the living room," Blake said.

"I call dibs on the end of the couch," she said.

Deke raised his hand. "I get the recliner for helping unload stuff."

Allie sat down at the kitchen table and unzipped her knee boots. "I've had all of these I can stand for one day."

Blake took one look at her mismatched socks and chuckled. "Good-lookin' socks there, darlin'. They make the outfit."

She held up her feet and wiggled her toes. "I've got another pair like them somewhere in the house but I can't find them. If Lizzy had pushed me toward Grady one more time, I planned to take off my boots in church to embarrass her."

"You are one wicked lady." Blake smiled.

"Not me!" Her smile was straight from heaven. "I'm just a carpenter who fixes roofs and does remodel jobs on houses."

"A beautiful, sexy carpenter who looks right gorgeous with a hammer in her hands," Blake said.

"Y'all going to jaw all day in there or are we going to watch our movie?" Deke called out.

"We're on the way and I don't want to hear a word about my socks," Allie said as she made her way from kitchen to living room.

Blake kicked off his boots and settled on the other end of the long leather sofa from Allie. Halfway though the movie she pulled her legs up and stretched them out toward him and he did the same, situating his on the outside. He moved his right one slightly so that it touched hers, and she didn't jerk it away or give him a dirty look.

Progress! By damn! That was progress.

A month ago he would have been telling some woman good-bye that he'd spent the weekend with, maybe saying that he'd call her with no intentions of ever doing so. Or maybe she'd walk him to the door and tell him that it had been fun but one weekend of fun with him was all a woman could handle. Tonight he was almost shouting because Allie hadn't moved her leg away from his. Toby wouldn't believe it or understand if he tried to tell him, and forget about saying anything to Jud. He was the loudest of the three about staying a bachelor until his dying breath.

"I'm pausing the show for a bathroom break. I'll bring in some beers on my way back," Deke said.

Allie shifted positions and her foot touched his hip. He picked it up and put it in his lap and began to massage it and suddenly, things weren't boring at all.

"God, that feels good," she said.

"I'm not God," Blake said.

"You know what I mean."

He pulled the other foot over and worked on it. "You are too tense, woman. Loosen up and enjoy life."

She eased her feet back and tucked them under her, pulling the sweater dress down to cover them.

"He's right." Deke set three beers on the coffee table and settled back into the recliner. "You should have more fun."

"Y'all are ganging up on me," she said. "Turn the movie back on. I like Crazy Cora more and more as the story plays out. I don't think she's nearly as crazy as everyone thinks."

Layers, Deke had said. Was one of Allie's layers nothing but a protective coating against men since her husband left her?

CHAPTER ELEVEN

On Monday morning five inches of snow had turned the countryside around Dry Creek into a winter wonderland. The wind had died down and there had been a glorious sunrise that morning. The weight of wet snow was heavy on the mesquite and scrub oak tree branches. Cardinals dotted the white landscape like little rose petals dropped from heaven to add color to the new monochromatic picture.

The beauty wouldn't last long. Cars, trucks, and other vehicles would soon leave their tracks. Animals had to leave behind footprints. Cattle would stir up the snow, and by nightfall, if the sun stayed out, what was left would turn to mud that would freeze by morning. But later didn't matter as Allie drove slowly from Audrey's Place to the Lucky Penny. Right then, that moment, when everything looked like a fairy tale, that's what mattered.

The Lucky Penny house was empty when she arrived and somehow it looked even worse without Deke and Blake there. Without those two big cowboys to talk to her or at least to each other while she listened, she noticed the ugly paint on the walls, the nasty stains on the ceilings, and the scuffed marks on the woodwork even more.

She sighed when she reached the bedroom and then smiled. It reminded her of Cinderella in her rags, kind of like the muddy mess the snow would make when it melted. But in a week, the room would be the princess in all her glory with its new paint job, pretty new ceiling, shiny hardwood floors, and that big beautiful king-size bed taking center stage. Then it would be as fresh and pretty as the morning with nothing marring the beauty of fresh-fallen snow.

The bare lightbulb would be replaced by the six-blade oak fan with a lovely school-glass light kit. It had been the last one in stock and on a seventy-five percent off sale so she'd bought it on a whim, and now she was having second thoughts. He might have asked what she'd do to the room if she had to sleep in it the rest of her life, but he hadn't meant she could go off half-cocked and buy something without even asking him about it.

First she had to tear out the nasty old before she could put in the shiny new. She smiled as she thought of her father saying those very words every time they started a new job.

As brittle as the old drywall was, it wouldn't be nice and come down in four-by-eight sheets. It would fall in chunks of every size that would throw white powder and mildew dust everywhere. She shut the door and opened the window.

Sure it would get cold but she'd dressed in thermal underwear, cargo pants, an old cotton western shirt, and insulated coveralls. She put her earbuds in and pushed the button on the tiny little MP3 player tucked into her pocket.

George Strait entertained her as she brought down the ceiling a piece at a time and then went back to remove all the nails from the ceiling joists. It was close to noon when she finished. The room was still filled with a fog of white powder and the old carpet would never be usable again, not with that much white powder ground down into the fibers.

With the music in her ears she didn't know anyone was in the house until Blake touched her on the ankle. She jerked the earbud out and frowned. "You scared the shit out of me. Don't sneak up on a woman holding a hammer."

He grinned. "Sorry about that. I called your name when I came in and a couple more times as I came this way. Want some help? The dozer is bogging down in the snow. Deke and Herman have plenty to keep them busy with what I've already got piled up. Crazy, even with the snow it's not as cold as it was over the weekend."

"There isn't any wind. That makes a difference. Got a hammer?"

"Of course."

She nodded. "Then yes, you can help get these nails out and then we'll be ready to hang the Sheetrock after we have dinner."

He was only gone a few minutes before he returned wearing a pair of coveralls like hers and carrying a hammer. "Seems colder in here than it does outside, don't it?"

"Yep," she said.

His biceps strained the seams of the camouflage coveralls as he popped one nail after another from the ceiling rafters. Keeping her eyes uplifted and concentrating on her own job was not easy for Allie. More than once, she found herself pausing to stare at the ease with which he reached up with that heavy hammer, hung the claw on a nail head, and pulled it free without so much as a grunt.

Riley had hated quiet. If they had nothing to talk about, then he turned on the television. Even if he didn't watch it, he wanted noise at all times. Blake seemed perfectly comfortable working in silence with her, and she liked that. The screeching sound of nail after nail coming out of an old rafter was better than music.

That's when she remembered the tiny player in her coverall's pocket and pulled it out, turned it off, and was returning it when they heard a loud rapping on the front door.

Blake laid the hammer on the floor. "Be right back. Can't imagine who is here."

The claw of the hammer was hung in a nail when Allie heard a familiar raspy giggle. She eased it back down and laid it on the top of the ladder. Two backward steps and her boots hit the floor. Five steps forward and she opened the door a crack and peeked. Yep, she'd been right. It was Sharlene and she was handing off a six-pack of beer to Blake.

She patted his cheek affectionately. "I was up in Wichita Falls over the weekend and thought you might need this. I know you have lots of food but a man cannot live by bread alone, he must have beer."

"Thank you." Blake's smile lit up the whole dingy room. "Bless your heart for thinking of me. And truer words were never spoken. I'll put this in the refrigerator. Want a cup of coffee to take the chill off?"

"No, darlin', not today, but I'm still waiting on your call." Sharlene rolled up slightly on her toes, cupped his face in her hands, and kissed him long, hard, and leaving no doubt tongue was involved. "Although, I might be willing to be late if there was something more than coffee involved."

Allie had to fight the sudden urge to throw her hammer at Sharlene. She did owe Blake. He had, after all, helped her pull nails for the last hour and a half, so she should help him out of the pickle. But then who's to say he wanted out of the situation? A streak of hot jealousy shot through her veins as she slammed the door into the bedroom and headed up the hallway.

"Hey Blake, is it time to put in one of those casseroles?" She talked loudly and put on her best innocent face. "Oh, hello, Sharlene. I was in the back room with the door shut and didn't realize you were here. Blake, is it time to warm up one of those casseroles for dinner?"

"I was just leaving," Sharlene stammered. "You think about what I said, darlin'." She winked at Blake and hurried out the front door.

"What took you so long?" he asked.

"Was it good?"

Blake frowned. "What?"

"How does kissing a smoker taste? I always thought it would be like licking the bottom of an ashtray," she said.

Blake's laughter echoed off the walls.

"What's so funny?" she asked.

"You are funny and you are right. I need a glass of sweet tea to get the taste out of my mouth. Want one?"

"No, I'm going to finish up that last corner so we can hang drywall after we eat. Holler when dinner is ready." She returned to the cold room, shut the door firmly, put her earbuds back in place, and went back to work. When Mr. George started singing "You Can't Make a Heart Love Somebody," tears came out of nowhere and streamed down her face. She crawled off the ladder, pulled the mask off, threw it on the floor with the broken wallboard, removed a glove, and brushed the tears away with her bare hand.

The lyrics reminded her of what Riley said when he finally admitted that he was having an affair. He said it was all her fault because she wouldn't stay at home and be a wife, especially since she couldn't be a mother. When she hadn't gotten pregnant in those two years, he said he'd go to the doctor for a checkup. He came home with the news it wasn't him so she didn't need to go. And like the lyrics of the song said, she couldn't make him love her.

She hadn't cried that day so why were the tears flowing now? She slid down the wall, bowed her head, and listened to the next song—"Today My World Slipped Away."

The song fit that day when Riley told Allie all about his new love, Greta. Riley said they had looked at each other across the top of that new Ford Mustang he had just sold her and he was smitten. She was the most beautiful, feminine woman in the whole world, and he had found his soul mate. Of course, it did help that she was a trust fund baby and he would be cashing in on that dividend check that came every month.

Why did she have to face off with all those memories that day? She wiped the tears again, leaving streaks of dust and grime on her cheeks like war paint. Her father's words came back again telling her to finish tearing out the old so she would be ready for the shiny new. Until that moment she hadn't realized how tightly she'd held on to the past, to the anger and the pain, but it had to go.

She raised her head and stared at the big gaping hole where the ceiling had been. Trusses, the bottom of roof decking, ceiling joists—all visible but the old ugly stuff had been ripped away. It was symbolic of what she had to do to move on with her life.

The old had been torn out of her heart and soul, but suddenly fear gripped her when she thought of taking a step forward. She'd been in limbo for so many years she didn't know if she could trust her feet to take even a baby step, she was so scared of falling on her face...again.

She looked out the open window at the bright sunshine and then up at the rafters. Instead of an answer to the multitude of questions plaguing her, she heard the back door slam and heavy footsteps coming down the hallway. She swiped a hand across her face to get rid of the last of the tears and stood up.

"Can we open the door?" Deke yelled.

She made her way across the cluttered floor. "It's a mess. Enter at your own risk."

The door eased open and warmth flowed in. Deke's silhouette filled the doorway. Leaning against the doorjamb with one leg slightly bent in those tight jeans, he was almost as dirty as she was. Twigs and leaves stuck to his flannel shirt as well as his hair.

"You got a lot done to be workin' alone." His gaze started at the hole where the ceiling used to be, traveled to the open window and carpet, and then slowly inched its way from her work boots to the top of her head. He grinned when he saw all the white dust in her hair. "Holy shit, Allie! You're going to grow up to look like your granny."

"Thank you so much for that, Deke! I may look like shit but I got the worst of the job done, and Blake helped me pull nails for more than an hour so that helped a lot." She smarted off back at him.

"Hey, I'm statin' facts not startin' a fight," he said.

"Good, because I'm sure not in the mood for a fight!" She pushed her way past him. "See y'all in the kitchen after I clean up."

When she looked in the mirror above the wall-hung sink in the bathroom, sure enough there was Irene Miller staring back at her. The streaks from tears mixing with dirt and dust had created pseudo-wrinkles down her cheeks. Her dark hair had a coating of white dust all the way to her scalp and her eyes were slightly swollen from crying.

That she looked like shit didn't bother her half as much

as the fact that Sharlene had seen her looking like that. She stripped out of her coveralls and left them lying on the bathroom floor. Her work pants and T-shirt were in good shape since they'd been covered up. However, the insulated underwear was getting pretty warm now that she was out of the chilly room. So she took off everything down to her underpants and bra and picked up a washcloth to work on her face.

One more glance in the mirror and she realized that she'd never brush all that grime from her hair. She found towels on the shelves above the toilet, along with shampoo. She pulled the curtain around the tub and hoped that the drain didn't clog. She hated doing plumbing work.

"I promise to wear a hat next time I take down drywall." She stepped into the tub and let the hot water rinse away tears, dirt, and dust from her body and hair.

When she finished, the woman in the mirror smiled at her. "Hello, I haven't seen you since before you married Riley. I thought I'd lost you forever."

The grin widened.

She redressed, leaving her work boots sitting on the floor beside her coveralls and long underwear. The phone in her hip pocket rang at the same time she stepped out into the hallway.

"Hello, Mama," she said.

"I need you to stop what you are doing by one o'clock. I have to take your grandmother to Wichita Falls this afternoon for a doctor's appointment. I forgot all about it until I looked at the calendar. You'll need to mind the store." Katy sounded frantic.

"It's okay, Mama. I'm at a really good stopping point. I've got the ceiling down in the master bedroom." Allie stopped and leaned against the wall. "Is one early enough? I can come on right now if you want me to."

"The main roads are clear from here to there but we're in for more snow tonight. I just want to get up there, get it done, and get home before the roads get slick. I'm not lookin' forward to driving in it. Are you eating dinner with Blake and Deke?" Katy asked.

"Yes, but I could eat whatever you've made in the store. It's no big deal," she answered.

"Go on and eat your dinner. One o'clock will be fine. Thank goodness the sun melted some of this already," Katy said.

Allie ran a hand through her hair and realized she hadn't taken time to brush it. "Want me to take her?"

"No, I have to be there to sign papers and talk to them about a new medication they want to try. See you in an hour."

She went back to the bathroom, ran the brush she found on the shelf beside the shampoo through her damp hair, and put it back on the shelf. Then she padded to the kitchen in her socks.

"Cinderella emerges." Blake set a pot of beans on the table. "I thought I heard the shower pipes rattling. Did you find everything you needed?"

She nodded. "Maybe I should have asked."

Blake patted her on the shoulder. "Friends make themselves at home. Your timing is great. Food's on the table. Beans with ham hock, fried okra, and sweet potato casserole."

Allie pulled out a chair and eased into it. "I'm hungry. You won't get any fight out of me."

"I'll do the honors." Deke picked up a ladle and filled Allie's bowl first. "Herman showed up this morning with a crew and I swear he's cutting and stackin' wood as fast as Blake and the bulldozer can pile it up."

"How are you doin' with the wood business, Deke?" Allie

scooped sweet potatoes onto her plate and added several spoons of okra to the side before passing both off to Blake.

Their fingertips brushed and sparks danced around the room. Life wasn't fair. Not thirty minutes ago Sharlene had her tongue in his mouth and yet, a simple touch had created enough electricity to jack her pulse up. Her mind wandered and she had to play fast catch-up when it came back to the kitchen and Deke was answering her question.

"I'm selling everything I cut to Herman right in the field. We made a deal. He's giving me five bucks less a rick than if I hauled it to Wichita Falls, but when you consider the time and the gas, I reckon I'm probably making money rather than losing it."

She nodded but her thoughts skipped backward to what her father said when they started a new remodeling job. Was Blake the new that she was supposed to be thinking about now that she'd erased the old?

Deke went on. "But it's going to snow again this afternoon, so when it starts we'll help you get the mess cleaned up in the bedroom and maybe even put up some ceiling. Chainsaws and snow in our eyes don't go together."

"I have to stop what I'm doing and go babysit the store this afternoon so Mama can take Granny to Wichita Falls for a doctor's appointment," she said.

Blake nodded. "When it starts snowing, we'll come to the house and do some work here."

Deke motioned toward her bowl. "We throw it out the window and if Allie will trust us, we can put up the drywall."

She shook her head. The beans were good, but she couldn't eat a second bowl. "That would be great, but after that last time don't you dare touch the bedding and taping."

Blake raised his eyebrows in question.

"I decided to surprise her once," Deke explained. "And I

had to sand it all off smooth so she could do it right. Some folks have an easy touch with that shit. Some of us flat out can't do it."

"You said it's a two-person job. I'll help Deke and we won't touch the bedding and taping. How's that?" Blake asked.

"That'd be great! I'd have a big jump on tomorrow if y'all could get it up." She almost choked on the words when she heard them out loud.

"Ain't never had too much of a problem with that." Deke laughed.

It was evident that Blake was biting his lip to keep from roaring. Boys! Their mind was always on sex! But then she couldn't fuss too much after the way she'd let her imagination go into places that would make Lucifer blush.

"Get your mind out of the gutter."

Then again, maybe she needed to mind her own advice. Blake had said that friends made themselves at home. Did he see her as a friend? Or maybe it was friends with benefits. After all he did have a reputation as being one of the wildest cowboys in Texas with his swagger and womanizing. Was she willing for that kind of friendship?

Well, by damn, she was the product of a whorehouse madam so maybe since she'd gotten rid of the past baggage it was simply her DNA surfacing. She might wind up with a reputation of being every bit as wild as Blake Dawson.

"When are you going to start fencing, Blake?" Deke asked.

"After I get the first eighty acres ready to plow up and plant, then I'll repair what fence there is around that portion so that Toby can bring in the first of the cattle in the summer. I probably should have waited to buy all those posts and barbed wire but I wasn't figuring on this kind of weather."

"They'll be here when you need them," Deke said. "That is, if that old ramshackle barn out there don't fall in where you got them stored."

"Soon as Toby gets here we'll need to put up a new barn, but at least it'll be summer and we won't have to think about it in rain, sleet, and snow."

Allie almost said that she could build them a barn, but summer was another five months away and after that episode with Sharlene, she wasn't committing to anything.

"So partner number two gets here in the summer?" she asked.

Blake nodded. "There will be two of us to begin getting the next couple of pastures ready for Jud to arrive by winter with the next herd. At that time we'll work on the rest of the ranch. It'll take a couple or three years to get it in top shape but we've got a schedule lined out."

"Then your brother and cousin will live here in this house with you until they get something else built?" Allie asked.

"Yes, they will. Since I got here first and I'm working alone, this house is going to be mine. They get to live in it until we're up and running a profit. They've already picked out a spot where they want to build when the time is right. Jud wants to put his house over on the other side of Audrey's Place and Toby wants to build back behind Audrey's Place. Allie, if y'all ever want to sell your twenty acres, we'd sure like to buy it."

Allie started shaking her head the moment he said the word *sell*. "Audrey's Place will never be for sale. It's our heritage and we'll pass it on down to our own kids."

"So you're planning on having children?" Blake asked.

"One of us will." She wasn't going to discuss that issue at the dinner table.

"Then I don't suppose Jud and Toby will care what you

are doing in the way of remodeling here at the Lucky Penny?" Deke asked.

"I don't think either of them would care if it was painted bull frog green as long as it was cool in the summer, warm in the winter, and had lots of food in the freezer," Blake answered.

Allie giggled. "How about pink with purple trim?"

Blake laid a hand on hers. "Now, that darlin', we might all balk at. Would you leave your van and trailer so we can throw the trash out on it? You can take my truck into town this afternoon." He removed his hand and refilled his glass with sweet tea.

She swallowed hard and nodded. Damn those sparks! Of all the cowboys to be in her sites when she finally tore out the old, it had to be Blake Dawson.

CHAPTER TWELVE

The aroma of chili met Allie when she entered the convenience store and she groaned. If she hadn't eaten those beans, she could make herself a chili pie with corn chips, cheese, and mustard, but now she was too full.

Katy picked up her coat and Irene's from the back of a chair behind the counter. "You are a few minutes early but the lunch run is over and there's still some left so if latecomers want a chili pie, you could probably still make about half a dozen, and the doughnuts have been there since early this morning so sell what's left at half price and…"

"Mama, I've got this," Allie butted in. "Go on and don't worry about anything. And if she's in a good mood after you leave and it's not snowing by then, take her somewhere to eat. You could use some downtime, too. You are frazzled."

"I don't usually forget these things." Once she and Irene were buttoned up, Katy led her mother toward the door.

"I can walk on my own," Irene protested. "Don't know

why we have to keep going to this damn doctor anyway. He don't give me pills or shots or do a damn thing for me. My hip still hurts and he don't even check it."

"It's not that kind of doctor, Mama," Katy said.

"A doctor is a doctor and he should treat a person's illnesses no matter what. Allie, I've got a bag of them white doughnuts in the back. You can have one but if you take any more, you are in trouble," Irene said.

Allie hugged Katy and opened the door for them. "You've had so much on your mind, it's a wonder it hasn't shut down. Go and don't drive fast."

"Thanks, darlin'." Katy blew a kiss her way.

Katy's car had barely cleared the parking lot when a bright red SUV pulled up and Allie slapped her forehead. Damn it to hell on a rusty poker! She didn't want to deal with Sharlene and Mary Jo this afternoon. Not after that morning.

Two women pushed their way into the store and hung their coats on the long line of hooks right inside the door. Sharlene's slim body looked great in skinny jeans and a tight knit shirt. Mary Jo, the brunette with blue streaks in her hair, had put on a few pounds since high school but she still had curves that made men turn for a second look.

Allie wanted to hide in the back room because there she was in the very worst pair of cargo pants she owned, a faded red T-shirt, hair that hadn't been styled, and no makeup. For the first time in years, it mattered to her what she looked like and she didn't enjoy feeling like the ugly duckling at a pretty white swan convention.

"Nadine is on her way," Sharlene smiled at Allie. "She's always late. You look different than you did a couple of hours ago."

"Amazing what a little soap and water can do. What are

y'all doing in Dry Creek on a Monday afternoon?" Allie asked.

"We all called in sick. Don't tell on us." Mary Jo laughed.

A second van came to a halt in the parking lot and Nadine hopped out with an orange Texas Longhorns umbrella over her head.

"Alora, darlin', would you please get us three big cups of coffee and a dozen of those doughnuts on the counter? And come on back here and sit with us? It's been too long since we've all four sat down and had a good old gossip fest." Nadine set the umbrella by the door and peeled back her yellow slicker to reveal red hair straight from the bottle.

"Make four of those chocolate," Sharlene yelled. "And Nadine is right. We haven't talked in forever."

Forever, her ass! They'd never been friends, not in high school, not since, and the only reason they wanted her to join them was to talk about Blake Dawson and the Lucky Penny. Besides she and Sharlene had seen each other a couple of hours ago.

"And four of them can be maple iced." Mary Jo said. "The weather man is saying the sun will come out later today and the main roads will be cleared even though I'll never understand why they go to the trouble when there's more on the way. I heard that it's already starting down around Abilene. Supposed to be here by suppertime and give us another four inches."

Mary Jo giggled. "I want more than four inches if I'm going to be snowed in with a cowboy. Tell me, Allie, what would I get if I got stranded with Blake?"

Nadine pulled out the fourth chair and patted the seat for Allie.

Allie fought the blush but she lost. It was on the tip of her tongue to tell Mary Jo to ask Sharlene, but she bit her lip to keep from spitting out the words.

"I think we've embarrassed her." Sharlene giggled. "But we do want to hear more about Blake Dawson and his brother. Blake is hot enough to make a virgin sin and I lost my V-card years ago. If Allie hadn't interrupted us this morning, I might have more to tell you." Sharlene went on to tell about how she was about to get Blake in a horizontal position when Allie came out of the bedroom looking like a bag lady.

Mary Jo laid a hand on the extra chair. "We really do want you to join us, Alora, even if you did upset Sharlene's plans. You do know she's got her eye on that cowboy and it's not a short-term deal she's lookin' for."

Nadine fanned herself with the back of her hand. "I swear to God, I get hot flashes every time I get a glimpse of him. I needed a fan Sunday in church and it was church! And you got to sit with him when your granny went all wonky. What was that like? Did you feel the heat from all that testosterone? Bobby Ray says that he won't last at the Lucky Penny and it might be best if he don't because there's liable to be a dozen marriages on the rocks if he sticks around very long."

"You are in love with Bobby Ray and planning to marry him. How can you talk like that?" Allie asked.

"I'm not dead. A dieter can look at the candy counter, you know." Nadine huffed.

"I work for Blake. End of story," Allie said bluntly.

"I'd gladly work under him." Sharlene giggled.

"Or on top of him," Mary Jo said.

"I've got news," Sharlene said. "Y'all remember Oma Lynn who graduated a year before us?"

"That tall blonde with braces who had two left feet?" Mary Jo asked.

"That's her. Well, she works at the Muenster bank and she says Blake Dawson... God, isn't that the sexiest name ever? It sounds like a name you'd hear on the CMA awards. I wonder if he sings." Sharlene sighed.

Nadine polished off the last of the doughnut and reached for a bear claw. "I bet he could make my body sing."

"Ain't no doubt." Mary Jo's laugh was high pitched.

Allie was torn between wanting to hear what they had to say and hiding in the back room out of sheer embarrassment. They were acting like they were still cheerleaders at Dry Creek High School. She sat down in the spare chair and crossed one leg over the other.

"Well, anyway, I called Oma Lynn to catch up. She was so happy to hear from me that she didn't even know I had an agenda." Sharlene reached for the last bear claw. "So I skirted around the issue and said that some dumb cowboy had bought the Lucky Penny. And she dived right in without me sayin' another word. She said that they call him the wild cowboy and his younger brother, Toby, is the hot cowboy and the cousin, Jud, is the lucky one."

Nadine almost choked on the bite of doughnut. "Good God almighty, you mean there's one even hotter than Blake? And they've got a cousin?"

"That's what Oma Lynn said," Sharlene said as she nodded. "And that his brother is going to show up here in the summer and the three of them are determined to turn that ranch's luck around. And one more thing, if I don't land Blake Dawson, then y'all better stand back because I will get Toby or Jud."

"Well, I can't wait to see the other two," Mary Jo said. "And now we want to hear about Blake. No detail is too small. How does he like his coffee? Black? With cream or sugar? Is he really wild? I heard he and Deke took some woman to Frankie's this weekend."

Allie leaned on the table with her elbows. "Who was the woman?"

Mary Jo shook her head. "Must've been some loose-legged old girl because you know what they say about Frankie's, but we can't find out and believe me we've tried hard to get someone to tell us."

Sharlene shook her head slowly. "I wouldn't even go there."

"Me, either. I've heard all kinds of things happen at Frankie's." Mary Jo shivered.

"You got any idea who they were having a threesome with?" Nadine asked.

All eyes turned to Allie. She squirmed in her chair and said, "You'll have to ask them. They don't tell me their dark secrets. Mainly we talk about drywall, paint, and shingles. Oh, and whatever food he brings out of the freezer for dinner."

Allie's phone rang and she fished it from her pocket. "Excuse me. Y'all need more coffee, help yourselves."

It didn't take a psychoanalyst to know they were talking about her and Blake when their loud voices dropped to whispers when she left the table.

"Fiona, thank you, thank you!" Allie said.

"For what?" her sister replied.

"The gossip triplets are here," Allie answered.

"What are they doing at the Lucky Penny?"

Allie sat down in the metal folding chair behind the counter. "Mama had to take Granny for an evaluation, so I'm minding the store this afternoon."

"Don't they have jobs?"

"They all called in sick," Allie answered.

"Lizzy has called me a dozen times in the past three days tattling on you for being really rude to some guy named Grady," Fiona said bluntly.

Allie nodded to herself. "If that sorry sucker was the only man left on earth, I still wouldn't like him."

"And Blake. If he was the last man on earth?" Fiona asked.

"I'd jump his bones." Allie laughed.

"Mama and Lizzy are afraid you are really going to fall for him. You aren't going to do that, are you? That place has never brought anything but bad luck to anyone who was affiliated with it, so think before you jump," Fiona begged.

Allie rolled her eyes toward the ceiling, then looked outside. The sun was still shining brightly in Dry Creek. It was hard to imagine that in a few hours the sky could go all gray.

"Allie, are you still there?" Fiona yelled.

Allie held the phone out from her ear. "I'm here. What if Blake is the one?"

"I hear he's got a reputation for wild cowboy ways, so he's definitely not the one for you, sister. After that crap with Riley, you're too responsible for that kind of relationship," Fiona said.

Well, that put the tally up to four who thought she was nothing but a plain old Jane who could never even get a wild cowboy to kiss her.

"Changing the subject. Remember when I told you when Riley left you that if Greta could break up a marriage, then she'd better watch out because someone could come along and Riley would leave her behind, too? Do you remember Denise Wilson who graduated with me?"

Allie didn't want to hear about Riley. He was the old that she'd taken care of that morning. Strange as it was, she'd rather be at the table with the gossip trio than listen to stories about her ex, but Fiona was only trying to help.

"She had an older brother who was Riley's friend, right?" Allie asked.

"That's the one," Fiona said. "She works at the dealership and rumor has it that Riley has been sneakin' around with Denise's younger sister, Suzanne. The kid won't listen to a damn thing. She's quit college and says that she's ready to settle down and be a mama."

"Holy shit! Is she pregnant?" Allie gasped.

"Not yet, according to Denise, but she and Riley have been going at it hot and heavy for more than a month. I've got to get to work now but tell me that even though he's hot, you're not interested in the cowboy and I'll tell Mama and Lizzy. That way they'll stop calling me," Fiona said.

Allie propped her feet on the counter. Crap! She was even wearing work boots and all three of those women at the table had on cute cowboy boots with their fancy jeans. "He's hot. I'm not interested."

"That don't sound like you mean it."

Allie laughed. "Okay, he's scorchin' hot. But I've got better sense than to get tangled up with someone that close to home. He's my friend and I like him." No way in hell was she mentioning Frankie's because her sister wouldn't only tattle, she'd make arrangements to send Allie off to a convent.

"You are interested. I can hear it in your voice. Dammit, Allie!"

"Tell Mama and Lizzy that I'm not interested in him and they'll leave you alone," Allie said. "And now I'm hanging up."

Allie hit the END button as Lucy Hudson walked into the store.

"Hey, Miz Allie, where's your mama?" She made her way to the milk and soda pop case.

"She had to take Granny up to Wichita Falls for a doctor's appointment."

"Ain't nothing else wrong with Irene, is there?" She carried two gallons of milk to the counter. "Don't have to buy this often but my milk cow ain't makin' as much as she did a month ago and them grandboys who are stayin' with me and Herman use a lot of milk. Might have to buy us another cow pretty soon."

"Granny is going for a routine checkup. That all you need today?"

"That's it. No, wait a minute. I'd better get a pound of bologna to make sandwiches for the boys tomorrow if the weather is fit."

"Won't take a minute. You sure a pound is enough?"

"Best make it two pounds. Them boys can put away the groceries," Lucy said.

Allie sliced and wrapped the order in white butcher paper, wrote the items on a yellow sales pad, and Lucy scribbled Herman's name on the bottom. Allie filed it under H with the rest of the Hudson bills for the month.

Lucy leaned over the counter and whispered. "I hear Sharlene is making a fool of herself with Blake and that Mary Jo ain't far behind her. Them two ain't cut out for ranchin'. It takes a strong woman to be a rancher's wife and them two are all about themselves, not helpin' a man make a livin'. You need to warn him or talk to Deke and get him to talk sense to that boy."

Allie was about to say it wasn't her place to warn Blake but Lucy inhaled and went on. "I like Blake and I hope he makes a go of it on the Lucky Penny. I'd hate to see him fail because he wound up getting roped by a woman with dollar signs in her eyes."

Allie nodded.

"Tell your mama and granny hello for me. I hope they get home all right. It's going to get slick out there," Lucy said.

"I will." Allie nodded.

Lucy winked, gathered up her bag of groceries, and hurried out to her truck.

"Well, that's done," Deke said, and looked up at the ceiling rafters. "All ready for her to start beddin' and tapin' come morning. Let's go to the store and get a cold soda pop. I bet Allie is bored to death on a day like this and she'll be glad for the company."

"Sounds good to me. Do they let dirty old cowboys like us in the store?"

"I expect we can go without shinin' our boots," Deke said.

The first flakes of snow were drifting down from the sky by the time they arrived at the store. Deke removed his weathered old cowboy hat and yelled, "Allie, if there's any doughnuts left put my name on them and bring them to the..." he cleared his throat and coughed, "back room where me and Blake are going to have a cold soda pop."

Allie cocked her head to one side. "What are y'all doin' in town?"

"We put in some hard work so we came to get a cold drink, darlin'." Blake grinned. "I could've cut more wood, but me and Deke decided to surprise you. The new drywall for the ceiling is up. Looks like hell but Deke tells me your magic touch tomorrow will do wonders. We're going to take the ceiling out down the hall and the living room this afternoon. Herman and his boys are still cutting wood but they'll have to quit pretty soon."

Blake noticed Sharlene at the table and was that Mary Jo?

"What is going on?" Blake asked when he and Deke had passed through a curtain into a back room. A twin bed was set up on one side with a recliner beside it facing a small television. Four chairs surrounded a table for four in the middle of the room. The blinds had been raised to let as much natural light as possible into the room.

Deke set two bottles of Coke on the table and explained the situation. "Irene stays in here part of the time, so they made it comfortable for her. But your question is about Sharlene, Nadine, and Mary Jo. Don't never encourage them with even a smile. Steer clear of them. If you need any help call me. They are trouble."

"Is this the voice of experience I hear?" Blake grinned.

"It's the voice of my older brother's experience. I learned from his mistakes and I'm passin' that bit of information down to you. Not only are they on the prowl most of the time, they kiss and tell, and they are Dry Creek's biggest gossips. And I heard Sharlene has already said that she's going to marry you, by hook or crook," Deke answered.

"Allie, darlin', we need to pay our bill. We're going to Wichita Falls for a spa afternoon. You want to go with us?" Nadine called out.

"Got to keep the store for Mama. Y'all have fun and be careful. You might get stuck up there if the weather gets really bad," Allie said from behind the counter.

Nadine giggled. "That is exactly what we are hoping and why we packed our bags in case of emergency."

Mary Jo handed her a twenty-dollar bill. "Are you sure there's nothing goin' on with you and Blake? I'm paying for everything today so take it all out of this."

Allie rang up the amount in the cash register and made the right change. "Smart ladies to go prepared."

"You didn't answer my question," Nadine said.

"Like I told you, I work for him. Deke helps me out when he can like he does on all jobs." If there was something going on, those three would be the last people on earth that Allie told.

"Good. I'd hate to see you get involved with the wrong person again like you did with Riley. Y'all never did go together. And believe me, honey, that cowboy is way too much for you to handle, especially since you couldn't handle Riley," Nadine laughed.

Tally was growing. Now it had five people on the list.

CHAPTER
THIRTEEN

Allie had been working all day Tuesday cutting and putting up insulation and she itched from her scalp to her toes, some of it real but a lot of it was imaginary since there was no way the insulation had gotten down into her socks and work boots. But still, it would be nice to take a quick shower before supper so she dropped all those itchy clothes on the floor and pulled the curtain around the tub.

Blake had taken a pan of pulled pork barbecue from the freezer and had invited her to stay for supper. Her mother, sister, and grandmother were at a ladies' meeting down at the church and they'd be there until well after nine, so no one would even know she'd spent the evening with Blake.

"Hey, throw your clothes out here in the hall and I'll put them in the washer. They'll be clean and dried by the time we finish supper." Blake's deep voice carried through the thick bathroom door. "My robe is on the hook on the back of the door. You can wear it until your stuff is ready."

She stood behind the door and shoved all her things out to him. Dammit! Now he'd know she wore plain white bras without a bit of lace and matching cotton bikini underpants. Nothing sexy about her; not one thing to catch a wild cowboy's eye.

The robe smelled like a mixture of Blake's shaving lotion and soap so she pulled it closer and inhaled deeply. Making sure it was securely belted around her waist and nothing was showing that shouldn't be, she glanced at her reflection in the mirror.

She felt totally naked even though she was covered from head to toe. The woman in the mirror with no makeup and wet hair wore white cotton underpants and a white bra and Blake would know it by now. There wasn't a damn thing she could do about it so she took the first step toward the kitchen.

"Come on in, Allie. I'm putting the food on the table," Blake called out.

She opened the door and sniffed the air. "Smells good."

Everything was normal when she got to the kitchen. Supper was on the table in disposable aluminum foil pans. A washer was running in the background and the coffee pot gurgled out the last bit of water. It was merely another meal at Blake's place but without Deke there and Allie wearing nothing but a robe—well that changed things a hell of a lot.

"Beer or sweet tea? I made a fresh pot of coffee for after with dessert, which is peach cobbler that came with the church ladies."

"Sweet tea," she answered. She didn't want a damn thing that Sharlene had brought into the house. "I love peach cobbler. I bet it's Ruby's recipe. That's what she always brings to church suppers."

"You look downright adorable in my robe and I bet you feel a hell of a lot better with all that insulation washed off you," Blake said. "After your things get washed and dried let's go outside and build a moon snowman."

"A what?"

"A snowman by the light of the moon."

She smiled. "That sounds like fun. It's wet enough to pack good and solid and there's enough to make a good snowman."

"You look beautiful," he said abruptly.

"I got to admit, I feel more than a little vulnerable, so you might want to keep your wild ways under wraps," she said honestly.

How did the conversation go from snowmen to her so quickly? She felt a blush coming on but she wasn't the only one with high color in her cheeks. Grown men did not get flustered, but Blake did. Then he laughed. "And what makes you think I've got an ounce of wild in me? I'm only a rough old cowboy trying to turn a ranch around and get the town of Dry Creek to accept me."

Allie sat down. "Oma Lynn. You ever heard of her?"

Blake's heavy dark brows drew together until they became one long line. "You mean the sweet lady who works at my bank in Muenster? Why are you asking about her?"

Allie dipped into the pot and filled up her bowl with pulled pork. "She grew up right here in Dry Creek. Sharlene, Mary Jo, and Nadine have gotten the scoop on you from her. She spilled the beans about you being the wild Dawson, your brother being the hot one, and your cousin being the lucky one."

Blake raked his hand down over his face. "Well, hell! I guess a man can't outrun his past, can he?"

"Just how wild were you?"

"Just how married were you?" he fired right back.

"Touché," she said with the briefest of nods.

"Guess we're both lookin' to make changes in our lives and forget the past," he said.

Did Allie hear him right? Did he say he wanted to make a change in his life? Could that possibly mean that Sharlene or Mary Jo weren't in his sights for a one-night stand or even more?

"Yes, sir. Would you please pass the cheese?"

He handed her the plate. "Anything for a beautiful lady. Thanks for having supper with me, Allie. The evenings get long if you and Deke aren't around."

Every time, without fail, that he called her beautiful her pulse raced and her heart threw in an extra beat. She took a deep breath before she spoke so he wouldn't know what crazy things he did to her nerves. "I know exactly what you mean about getting lonesome. Lizzy is so involved with wedding plans and the evenings are tough for Granny. If she does have a lucid moment it won't be after dark. And Mama gets dragged into the wedding business so even though there's four of us over at our place, I still get lonely."

He gave her one of those brilliant grins that electrified the whole room. "Well, darlin', you are welcome here anytime of the night or day." He stood, walked over to move Allie's clothes from the washer to the dryer, then came back to the table.

She drew his robe even tighter around her chest, glad

that the plush material covered up the effect he had on her aching breasts. She was flirting with the devil, but he was so damn enticing that even a glance drew her to him like a wayward saint to the warmth of hell's blaze. Allie had sure never been any kind of saint, but she really should slow down and quit taking such giant steps toward the fire.

"You've got that faraway look on your face again. Is Lizzy arguing with you?" Blake asked.

"No, she's been quiet this evening. It was me fighting with me," she said honestly.

"About what?"

Blake picked up a pickle and bit into it. "Want to talk about it?"

"No, I'm tired of analyzing everything to death."

Blake handed her the rest of the pickle. "It's dill and I thought it was a sweet pickle. You finish it. You like dill."

Without even thinking about it, she popped the rest of the pickle into her mouth. Was that something that friends did? She didn't share her food with Deke and they'd been friends for more than a decade.

She was still chewing when the front door burst open and Irene stomped in wearing a pair of bright red rubber boots, a cowboy hat, and a long denim duster, all covered with snow.

"Walter, where in the hell are you?" she yelled.

Allie jumped up so quickly that the robe's belt loosened and the top fell back, showing the top half of her breasts. Blake and Allie met Irene in the living room and she took one look at Allie, doubled up her fist, and shook it at Blake.

"Damn it, Walter! I'm going to kill you with my bare hands for cheatin' on me."

Allie took a step forward and grabbed her grandmother's hands. When she did even more of the robe opened up.

"Granny, this is Blake and I'm Alora Raine. I'm your granddaughter and this man is not Walter," Allie said sternly.

"You are naked under that robe," Irene hissed.

Allie continued to hold her hands. "Yes, I am. I've been working in insulation all day and my clothes are in the dryer right now. I'll get dressed as soon as they are done. We'll call Mama to come get you."

"My mama has been dead for years so you can't call her. Silly girl, there ain't no phones in heaven." Irene eyed Blake seriously. "You aren't Walter, are you? Who are you again?"

"I'm your new neighbor, Blake Dawson. Allie is doing some carpenter work for me," he said.

Allie groaned when she heard a vehicle coming to a stop outside. Thinking about having to explain to her mother why she was wearing nothing but a robe was enough to make her want to run home in four inches of snow in her bare feet. If that old adage about how that man plans and God laughs was true, then the Almighty must be howling up in heaven right now.

High heels on the wooden porch didn't sound like her mother's footsteps but then maybe Katy had gotten dressed up for the church thing and hadn't had time to kick off her Sunday shoes. It didn't matter if she showed up in rubber boots or her best dress shoes as long as she took Granny home and didn't throw a hissy about the way Allie was dressed.

Allie let go of her grandmother's hands and put the robe to rights. The cutesy little rap on the door sounded like da-da-da-da-da and then a da-da should have alerted Allie that it was not her mother.

Blake yelled for the visitor to come on in. The door swung open and a cold north wind pushed Nadine into the room. She wore her best Sunday coat and high-heeled shoes, and she carried an apple pie in her hands.

"Blake, darlin', I brought you a pie. Oh. My. God!" She looked from Irene to Blake and then to Allie. "I didn't know you had company."

Irene poked her on the arm. "What the hell are you doing here? Does Bobby Ray know you are out at this time of night flirtin' with a married man? He'll call off the wedding if he finds out and I'll tell him next time I see him."

"Blake is married?" Nadine frowned.

"I'm not married," Blake answered.

Nadine shoved the pie into his hands. "I just dropped by to bring you another apple pie and welcome you to Dry Creek."

"Thank you," he mumbled.

More noises out in the driveway meant Katy was really coming to take Granny home this time. After this shit with Nadine, it would be wonderful to get the whole ordeal finished and go home with her mama and Granny. Hopefully, her things would be dry by then.

The knock came to the door and Blake opened it.

"May I help you?" he asked.

"Nadine?" Her fiancé, Bobby Ray, pushed his way past Blake and into the house. He stopped so quick that his boots squeaked on the floor. His eyes went straight to Nadine. "What are you doing here? You're supposed to be at that ladies' thing at the church?"

"I came to see Allie," she said quickly. "She wanted to taste my apple pie so I brought one to her."

Bobby Ray, a tall man with a full black beard and a beer

belly, crossed his arms over his chest. "Why here and not over at Audrey's Place?"

"Lizzy was at the church meeting and said she was doing some work here and when I called her, she said to bring it here," Nadine lied.

"I asked about the pie recipe when she and Sharlene and Mary Jo came in the store yesterday for coffee. It's awful sweet of you to bring one to me," Allie said.

Bobby Ray tilted his head toward Blake. "Why is Blake holding it and why are you dressed like that?"

"He's holding it because"—Allie nodded toward her grandmother and lowered her voice—"she thought it was for her and she hates apple pie and she's on a tear tonight and we were afraid she would throw it at Nadine and ruin her coat." The sentence came out in a rush. "And why I'm dressed like this isn't a damn bit of your business, Bobby Ray."

"That's right." Irene slapped him on the shoulder. "Don't you dare call my granddaughter a slut! What exactly are you doing here? Did you get drunk and lose your way to Audrey's Place? Well, it ain't a whorehouse no more but we all know that you chase anything that's got a pair of panties up under their skirt."

"Granny!" Allie said.

"It's the truth." Irene tilted her chin up defiantly.

Nadine frowned as both hands popped on her wide hips. "Bobby Ray?"

Bobby Ray's cheeks turned fire engine red. "She's off in another world. Don't listen to her."

Nadine pushed him on the chest. "Have you been cheatin' on me?"

"Hell, no! If anyone is cheatin', it's you. I don't believe this cock and bull story one bit about bringing that pie to Allie." His voice got louder with each word.

Irene took a step between them. "If you are going to shout in Walter's home, then get the hell out in the yard. If you wake his cantankerous old bitch of a mama, I'll shoot the both of you."

"I came over here to ask Blake if I could cut up some of that wood he's givin' away for free. I didn't come to fight with you, Nadine." Bobby Ray crossed his arms over his chest.

Blake set the pie on the coffee table. "You're welcome to all the wood you want. Herman and his crew have been taking a lot of it but believe me, there is plenty more coming soon as I can get it dozed down."

Allie heard another vehicle. It had to be her mother this time. Or maybe it was all the ladies of the church bringing another round of food to replenish what Blake had used. It didn't matter. Tomorrow morning the fact that she was in his house, wearing his robe and nothing else, would be the headlines of the gossip vine.

This time there was no knock. A tall blonde plowed into the living room. Wearing a floor-length black leather coat, tight skinny jeans, and a gorgeous red sweater, the woman ignored everyone. She set her eyes on Blake and made a beeline for him, slung her arms around his neck, and kissed him. It wasn't a sister kiss but a long, lingering one that involved lots of tongue and her leg wrapped around his.

When the kiss broke, her eyes lit on Bobby Ray, standing there with his hands in his pockets and looking at the ceiling. "Bobby Ray Wilson. I haven't seen you in a whole month, darlin'. What are you doing here? I swear the world gets smaller every day."

Bobby Ray stammered. "What brings you here, Scarlett?"

"Long story but it don't have anything to do with us, darlin'. I told you that we were through the last time I saw you, remember? I don't date married men or engaged ones. You were a naughty boy. You should have told me you were engaged before we spent the weekend together," Scarlett said.

Nadine drew back her fist and if Blake hadn't taken a couple of long strides forward and blocked it, she would have broken Bobby Ray's nose right there.

"Turn me loose. I'm going to kill him," Nadine screeched.

"Who is that screeching bitch, Blake?" Scarlett asked.

"This would be Bobby Ray's fiancée, Nadine," Blake said.

Scarlett slapped a hand over her mouth dramatically. "Oops."

Nadine shook free of Blake's grasp and tiptoed so that her nose was only inches from Bobby Ray's. "You son of a bitch."

"That would be calling the pot black after this little escapade, wouldn't it? You're running around taking pies to men after dark. I bet you didn't make me a pie, did you?" Bobby Ray said.

Scarlett ignored them. "And this one wearing my favorite robe, sweetheart? Who is she?"

Allie would have taken the robe off and stomped on it with dirty boots if she'd had another piece of clothing underneath. "I'm Alora Raine Logan. I happen to be working on this house and it's none of your business why I'm wearing this robe."

Scarlett looked down on Allie, her blue eyes so cold that Allie could feel the chill behind them. Her voice was sweetly sarcastic when she said, "It's nice and warm and tickles all the right places, doesn't it? Gets you real ready for the bedroom."

Allie met the challenge without backing down an inch. "Who are you?"

"I'm Blake's wife and this is my yearly booty call," she said.

CHAPTER FOURTEEN

The entire room went so quiet that Allie's ears ached. Did that hussy just say she was Blake's wife? Allie whipped around and stared at him.

"Ex," Blake said quickly.

A loud rap on the door frame took everyone's attention in that direction. Katy Logan stepped inside without waiting to be invited. "Have you seen...oh, there you are, Mama. It's time to go home now. What the..." Katy's eyes came close to popping out of the sockets when she saw Allie.

"It's a long story," Allie said. "Come on, Granny. I think it's time for us to go home."

Irene sat down in the rocking chair. "Why? I like this party. It's exciting. When are they bringing out the birthday cake and ice cream? I want cake."

"We've got chocolate cake waiting for us at home. I'll get my boots and I'll see to it your robe gets brought home tomorrow," Allie said coldly without even looking at Blake.

"Allie, let me explain," he said.

Her shoulder bumped his as she stomped toward the bathroom to get her boots, but she didn't look back. "Enjoy your booty call. I'll get my boots and get out of your way."

"Is this your new girlfriend?" Scarlett asked above the argument still going on between Bobby Ray and Nadine.

"That is none of your business. All of you need to leave," Blake yelled above the din.

"Well, Walter, don't go screamin' at me like that. You invited me for cake and ice cream. I didn't bring all these other fools. It's not my fault," Irene huffed.

Allie marched back up the hall in boots that were unlaced, took her grandmother's hand, and helped her up out of the rocking chair. "Come on, Granny. We'll have cake and ice cream and you can even blow out the candles."

"Is it my birthday?"

"Not yet, but we'll practice for when it is," Allie said.

The moment they were alone in the house, Scarlett draped her arms around Blake's neck and rolled slightly up on her toes to kiss him on the lips. One hand braced against his chest while the other one worked on his belt.

"A year is too long," she whispered. "We have to start taking care of this every six months."

He pushed her away and ran a palm over his mouth, wiping the kiss away. "Get out, Scarlett, and don't come back."

"You can't resist me. You never could so don't give me that song and dance. I've looked forward to this for a month. We always get together right after New Year's to celebrate the fact that our parents were smart enough to get our drunken marriage annulled."

He opened the door and pointed. "Out!"

"You can do a hell of a lot better than that mousy-lookin' little creature."

"One more time. Out!" He raised his voice so loud that Shooter whimpered.

"Okay, then," she growled. "Since you are in a pissy mood, I'll leave. Don't tell me that someone is about to tame you. I didn't think that could be done." She headed toward the door.

Blake locked the door behind her and threw himself back in the recliner. "Dammit! Maybe this place is unlucky after all."

Shooter gobbled down the apple pie and licked the glass pie plate clean. Then he curled up in front of the fireplace, his big brown eyes looking up at Blake.

"You're not in trouble, boy. I was going to heave the thing out in the yard," Blake mumbled.

Shooter's tail wagged a few times.

"Now I have to explain the whole thing to Allie."

The doorknob rattled and Deke yelled from the other side, "Hey, man, are you alone in there?"

Blake rushed to the door and slung it wide open. "Where in the hell were you thirty minutes ago when I needed you?"

"What do you need done?" Deke asked. "Or are we going somewhere to dance and flirt with the ladies?"

"I needed you to referee." Blake ushered him inside and told him the rest of the story.

Deke removed his coat and tossed it behind the recliner. "Man, I can't believe all that happened tonight but I'm damn glad that Allie and even Irene were here when Nadine showed up. If you'd been alone and Bobby Ray hadn't decided to come around and ask about firewood, you'd have been in trouble."

"If I can tell Scarlett to go away, and Sharlene and Mary Jo, I reckon I could get rid of that redhead." Blake plopped down on the sofa. "There's still food on the table if you're hungry."

"Already ate but don't put it away. I might get into it later," Deke said. "Do you like Allie? I mean as in *like* her, not as in like her as a friend and neighbor? It seems to me you might have developed some feelings for her."

"Why are you asking?"

The dog on the television barked and Shooter's head popped up. "See, even Shooter thinks something is going on and he's voicing his opinion. The reason I'm askin' is because she's like a sister to me and I don't want to see her hurt, and you just now told me about this once-a-year booty call and I bet this is the first time you turned it down."

"I could never hurt Allie. I . . ." Blake hesitated. "Yes, I do like her a lot."

"You'd best be real sure before you make that statement because as good of friends as we've become, if you make her cry, I'll have to hurt you," Deke said seriously.

Blake went to the kitchen and brought back two open beers. He handed one to Deke and downed a third of his before he settled into the rocking chair in front of the blazing fire. "You don't scare me as much as this crazy feeling inside me. I didn't move here with intentions of getting involved in any way with a woman. I should back away from her completely. She's already got baggage in her past and she don't need an old cowboy like me, and besides my brother and I have a rule about dating women too close to home," Blake said.

"That's not your decision to make. It's Allie's."

"After tonight I'll be surprised if she even comes back to finish the bedroom."

"Man, I would have loved to have been here to see it but I'm more than a little mad at you for kicking that tall blonde out in the cold. I would have gladly let her come to my house for a booty call." Deke laughed.

"Start talkin'," Katy said the minute they were in the house.

Irene clapped her hands like a child. "Cake and candles and ice cream."

"We'd better take care of this first or she'll be a nightmare the rest of the evening." Allie led the way to the kitchen. She found a package of two chocolate cupcakes in the pantry, unwrapped them, and put them on a decorative disposable plate before carrying them out to the table where Irene waited.

"Candles?" She frowned.

"Right here." Katy brought them to the table with the container of ice cream.

Allie poked a candle in each cupcake. "Now blow 'em out, Granny."

"Practicin' for my birthday, right? That means you have to sing to me."

"You get them both with one breath and we'll sing," Katy said.

"What's going on? It's not Granny's birthday." Lizzy carried her damn wedding planning book into the kitchen. It was a thick three-ring binder with everything from pictures of centerpieces to candles to honeymoon places, all arranged neatly with tabbed dividers.

Allie hated the sight of the thing, hated everything about it from the pictures of the lavender dresses to the tuxedos that Mitch and Grady would wear. The wedding would be held in the Dry Creek church with the reception in the fellowship hall, not in a big city cathedral.

"I thought we'd talk about the ribbons for our bouquets tonight, but I see you are all crazy." Lizzy pouted.

"We are practicin' and if you don't like it, go away," Irene said.

"Practicin' what?" Lizzy asked.

"Granny's birthday," Allie answered.

She blew out both candles and Katy started the birthday song. Lizzy and Allie sang with her all the way to the end.

Lizzy poked Allie on the arm. "What are you doing in that men's robe and why does she think it's her birthday?"

"It's a long story. Come on upstairs to my bedroom while she eats and I'll tell you." She didn't want to confide in her sister, but by morning the rumors would have the story blown so far out of proportion that she might as well come clean.

Lizzy followed Allie to her bedroom and sat on the edge of the bed. "Well?"

"I'm going to get dressed first so be patient." She stepped inside the big closet and shut the door. Like always, she'd held up good under pressure but now that it was over, her hands shook and her stomach hurt. Her skin turned clammy and tears filled her eyes, but she refused to let them spill. She pulled on a pair of underpants and an oversized nightshirt that stopped midway down her thigh.

"You going to take all night in there?" Lizzy called out.

Allie pushed the door open and lay on the bed, curled up in a C with the pillow under her head. "Might as well stretch out here beside me. This might take awhile."

Lizzy fell back on the bed. "What have you done? Don't tell me that was Blake's robe you were wearing down there. I thought it was one of Daddy's old ones but it was that cowboy's, wasn't it?"

"It is and there's a reason I was wearing it but believe

me, sister, I will not be wearing it ever again." She told the story from the time she finished the room, only leaving out the way his robe touching her bare body made her feel.

"Holy sweet Jesus," Lizzy exclaimed. "Do you know what the gossip hounds are going to do with that before morning? To get the heat off herself, Nadine will call Sharlene and Mary Jo and they'll spread the news to everyone else, and by morning you will be having an affair with that cowboy. You might as well have gone on and slept with him."

"Well, shit! Now that I have your permission, maybe I should go over there and boot that tall bitch out of his bed and have a turn with him," Allie said sarcastically.

"Oh, hush! That hussy actually said that she'd worn that robe?" Lizzy hissed.

Allie nodded. "She did."

Lizzy slid off the bed. "Put on some jeans and some boots. We are going to burn the damn thing out in the backyard right now. I may not agree with you but by damn, you are my sister and no one is treating you like that."

"That won't solve anything. She is part of his past, like Riley is mine."

Lizzy went straight to the closet and picked the robe up from the floor. "I don't give a royal rat's ass. There's going to be a robe burnin'. I'll do it if you don't want to." She paused. "Oh. My. God. You have fallen for that cowboy, haven't you?"

Allie shrugged. "I like spending time with him but I wouldn't say I've fallen for him. That involves more than wearing his robe while my clothes are in the washing machine. Which reminds me, why wasn't Granny with you at the Lady's Circle meeting?"

Lizzy glared at the robe now lying on the floor. "No one

showed up so we came on back home. We didn't have a meeting after all."

"Nadine said she was there and you told her I was working over at the Lucky Penny."

Lizzy's eyes rolled toward the ceiling. "Before or after Bobby Ray showed up? She was trying to save her own ass and you helped her out, so she owes you big time. And don't change the subject. Answer me."

Allie sighed. "You sound like Granny when your voice goes all high and squeaky. I like Blake. He's a good person, Lizzy. Tonight wasn't his fault. It was one of those crazy cluster things that happen all at once."

"Depends on the booty call woman, don't it? I wonder if he sent her packing or if she's over there right now." Lizzy's fists were clenched. "Lord, I'd like to hit her or him or even Nadine. Do you realize what kind of gossip is going to be going through town by morning?"

"I need to sort it all out. Can you give me a few days to do that before you start bitchin' about it? Or before you go hittin' someone? Remember you're going to be a preacher's wife."

Lizzy set her mouth in a firm line. "Fire starts in ten minutes. That's how long it will take me to stuff this in the fire pit and douse it with gasoline."

"Wait till I get my jeans on. If that hussy had it on her body, then I want to see it burn," Allie said quickly.

"That's my sister. The one I knew before Riley broke her heart." Lizzy grinned. "And you promise you won't ever go back over there?"

Allie left the bed and jerked on a pair of jeans. "Hell, no! I've got things to say to him."

"Well, shit! You like him more than a little bit if he makes you that mad."

Allie pulled her dark hair up in a ponytail. "Maybe so. I'll have to figure it out but right now we've got a robe to burn. Wonder if he'd like to see it or maybe smell the smoke?"

"Wind is blowing toward the south. Call him once we get it lit and tell him to step out on the porch," Lizzy said. "He'll probably tell you to keep your scrawny ass on your side of the fence from now on."

They set the robe on fire and despite feeling childish and more than a little bit like a teenager instead of a twenty-eight-year-old woman, Allie did call Blake. He answered on the first ring and she told him what she and Lizzy were doing.

"Fine by me," Blake said. "But next time you need to wash some insulation out of your clothes you need to remember that you'll have to run around naked. I have no problem with that. None whatsoever."

"I will always have an extra set of clothing from now on."

"Then that means you're going to finish the job you started?"

Allie drew in a long breath. "I don't let tall bitches keep me from doing a job. Just tell her to stay out of my way tomorrow morning."

"She's gone and I don't expect she'll ever come back. Deke says to say hello."

"Hello, Deke, and good night, Blake."

She pushed the END button and bit back the grin so that she wouldn't have to tell Lizzy what he'd said.

CHAPTER FIFTEEN

Allie called Blake the next morning to tell him that she had to mind the feed store because Lizzy had come down with the flu overnight. That meant Katy took Granny to the convenience store with her and Allie would be on the other end of the block at Lizzy's store all day. The sun was out again but the temperature was below freezing so there wouldn't be a lot of melting going on that day.

She got his voice mail and left a short message.

She tried again at midmorning but got the same message, and her mind immediately went to the tall blond bombshell who might have returned and sweet-talked her way into Blake's bed. It was his bed and his life so it wasn't a damn bit of her business, but it didn't keep the envy at bay. Besides she'd known Blake less than two weeks so what gave her the right to be jealous.

Wearing his robe did not give her any rights over him. Lighting it up might have burned any bridges between them anyway. She grabbed up a dusting rag and went to work on the shelves in the Dry Creek Feed and Seed Store. As bad as she hated cleaning, she needed something to do so that the hands of the clock would move. Starting on the side where all the supplies were kept, she straightened, wiped out a month's worth of dust, and grumbled.

She shouldn't worry about killing Mitch. He expected a spotlessly clean house and three meals on the table and Lizzy to wear high heels the whole time she was making that happen. After the first week, she'd kill him. Poor old sumbitch had no idea what he was getting into. Of all three Logan sisters, Lizzy hated cleaning the most.

"Anybody here?" A voice startled her so badly that she threw the dust rag straight up with a squeal. Gravity brought it back to Lucy's hands and she held it out to her.

"Just because I caught the damn thing, don't mean I'm going to use it."

Allie laid the rag on the shelf. "What can I do for you today, Miz Lucy?"

"I need to buy a chainsaw blade for Herman. He called me when I was elbow deep in makin' bread for the week to tell me to bring a new saw blade out to the Lucky Penny for him. Thinks he can't waste a minute coming to town to get it, but it's okay to interrupt what I'm doin'," Lucy fussed.

"Got to cut wood while the sun shines. This is just the middle of January. We could have lots more winter before the robins come around to stay," Allie said.

"And it would be a sin if one chunk of mesquite wasn't in his wood yard." Lucy winked. "Men! Can't live with 'em and God says we can't shoot 'em when we get done with 'em. And while I'm here, I need a new extension cord."

"The big orange industrial one or one of these brown and

white ones?" Allie pointed to the shelf where they were displayed.

Lucy glanced back toward her office. "Give me one of them white ones then. And put it on our ticket. Where's Lizzy?"

"She's down with that stomach virus that's going around, but it only lasts a couple of days so she'll be back by Friday." Allie rang up the bill and laid Herman's copy on the counter.

Lucy scribbled his name on the bottom of the ticket. "Tell her to get well soon and to keep that shit at Audrey's Place. Us old folks don't bounce back like the young do. And I sure hope Irene don't get a dose of it."

Allie filed the ticket in a box under the counter. Lizzy could take care of entering all that into the computer later. It was double work but the old folks in town didn't trust the new way of doing business, so Lizzy and Katy both still made out handwritten tickets for them.

Lucy pointed to the radio on the counter. "I'm glad that Lizzy plays old country music in here. I hate going into a store and that new stuff is playing. It makes my ears hurt."

"Daddy always had the classic country station playing," Allie said.

"I know he did. I liked it then and I still do. It don't get no better than Conway and Loretta." Lucy smiled. "You know folks in town say you are on a fool's mission fixin' up that house for Blake, don't you?" Lucy changed the subject abruptly.

"I'm not surprised. Hey, do you remember someone named Walter who lived on the Lucky Penny maybe thirty years ago?" Allie asked.

Lucy nodded. "Remember him well. Tall, lanky old boy with dark hair and glasses. Him and his mama bought the ranch and lived there a year, maybe two, and then like all the rest of the folks who've lived there, they moved on. Can't recall his last name but his mama was one of them women that always had something wrong with her. I wanted to wring her neck for pretending to be sick all the time. Woman who could eat as much as she could at a church social, why there wasn't a damn thing wrong with her. She just had to act like that to keep Walter under her thumb. Tell all the ladies at Audrey's Place I hope they stay well."

Allie plopped down in the lawn chair behind the counter. "So Walter isn't a total figment of her imagination."

"No, Walter was very real," Lucy answered and waved as she left the store. The business phone rang and Allie reached for the cordless sitting beside the cash register. "Dry Creek Feed and Seed," she answered.

"I forgot to tell you that the vet supply guy isn't coming this month and what's on the shelf is all we've got until he gets here the first of February. If someone needs more than what's there, I can make a run up to Wichita Falls but it'll take me a couple of days to get it," Lizzy said.

"Drink your hot tea and stop worryin'. I can run this store for a day or two," Allie said. "Lucy is the only customer that you've had and she bought an extension cord and a chain for Herman's chainsaw."

"Mitch was coming into town to see me tonight and now he can't," Lizzy moaned.

"None of the rest of us have caught whatever you have. Maybe it's not a bug but wedding jitters. Or maybe you're pregnant," Allie said with a wicked grin.

"Alora Raine Logan!" Lizzy yelled into the phone.

Allie held it out from her ear. "Are you telling me it's not possible? Good God, Lizzy. You've been dating this man for a year."

"We entered into a covenant when we got engaged. We will abstain until our wedding night," Lizzy said.

"Well, that explains a lot." Allie laughed. "Your bitchy mood. And your sharp tongue and that hangdog look on your face all the time. You need to get laid."

"I'm abstaining for the Lord," Lizzy growled. "You are doing without because you…"

Allie's jaw set in anger. "Because I'm ugly as a mud fence? Because I have no sex appeal? Because I am a carpenter? Be careful, Lizzy. I'm minding the store for you and I could rearrange everything or maybe I could shuffle all the stuff in the bill box under the counter."

"You wouldn't dare!" Lizzy huffed.

"Oh, I would and you know it," Allie said.

"Mitch is going to be your brother."

Allie shook her head emphatically even though no one could see it. "He's going to be your husband, not my brother, and I will be every bit as nice to him as you were to Riley."

"I never did like that bastard," Lizzy grumbled.

Allie stood up and carried the phone with her to the first round rack of clothing. "Point proven. I'm going to work on straightening and putting up stock on the clothing side. You need to look around before you order. You've got four orange hoodies in a two-X size and only one in a small."

"Those will be gone by the end of next week and the small will still be hanging there. I ordered it for Sharlene's brother and he broke his leg and can't hunt this year. Thanks for the cleanup. Bye," Lizzy said in a rush and the phone went silent.

Allie didn't need an explanation of the quick end to the call and hoped that she didn't catch whatever sent Lizzy to the bathroom every fifteen minutes. She looked back through the clothing area of the store. Hunting jackets, hoodies, jeans, and one rack of cute little western shirts for women.

"I need coffee before I tackle this," she said.

After a quick trip to the office/kitchenette, she propped a hip on the tall stool behind the cash register. She had taken the first sip when the door opened, and she looked across the store into the eyes of her ex-husband, Riley. His light brown hair was longer, almost touching his shirt collar, and he'd gained at least twenty pounds, most of it around his midsection right above his belt. All in all he looked like warmed-over shit and that put a big smile on her face.

"Hello, Allie." He smiled back at her.

She wiped the grin off her face instantly. "What brings you to Dry Creek?"

His soft-soled shoes didn't make a sound as he crossed the floor. She didn't recognize that shaving lotion, but it smelled like he'd taken a bath in it and it cost more than a buck ninety-nine at Walmart.

"I came to talk to you, darlin'," he said smoothly.

She recognized his attempt at seduction, but her bullshit radar jacked all the way to the top of the red alert. She crossed her arms over her chest. "That ship sailed a lifetime ago, Riley. I don't have anything to say to you nor do I want to hear anything you say to me."

"But all ships eventually come back home after their adventure." He placed his palms on the counter and locked gazes with her.

Riley had been her high school sweetheart. He'd made her feel special. She'd landed the quarterback of the football team and he treated her like a queen. They'd married right before her nineteenth birthday and divorced about the time she was twenty-two.

"I understand you've been flirting with the new owner over at the Lucky Penny and got caught last night after a hot little rendezvous." His smile was so sarcastic that it chilled the whole store.

The Riley she married, the one who'd looked into her eyes with such love on their wedding day, was not the man on the other side of the counter. He was the stranger who came home one day and told her he was in love with another woman. There was no way he could ever, ever worm his way into her heart again.

She sipped her coffee. "I understand you've been keeping even later hours with a minor and that your nights are a lot hotter than mine."

"She's of age," he protested. "And I didn't come here to talk about Suzanne."

"What did you come to talk about?" Allie asked. "Do you need a sack of chicken feed or maybe an extension cord? I can help you with that, but anything else you'll have to get that from your wife or your newest soul mate."

His thin mouth clamped shut until it was nothing more than a slit. Fantastic! Paybacks were a bitch but they could be so sweet.

"I want to talk about us," he said through clenched teeth.

Allie shook her head. "There is no us. Hasn't been in seven years. There is me, and what I do or do not do isn't a damn bit of your business. There is you, and I couldn't care less what you do."

"Come on, Allie. We've been in love since we were in grade school," he said.

"Like I said, that ship sailed. Matter of fact, I believe it sunk in a storm and there's nothing left of it," she told him. "You were a sweet guy at one time, but you changed. I'm looking ahead not behind."

"We were good together. We could be again." His voice dropped to a whisper. "We could start fresh like Bobby Ray and Nadine."

"Bobby Ray." She twisted her mouth to the side. "So he came running to your house when Nadine threw him out last night, did he? I wondered how you got your information so quick."

Riley reached across the counter and touched her cheek. "Don't do that with your mouth. It makes you look like an old woman. Bobby Ray stayed with me last night. Nadine cheats on him, too, so she doesn't have room to bitch. I'm sure that somewhere in our marriage you had a little fling."

Allie slid off the stool, reached under the counter, and brought up a small twenty-two-caliber pistol. She shoved it up against Riley's nose and he took a step back.

"Do not ever put your hands on me again. I don't care if I look like an old woman or like warmed-over shit. If you touch me again, I will shoot you and enjoy watching you die before I call nine-one-one," she said.

"Well, hell, Allie, you do that with your mouth too much when you are angry," he said. "I was only trying to help like I did when we were married and I gave you advice."

She lowered the gun and laughed out loud.

"What's so funny?" he asked.

"You are a regular comedian today," she said between giggles. "If I cheated on you, I wouldn't tell you. If I didn't, I wouldn't tell you. Go home, Riley. It's been over with us for a long time. And you weren't giving me advice, you were putting me down that last few months so you wouldn't feel guilty about cheating on me."

"I want you back, Allie. I'll treat you right this time. I'll let you work," he begged.

She shook her head slowly from side to side. "Sometimes

it's too late to do what you should've been doing all along. Door is closed, Riley. Let me work, indeed! Are you dumb-ass crazy?"

His face turned scarlet with rage. "Don't you talk to me like that and don't laugh at me."

She brought the gun back up, only this time she aimed it at his crotch. "Give me a reason."

The cowbell attached to the front door rang loudly. He took two steps back but she readjusted the gun, hoping her aim would put a hole through both balls with one shot.

Nadine stopped at the end of the counter. "What in the hell are you doing in town, Riley? And don't be givin' me that look. I heard that Bobby Ray holed up in your place last night. He's back home now, but we've had a come-to-Jesus talk." She turned to Allie and asked, "What's he done that you've got a gun on his stuff?"

"He raised his fist at me," Allie said.

"Then shoot him and I'll be your witness," Nadine said.

"He came to give me a second chance," Allie said. "You want to spread the news so Suzanne knows what kind of man she's quittin' college for?"

"Are you crazy? She can damn sure do better than you." Nadine got right into his personal space and poked him in the chest.

"I don't know what gave her that idea. I'm a happily married man. I dropped by because I was in town. She's lying. I would never hit a woman." Riley pulled himself up to his full height of five feet eight inches. "I'll be going now. I don't have to take abuse from either of you."

"No, but I reckon Greta and Suzanne might have some that you'll have to take when they both hear you've been down here trying to get back with your ex," Nadine told him.

He almost made it to the door when Irene rushed inside

and stopped right in front of him. She stomped one foot on the wooden floor.

"You bastard. What in the hell are you doin' in my store?" she demanded. "I hope God strikes you graveyard dead. And God hears the prayers of little children and crazy old women, so you'd best get on out of here."

"I'm leaving." He turned back to give Nadine an evil smile. "You ever tell her about us?" The slamming door echoed through the store like a shotgun blast.

"Did you screw him, too?" Irene turned on Nadine.

Nadine blushed and covered her face with her hands. "I'm so sorry, Allie."

"Before or after we were married?" Allie asked.

The sobbing started.

"I asked a question," Allie said loudly.

"After," Nadine sobbed. "But only two times. He said that you couldn't keep him happy, that you hated sex and wouldn't even sleep with him. But I wasn't the only one, Allie."

"Sharlene?"

Nadine dropped her hands and nodded. "But before y'all were married."

"And Mary Jo?"

"Right before Greta," Nadine whimpered.

Irene threw up her hands in disgust and went straight back to the office where she sat down in the office chair and turned on the television. Allie could barely think straight, but she made a quick call to her mom to let her know Granny was safe and sound before turning toward Nadine.

Nadine froze in the spot where she'd been standing when Riley was still there. "I am so sorry. I came to town to 'fess up to you. Honest, I did. I heard you were runnin' the store for Lizzy because she's sick, and I came in here to tell you that I won't be flirting with Blake Dawson anymore. I didn't know you were interested in him and I feel so guilty for what I did with Riley, I'd never do that to you again, Allie. You deserve better."

Allie should feel something other than indifference. Four women including Greta had slept with her husband either before or after she married him. One was standing right there within slapping distance. She should hate her but the only thing she felt for Nadine was pity. "Well, thank you for that but you should be thinkin' about your wedding instead of my feelings."

Nadine took a step toward the counter. "You have always been too nice. We were all so jealous of you in high school and then afterwards when you married Riley. Every girl in school was in love with him and he chose you. We all hated you for that."

Allie wasn't in a hugging mood so she hoped to hell Nadine didn't come around the end of the counter and expect to have a girly-type hugging fest. "Don't look like much of a catch now, does he?"

Nadine's chin quivered and more tears rolled down her cheeks, leaving long streaks of black mascara in their wake. "I'm bored. I want my own café, but that's not going to happen. Bobby Ray wants me to quit my job when we get married. If I'm bored now, just think what it will be then. I'm so jealous of you. Always have been because you have something that is yours and you work for it and you are happy."

Allie's mind went into high gear. "Rent one of the empty buildings and put in a café. We could use one in Dry Creek. You might not make a million dollars a year, but it will give you something to do. I've eaten your cookin' at the church socials and you're good at it."

"I'm not as smart as you. I can cook but a business requires book work and I never was real good in school," Nadine said.

"Sharlene is good at bookkeeping. She works at a bank and could help you with that," Allie said.

"Do you really think I could do this?" Nadine whispered.

"Yes, I do," Allie said.

Nadine cocked her head to one side. "You reckon your mom would rent the old café building to me? It's already set up with a kitchen. Would take a lot of cleanup but it would cut down on start-up cost."

"Go ask her. She might even rent to own so that if you get it going good you could buy the place from her," Allie said.

"Why didn't I think of that rather than hating you for having what I wanted?" Nadine asked.

Allie laid a hand on Nadine's arm. At first the woman flinched and then she grabbed the hand and brought it to her cheek. "Like I said, you've always been too nice."

"I can be a real bitch. Ask my sister if you don't believe me. Or ask Deke or Blake. But the past is gone and today is all we get. You might want to talk to Bobby Ray before you talk to Mama. He's a lot like Riley in that he expects his little woman to stay home and raise kids."

Nadine took a deep breath. "Right now is the perfect time to do this because he won't tell me no. Not after last night. Thank you, Allie. You might have saved my sanity."

Allie looked out the front window at the buildings across the street and imagined all of them with clean windows and prosperous businesses. "Think Sharlene would want to rent one of the buildings? Or maybe Mary Jo? We might turn this town around if all the women who are bored had something to keep them busy."

"Lord, honey, Mary Jo can cook, but not like Nadine. But,

oh, my gosh, Allie, she might put in a beauty and barbershop combination in the old barbershop. I'm going to talk to her and Sharlene, too." Nadine clapped her hands like Irene did when she got a chocolate cupcake.

Allie followed her to the door. "Just remember, you aren't going to get rich here in Dry Creek but it might make you feel a lot better."

The door had barely shut behind her when Allie's phone rang. She recognized Deke's number and answered after the second ring.

"Are you holding a grudge? This isn't like you, Allie," Deke said bluntly.

Riley? Nadine? How did Deke know all that so quickly? "Grudge for what?"

"Come on. All last night wasn't Blake's fault so why didn't you show up for work this morning? He told you he kicked that ex of his to the curb after you left and I believe him," Deke said.

"Well, it damn sure wasn't my fault!" she shot right back at him.

"I didn't say it was. It wasn't anyone's fault, so why aren't you on the job today?" Deke asked.

Blake yelled in the background. "Hey, Deke, I've got five messages from Allie. Her sister is sick and she's down at the feed store. I left my phone on the kitchen table this morning."

"What's the matter with Lizzy? Did she finally wake up and realize that she's engaged to a jerk and it made her sick to think about what a fool she's been?" Deke asked.

Allie popped up on the counter and crossed her legs Indian-style. "I want to go back to what we were talking about before. Why did you take Blake's side first? I've been your friend a hell of a lot longer than he has."

"Yes you have and that's why I didn't like it when you were sinking back into that ugly mood you got in after the divorce," Deke said. "I was afraid you'd lose your mind that first year after Riley left."

Allie didn't want to talk about the past. "So I'm ugly?"

Deke lowered his voice to a whisper. "I did not say that. I said you were in an ugly mood and you're not going to twist your way out of this. If you didn't like Blake and I mean more than a friend, you wouldn't be carryin' on like this."

"You are acting like a girl." She laughed.

"I'm your best friend, so I have to act like a girl for you to listen to me. Just don't ask me to wear pink taffeta and be your bridesmaid when you get married again. I draw the line at that," he said.

"Darlin', you don't look good in pink taffeta. I was thinking purple silk, something with a big skirt and a sweetheart neckline," she teased. "And FYI, I'm not getting married again and if I did it would involve a twenty-minute trip to the courthouse in Throckmorton, not a big wedding. Go eat your dinner and get back to work. With any luck I'll be back on the job tomorrow morning."

Deke lowered his voice to a whisper. "The hussy did not come back last night. And Bobby Ray spent the night at Riley's place, but he and Nadine made up this morning."

"Gossip travels fast," she said.

"Nothing speedier in the whole world especially with the help of a cell phone and texting. Got to go."

"Bye, Deke, and thanks for the call."

"You betcha and Blake is yelling for me to tell you that he will call you back soon as we get done eating dinner."

Allie's coffee had gone lukewarm, but she sipped it anyway. The first tinkling, haunting sounds of the piano announced a song by Conway Twitty started on the radio. She tapped a finger on the counter to the beat in her head. He sang about standing on a bridge that just wouldn't burn. Allie shut her eyes and pictured an old wooden bridge. Riley stood on the other end with his arms open wide, a smile on his face, beckoning to her to take the first step. In the vision, she took out an imaginary chuck of blazing firewood and set the damn thing on fire.

"Good-bye, past. Hello, future," she mumbled.

Blake was in the dozer with Shooter right beside him when he called Allie. She was out of breath when she said, "Hello."

"Busy at the feed store today?" he asked.

"Quiet except for a little drama this morning and then I had a run this afternoon for feed. I was in the back of the store making tickets for half a dozen ranchers who were loading their trucks when I heard the phone. I'd left it on the counter beside the cash register," she explained.

"I can call back," Blake said.

"It's okay. I can talk," she said. "Everything is taken care of right now. Granny is watching television and eating doughnuts in the office, while Mama has her usual school lunch rush. Hey, guess what? Nadine may open up a café here on Main Street."

Blake put the phone on speaker so he could talk and drive at the same time. "I wanted to tell you that Scarlett left right after you did last night. I guess a person can't run from their past, can they?"

"Riley came in here this morning wanting to give me a second chance. Then that old song by Conway played on the radio. Remember 'A Bridge That Just Won't Burn'?"

"No but I can understand the title after last night," Blake said. "Are we okay, Allie, until we can talk face-to-face?"

"Did you hear what I said? He wants to give me a second chance; not me give him one." Allie's tone changed.

Blake chuckled. "Now I understand."

"I'll be back at work tomorrow or Friday at the latest. My goal is to have your bedroom done by Saturday evening," she said. "We can talk then."

"And then you'll go out with me for dinner and a movie. Maybe up to Wichita Falls?" he asked.

"Tell you what. I'll go out with you when I have that room done. It can be our celebration," she answered.

Blake pumped his fist into the air and Shooter barked. "I could help you so it would be done by Saturday night."

"How good at painting are you?" she asked.

"I can roll paint just as good as anyone and I'll be more than glad to help out."

"And now I have a customer so I'd best get off the phone. Thanks for calling, Blake, and yes, we're okay for right now."

It was another rancher needing a pickup load of feed and that didn't take long. Allie checked on Granny and then went back to her stool. She should have been dancing a jig around the store that Blake had asked her out, but instead she had a rock in her chest.

"It's because I'm falling right back into the same pattern I had with Riley. He calls the shots and I do the dancing," she mumbled.

"No, you are not going dancing," Granny said at her elbow. "You are not going to a bar where they do that hoochy-cooch dancing. Your sister is marryin' a damn preacher and you'll ruin her reputation. I'm going back over to your mama's store. She made pinto beans and ham this morning and I'm hungry for more than doughnuts."

Allie helped her into her coat and followed her to the

door, stepped outside in the bitter cold and watched her until she was safely inside the convenience store, and then went back to her fretting stool. It was only dinner and a movie with a friend; it wasn't a date. Not even after all those hot kisses, it still wasn't a date. She'd ask Deke to go with them to prove that it was friendship and not the beginnings of a relationship.

CHAPTER SIXTEEN

Blake made sure his phone was fully charged and in his shirt pocket instead of leaving it on the kitchen table. He could hardly believe that it was Friday. In ten days his house had gotten a brand-new roof and his bedroom was getting a fine remodel. Things were falling into place even better than he could have hoped for when he first moved to the Lucky Penny. He had missed seeing Allie the past two days while she worked at the feed store but he hoped she'd be back at the Lucky Penny that day.

He'd barely crawled up in the dozer when the phone rang, and he hurriedly pulled it from his pocket and smiled brightly when he saw that Allie was calling.

He answered before it rang the second time. "We've got to stop all this talking on the phone. I miss you, Allie. I miss seeing your gorgeous smile and having you sit beside me at the dinner table. I miss talking to you. It's not the same around here without you, and Deke is getting depressed. Poor old Shooter misses you, too."

"I'm at the store today," Allie said. "Not the feed store but Mama's place. Lizzy finally felt well enough to go to work, but Granny is lethargic so Mama took her back to the doctor to make sure she's not coming down with the stomach bug. She was afraid to let it go over the weekend. You and Deke want to come into town for dinner? We've got a big pot of taco meat simmering and we're serving tacos with pinto beans and dirty rice. I'll treat today. If you wait until the school rush is over, I can even sit down and eat with you guys."

Blake smiled and nodded to himself. She talked too much when she was nervous. He wanted nothing more than to hug her, to calm her from whatever was creating turmoil in her life, but most of all he wanted to be near her again. Even if he couldn't kiss her or hold her, he wanted to share space with her, be able to look at her. It seemed like a hundred years since that craziness when Scarlett showed up at his house and even longer since Allie stormed out past him in that damn robe. He was glad she'd burned the thing. He never wanted to see it again.

"What time? Can I bring the beer?" he asked.

"Twelve thirty or after and yes on the beer. I can't sell it but I could sure drink one with dinner. Looks like our bedroom celebration will have to wait until the first of the week. There's no way I can get it finished by Saturday," she said.

"Bedroom celebration, darlin'?" he asked.

"We're going out to celebrate finishing your bedroom. Did you forget? I thought we'd ask Deke to join us so he won't feel left out," she said quickly.

"No, I hadn't forgotten. I was teasing you and darlin' I don't do threesomes," he said. "I'll see you at dinner. I'll be the one with three beers and a lean and hungry look on my face."

In the middle of the morning he got a text message from Toby, saying that he was leaving Muenster as soon as he could get away that evening and driving up to the Lucky Penny for the weekend.

He couldn't wait for Toby to arrive at the ranch so he could see the progress Blake had made. But most of all he wanted to introduce him to his Allie.

"My Allie," he muttered. "I only wish she were mine."

Allie was so busy making lunches from eleven thirty until five minutes before the final bell rang down at the school that she didn't have time to look up. When the store finally cleared she sat down at a table and propped her legs up on an empty chair.

She wished she was painting walls at Blake's place rather than running the store, but family helped family, even when they didn't like it. Too bad Lizzy or her mother didn't know a hammer from a dishrag so they could return the favor when she needed help.

"Hey," Deke called out as he and Blake pushed their way into the store. "Looks like we timed it about right. There's some big black clouds gathering up down in the southwest and I got a text from a friend in Throckmorton who says we've got freezing rain on the way by midnight, so we're in for a blast. Cold wind is coming down from the north and rain from the south. Won't be no more workin' outside today."

Allie's heart kicked in an extra beat when she saw Blake, and her pulse went from low to high gear in less than five seconds. It was the first time she'd seen him since that horrible night. He stopped a few feet from her and she searched his expression, hoping that they were truly all right and the whole scene wouldn't be awkward between them.

"Crazy how the weather affects what we do, isn't it? Take off your coats and hang them on the rack in the back. Dinner is on the stove. Help yourselves." Her voice sounded normal despite the way her heart was flopping around like a fish out of water inside her chest. She started to get up but Blake shook his head.

"Keep your seat. I'll bring you a plate. One or two tacos?" He smiled and erased all doubts from her mind.

She held up four fingers. "No beans and extra dirty rice, but I'll make my own plate and we'll take them to the back room where it's a little more private."

"She's bored." Deke laughed. "When she's bored she eats and she gets cranky and picks fights. When she's nervous she talks too much. She's not made to run a store. Hey, neither Blake nor I can't work outside anymore with this weather comin' on so how be I run the store for you and you go on home with Blake and do some paintin'. It might keep you from goin' plumb batshit crazy."

Allie jogged over to Deke, put her arms around his neck, and hugged him like a brother. "I love you, love you, love you! You are my very best friend and I owe you one."

"I guess I could tear out some hallway ceiling while you paint." Blake removed three beers from the pockets of his work coat and set them on the table. A twinge of jealousy reared its ugly head when she told Deke that she loved him and said that he was her best friend. Blake wanted that spot even if he wasn't going to admit it out loud.

"That sounds wonderful. Now let's eat so we can get out of here and go to work," she said.

Blake nodded toward the doughnuts. "Can we have them for dessert?"

"No!" Deke called out from the back of the store. "You'll want ice cream to chase the picante sauce that we're going to put on these tacos. Katy makes it from her own special recipe and believe me, you will want ice cream. We'll each pick a pint of our favorite flavor from the freezer."

Blake removed his coat and hung it on the back of a chair and headed for the back room with Allie right behind him. In a few minutes she and Blake were sitting on one side of the table with Deke at the end. Blake's leg was jammed tightly against hers and electricity, that had nothing to do with the thunder and lightning outside, rattled through her body jump-starting her pulse into racing again just when it had slowed down to normal.

"Damn fine tacos," Deke said between bites. "Herman and his boys are practically carrying off ever' bit of the mesquite that Blake is clearing out. I've made a hell of a good livin' sellin' my wood to him this week, but this damn weather will slow us down for the rest of the week for sure. Freezing rain on top of snow makes a big mess."

Blake finished his first taco and sipped his beer. "Once things thaw out, it's going to be easy to turn the land the way they're cleaning it up. I might even have eighty acres in alfalfa when Toby brings in the first round of cattle. We can put them on forty to graze and make hay from the rest. Then come fall when Jud gets here, we'll have more land ready. It's going better than I thought it might. These are good tacos. What's your secret, Allie?"

Allie picked up her second one and turned to look at Blake. "Not my secret but Mama's. She makes her own seasonings for the meat, but there's a possibility that she won't be cooking much longer here in the store."

Deke frowned, drawing his forehead down to turn his hazel eyes into slits. "I don't want to hear that. What are we going to do for a place to have coffee or to grab food at noon if Blake ain't cookin'?"

"Nadine is opening up the old café. Hopefully by the end of the month. It all happened really quick. She's leased it from Mama and if things go well after the first year, she's going to buy the building," Allie said. "And she's trying to talk Mary Jo into putting in a barber and beauty shop across the street."

Deke held up a finger. "And Sharlene? Is she putting in a brothel? That's what we need most."

Allie slapped him on the arm. "No, but Nadine is talking to her about a day care center in the old clothing store. It's got a lot of room and it wouldn't take much to convert it and Sharlene is real good with kids. And besides who needs a brothel when it appears that menfolk can get all of that around here that they want for free."

"Alora Raine!" Deke pretended to be shocked.

Blake glanced out the window. "Wouldn't it be something if all these empty buildings were filled with businesses?"

Deke chuckled. "You best hope for one miracle at a time. Turning the luck of the Lucky Penny is enough for you to worry about right now."

CHAPTER
SEVENTEEN

Herman waved from the window of his trailer loaded high with mesquite wood when Allie and Blake passed him on the way to the ranch. Travis Tritt was singing "Love of a Woman" on the classic country radio station and Blake kept time with his thumbs on the steering wheel.

Allie tapped her foot to the beat and was so wrapped up in her relief to get away from the store that she didn't realize they were at the Lucky Penny until Blake parked the truck and jogged around the front end to open the door for her.

She stepped out in four inches of snow that wasn't so pretty anymore with tire tracks zigzagging everywhere across it. Shooter bounded off the porch, his tail wagging as if it was a lovely spring day. A rabbit peeked out from behind a fence post and the dog went into instant point, quivering only slightly until the bunny bounded and the race was on.

"I vote that we build a snowman before we go inside to work," Blake said. "I don't know about you but the last time I built a snowman I was still a kid."

She pulled her gloves from her coat pocket. "We've had snow and ice and bad weather in this part of the state but the last time my sisters and I built a snowman was the year before I graduated high school. Fiona was still in junior high and I really thought I was too old to play in the snow."

"And today," Blake asked.

"You got a carrot for his nose?" She grinned.

"I sure do. Let's build him in the backyard. That way I can see him from the kitchen windows," Blake said.

The wet snow packed together beautifully. Soon she had a start the size of a basketball and she started rolling it on the ground. When it was big enough for a base she looked over her shoulder to see that Blake had already positioned the bottom of the snowman in the middle of the yard. From the size of what he'd made, her donation would be the mid-section.

Wiggling her shoulders to get the kinks out, she looked for him but he was nowhere. She hadn't heard the back door open or close so he wasn't in the house, but then she'd been thinking about burning bridges again. Suddenly two strong arms wrapped around her waist from behind. Shooter came out of nowhere and should've stopped quicker because when he threw his paws up on her chest, the momentum took all three of them to the ground.

Shooter popped up on his feet immediately, sent snow flying in an instant mini blizzard when he shook from head to toe, and then bounded off to chase after something else.

When the snow settled, Allie was on her side, pressed against Blake's long, muscular body, and his arms were tight around her. She reached up and brushed flakes from his thick eyelashes. The vibes between them were so strong that she wished she had fallen into bed with him instead of into a snowdrift up next to the house.

If that had happened would it satisfy the lust? She needed a little taste of what he had to offer to prove that all men were alike when they were stripped down, then she would be over this crazy schoolgirl infatuation that kept making her go all ga-ga when he was close. But Allie Logan had no idea how to initiate a booty call.

Blake pulled her even closer. "It makes for a cold bed but I like the way you fit into my arms."

"Me, too," she whispered. "But right now I feel a freezing mist starting to fall. If we're going to finish this old boy so he can get a coating of ice over him tonight, we'd best get on with it. You've got the bottom layer ready. I've made the middle. All we have to do is put them together and make him a head. Then it won't take long to put a hat and scarf on him and give him a face. And I'm talking too much again."

"Nervous?" He pulled her up with him when he sat up.

"Yes."

He tipped up her chin with his fist and kissed her. The heat when their lips met came close to melting all the snow in the whole state. His tongue teased its way into her mouth, creating bright sparkly things that floated around them in multi-colors like a fireworks display in July.

When he broke the kiss, she leaned against his shoulder, every nerve ending standing on edge, every hormone begging for more. She didn't care what common sense said, she wanted him to kiss her again.

"You don't ever have to be nervous around me, Allie," he whispered.

Then instantly he was on his feet with his hand extended

toward her. She put her glove in his and wasn't the least bit amazed at the effect even that much of a touch had on her.

"Let's get this snowman done so we can get inside before this misty freezing rain gets worse," he said.

The snowman was six feet tall and quite the cowboy with his red plaid scarf and old straw hat. He had a carrot for a nose and blackened wood chips for eyes and mouth, and mesquite limbs for arms. And a coating of freezing rain was already putting a shine on him when Allie and Blake hurried into the warm house.

The second the door shut behind Blake, he wrapped his arms around her and hugged her tightly to his chest. "I miss you so much when you aren't here every day," he whispered into her hair.

"Me, too," she said softly.

"I want more than friendship, Allie." His voice was hoarse with emotion.

"How much more?" She tilted her head back to see his face. His dark lashes fluttered and his mouth opened slightly. She tiptoed and moistened her dry lips with the tip of her tongue. His lips found hers in a hard, demanding kiss that made her knees go weak and all she could do was pant. Her arms snaked up around his neck and she arched her body against his so tightly that air couldn't find a way to get between them.

His eyes were closed as the kisses grew even hotter. His hands found her cheeks and gently held her face still as he made love to her mouth.

"Oh, my God!" she panted when he finally scooped her up in his arms. "I feel like my insides are a boiling pot of heat and desire."

His chuckle was as hoarse as if he was a lifetime smoker. "Is that a pickup line, Allie?"

"It's a fact. Where are you taking me?" she asked. "Please say it's to your bed because Shooter is on the sofa."

"Say no now if you are going to," he whispered.

"I couldn't say no even if I wanted to," she said softly.

Instead of turning into the room where his king-size mattress took up most of the floor he carried her into the bathroom and set her on the floor. "You are simply beautiful, Allie, and you deserve so much more than a slam-bam-thank-you-ma'am. We've got all afternoon so I want to make this last. First a nice warm bath together."

"Are you serious?" she asked.

He bent and captured her lips again. And this time it was a whole new experience, as if they'd never shared kisses before. Would it always be this hot and heavy or would it burn itself out after the first sex session?

"Are you telling me you are a bath virgin?" he asked.

"My name is Alora Raine Logan, and I'm a bath virgin. But I'm willing to give it up today, January fifteenth. Oh! Fifteen is my lucky number. This is good."

He set her down and removed her coat. "I'll be gentle."

She pushed the sleeves of his jacket down and threw it in the corner with her coat. "I might not be."

He pulled her to his chest again. Unfastening her shirt, one button at a time, he lingered over the exposed skin, kissing and tasting every inch as it was revealed. "You are so beautiful." He unfastened her jeans, slid them down along with her cotton underpants, and tossed them into the clothing pile.

She didn't argue because anything resembling words had suddenly left her brain. Her knees were weak when her bra flew through the air and landed near her jeans. He picked her up and carried her a few feet to an old ladder-back chair and sat down with her straddling his lap.

"Bath?" she gasped.

"Not yet. I need to touch you and feel all this glorious skin." His hands were everywhere, burning as they went and heating up every fiber of her being. She had no idea that foreplay could be this much fun.

"If it's going to be a bath for two, then I'll have to return the favor." She tugged his flannel shirt free from his jeans. Starting at the top, she popped all the snaps in one fell swoop and pushed it off his shoulders. When it joined the pile of clothing in the corner, she ran her fingertips through the soft dark hair on his chest, slowing down when she reached his taut nipples.

"You drive me crazy, Allie. I've wanted to touch you since the first time I laid eyes on you," he said.

"I thought I wasn't your type," she said.

"So did I but I was wrong."

She arched against him and groaned loudly. "I'm not so sure I can wait for a bath."

"Anything worth doing is worth doing right."

He stood her up on the bathroom floor and took her by the hand, led her to the tub, and turned on the water. "Put your hand down here and tell me when it's warm enough."

"Are you talking about water or something else?" She bent forward and he strung kisses from her neck, down her back, across her hips, and to her knees.

"And you called me wild?" He chuckled.

She stuck her hand under the running water. "You probably need to put ice in it."

"Oh, no, darlin'. I want you to be every bit as hot as you've made me. You are so beautiful that it flat out takes my breath away."

She didn't care if he'd used the same lines on thousands of women or if he'd gotten a bum rap when it came to his reputation and wasn't as wild as everyone said. She wanted to finish what they'd started.

"Do I really make you hot?" she asked.

He shucked out of his boots, socks, jeans, and underwear, and stood before her every bit as naked as she was. She gasped and moved closer to him, her hand reaching out to encircle an erection that was so ready it pulsated. "That's hotter than the water. It might make it boil when it gets into the bath."

"Oh, darlin', we might need that ice after all." He scooped her up and put her in the tub.

He crawled into the ancient old claw-foot tub with a sloped back, with her facing him, their legs touching.

"Don't ever get rid of this tub," she said.

"Don't intend to." He grinned.

She moved her foot slightly and found him still hard as steel, and using her foot to steady things, she softly massaged his erection with the toes of her other foot.

"Sweet Jesus, you're not a bathtub virgin at all," he said.

"Yes, I am. It must be some of the DNA from my Audrey's Place ancestors rising to the top, and I have to admit I like it," she whispered.

He picked up the sweet-smelling soap, lathered his hands, and then began giving her a bath with his bare hands as the water continued to fill the tub. She'd never known such raw nerve endings as when his slick, soapy hands caressed her breasts, her toes, and her inner thighs.

She flipped around until she was sitting in his lap, her arms around his neck, fingertips toying with his wet hair, and legs wrapped around his waist. Then she moved one hand down to turn off the water and the other one slipped between them to guide him into her.

"Are you sure?" he asked her. "We can wait for protection."

"That feels too wonderful to stop." She arched against him and brought his lips to hers, latching on to them in a hungry kiss. "Besides, I trust you. And I can't have children anyway."

She saw a cloud of sadness flash through his eyes and rolled her hips to keep him distracted. "Allie...God that feels good." He moaned and clasped her hips with his hands, his mouth seeking hers again.

They rocked together until she arched backward so far that her hair dragged into the water, and then an explosion like she'd never felt before consumed her body, leaving her limp. Satisfaction was instantaneous for both of them. He growled her name, all of it—Alora Raine—as he came into her.

She laid her head on his chest and melted against him. "That was wonderful."

"That was only the opening credits. Now we'll take this to the bedroom and have the full movie." He rose up from the water like a warlord of some ancient country, threw her over his shoulder, and carried her, soaking wet, to the bedroom where he kissed her butt before he flipped her on the mattress and dried her body with the top sheet.

"I'm ruining your bed." She tried to wiggle away.

"It's all washable." His mouth found hers again and the second round started with less foreplay and a lot more pure old wonderful, wild cowboy sex. She could hardly believe it when they both reached the edge of the cliff at the same time for the second time in an hour and dove into that gorgeous afterglow together. So much for a one-time satisfying of the itch she had for Blake Dawson. She hadn't even begun to scratch the surface of the yearning down deep in her body.

He rolled to the dry side of the king-size mattress and pulled the bedspread up over them. Holding her with one arm and stroking her face with the other, he said, "There are no words. Is this what you girls call afterglow?"

"So you were an afterglow virgin until now?"

"I guess I was," he answered.

"Me too." She yawned.

She awoke to the click of the clock as another minute passed. With a start, she sat straight up in bed, only to find herself alone. It was straight-up five o'clock. Had she dreamed the whole afternoon? If so, she didn't want to wake up.

"Hey," he said from the doorway. "We got so involved that I forgot to tell you that my brother, Toby, is on the way for a visit. He'll be here in half an hour."

"Oh my God, I had no idea we slept so long! I've got to go home." She was frantic. She didn't want to be there when his brother arrived, especially not with a smile that she couldn't wipe off with a dose of alum-laced lemonade.

"You don't have to." He wore his jeans but no shirt and held a brown robe in his hands. "I got it for Christmas and I promise it's never been on another woman."

"It'll have to wait. I really have to get dressed and go home." She hopped up from the bed and stood before him, comfortable in her nakedness. "And before you offer to drive me, I think it would be best if I walk. I need to have a reason for the blush on my face."

He opened his arms and she walked into them. "You are amazing as well as beautiful, Allie. Can you come back later and meet Toby? He's staying all weekend and I want him to meet you."

"Of course I want to meet him, but not right now," she said. "Bring him to church on Sunday. It will show the folks in Dry Creek that y'all ain't as wild and hot as they heard. I hope they don't ask me any questions. I'd hate to lie right there in the church house about how hot and wild you are," she said.

He laughed out loud. "Please let me take you home."

"No, sir. I meant it when I said that about this blush on my face. It screams sex and Lizzy will bitch until she runs out of breath. It's not that far and my knees aren't so weak that I can't climb a fence."

"I'll build a stile over it next week," he said.

"You will not! Everyone in town would talk about why. Besides as wonderful as this was, we both need to think about it, Blake. It might be smart for us to stop now before one of us kills the other one."

"What?" He frowned.

"A few more weeks of something that hot will set one or both of us on fire and all they'll find will be ashes and teeth," she said as she grinned.

CHAPTER EIGHTEEN

The Bent Spur, a cowboy bar that Toby and Blake found just over the border into Wilbarger County, Texas, was hopping that Friday night. The parking lot was full enough that they had to park Toby's truck at the outer edge and the music so loud that Blake felt the ground pulsating under his boots.

"We'll have to remember this place. I already like it," Toby yelled above the din when they pushed open the double door and joined the noisy crowd.

A tall blonde dressed in skintight jeans, a top that dipped low enough to reveal two inches of cleavage, and a provocative look in her eye quickly crossed the floor in a man-teasing wiggle and ran a hand down Toby's forearm. She looked up at him, batted her blue eyes, and smiled brightly.

"Hey, cowboy. Wanna dance?" she asked in a husky voice.

"Absolutely, sweet darlin', but let's get a beer first," Toby said.

The woman looped her arm in Toby's and wove her way through the line-dancing couples to the bar with Blake bringing up the rear right behind them. Toby ordered two beers and the woman asked for a double shot of Jack on the rocks.

"Hey, what are you doin' here?" Deke turned around on the bar stool.

"Toby, this is Deke. Deke, my brother Toby. And this is?" Blake nodded toward the blonde sitting beside him.

"This is Lisa," Deke said. "That would be her twin sister with the double shot of Jack sitting beside Toby there."

"Fine way to start the night," Toby said.

"Depends." Blake sipped his beer.

"You sick or something?" Toby asked.

Blake smiled and held up his beer in a toast. "Been workin' hard all week."

Toby frowned. "You've never been too tired to party after a week's work before."

The blonde wrapped her arms around Toby's neck. "Forgot to tell you my name and here you already bought me a drink. I'm Laney, darlin', and I understand that you are Toby. If you ain't the hottest thing I've ever seen. Come on and dance with me, cowboy."

Toby set his beer down on the bar, winked at Blake, and two-stepped across the floor with the woman who'd pressed her body so close to his that air would have had a hard time wiggling its way between them.

Conway Twitty's voice sang "I See the Want to in Your Eyes." When Twitty mentioned that he saw the sparkling little diamond on her hand, Blake instinctively looked for a ring on Laney's finger.

"Neither of them are married," Deke said. "Hey, girl, this here old cowboy's feet are aching to dance." He held out his hand to Lisa, she threw back the rest of her drink, and they disappeared in the crowd of dancing folks.

A short redhead popped her butt on the bar stool Lisa had vacated and smiled at Blake. "You must like Conway."

"What makes you think that?"

"You're keeping time with your thumb on your beer glass."

"I do like him." Blake nodded. The lady was a cute little thing and her eyes said that she was interested, but something wasn't clicking.

She leaned closer to him and touched his cheek with her fingertips. "Well, darlin', so do I and for the next half hour that's what we're going to hear because I plugged a bunch of money into the jukebox. Buy me a drink to celebrate our mutual love of Mr. Twitty?"

Blake held up a hand and the bartender quickly made his way to that end of the bar. "This Conway-lovin' lady would like a drink."

"Long-neck Coors, in the bottle," she said.

Blake laid a bill on the bar and pointed to his glass. "Refill, please, of the same."

"I'm Kayla. Thanks for the drink. You could ask me to dance," she said.

"Got two left feet," Blake said. What was the matter with him? He should be already on the dance floor with Kayla wrapped around him like a pet python.

She took his hand and tugged at it. "I don't believe you."

"Don't say you wasn't warned." He took another sip of his beer and let her lead him out onto the dance floor.

She melted into his arms as the jukebox played "Rest Your Love on Me."

She rose on her toes and breathed into his ear. "Like the words of the song says, I'd like to put my worries in your pocket and rest my love on you all night. I see some sadness in those green eyes, cowboy. Let me make you happy tonight."

"I bet you tell all the old ugly cowboys that," he said.

"Darlin', whoever told you that you are ugly has shit for brains." She laughed. "You didn't tell me your name."

"Blake Dawson."

"Blake and Kayla. Goes together real good, at least for one night."

A tall brunette moved into Kayla's place and looped her arms around his neck when that song ended and Conway started singing "House on Old Lonesome Road."

"It's my birthday and my friends dared me to come over and dance with you," she whispered. "I have a boyfriend at home."

He twirled her out and brought her back to him and even dipped her at the end of the dance. "Happy birthday, darlin'. Your boyfriend is one lucky feller."

Blake made his way to the men's room where he checked his reflection in the mirror. It was the same face that he shaved every morning, same dark hair, and same green eyes, so why in the hell wasn't he having a good time. He felt his forehead. No fever so he wasn't sick.

Singing, "I May Never Get to Heaven," Conway's voice came through the speaker above his head. The lyrics said that he might never get to heaven but he once came mighty close. Blake shut his eyes and visualized Allie lying next to him on the mattress/bed. Could that have really only been a few hours ago? It seemed like nothing more than a dream or a little taste of what Conway was singing about. Any of the women he'd met that evening would give him a good time, but all he wanted was to go home to Allie.

"Where you been?" Deke motioned him to the end of the

bar and pointed at the empty seat on the other side of Toby when he returned to the bar. "Me and Toby been havin' us a good time."

Six weeks ago, he would have been in heaven, but that night, even with the toe-stomping line dancing, he felt as out of place as a hooker on the front row of a tent revival. Then of all things that Mama Fate could throw at him, Blake Shelton started singing "Home."

Blake fished his phone out of his back pocket even though it hadn't vibrated or rang. "Excuse me. I have to take this, so I'll step outside."

He sucked in the cold, clean night air and leaned against the porch post. The lyrics of the song said that he felt like he was living someone else's life, that another day had come and gone and he wanted to go home. He talked about being surrounded by a million people and yet he felt all alone.

What in the hell was wrong with him? He should be in there flirting with all the women, making passes at the ones who were across the room with another cowboy, and picking out the three he would choose among. The lucky one would go home with him. He didn't usually run from women and yet there he was thinking of going home without even a telephone number.

And why did every damn song remind him of Allie in some way?

Another song started but the last one about going home was stuck in his mind so strongly that he couldn't hear anything else. He wanted to be home with Shooter, maybe working alongside Allie. Hell, pulling nails out of the ceiling made him happier than he was right now.

"Shit," he muttered. "I've turned into the designated driver."

Toby poked his head out the door and asked, "Something wrong? The redhead said you got an important call."

"Nothing's wrong." He paused. "Actually, everything's wrong. Think you could catch a ride home with Deke? I'm just gonna head home," Blake said.

"Sure thing. I know he won't mind. We might even leave here and go find a quieter place with Lisa and Laney," Toby said.

"Have fun," Blake said. "See you at home. Keep in mind that you're sleeping on the couch."

"I don't mind stackin'." Toby laughed.

It wasn't fair.

Lizzy had flat out sabotaged Allie and she was miserable as hell sitting in the living room watching a damn old boring movie with Grady and Mitch, but there wasn't anything she could do to get out of it. And it was Friday night! She could be at Frankie's with Deke and Blake like last week.

As luck would have it, Granny had even turned in early and wasn't wandering through the room. She'd tried to get her mother to stick around and watch the movie with them but oh, no, she went to bed with a book. So now Allie was stuck on the sofa with Grady's arm around her.

She made an excuse to go to the bathroom and slid down the back of the door, sitting on the floor with her knees up and her face buried in her hands. Three hours earlier she'd been sleeping in Blake's arms with the most beautiful afterglow in the whole damn world surrounding them.

"You okay in there?" Lizzy asked from the other side of the door.

"No, I think I'm getting that bug you had," Allie said.

"Well, crap! And you and Grady were having such a good time. I guess you'd best go on up to your room so you don't give it to him and Mitch," Lizzy said. "I should've known you were catchin' it when you came in from the

Lucky Penny with scarlet cheeks. I'll tell Grady. He'll be disappointed."

"Sorry," Allie lied.

She waited to stand up and sneak up the stairs to her room until she could hear the drone of Lizzy's voice in the living room. Once inside her room she couldn't sit still. Pacing from one side to the other, she wondered what Blake was doing right then. Were he and Toby watching some old western movie and drinking beer? Was Shooter as glad to see Toby as he was to see her nearly every day lately? Or were they all three out with a flashlight showing Toby all the work that Blake had gotten done the past few weeks?

She turned on the radio to the classic country music station and curled up in the old overstuffed rocking chair in the corner, slinging her legs over the arm. Granny had rocked her to sleep in this same chair when she was a little girl and it always brought her comfort to sit in it, but not that night. She went to the window, pulled back the curtain, and looked outside and then picked up a book from her nightstand. It didn't interest her so she put it back.

The DJ announced that the next hour would be a tribute to Alan Jackson and if anyone had requests to call in. Then he started playing, "Small Town Southern Man."

She couldn't listen to the song because it was too sad in light of how badly she wanted Blake Dawson to be that small-town Southern man who'd be content with a wife and small-town living. She turned the radio off and hit the POWER button on the television remote.

"Well, shit!" she mumbled as Alan Jackson's video for the same song showed up on CMT. "Evidently, I'm supposed to listen to this."

Tears rolled down her cheeks as she watched the video from beginning to end. She wanted what those two people had in the video portraying their lives from the time they danced together the first time until the day that death came calling for the small-town Southern man.

She wondered if Blake Dawson could ever be tamed into a man who'd only love one woman. And if he could, would she ever trust him? It seemed as if everywhere she looked these days, someone was cheating on the person they'd vowed to love forever.

The next video was Blake Shelton's "Goodbye Time." Every single word scared the crap out of her. She had to see Blake tomorrow, to explain that the sex they'd had could never happen again because she couldn't bear to spend years with him only to wake up one day and have him tell her that the feeling was gone.

Someday when she was an old woman with gray hair, sitting on the porch and watching the seasons come and go, she would remember this beautiful day when a man made her experience that wonderful thing called afterglow. She'd smile and hold it close to her heart and be grateful that it was untarnished and beautiful.

She fell asleep in the chair as Miranda Lambert sang, "The House That Built Me." Her last thought as her eyes drooped was that Audrey's Place had built her and it was where she belonged...forever.

CHAPTER NINETEEN

Blake awoke to the sounds of giggling women in the living room on Saturday morning. Two weeks ago he hadn't even known Allie Logan and he'd been dreaming of her when the sound of women awoke him. He reached for her in that drowsy moment before sweet dreams become cold reality. All he got was a handful of pillow.

The laughing turned into conversation and he heard his brother's name and then Deke's mentioned. Surely they hadn't brought those two sisters both back to the Lucky Penny.

He sat up so quickly that the room did a couple of spins before it came to a stop. "Dammit! I didn't drink that much." He reached for his jeans and tugged them up over his naked body.

Two women were in the living room giggling about how much fun they'd had the night before. Toby was singing in the bathroom—an old tune called "I Always Get Lucky with

You" at the top of his lungs—off key and out of tune but with the gusto of a drunken cowboy. He raised his hand to knock on the door and Toby slung it open. Wearing nothing but a towel around his waist and a smile, he winked at Blake, stood to one side, and motioned him inside.

"You missed a damn good time," he whispered.

"It sounds like it." Blake took a long time washing his hands and combing back his dark hair, hoping the whole time that the women would be gone when he finally went to the living room.

No such luck.

The aroma of coffee, frying bacon, and sausage floated down the hallway and with it came feminine voices. Toby was making his famous morning-after breakfast for the ladies. Blake stopped by his room long enough to pull an oatmeal-colored thermal shirt over his head and put on a pair of thick socks. He was hungry and Toby made a mean skillet of sausage gravy, and his biscuits were every bit as light as his granny's.

"Where's Deke?" he asked as he headed for the coffeepot.

Laney pressed her body against his side. "Too weak to crawl out of bed. We could take our breakfast to your bedroom."

"I'm sorry I forgot y'all's name." Blake yawned.

Laney laid a hand over her heart and then wiped at an imaginary tear. "Well, if that ain't a slap right in the face."

The other one patted him on the shoulder. "I'm Lisa, darlin', and this one who brought Deke to his knees last night is my sister, Laney. But now that Deke's out of commission for a while..." She raised an eyebrow suggestively.

"Thanks, but no thanks. I'm only here for the morning-after food," he answered.

"I told you." Toby grinned. "He's got bit by the love bug."

"I betcha a little lust bug could knock that shit out of your head, darlin'." Laney ran a hand down his back and squeezed his butt cheek firmly. "Well, I do believe this cowboy is going commando this morning. I don't feel anything but jeans and good tight ass."

Blake stepped away from her, filled a cup with steaming hot coffee, and sat down at the end of the table. "Like I said, no thanks, Miz Laney."

"Well, I know when I'm defeated but if you ever change your mind, my number is on that old calendar over there."

A loud clap of thunder awoke Allie with a start. She grabbed a pillow and crammed it over her head, but the next lightning flash only heralded a rolling thunder that sounded as if it was dumping a load of potatoes on top of Audrey's Place. Her phone rang right at the end of the noise. She pushed back the covers and threw the pillow in the direction of the rocking chair.

"Why in the hell are you calling me?" Allie growled into the phone.

"Good morning, sunshine." Lizzy laughed. "Breakfast is ready and I don't want to eat alone and I didn't want to come back upstairs. Mama and Granny have already left for the store. Crawl out and come on down here. I made crunchy French toast."

Allie's stomach growled. "I'm on the way."

The sun peeked from behind a bank of dark, fast-moving clouds, sending a few rays through the glass in the front door. Allie stopped long enough to stretch and feel the warmth on the foyer floor against her bare feet.

Lizzy stuck her head out of the kitchen. "Your toast is getting cold while you play in the sun. Weatherman says we've got more bad weather on the way later this afternoon.

Be glad you are at least working inside over there at that abominable place."

So much for hoping that Lizzy was ready to bury the hatchet. She had an agenda up her sleeve, and that was the reason she'd made Allie's favorite food. Suddenly, her favorite breakfast didn't sound so good after all.

Lizzy did give her time to sit down and at least get the first bite in her mouth before she pulled out a chair across the table from her, sucked up enough air to deliver a Sunday-morning sermon, and started talking. "I knew you weren't sick. You flat out lied to get out of spending time with Grady. And all for nothing because I've already heard the gossip this morning, and your little Lucky Penny bubble is about to bust wide open."

"What in the devil are you talking about?" Allie asked.

"Blake's brother arrived last night and the two of them and Deke went bar hopping up near Wichita Falls. Deke brought a tall blond hussy home with him. I did have such hopes for him turning his life around when he started coming to church pretty regular, but now that the infamous wild Dawson has become his new best friend, I swear, he's on a joy ride straight to hell," Lizzy said.

"Are we being judgmental this morning?" Allie was sure glad the gossips hadn't been hiding outside the window when she and Blake had been tangled up in his sheets.

"I'm stating pure facts and I'm tellin' you that..."

"What if I told you I spent yesterday afternoon having hot pig sex with Blake Dawson?" Allie asked.

Lizzy slapped the table hard enough that her coffee sloshed out. "Now look what you made me do. Sometimes, you make me so mad I could shake you, Alora Raine."

Allie shrugged. "It's a sister thing or maybe it's a middle-child thing. Do you think maybe you should see a therapist for your control issues?"

Lizzy jumped to her feet and grabbed a fistful of paper towels. "It's not a middle-child thing. Fiona doesn't make me as mad as you do. There's no way you really slept with Blake Dawson. One, you're too smart to do something that crazy, and two, he's a one-night-stand kind of guy. You're not wild enough to be his type."

"Deke says the same thing, so I guess if Lucifer's protégé and God's right arm say it's so, then it must be true." She continued eating her breakfast but down deep she wondered if Toby and Blake had brought home women from the bar, too.

"Go on and ruin your life again," Lizzy huffed. "I'm trying to warn you, but I can only be the watchman. I can sit in the tower and tell you what I see coming, but I can't make you steer clear of it."

Allie picked up her empty plate and headed to the sink with it. "Well, sister, you enjoy the view from your tower. I'm heading over to that abominable place to paint. See you at supper."

* * *

Allie parked beside a truck but didn't pay a lot of attention to it, figuring it was Toby's. A streak of lightning so close that the air crackled sent her running to the porch. She slipped inside the front door to the sounds of people talking in the kitchen. She quickly removed her yellow slicker, hung it on the coatrack, and replaced her rubber boots with her work boots.

Shooter hopped off the sofa. Tangled sheets and a blanket gave testimony that Toby hadn't gone back to Muenster early that morning and was one of the voices in the kitchen. She thought that she recognized the other voice as Deke's. She didn't really care how much testosterone was sitting around the table; she only wanted a cup of hot coffee to wrap her hands around before she started to work in Blake's bedroom. She intended to have the walls and trim painted today. The doors would have to wait until Monday, but by the middle of next week her goal was to have that room completely done and the living room and hall ceilings ready to texture. Then she and Blake would really have something to celebrate.

Her line of thinking stopped abruptly when she walked into the kitchen and saw the man at the stove had a woman draped around him like a snake, one hand on his butt, the other pressed against his chest as she kissed him.

Allie whipped around, feeling a blush burning her cheeks, only to see Blake sitting at the table with another blonde who looked almost identical to the one plastered against the man she could only assume was Blake's brother, Toby. She risked another quick glance and saw that Toby had the same face shape, hair color, and smile as Blake, but his eyes were blue and he had a faint white scar across one cheek.

"Where's Deke?" she asked, her brows furrowing into a single line.

"At home, I guess." Blake quickly pushed back his chair and stood up. "Allie, I didn't know you were coming to work today."

"Evidently not," she said. "I'll get a cup of coffee and go on to the bedroom to work. Y'all don't let me interrupt."

Her work boots sounded like shotgun blasts with every step as she crossed the kitchen, poured a cup of coffee, and carried it down the hallway. She shut Blake's bedroom door behind her and sat down on the dirty carpet with a thud, hot coffee sloshing out. Her hands shook so badly that she finally set the cup down and put her head in her hands.

"Allie? Can I come in please? We need to talk." Blake said from the other side of the door.

"It's your house," she said.

He slipped into the room, shut the door behind him, and sat down in front of her, keeping a foot of space between them. Before he could say a word, another knock on the door startled both of them. "Hey, is Walter hiding in there? I've got a sweet little lady out here hunting for him. I told her we don't have a Walter here, but she doesn't believe me."

Blake rolled up on his feet and offered her his hand. "What you saw wasn't what was happening."

She ignored the hand and got up on her own, leaving the coffee behind.

Irene slung the door wide open and marched inside with her hands on her hips. A pair of Lizzy's designer jeans hung on her skinny hips and the red-sequined top that Allie wore to the church Christmas party a few weeks before had slipped off one shoulder, letting a white bra strap shine right along with her veined skin. Her thin gray hair hung in wet strands and the makeup she'd applied streaked down her face settling in the wrinkles. The jeans were soaked as well as the sequined top and her poor frail body had a faint blue cast from the cold wind and rain.

"What in the hell are you doing with another woman in this house, Walter? Three of them to be exact and those two in the kitchen are barroom Rosies if I've ever seen one. This one might look decent but she's in your bedroom behind closed doors and where is the furniture?" Irene stopped for a breath and slapped Blake on the arm. "You've got some explainin' to do. I swear to God, I don't know why I even bother with you. It's a wonder your mother hasn't taken a fryin' pan to those bitches."

Toby cocked his head to one side just like Allie had seen Blake do when he found something amusing. Well, her grandmother was not funny, and the disease that was eating holes in her memory wasn't a bit comical.

"Breakfast is served. Laney and Lisa are already digging in. There's plenty for all y'all," Toby said.

"Is this one of your lazy-ass brothers? Where is your mother?" Irene demanded.

"Granny, this is not Walter. It's Blake Dawson and his brother, Toby Dawson. I'm Allie, your granddaughter, and those women in the kitchen are not here to see Walter," Allie said.

"I'm ready to go home now. I'm cold and I'm hungry." She looped her arm through Allie's and marched past Toby, with Blake right behind them. They'd barely made it to the living room when Katy knocked softly on the door, pushed it open, and sighed.

"I figured I'd find you over here. Good God, Mama! If you don't get pneumonia from getting out in that getup, it'll be a miracle. I'm surprised you didn't fall and break a hip on the ice." She grabbed Allie's yellow slicker from the coatrack and slung it around Irene's shoulders.

"Allie was in the bedroom with that man," Irene tattled. "And I'm not old. I can damn well climb over a fence any old day of the week and the ice broke when I stepped on it so stop your bitchin'."

"It's the room I'm working on," Allie explained.

"Introductions?" Toby asked.

"Sorry." Blake grinned sheepishly. "This is Allie, the

woman who's redoing the house and who put the roof on for us. This is Katy, her mother, and this is Irene, her grandmother. Ladies, this is Toby, my brother and business partner in the Lucky Penny."

So she wasn't his friend Allie, or his neighbor Allie. Heaven forbid that she might be his girlfriend Allie. Hell, no! She was the woman who was redoing his house. Lizzy had been right all along. She didn't have enough sense to know not to wade right into hell.

Toby kissed Irene's hand, shook hands with Katy and with Allie, and said, "I'm right pleased to make your acquaintance, ladies."

Irene's eyes started at Toby's toes and traveled slowly up his long legs to his zipper, hesitated a brief second, and went on up to the top of his head. "Are you kin to Blake?"

"Yes, ma'am. He's my brother, and I'll be moving into the house with him in a couple of months," Toby answered.

"Who are them cheap barroom Rosies in the kitchen?" she asked.

"Just a couple of women who followed me and Deke home last night," Toby said.

"Like a couple of dogs in heat, I suppose," Irene said.

Toby chuckled. "Don't let them hear you say that."

"I'll say whatever the hell I want. Truth is truth, don't matter if you pour chocolate syrup or cover it up with fresh cow shit, it's still the truth."

"Lord, help us all," Katy moaned. "Allie, you'll have to stay home with her today. You know how she gets after she runs off and comes over here. I can't manage her at the store, and Lizzy sure can't keep an eye on her on a Saturday at the feed store. That's her busiest day."

"I thought she was with you at the store. Lizzy said you'd taken her," Allie said.

Katy shook her head. "I did but she stole my car keys, slipped out the back door, went home and obviously changed her clothes, and here she is. I had to get Nadine to loan me her van to come get her. The car is parked at home. You can come get me at five."

"I'll be there," Allie nodded. "Go on back to the store. I'll take her home and get her warmed up."

"We need to talk," Blake whispered.

"Nothing to talk about." Allie took off her work boots and slipped her feet back down into the rubber boots.

"Later."

"Probably not," she said.

He pulled a heavy jacket from the rack and held it out to her. "I tell you, it's not what it looked like. Take my coat. You can't go out there without something to keep you warm. That rain is cold."

She shook her head. "I come from sturdy stock. I'm not sugar or salt, so I don't melt in cold rain. See you in church tomorrow."

"And you and your brother are welcome to come home with us for lunch," Katy said as she escorted Irene out onto the porch. "I won't take no for an answer."

"We'd love to have Sunday dinner with y'all," Toby said.

"Tell Deke, too," Katy threw over her shoulder.

"You sure you want to do that?" Allie asked Blake.

"Wouldn't miss it for the world, would we, Toby?" Blake said. He turned to his brother. "Now can you please get rid of yours and Deke's women so we can take a drive around the ranch? It might be sleeting, but you can still see what I've gotten done around here." Blake talked to Toby but most of it was for Allie's ears.

"Lookin' forward to it, ma'am." Toby nodded toward Allie.

Blake laid a hand on her shoulder. "I did not..." he started.

She shrugged it off.

"I don't care." She closed the door behind her.

CHAPTER TWENTY

Is that the woman that's got your heart in a twist?" Toby asked.

"What makes you think that?" Blake asked.

"You've got that look in your eyes."

Blake shrugged.

A lot of good it would do him if he did fall in love with Allie. She'd declared that she didn't care. Just when he was contemplating hanging up his wild ways and entering into a serious relationship with a decent woman, she said that she didn't care. Blake Dawson, the player, had been played.

"What's on your mind, big brother?" Toby asked. "What happened in that bedroom?"

Blake shook his head. "I'm not totally sure, but I believe the tables got turned on me and it's one strange feeling. I don't want to talk about it right now. We don't have time for women."

"Except for Laneys and Lisas, right?"

"Not even for that if we're going to get this place in shape in four years like we said we'd do," Blake said.

Toby headed for the kitchen. "Man, I'm not goin' celibate for four years, not for this ranch, not for you, and not even for God. And you ain't, either, because when you go a month without a woman you get cranky as hell."

"Who's goin' a month without a woman?" Lisa asked. "We've been poutin' because y'all weren't here to share this breakfast with us and now it's time for us to go. We've both got appointments at eleven in Wichita Falls and the roads are probably getting icy. But don't pout, darlin's, we'll be in touch. You can't get rid of us. We know where you live."

Laney wrapped her arms around Blake's neck and laid her head on his chest. "Next time, darlin', I'll prove that lust can get rid of that love bug faster than hittin' delete on the computer. You boys stay ready and maybe we'll see you at the bar in a couple of weeks."

Lisa tiptoed and kissed Toby on the cheek. "It was fun. It was real. It was real fun, but next time, talk your brother into joining us."

"I'm not into the kinky stuff." Toby chuckled.

"Then we'll get Laney to join the party and call it an orgy, not a threesome," Lisa said huskily. "Mmmm, thinkin' about that makes me go all soft and mushy inside."

"We could invite Deke if we're having an orgy," Laney said.

"Dammit!" Blake doubled up his fist and hit his palm with it as soon as the women were gone. "I don't want those two comin' around here. I'm trying to build a relationship with the community, not start a whorehouse."

Toby laid a hand on Blake's shoulder. "Amen to that and I won't let it happen again. I had too many beers and wasn't thinkin' straight. Let's go eat breakfast if those two women left anything for us. And then we'll take a look at what you've done. I'd planned on helping you clear off some mesquite or repair fence but it's rainin'. I guess we could tear down the ceilings in the hall and living room," Toby said.

"And put up the new," Blake said. "Even if my carpenter doesn't come back, that would be a start. You any good at bedding and taping?"

"I got the bedding part down real good but like I said, I'm not into the kinky shit. Why wouldn't Allie come back?"

"I'm not sayin' another word except to say that you have not lost your touch with these biscuits, brother," Blake said.

Lizzy met her mother, grandmother, and sister at the door. She clucked her tongue like an old hen or an old woman when she saw her grandmother wearing jeans and a sparkly top, with a yellow rain slicker flopping open with every step. "I'm not even going to ask. I'm going to work and we'll talk about it this evening."

Katy glanced nervously toward Allie. "Store should have opened thirty minutes ago. If I don't get down there, the gossip will be flyin' over town like Santa Claus at Christmas."

"I've got it. Both of you get going. I'll get her dry and fed, then I'll watch her like a hawk. It's not my day to clean, but I'll take care of the house cleaning for you, Mama," Allie shooed them both out the door.

Lord only knew, she needed something to keep her mind occupied that day or she'd go crazy. She'd never known such acute jealousy as she did when she saw that two-bit, brazen blond hussy who looked like she was about to kiss Blake. She hadn't even been that angry when Riley came home and told her that he was in love with another woman.

"My tits are frozen," Granny said. "Help me get out of

these hooker clothes and into a warm shower. Why'd you tell me to wear this shit anyway? You know I'm old."

Allie pulled the ruined sequin top up over her grand-mother's head and marched her to the shower. When she was tugging the jeans down from her granny's hips, she realized the old girl had on two different shoes. One was a brown sneaker that belonged to Katy. It was laced properly and tied in a perfect little bow. The other was a lovely black-velvet flat that Lizzy kept for special occasions. Lizzy would gripe for days, but there was nothing to do but toss them in the trash now because they were ruined.

"Granny, where did you find this shoe?" Allie asked.

"Me? You're the one who put me in that ridiculous outfit and then let me go out in the weather so don't ask dumb questions. I've got more sense than to pick out shit like that," Irene fussed. "I can take off my own underpants and bra. You put a towel on the vanity and when my bones are warm, I'll come out and get dressed."

Allie sighed. "How about a nice warm sweat suit, too?"

"Okay but don't you give me none of that stuff that looks like hooker clothes. I keep telling you, I'm not Audrey."

"Yes, ma'am," Allie said with a nod.

She laid the clothing out and then sat down in the rocking chair beside the window in her grandmother's room. She could hear her grandmother singing something about the love of her life. Allie wondered if it was something she made up or if the song had been popular back in her younger life.

Leaning her head back staring at the ceiling she replayed that introduction. She was the carpenter, nothing more or less. Blake didn't throw an arm around her shoulder or even wink when he said that. The moment had brought the truth to the surface. She was nothing more than another notch on his bedpost.

The headache started with a jabbing pain in her right temple and traveled across her forehead around to the back of her skull. She shut her eyes and put her hand over them to keep out the light. She didn't even try to open them when she heard the shower stop or when her grandmother grumbled about the ugly pink sweat suit that was laid out for her.

She did open them when her granny kicked the rung of the rocker. "What the hell's wrong with you? Surely you haven't let that boy next door get in your pants and give you a guilty headache. If you have, I hope to hell you used protection because your mama will crap little green apples if you get pregnant."

"Granny, come sit down at the vanity and let me blow-dry your hair and curl it for you. It looks pitiful," Allie said.

Irene clapped her hands. "And my fingernails and toenails, too. Let's have a beauty shop day. I could trim your hair and put it up in sponge rollers."

Allie wouldn't let her grandmother near her hair with a pair of fingernail clippers much less scissors, and she doubted if there were any sponge rollers left in the house. It had been years since she'd seen even a stray one.

"Let's do you all up pretty first and then we'll talk about my hair and nails. It might be time for dinner by then, and I was thinkin' about chocolate chip pancakes." Allie evaded the idea with expert precision.

Irene clapped louder. "I like it when you stay home with me, Allie. You know I can't remember too good these days. Sometimes whole days get away from me."

Allie gave her a hug. "You smell like baby powder."

"It's a nice clean scent that goes well with any perfume," Irene said seriously. "I bet I've told you that a hundred times."

Allie led her to the vanity and set her on the cute little

brass stool with a pink velvet pillow. "Yes, you have, but it takes a lot of tellin' for me to remember. Now, while I do your hair, you can tell me stories about when you were a little girl."

Irene prattled on, telling tales of her childhood that Allie had heard dozens if not hundreds of times. Letting her own mind wander while she curled her grandmother's thin gray hair and did her nails in the bright pink nail polish that she liked, she kept going over and over the details of that morning. Did she miss a sly wink? She slowed the events down and could honestly say that he had not even looked her way when he introduced her as the woman who'd been working on his house.

"And then you grew up and married that sumbitch." Granny's final words brought her back into the present.

"Yes, I did," Allie said, and her phone rang.

Granny stuck out her lower lip in a pout. "This is supposed to be our day. Don't you dare invite that boy from next door over here. He'll get in our way and ruin everything."

Allie checked the ID hoping it was Blake, but no such luck. "It's Fiona, Granny, not Blake."

"Give me that phone." The older woman jerked it out of her hand. "Fiona, Allie did my hair and my nails and I'm all pretty for you to come home this weekend. Are you on the way? I miss you so much. When was the last time you came home? It's been five years hasn't it?"

A pause and Irene set her mouth in a firm line. "Bullshit! You were not home at Thanksgiving. I might be old, but I ain't stupid. I know... who in the hell is this? I don't want any magazines so stop calling here."

And like that, in the blink of an eye, Irene was off in another time warp. "Take this phone and tell those people that I'm sick to death of them buggin' the shit out of me about magazines. And they are not getting my credit card number, either."

"Fiona?" Allie said. "Are you still there?"

"Mama called and told me about Granny running off again this morning. I bet she was a sight in that getup. And she said that Blake looks at you like he could eat you up, her words, not mine. And that she invited him to dinner tomorrow after church so she could see y'all together. She's worried about all this, Allie," Fiona said.

Allie had forgotten about dinner the next day. She couldn't face Blake that soon. She would plead a headache, which might not be a lie the way it was pounding right then, and stay home from church. As soon as the family left, she would run away to Deke's and stay there all day.

Fiona raised her voice. "Are you still there? You didn't hang up on me, did you?"

That's when Allie heard the cling of a cash register in the background and lots of people talking at once. Fiona worked in a prestigious law firm in Houston, so why were there noises like a fast food place in the background?

"Where are you?" Allie asked.

"At work," Fiona said quickly. "Well, not actually at work. I'm at a coffee shop right next door getting a mid-morning cup of coffee."

Allie tried to blink away the headache, but it didn't work. "I thought I heard cash register noises."

"Got to go. Just wanted to let you know that Mama is watching you close. See you at the wedding this spring," Fiona said.

Allie hit the END button and shoved her phone back into her pocket. She heard a soft snore, more like a kitten's purr, and turned to find Irene curled up on her bed in a ball, sound asleep. Figuring it was a fine time to straighten her grandmother's room and keep an eye on her at the same time, Allie, hurried off to the utility room for her basket of cleaners.

"Poor old darlin'," she mumbled, "it has to be hard on her doing all that time travel. I can not imagine living in so many worlds every day."

She'd finished cleaning the bathroom and had started dusting all the empty perfume bottles on Irene's dresser, when her phone rang a second time that morning. Expecting it to be Lizzy after she got the gossip of two women keeping three men company the night before, she was surprised to see Blake's number flashing on the screen.

"Hello," she answered cautiously. "If you're calling about the bedroom, I told you in the beginning that I'd have to take days off for family pretty often."

"We're going to take down the ceiling in the hall and living room and put up the new drywall. I'm not getting into the bedding and taping, though. We figure we can do this much and come Monday it will be ready for you. Deke is coming over soon as he gets his chores done to help us, too. But that's not why I'm calling. We need to talk, Allie."

"You're coming to Sunday dinner. We'll talk then." She picked up a tarnished silver hairbrush and dusted under it.

"Are we still on for a celebration when you finish the bedroom?"

She had to scramble to hold on to the phone and the brush at the same time. "I have no idea. Wouldn't you much rather go to a bar and pick up a bimbo and have dinner with her, rather than the woman who is working on your house?"

"What are you so mad about? It's me who has the right to be mad since you said you didn't care. What am I, Allie? A notch on your bedpost?" His tone turned edgy.

She shut her eyes against the headache that threatened. "I'm not fighting with you on the phone, Blake Dawson."

"Then I'll come over there and we can fight in person."

She didn't want to see him or talk to him, on the phone or in person, until the steam stopped pouring out of her ears. He'd accused her of being nothing more than one of those bar bitches who'd go to bed with anything that had a penis. Notch on her bedpost, indeed! If they compared, hers would have two notches where his would look like a carved-up totem pole.

"I think we'd both best cool off before we see each other," she said tersely.

"Maybe so. I'll see you in church," he said, and the phone went dark.

CHAPTER TWENTY-ONE

Allie woke up with the determination that she would not go to church and she would not have Sunday dinner with her family. She planned a shopping trip to Wichita Falls where she would check out all the after-holiday sales and maybe take in an afternoon matinee.

She went through six outfits that morning before finally settling on a long straight skirt in brown and beige chevron stripes and a sweater the same color as her eyes. She curled her hair and applied makeup, glanced at herself in the mirror, and decided she was entirely too bland. She traipsed across the landing to Fiona's room and rifled through the accessories she'd left in her closet. She tried on a pretty scarf but the damn thing choked her. Finally, she settled on a heavy gold necklace with a set of crossed pistols, covered with sparkling fake diamonds.

"Making a statement, are you?" Lizzy said from the doorway.

"Dressing up a ho-hum look," Allie answered.

Lizzy's smile was actually sweet that morning. "I hope you've finally seen the light and those pistols are a sign that you're ready to shoot the cowboy next door."

Allie whipped around so fast that she dropped the scarf she'd tried on. "Why would you say that?"

Lizzy hugged Allie. "I heard about what happened yesterday morning and I was right. Blake was just leading you on."

Allie changed the subject. "You look pretty this morning. Red has always been your color."

Lizzy smoothed the front of the red sweater dress. "I came to borrow a scarf from Fiona to dress down all this red. It's kind of loud for a preacher's wife, don't you think?"

Allie brushed past her on the way out of the room. "You already toned it down with those black leggings and boots. If you really wanted to look like a hussy, you could have worn fishnet hose and spike heels. And you'd better remember to put whatever you borrow right back where it was. I'm pretty sure that Fiona takes inventory every time she comes home."

"How we could all three have the same parents is a complete mystery," Lizzy said. "Oh, yeah, I invited Grady and Mitch to Sunday dinner. Mama said she's invited the neighbors. I figure it will be a good time for you to see the difference between a man of God and a wild cowboy."

Allie bit her lip to keep from smarting off, but she did touch the pistols and wish for one second that they fired real bullets and that God would look the other way. If she didn't go to church, Blake would think she was running from him. If she did go, she'd have to endure the business of talking to him as well as Grady. Lord, why did life have to be so complicated?

She still hadn't made up her mind what she was going to do when she reached the foyer. Granny sat ramrod straight in the chair beside the foyer table. She was dressed in a cute little navy blue pantsuit and her shoes matched. Her hair was combed back in waves and her lipstick had settled into the wrinkles around her mouth.

"I don't want to go to church," she whispered.

"Me, either. Let's run away," Allie said softly.

"We can't. We are strong women and we don't run from our problems," Granny said.

"What is your problem?" Allie asked.

"I forget where the bathroom is, but I can depend on you to remember, can't I?"

Allie sighed. "Yes, Granny, I will sit beside you and remember for you."

Snowflakes drifted to land among a few dead leaves, blown in from the scrub oak trees across the street from the church that morning. Would winter never end? Allie was so ready for spring, for the sound of birds chirping instead of sleet pounding on the metal house roof, to sit on the porch swing in the evening instead of having to be inside all the time.

Allie, her mother, and grandmother had all gone together in Katy's vehicle. Lizzy had tried her best to fix it so that Allie would ride in the backseat with Grady in Mitch's truck, but Allie had sidestepped the issue by saying that she'd help with Granny.

When they reached the church, Allie manipulated it so that she sat on the end of the pew next to her grandmother. Katy was next in line and then Lizzy with Mitch beside her and Grady on the far end. Lizzy didn't spare a bit on the dirty looks, but Allie could endure those if she didn't have to sit beside Grady.

She glanced over her shoulder after the announcements were made and the preacher was making his way from the short deacon's bench to the pulpit. Deke, Toby, and Blake were all sitting in the back pew. It was the first time that antsy feeling hadn't forewarned her that he was in close proximity. Did that mean that whatever they had—friendship, relationship, or one-night fling—was over?

Deke waved.

Toby smiled and nodded.

Blake looked straight ahead.

She whipped back around and from that moment, the preacher might as well have been reading the dictionary because Allie didn't hear a single word.

Like a record playing on a loop, she kept hearing that television commercial from a year ago. It advertised a dating site and said that love didn't come first, but like did. She argued with it, saying that it was a little late for that since she and Blake had already had sex. But the damn commercial took on a life of its own and fought with her.

Sex, like, and love are three different things, it said.

That stumped her train of thought completely as she analyzed the statement and decided it was right. Sex, like what Deke and Toby had Friday night or what she and Blake had on Friday afternoon, was a very different thing from like or love.

But what about the sex Blake and I had? What does that mean? She didn't get an answer from the commercial or from the preacher who was preaching from Psalms Twenty-three that morning.

She liked Blake as a person, as a hardworking rancher, but she was not going to be the friend who hopped over the fence for booty calls whenever Blake wanted a quick romp in the hay. If that's what he wanted, he could call his ex-wife, Scarlett, to warm up his bed.

She folded her hands in her lap and tried to listen to the preacher. It didn't work because within seconds, she was back to the argument. She'd followed her heart when she married Riley and intended to be his wife until death parted them. But she'd learned after two years that physical death wasn't the only way to end a marriage. It could simply die in its sleep or it could be murdered by a two-timin' husband.

That antsy feeling that said someone was staring at her made her look over her shoulder. Blake's lips curled into a smile when their gazes locked and held for several seconds. When she started to turn back around, she caught Grady's gaze from the other end of the pew. It had the intensity of a hungry hound chasing a rabbit and made her skin crawl.

Trust my heart when it failed me? Trust my sister's advice when it makes me want to run for the hills? Maybe I should simply forget all about men and become a nun. I bet a convent could use my skills as a carpenter.

If the pistols resting between her breasts could have fired for-real bullets, Allie would have aimed, fired, blown away the smoke, and toted her sister's lifeless body out to the back side of the twenty acres known as Audrey's Place for the buzzards to feast upon when the family got back to Audrey's after church.

Damn Lizzy's sorry ass to hell for eternity. Allie didn't even care that she was damning a soon-to-be preacher's wife or that the little dinner place cards done up with pictures of hearts were a right cute idea. She was sitting smack dab between Grady and Blake and Lizzy had done the planning.

Every ugly deed does have its comeuppance. Lizzy got

hers because the only place left for her to sit was between generic old Mitch and hotter'n the devil's little forked tail Toby Dawson. It would serve her sister right to be as miserable as she was.

Her mother sat at one end of the table. Granny sat at the other end and on each side there was a sister between two men. If that didn't set Granny off into a cussin' fit or else send her back to talking about Walter nothing could.

"Nice to have a full table today." Granny picked up the basket of hot rolls, put two on her plate, and passed them to her right. "Lizzy, why are you sitting between a preacher man and a hot cowboy? Are you trying to figure out which one you like best?" She leaned forward and whispered. "I'd take the hot cowboy. He'll be more fun."

It was as if someone pushed a MUTE button. One second conversation flowed, then presto, everything went quiet. The silence was every bit as deafening as it had been over at the Lucky Penny when that hussy announced that she was Blake's wife.

Toby finally broke the awkward silence. "Did you make these biscuits, Miz Irene? They taste just like my granny's and everyone loves hers down around Muenster."

"Muenster...Texas or Oklahoma? Where is that place? Is that where the Amish people live? We ain't of the Amish faith, not that there's anything wrong with that if you are. Mitch, here, has some of that in his blood, don't you, Mitch?" Irene said.

"No, ma'am. Not me," Mitch said quickly. "I'm all for keeping the word of God but I do like electricity and modern plumbing."

"Hmmm." Irene pursed her lips. "Way you treat Lizzy, I figured you'd come from one of those strict religions. Oh, well, here you go." She passed the green beans to Toby. "They're real good. Katy cooks them with lots of bacon and onions."

"Thank you," Toby said.

Allie caught Lizzy's sharp intake of breath when Toby passed the bowl off to her. She took out a heaping helping of beans and gave them to Mitch. And nothing happened when Mitch's fingers deliberately covered Lizzy's: zilch, nada, nothing at all. So the sexy cowboy did affect Lizzy. Yes, sir, paybacks were definitely a bitch.

Before the beans made it to her, Grady slipped his hand on her thigh and squeezed as he whispered, "You look lovely today. I like you all dressed up much better than in those ugly cargo pants. You should do it more often."

Zilch. Nada. Nothing at all, other than a major irritation until she picked up his hand and put it back in his lap. "Thank you but I'm much more comfortable in my work clothes."

"Why are you talking about britches at the Sunday dinner table?" Granny asked. "In my day, ladies wore dresses and they only put on britches to ride horses or do chores outside on the farm."

Blake's knee pressed against hers and his simple touch jacked her blood pressure way on up there. She felt like Abigail in her favorite LaVyrle Spencer novel, *Hummingbird.* The sensible choice was the man Abigail was nursing back to health in the downstairs part of her house. But the one that made her heart sing was the bad boy upstairs with a bullet hole in his body. The one who called her Abby and set her free from the strict rules of society, the one she couldn't wait to talk to every day.

Grady called her Alora. Formal. Rigid.

Blake called her Allie. Sensible. Happy heart.

She understood the character Abby so much better that day.

"Penny for your thoughts, Allie," Blake said.

"I'll pay a dollar for them, Alora." Grady grinned.

Allie glanced at Lizzy. "I might sell them to the highest bidder and use the money to buy whatever is making my sister blush."

"I'm not blushing. It's hot in here from all the cooking," Lizzy stammered.

"Does Walter still live at the Lucky Penny?" Irene blurted out. "Has his mother died yet? I get confused about time and I can't remember if he moved."

Allie leaned forward, ignoring both men, and said, "No, Granny, Walter moved years ago. I don't know if his mother is still living or not."

"Probably is unless someone drove a stake through her heart. I might take a Sunday afternoon walk over there and see if Walter is still there," she said.

"Not today, Mama. You have to stay here and chaperone the kids while I drive up to Wichita Falls for supplies. When are you moving to the ranch, Toby?" Katy asked.

"I'm hoping to be here by the first of June. With two of us and a hot summer, we should get lots done. Then our cousin, Jud, will join us about Thanksgiving time," Toby answered.

Katy nodded. "Sounds like you've got things planned out pretty good."

Irene shrugged. "Who were we talking about?"

"Blake's brother, Toby, the one right there." Mitch narrowed his eyes at the elderly woman. "...Is arriving in June if Blake is still living on the Lucky Penny and their cousin will join them at Thanksgiving."

"Don't look at me like that. We don't like each other but this is the Sunday dinner table," Irene said, raising her voice.

Blake reached over and laid a hand on Irene's arm. "I hear that you took care of the three sisters right here in this house while Miz Katy worked. Tell me some stories."

She gave Mitch a dirty look and smiled at Blake. "They were a handful for sure. When there's three, there's lots of whining and giggling."

Irene's mind stayed crystal clear as she told stories from the past. Blake's laugher was genuine. Mitch's lack of even a smile showed that he was bored. When they'd finished eating, Katy brought out two pies—apple and cherry—for dessert, along with a container of ice cream and caramel topping.

"Lizzy likes her apple pie with a crown." Irene smiled. "That's what she called it when she was a little girl and said apple pie was princess food and the ice cream was the princess's crown."

"Me, too." Toby nodded. "But Blake likes cherry better. He never did like apple pie. That's when the family knew for a fact there was something wrong with him. All cowboys love their mamas, pretty girls, and apple pie."

"Two out of three ain't bad, though," Blake said.

"Not me. Too many fat grams and calories," Mitch said. "We'll have to watch those or we'll be as big as circus clowns, won't we, darlin'?"

Allie placed a well-directed kick right on his shin and immediately apologized. "Oh, excuse me. I'm so sorry." She flashed a sarcastic smile across the table.

"I think Lizzy and I will forgo dessert and have coffee in the living room while we set up the Monopoly game." He glared at Allie.

"Yes, darlin'." Lizzy pushed back her chair.

He did the same and slung an arm around Lizzy's shoulders.

Allie could see why her granny thought the man should be planted six feet under. It wasn't a loving arm around her sister, but a possessive, controlling one.

"How about you, Allie? Shall we take our coffee to the living room with them?" Grady asked.

"Hell, no! I'm having both kinds of pie with ice cream. I'll save you a chunk of apple for later, Lizzy," she called out.

Lizzy gave her a weak grin as she poured two cups of coffee and handed one to Mitch before she followed her fiancé out of the kitchen.

"So what are you guys doing this afternoon?" Katy asked Blake. "I hear you tore out some ceiling and put up some new yesterday."

"We are going to take advantage of the sunshine and look at the ranch." He turned slightly and touched Allie on the arm. "Want to go with us?"

"I promised I'd watch Granny this afternoon, so I can't leave."

Irene pointed at Allie. "It's not nice to whisper. Who is that sitting beside you anyway? Is that one of Walter's kids? When did he get married?"

"This is Blake Dawson," Allie said. "He lives over at the Lucky Penny now."

"I'm confused again," Irene said.

Blake smiled at her. "It's okay. We all get things mixed up some of the time."

"You are a good boy," she said. "I want cherry pie with ice cream and chocolate syrup on top."

Toby was in the truck with the motor running but Blake lingered behind to talk to Allie. "I really want to explain about yesterday. Deke took a woman home and she had the car for both of them, so she came to get her sister and thought she could seduce me..."

Allie held up a palm and said, "Enough. I told you I don't care."

"And what does that mean?"

"It means..."

"Hey, Alora, darlin'." Grady pushed his way out the door and in between them. "We're waiting on you. We can't start the game without you."

"I'll be there in five minutes," she said.

"Go on now since you don't care," Blake said bluntly.

"Care about what?" Grady asked.

"Nothing," Allie answered quickly.

"Guess that sums it up then." Blake settled his black cowboy hat on his head and marched off the porch, his boots making a cracking sound on the wood with each step.

"Is that over now?" Grady asked. "It needs to be. He's not the man for you, darlin', and I'm glad that you don't care about him. Now come on inside with me and I'll show you a proper good time." He slung his arm around her.

She shrugged it off but not before Blake turned around. The expression on his face said that he was finished with her and that he didn't even care if she came back to finish re-modeling his house. It was over and done with and all that was left was Grady.

Sensible.

Sad heart with no song.

"Y'all are going to have to play without me," she said around the lump in her throat. "I promised to read to Granny while she falls asleep for her Sunday nap. If she isn't rest-less, I'll check in with you later."

Grady kissed her on the cheek. "Okay, sweetheart."

She shivered from disgust instead of desire and wiped it away with the back of her hand as she went to the kitchen. Katy was busy clearing the table. Half of Granny's pie was done and she had that blank look on her face that said she wasn't sure where she was.

"Go on, Mama. I'll do this while I wait on her to finish. You can be halfway to Wichita Falls by the time that happens and I need something to do," Allie said.

"Have you been crying?" Katy asked.

"Not yet, but I might start when the anger dies down. Blake and I had an argument."

Katy hung a kitchen towel on the hook. "About what? Are you going to finish the job over there?"

"I told him I didn't care and..."

"Care about what?"

Allie put a hand on her forehead but it didn't ease the pain throbbing in her temples. "I'm not sure. It's complicated."

Katy handed her the dishtowel. "You'd best uncomplicate it before Grady pushes his way into your life. I pray every night that you don't let him talk you into a relationship."

Allie shivered. "You'd rather have Blake than him? And yes, I am going to finish the job. Whether we are friends or not doesn't mean I can't work for him."

"Honey, I'd rather have Lucifer than Grady. He's got shifty eyes." Katy cut her eyes toward Irene. "You'll have to keep a close watch on her."

"I'm going to read to her and then sit in the rocking chair in her room and reread that LaVyrle Spencer book about Abigail this afternoon," Allie said.

Katy nodded. "And figure out what you meant by you don't care, right?"

"I hope so, Mama."

Granny was asleep before Allie finished reading the first page of *The Velveteen Rabbit,* which was her new favorite book these days. The roles had been reversed because Allie remembered Granny reading that book to her when she was a child.

When she heard the first soft snore, she put the book aside and picked up *Hummingbird* by LaVyrle Spencer. After reading five pages and not comprehending a single word that she'd read, she laid it aside and decided to straighten Granny's closet.

But first she was going to call Blake and try to explain to him what she meant by she didn't care. It wasn't that she didn't care for him, but that she didn't care who Toby and Deke slept with and that Blake didn't owe her an explanation for their actions. There, that was easy enough to put into words, now wasn't it?

And then she was going to confront him about the way he'd introduced her to his brother. He didn't have to say they'd slept together, but he damn sure could have done better than saying she was the woman who was remodeling the house.

She hit the right number and the call went straight to voice mail. No way was she going to talk to a damn recording about something that important. She waited two minutes and called again. Same thing.

She ended the call before the message even finished and called a third time. That time Blake answered.

"This is not a good time, Allie," he said gruffly.

"I don't care."

"You say that often, don't you?"

"What?" she asked.

"I don't care."

"I meant I don't care if it's not a good time. We need to talk, Blake."

"This time I don't care to hear the explanation. We need some breathing space before we talk again. That dinner was the most awkward thing I've ever had to endure." The line went dead and she slung the phone on the bed.

"Dammit!" She wanted to scream, but the whisper had to do. Waking Granny always made her cranky.

She slung open the closet doors, sat down on the floor, and started arranging the piles of shoes into some kind of order. She found three bars of soap tucked down in the toes of shoes that Granny hadn't worn in five years or more. A shoebox held a ziplock bag full of miniature chocolate bars that had long since gone white with age, two washcloths, and a can of root beer.

When she'd first started hoarding things, they'd asked the doctor about it and discovered it was a symptom of the disease. Folks got paranoid and thought people were stealing their possessions so they hid them.

Then she found the full bottle of Jack Daniel's in one boot and a bottle of Patrón tequila in another boot. Granny must have found them in Fiona's room because Katy didn't drink, Lizzy was too self-righteous to even have a beer these days, and Allie damn sure hadn't brought the bottles home.

She opened the bourbon first and took a long swig and then tried a taste of the tequila. She liked the bourbon better, but it might hurt Mr. Patrón's feelings if she didn't share her attention between him and Mr. Jack.

A sip of Jack for the wild cowboy.

A sip of tequila to wash the youth director out of her world.

Equal time, she thought as she twisted the cap off the Jack for another gulp.

"Bless Granny's heart for hiding things," she said as she leaned against the wall and got serious about the sharing process.

CHAPTER TWENTY-TWO

A picture of Nadine with that apple pie in her hand snuck across Allie's mind. She tucked her chin to her chest and glared at the tequila bottle in her left hand. How in the hell had she drunk half a bottle of that, too? Did Nadine drop by and help her?

"Well, here's to Nadine and apple pies that Blake doesn't like. But he likes pretty girls and his mama." She clinked the two bottles together in a toast. "Some friend I am. Nadine has been down there working on that shitty old building for days trying to turn it into a café, and I haven't even stopped by to check on her."

"Who are you talkin' to?" Granny asked as she slung her legs over the side of the bed. "I'm going to the kitchen for more pie. Want me to bring you some?"

"No, thank you. I'll be right behind you."

Allie frowned as she held on to the furniture and walls and made her way to the door. Lizzy could watch Granny for the rest of the afternoon. After all, she was only playing that boring as hell game of Monopoly. Now if she'd been up in her bedroom having wild, passionate, afterglow-producing sex with Mitch, Allie wouldn't expect her to watch Granny. But between boring sex and boring Monopoly, Allie would probably choose the board game, too.

She giggled at the idea of bored and board being pronounced the same way. Then the laughter died and sadness set in. Poor darling Lizzy wasn't ever going to experience the kind of sex that Allie had had with Blake. She loved her sister even if they weren't best friends. They should fix that and Allie would make the first step. She carried the two bottles out into the foyer and yelled her sister's name.

"My God, you are drunk. On a Sunday, no less," Lizzy gasped when she saw her sister leaning against the wall.

"Shhhh, don't yell. Mitch will hear. He'll pray for me and I don't want God to know that I've been drinkin' on Sunday." The words were slurred but at least she was standing on her own two feet.

"Mitch and Grady left a long time ago. Granny and I are about to have a slice of pie. She said you were cleaning her closet. You smell like a liquor store." Lizzy's pert little nose curled up. "You are drunk. You were supposed to be watching Granny, not getting drunk."

Allie giggled. "I'm not drunk and I love you, Lizzy. Don't marry Mitch. You won't ever have mind-blowing sex with him or know what an afterglow is. He's boring as a board game." She hugged her sister. "Let's bury the hatchet and have a drink to toast being best friends." She held up the two bottles and clinked them together. "Which one will it be? Señor Patrón or bad, bad boy Jack?"

"Neither one." Lizzy made a grab for the liquor. "Give me those bottles and go sleep it off in your room."

Allie hugged them to her breast like long-lost relatives. "Hell, no! I'm going to town to have a drink with Nadine. I'm dis...dis...appointed in you, Lizzy. Nadine will be my best friend if you won't and you ain't going to be happy ever, not ever."

"You can't drive drunk," Lizzy protested.

"I tell you, I'm not drunk, but I will be by the time I finish up my visit with these two. You take care of Granny. If she runs away, you'll answer to Mama." Allie picked up her purse from the foyer table and staggered out the front door. She heard Lizzy talking to her mother on the phone, but her sister could talk to Jesus, God, and Moses for all she cared. She needed a best friend and Nadine would be glad to drink a toast with her.

Besides she hadn't been a good friend to the woman. No doubt, Nadine would be at the store building because she wanted to open the café in another week. It was absolutely imperative that Allie tell her that all cowboys didn't like apple pie. They liked their mamas and pretty girls but some of them liked cherry pie or maybe even lemon meringue, but not to depend on apple pies. A friend would be honest with Nadine and tell her that.

She put the bottles between her legs, backed her thirteen-year-old pickup truck out of the driveway, and widened her eyes, being careful not to blink except when totally necessary. She'd prove to Deke that she could hold her liquor, prove to Lizzy that she wasn't drunk, and Blake Dawson could go to hell for not letting her explain.

When she made it to the end of the lane, she put her foot on the brake. Left was town. Right took her to the Lucky Penny. Or was right town? She wasn't drunk. She knew that Blake didn't like apple pie. If she was drunk, she wouldn't remember that. She twisted the cap off the Jack and took a long gulp. Everything was clear as a bell and the whiskey didn't even burn. She could hold her liquor. All she needed was bad boy Jack to clear her mind.

She whipped the truck to the right and was singing with the radio when she made another right into the Lucky Penny lane. She held up the bottle of Jack when Travis Tritt sang that the whiskey wasn't workin' anymore and nodded when the song's lyrics said that he needed one more honky-tonk angel to turn his life around.

She'd be a honky-tonk angel. She could be as wild as Blake. She thought she was stomping the brakes when she realized she was in front of the house at Blake's ranch. She really did, but when she yelled "whoa," the truck kept moving.

She hit the pedal harder, but the damn thing wouldn't listen to her. It was a hell of a time for the brakes to go out but she had to protect her two bottles because she and Nadine were going to have a drink to their friendship. Only Nadine wasn't putting in a café at the Lucky Penny. The truck busted through the wooden fence circling the yard and ground to a stop when it hit the porch, the solid foundation putting a huge dent in the front and a hole in the radiator.

"Well, shit!" she mumbled as her head hit the steering wheel. "Shhh! Shut up!" She slapped the steering wheel. "I went the wrong way. Shut up or Blake will find out."

Blake and Shooter were alone in the house. Toby had gone home a couple of hours before and the house was too quiet. Suddenly the whole house trembled, and Blake grabbed the wall and hung on, not knowing what to expect next since he'd never experienced an earthquake before. Shooter darted into the bedroom and tried to dive under the bed, but the mattress was still on the floor. He yipped and huddled in the corner, his paws covering his eyes.

When nothing else happened, Blake let go of the wall and checked the ceiling. The roof hadn't fallen and the new ceiling didn't show signs of cracks. The floor beneath him was solid once again. Was that a horn blaring outside?

Shooter whimpered but he didn't move.

"That wasn't an earthquake. Someone rammed into our house." Blake ran down the hall, across the living room, and out onto the porch.

"What the hell?" He didn't recognize the older model small truck. He'd never seen the baby blue vehicle with rusted-out spots along the bottom of the fenders, but there was definitely a person in there and she was not moving. He jogged to the truck, through an inch of snow in his socks, to check the body for life.

Allie raised her head enough to stop the horn when he slung open the door. "It's okay if you don't like apple pie." She fell out into his arms. Two bottles landed on the frozen ground. The square one with a black label landed on its side, a few drops spilling out onto the ground but most of the remainder held secure by the shape of the bottle. The Patrón landed right side up, resting there as pretty as if it was sitting on the top shelf behind a fancy bar.

He reached inside and turned off the engine and then carried her into the house. She was snoring loudly and smelled like a whiskey barrel when he laid her down on the mattress. Shooter sniffed her, tucked his tail between his legs, and made a beeline for the living room.

Blake chuckled and she roused slightly.

"Blake hates apple pie, Nadine. He loves his mama, though."

"Shhh! Shut your eyes," he said.

She sat straight up without opening her eyes and began weaving from side to side. "Can't have sex with all these clothes on." She slurred her words, but Blake understood most of them. "Poor Lizzy. Board games make boring sex."

He swiftly removed her sweater and unzipped her skirt before sliding it down her legs. She opened her bloodshot eyes and cocked her head to one side. "I love you, Blake."

He whipped his T-shirt off and pulled it over her head, pushed her back onto the pillows and covered her up. "Sleep, darlin'. Tomorrow you'll have a headache, but you won't remember much of what you said. What on earth made you hit the bottle anyway?"

"Apple pie," she mumbled. "You don't like apple pie."

He lined a small trash can with a plastic bag and set it beside the bed. Then he removed another T-shirt from a dresser drawer, jerked it over his head, picked up the book he'd planned on reading that evening, and settled himself on the other side of the king-size mattress. She was drunk off her ass, and she wouldn't remember saying it but that was okay. She was beside him and for right now, she did care.

The sun had sunk below the window ledge when the notion struck that he should at least let the folks over at Audrey's Place know where their prodigal daughter had landed. They probably didn't need to know the particulars, like the fact that one of them had a truck that was most likely totaled sitting in his front yard. Or that she was passed out cold and snoring like a two-ton grizzly bear.

He laid his book to the side and reached for his phone on the nightstand. It slipped out of his hands and skittered its way across the hardwood floor. Allie roused up and opened one eye. "Ouch. My head hurts. Afterglow isn't supposed to give me a headache."

He slid off the mattress, picked up the phone, made his

way around the bed to her side, and kissed her on the fore-head, but she was already snoring again. He called her number but it went straight to voice mail. Then he remembered the number on the side of the van and called it.

"Hello." Irene's thin voice filled his ear. "Who is this?"

"This is Blake Dawson from the Lucky Penny. Could I talk to Katy or to Lizzy?"

"I don't know you, and who is Katy? Are you the law? Well, we ain't run no whorehouse here in a long time, so stay the hell away from Audrey's Place." The clink of her hanging up the phone receiver banged in his ear.

"Guess some folks still have a dial-up phone." He called the number again.

Irene screamed into the phone. "If this is the law, you can go to hell. We ain't runnin' moonshine, either, and we done closed up the whorehouse."

He could hear Lizzy yelling in the background. "Granny, who is that? Is it Nadine? Is Allie with her?"

"Who is Nadine and what are you talkin' about? It's the law. They're over at the Lucky Penny. I bet that damn Walter has told them that we used to run a whorehouse here," Irene said.

Lizzy's frazzled voice finally asked, "Nadine, is Allie with you?"

"This is Blake, Lizzy. Allie is over here."

"She's drunk, Blake. Bring her home. Don't let her drive. That old truck of hers doesn't even have air bags and the tires are bald."

"She's out cold and moving her will probably make her start upchucking so why don't we let her sleep it off over here," Blake said. "I promise I won't let her drive and I've got a damn fine recipe for a hangover that I'll give her when she wakes up."

"Please don't tell anyone that she's a drunk. I'm marryin' a preacher, you know," Lizzy said.

"Wouldn't dream of saying a word," Blake said. "I'll drive her home when she's sobered up tomorrow morning."

"She's trying to ruin me," Lizzy got out before Irene wrestled the phone from her.

"Walter, is that you? I told you not to call this number. What in the hell are you thinkin'? Is the law over there?" Irene's shrill voice blasted through his ears.

"Give me that phone, Granny," Lizzy demanded.

The loud bang in his ears said that Irene hung up a second time.

He tiptoed to the kitchen and made himself a sandwich, carried it to the living room, and turned on the television. The weatherman said that they'd have thunderstorms through the night and most of the day on Monday. He watched two episodes of *Family Feud* and a couple of reruns of *NCIS*, but his mind kept running in circles and Allie Logan was right in the middle of all of it.

Shooter went to the door and whined so he let him out for his evening run and checked the truck one more time. The front end was smashed up, but it didn't look like it would leak if it rained. Just in case there was something important in the cab, he took a look. The only thing in there was a candy wrapper on the floor, the lid to the bottle of Jack Daniel's, which was still lying on the ground with golden liquid in it, and Allie's purse.

He slung her purse over his shoulder and picked up the lid, recapped the liquor bottle, and carried both into the house. "No need to waste good Jack."

Shooter finished his business and dashed into the house, almost tripping Blake on his way to the kitchen.

"You don't have to break my leg. I wouldn't forget your midnight snack."

Shooter sat up on his hind legs and begged.

"Okay, you rascal." Blake laughed. "You get two pieces of bologna for that trick. But when you're too fat to run this spring, it won't be my fault."

Allie's eyes popped open and then snapped shut again as she grabbed her head and rolled up into a ball. Her mouth was dry and tasted like a dirty bathroom smelled. She tried to swallow but gagged instead. Clamping a hand over her mouth, she tried to get up and rush to the bathroom, but knew she wouldn't make it. She grabbed the trash can beside her bed and dry-heaved until her sides ached, but nothing came up.

She'd never had the flu like this before and she damn sure did not have time for it now. She had to paint Blake's bedroom and then texture the ceiling in the hall and living room. She set the trash can back on the floor and fell back on her bed.

Shooter bounded across the floor and onto the mattress, started at her chin and slurped all the way to her forehead, his dog food breath causing her to gag again. How in the devil did Blake's dog get in her house and to her bedroom?

She pushed him away and opened her eyes slowly, shielding them with her hand against the light pouring in the window. Then a streak of lightning lit up the sky, followed quickly by a boom of thunder that made Shooter drop and shove his head under the covers.

"God, that's loud." She moved her hands to her ears. "Oh. My. God. I'm in Blake's bed. How did I get here and what have I done?"

"Truth or a pretty princess story?" Blake asked.

Her chest tightened at how sexy he was, standing there like a mythical god with pajama pants riding low on his hips, a wife beater shirt stretched out across his muscular chest, and barefoot. She told herself that men did not have sexy feet but when she looked back at his, they really were. His hair was tousled like he'd gotten out of bed after a night of wild sex. Oh, God, did they have sex?

"Truth?" She pulled herself up and propped her back against the pillows.

"Don't even want a little bit of the pretty story?" he asked. "I worked one up for you about a princess who was poisoned by her wicked sister who was going to marry a preacher." He grinned.

The laugh made it past her chest and partially out of her mouth before it stopped and she grabbed her head again. "Just the truth."

"You got drunker than a rabid skunk, drove your truck over here, and evidently you didn't want to walk across the yard so you parked right up next to the porch, and passed out cold in my arms. So I put you to bed, and now it's time to get rid of the hangover." He poured honey from a cute little bear-shaped bottle into a spoon and said, "Open your mouth."

She clamped her mouth shut and mumbled. "Will it make my headache stop?"

"It's the first step. Open up." He started toward her mouth and she obeyed. She didn't care if it was arsenic, as long as it made the throbbing between her eyes stop without killing her.

"Don't move. Next step is coming up."

Shooter peeked out from under the covers.

She tucked her chin down and glared at him. "If it's gravy, you can have it all. I'll gag on gravy this morning. Just thinking about it makes my stomach churn."

"It's not gravy. It's really strong black coffee and two aspirin. This is a four-step program, but it works." Blake carried in two cups of steaming hot coffee.

He handed her two aspirin, his fingertips tickling the palm of her hand. She tossed them into her mouth and swallowed them with the first sip of coffee. He was right about it being strong. It could melt enamel off her teeth if she held it in her mouth too long.

"Where did you get the liquor?" Blake asked.

Allie shut her eyes tightly. "Granny hides things. I found it in her closet when I was straightening her shoes. Where is it?"

"About half of the Jack is gone and maybe a third of the tequila."

She groaned. "I've never been drunk and believe me I won't be again. What did I say or do."

"We had a great talk and cleared up that shit about you saying you didn't care and then you did some real good snoring."

She knew exactly how her grandmother felt because she couldn't remember a damn thing about a talk of any kind. She remembered finding all sorts of things in the closet and drinking from the two bottles. Then there was an argument with Lizzy in the foyer. And then she was going to talk to Nadine but nothing about a talk with Blake came to mind.

"We did?" She opened one eye.

Blake grinned. "Of course we did. You drink the rest of that and don't move. I'll bring the third dose back in a few minutes."

As he left the room, a clear memory flashed and both eyes opened wide. "Oh, no! I wrecked my truck!" She set the coffee on the floor and threw her head back against the pillows with a groan as her stomach did a flip-flop and the memory of her truck rammed into the house came clear. "Plowed right into the house and the horn was so loud."

Shooter moved over and laid his head in her lap. She propped up enough to continue to sip her coffee with one hand and scratch his ears with the other.

"Scrambled eggs and toast." Blake returned carrying a plate of food.

She couldn't eat eggs. Lord have mercy! Was he trying to kill her? "I can't eat eggs. My stomach can't handle them. I'll try a few bites of the toast."

Blake picked up the fork. "No, ma'am. You will eat every bite of the eggs. There's only two. Big men like Toby or me, well, we have to eat four."

"I can feed myself," she protested.

"You handle the coffee. I'll do the feeding." He grinned.

Sensual. Sexy. Hot.

Those words came to Allie and they had nothing to do with the eggs that Blake kept putting into her mouth. There was something sensual and sexy about a man feeding her breakfast in bed, even if it was a hangover cure. Not once in the two years she'd been married to Riley had he ever brought her breakfast in bed or fed her. But she didn't want to think about Riley; she wanted to focus on the man feeding her the hangover cure.

"No!" she said.

He put another bite into her mouth. "No, what?"

She swallowed quickly. "We are fighting. You shouldn't be nice to me."

"We got all that settled last night," he said.

"I don't remember it and until I remember it's not settled. Four steps? What's the last one?" she asked.

"A banana and then a warm shower," he said. "Don't snarl your pretty nose. Trust me! It works."

She blinked several times. "How did you figure all this out?"

"Internet," he said. "After a few hangovers I did some research and found a combination of cures that works. You plannin' on usin' it real often?"

She shook her head very slowly. "I like a beer. I even like a shot of Jack. I'm not so much into tequila, but it was there and I didn't want it to feel left out. But until right now I've never been drunk and it isn't ever happening again."

He put the last bite into her mouth and kissed her on the forehead. "Good girl. Now for the final step, and then you can take a shower. There's an extra toothbrush in the cabinet. Still in the bubble pack. You'll be ready for it after you shower. I'll get another pot of coffee going while you do that."

Her eyes fixed on his fine-looking butt under those loose pajama pants as he left the room again. Surely she wasn't imagining or hadn't merely dreamed that they'd had sex on this very mattress. She drew her eyebrows down and flinched when that brought another pang between her eyes. What was today? Had she been there a day? A week?

Shooter hopped off the mattress and made his way up the hallway, probably to stretch out in front of the fireplace since the lightning and thunder had stopped. Was that an omen? The storm was over and it was time for her to go home and face the music from her family, and why was it thundering at this time of year? There was snow on the ground for heaven's sake.

She would eat the damn banana and she'd have a shower and gladly brush her teeth, but then she and Blake were going to have a talk. And this time she would remember every word, every nuance, and every expression on his face.

"Every single damn word," she mumbled.

"Word about what?" he asked. "It's snowing again and you don't feel much like texturing a ceiling, so I vote we cuddle up on the sofa and spend the day together. We can turn off our cell phones and pretend we're stranded on a desert island."

"How long have I been here?" she asked.

"Since late last evening. Today is Monday."

Had they cleared things up? If not, then why was he being so nice? "I've always wanted to get lost on an island. Hand me that banana and get the canoe ready for us to row to the island."

Did she say that out loud? Good lord! What was the matter with her? They still had to clear a hell of a lot of things up before she cuddled up with him on the sofa all day.

He tossed it toward her and she caught it with both hands. "It's working. My headache isn't as bad."

"I'm the hangover guru. Stick with me and I'll take care of you," he said.

"Sounds to me like you're a guy who's used that line many times," she said, grabbing her aching head.

"Maybe I should write country music about curing hangovers." He extended his hand and helped her off the mattress. "Finish the banana on the way to the shower. Everything is laid out and ready for you."

CHAPTER
TWENTY-THREE

Hot water washed away more of the headache, but it didn't do much to take away the guilt. What had she been thinking? She'd been put in charge of her grandmother for the afternoon and she'd failed...again.

Alora Raine Logan was a failure and she admitted it. Strip stark naked, standing under the shower spray on the Lucky Penny, which was every bit as appropriate as an AA meeting for alcoholics. She had failed in her marriage—couldn't hold Riley's interest. Failed as a daughter—proved she couldn't be trusted. Failed as a sister—weekends were the only time Lizzy got to spend with Mitch.

"Sorry sumbitch that Mitch is, he's *her* sumbitch." Allie wiped at the tears streaming down her cheeks.

She slid down into the bathtub and curled up in a tight little ball, sobbing as the hot water streamed over her body. She didn't hear the little plastic rings holding the shower curtain slide across the rod. She had no idea anyone was in the bathroom until Blake was in the tub with her. Still dressed in pajama pants and a knit shirt, he sat down behind her and gathered her into his arms. One minute she was sitting on the hard porcelain of an old bathtub, the next she was curled up in his lap, her cheek against his chest.

She started to say something, but he put a finger over her lips.

"The depression is the alcohol talking, not Allie Logan. Whatever happened is water under the bridge. Burn the damn bridge and forget the past," he whispered.

His words were so poetic that they brought on a fresh batch of tears. She didn't care if it was just another line he'd used. Didn't care...they were the words that had started all this to begin with.

"I do care," she said between sobs.

"About what?" He brushed strands of wet hair from her face.

She took several seconds to get her thoughts together. "I care about Lizzy and Mama and Granny. I don't care if you are telling me pretty words that you've told lots of women before me. I don't care about your past. I'll burn those bridges for you if you'll hand me a stick of firewood and a match."

How he managed to stand up in a slippery, wet tub with her in his arms, then step out without falling, was a miracle. But suddenly, she found herself wrapped in that brand-new robe he'd talked about and her hand was in his, letting him lead her to the living room. He tossed a quilt over the sofa and motioned for her to sit. She obeyed without arguing and he carefully brought the ends of the quilt up around her legs.

"Don't go away." He smiled.

Leaving wet footprints on the floor and dripping water as he disappeared into his bedroom, he whistled a tune that she recognized as "Honey Bee" by Blake Shelton. In a few minutes he returned, dressed in gray sweat bottoms and a long-sleeved thermal shirt. He carried a towel in one hand and a hairbrush in the other.

"Slide forward about a foot," he said.

When she did, he settled in behind her, one long muscular leg on each side of her body. He towel-dried her hair and then massaged her scalp with his fingertips. Holy smoking shit! Her body felt like a rag doll and yet every nerve was on high alert, wanting more, begging for his wonderful hands.

"Mmmm," she murmured.

"Is it making it better?" he drawled.

He started brushing her hair and a whole new set of emotions surfaced. She was afraid to move an inch for fear she'd find out this was all a dream and she would wake up with that grinding hangover, or worse yet, in her lonely bed at home.

His hands grazed her cheeks as he pulled her damp hair back to run the brush through it. Then he leaned forward and kissed her softly on the side of her neck.

"We were going to talk," she whispered.

"We are talkin', darlin'. We'll use words when necessary," he said softly.

No one had ever cared enough about Allie to sit in a tub with her when she was crying or brush her hair, much less talk to her without using words. Sitting there with her eyes shut, feeling Blake's long legs against her body and what had to be an erection pressing against her back, she couldn't help but wonder if the third time was the charm. First there was Granny's Walter. Then there was Katy's Ray. And now there was Blake, who was the third. If it was a real fairy tale, the prince would come along and win the princess.

"Now that's as far-fetched as anything can be," she murmured to herself.

"What?" he asked.

She clamped a hand over her mouth. "Did I say that out loud?"

"You did. Want to explain?" he asked.

She shook her head and leaned back so she could look up into his eyes. "Do you have your contacts in place?"

"No, ma'am, and I'm blind without them or my glasses so my hands are seeing for me this morning. They tell me that you are beautiful beyond words." He smiled.

"And when do you wear glasses? After a Friday night of bar hopping?"

He reached behind him to the end table and put his glasses on. "Or on a nice rainy day so I can see you better. I don't like them but they come in handy when my allergies act up."

"I like them on you. They make your eyes even greener."

"Then I'll throw away my contacts and wear them every day just for you," Blake said sincerely.

In all the fairy tales she'd read or that Granny had read to her in her youth, the prince had never worn glasses or been nearsighted. This had to be reality.

"You don't have to do that, Blake. Do you always believe what your hands say?" she teased.

"Not always but my heart never lies to me and it's in agreement with my hands," he whispered.

"Oh!"

He stopped and kissed her hair. "I'm sorry. Did I hit a tangle?"

"No, I should call Mama and Lizzy. It's a wonder they haven't called out the militia already," she said.

He pulled the brush to the end of her dark hair and then

laid it on the end table. "I talked to Lizzy last night and your mother this morning. They know where you are, that you are alive, and that I'll bring you home sometime later."

"I can drive myself home. I drove over here drunk, so I reckon I can get back when I'm sober," she said.

"Not in that truck out there with the front end caved in. You're lucky that you didn't hurt yourself, but then God protects drunks and fools," he said with a chuckle.

She crawled off the sofa and pulled the robe tightly across her bare breasts. "I was hoping that part was a dream. Did I really wreck my truck?"

"You did, darlin'," he answered. "Look out the window. Is that the one you bought when you were sixteen?"

When she peeked through the blinds, she expected another burst of tears. She'd saved money from working with her dad to buy that truck and now it was totaled. Sure, she could probably find used parts and have someone fix the thing, but was it worth it? Was this an omen that she should let go of all the past?

"I'm sorry." Blake's arms circled her waist and he buried his face in her hair. "I'm sure it means a lot to you, but it will take a fortune to fix it."

"Thank God the folks who built Audrey's and this house as well put them on a good solid foundation." She leaned back against his chest. "It's time to say good-bye to that truck and send her off to that great junkyard in the sky."

"She will be able to visit with my first wrecked vehicle that looked a whole lot like her. Only I was eighteen and probably drunker than you were last night. Shooter and I thought we were experiencing our very first earthquake."

"What happened that you got so drunk? And did it really shake the house that hard?"

"Second question first." He led her back to the sofa, sat down, and pulled her into his lap. "Yes, it did, and I figure from the way that front end is caved in that you hit the gas instead of the brake. If you'd been sober, you would have stiffened up and come out of it with a whiplash at the least, but you were limber as a wet noodle. I did find a couple of bruises up under your arms where you must've hit the steering wheel but that's all."

She pushed up the sleeves of his robe and sure enough there were two long, skinny strips of purple under each arm as if she'd hugged that steering wheel at time of impact.

He kissed each bruise and pulled the sleeves back down for her. "Other question. My folks called a lawyer and he took care of things. I knew they were right. Hell, I knew I was making a mistake when I was standing there drunk and saying my vows to love, honor, and respect Scarlett." He wrapped his arms around her even tighter. "But it didn't make it sting any less for them to treat me like a child so I went out that night and got drunk again. I spent three days in the hospital with a concussion. When I saw my truck after they'd pulled it from around the big pecan tree, I decided I'd never drink that much again."

"Did you keep that promise to yourself?" she asked.

"Almost all the time. Nowadays, three beers is my limit. If I have a shot of Jack, then two beers is my limit."

She readjusted her position until she was sitting in his lap, tilted her chin up, moistened her lips, and wrapped her arms around his neck. "Me, too. I'm making that promise to myself and sealing it with a kiss from you right here and now."

Lips met lips in a fiery kiss that erased the argument. Tongues did a mating dance that included forgetting and forgiving, leaving Allie and Blake in a wonderful vacuum with room for only two beating hearts. The heat between them burned away the bad feelings and nothing mattered but the future.

"Wow! Just wow," he said.

"Was it as good for you as it was for me?" she asked.

He traced the outline of her lips with his forefinger. "Better. So we've made our pact that we aren't getting drunk off our asses ever again. Does that mean we're going to watch each other's backs to be sure we keep our word?"

She stood up and moved to the other end of the sofa. There was no way she could keep her mind on a conversation with his warm breath on her body and his arms wrapped securely around her waist.

"I like you, Blake Dawson." She settled down with her back against the arm and sitting Indian-style, the robe covering her legs. Her heart said that she loved him, but she wasn't totally sure that there weren't a few drops of whiskey and tequila left in her blood that might be influencing the major organ in her body.

"I like you, too, Allie Logan," he said, and smiled.

"Why?"

"You said it first so you have to tell me why you like me first. And I'm leaving my glasses on so I can see you, because your face does not lie."

"Oh, really?"

"Yes, ma'am." He stared into her eyes. "Just how far does this 'like' business go?"

She inhaled and let it out slowly. "It's real hard for me to trust anyone, and I have commitment issues after two years with a husband who left me for another woman. He was a lot like Mitch. He manipulated me into giving him what he wanted and made me feel guilty when I didn't cave in. The only thing I refused to do was quit working, and that was a big thorn in our marriage."

"Riley abused you?" Blake asked.

"Yes, but I was young, naïve, and very stupid. I didn't know that it was abuse. He'd sigh and say that he wished my job at least let me dress like a lady instead of a homeless person. But he had good qualities and we had good times. It wasn't all bad. I guess that's why I didn't see the infidelity when it was right before my face."

"That's just wrong," Blake whispered coldly.

She could feel the last of the ice chipping away from her heart. Was this what it was like to have a best friend, someone that a person could tell anything? "I don't think my heart was broken but more relieved that I didn't have to keep having the fight over my working situation. But my pride was in shambles. It was two years before I went out on a date and I figured out real quick that I didn't believe a nice word the man said. It wasn't him but me. I didn't trust men."

"And now?"

"I like you and I trust you, but I want to know why you introduced me to your brother as the woman who was fixing this house instead of your friend or since we'd been to bed, as your girlfriend," she said.

He moved down the sofa and took her hands in his. "It was an awkward situation, Allie. Those women from the bar were in the kitchen. Your granny showed up looking like a half-drowned old madam. Don't look at me like that. You know I'm tellin' the truth. And then your mother came to get her. I wanted to tell you that I hadn't slept with you and then turned around and slept with one of those women, but I couldn't with all of them standing so close. And I didn't think you'd want them to know that we'd had sex, and I didn't know how to introduce you. And I'm battling this idea of us when you live so close."

"What does my living close have to do with anything?" she asked.

"If things didn't work out between us and there were hard feelings, well, we are neighbors. It's complicated."

Sitting there with her small hands tucked into his big ones felt right as if that's the way life should be. "I don't want you to leave the Lucky Penny, so please make it work. I've opened my heart to you. That's why I like you, Blake. I can talk to you. I can argue with you. I can be drunk and shake the hell out of your house and you don't judge me. You don't talk down to me or make me feel like less of a woman because of what I do."

He leaned forward and cupped her face in his hands. "You've had Deke as a best friend, but I've never had a best friend who was a woman, so this is all new territory for me. Why do I like you? Let me count the ways."

She pulled a hand free. "You don't have to be complimentary. Just knowing that you consider me a best friend is enough reason to like me."

He captured her hand midair and kissed the knuckles. "What I feel for you goes far above 'like,' Allie Logan. I don't know if it's love because I've never really been in love before. But believe me when I tell you that I admire you for what you do. I think it's downright sexy the way you can crawl up on a roof or fix a ceiling and honey, those cargo pants turn me on."

"Kind of like that song 'She Thinks My Tractor's Sexy'?" she said. "Only in reverse? He thinks my cargos are sexy?"

"You got it. You can do all those things and then when we

are in bed, you make me feel like I'm the greatest lover on earth."

Allie's smile grew wider. "That's because you are. And speaking of that, since we're best friends, does that mean we can't see if you're still that great in bed? Like right now?"

"Allie, I want more from you than booty calls. If we weren't both close to thirty, I'd say this is where I'd ask you to go out with me." He chuckled.

She pulled both her hands free and cupped his cheeks in her hands. "We haven't even been dating. You know that commercial that says like comes before love?"

His hands covered hers. "I've seen it on television a couple of times."

Allie leaned forward and kissed him on the tip of the chin. "I'm not so sure I believe that. I think maybe they get mixed up sometimes and sometimes they arrive at the same time, but right now I don't want to think about any of it. I want to go to bed with you."

He was a blur as he stood up and then suddenly she was in his arms and they were headed down the hallway. He kicked the bedroom door shut with his bare foot and laid her gently on the mattress.

"I think that can be arranged." He tugged the belt of the robe and laid the sides back. She shivered, not because of the cold wind howling outside or the rain pouring down on the new roof, but in anticipation of what was to come.

When he removed his pajama pants her eyes went to the rock-hard erection and then upward as the shirt came off. They locked gazes and he started to stretch out beside her but she shook her head.

"You're saying no?" he asked.

"I'm saying that we've had foreplay. I want you." She

pulled him down and wrapped her legs around his waist, wiggling just right so that a good firm thrust took him inside her.

He braced himself on his elbows and started a steady rhythm complete with hot and heavy kisses that had her panting and rocking with him after the first few seconds. It didn't surprise her one bit that this time was every bit as good as the last, but she didn't dwell on anything but satisfying the deep need inside her body as she finally let go of all the past and trusted her heart and soul to the bad boy on the Lucky Penny.

The last time they'd had sex she felt as if she were in a vacuum where no one else was allowed but her and Blake. This time it went beyond that into a place where nothing, not a single thought or a worry of any kind, entered her mind. She and Blake were on a sexual journey. She could see the strength in his strong arms when he rose up above her. The intensity in his eyes when she looked deep into them kept nothing back and gave her free access to delve all the way to his soul. His weight felt right when he eased down on top of her and then they were rocking together in a world where past and future didn't matter. Only the present was allowed and it was glorious.

Time stood still. Wandering thoughts didn't exist. Nothing was more important than satisfying that deep need driving them to the top of a climax. Then with a groan and a final thrust they dived over the edge together, her fingers tangled in his hair, his lips on that soft spot on her neck. Before either of them could stop panting, the soft afterglow folded around them like a warm blanket.

He rolled to one side and pulled her against him until her head rested on his chest. "When I can breathe," he panted, "I will tell you how wonderful that was."

"When you can breathe..." she panted between words, "you can kiss me and we'll start all over again."

"You are amazing, Allie," he whispered softly.

Getting enough of Blake Dawson might be a lifetime job. She was up for the challenge if it meant winding up in bed like this several times a week...or a day!

CHAPTER TWENTY-FOUR

Blake and Deke had already gone when Allie let herself into the house and went right to work that Tuesday morning. At noon the ceiling was painted, the walls were finished, and she was working her way around the floor doing the wood-work. The door into the bedroom and the one that hung on the closet had been removed and were resting on sawhorses in the third bedroom. Now that some of the Sheetrock had been cleared out, she used that room to sand and then paint one side of the doors before she had started the ceiling that morning. Her goal was to turn them over and paint the other side before she left that evening. Then the next day she would hang them before she started texturing the hallway and living room ceiling.

She'd really dodged a bullet the day before with the gossip hounds in Dry Creek. The big news in town right then was the grand opening tonight of Nadine's new café. It had only taken a lot of elbow grease and a big trip to the grocery wholesale store to get the place up and running. Katy had helped her cut through a ton of red tape to get a license and rumor had it that Sharlene and Mary Jo were taking vacation time from their jobs to help out the first week as waitresses and dishwashers.

Of course Nadine's business venture was only part of what was keeping all the phone lines heated up that week. Sharlene was still thinking about cleaning up the old clothing store for a day care center because she was tired of the banking business and Mary Jo was continuing with plans for putting in a beauty and barbershop combination in the building between the café and the feed store.

Some folks thought those three women should be hauled out of Dry Creek by the boys in the white jackets. Others cheered for the ladies and whispered over the backyard fences that Blake Dawson might be the luckiest thing that had happened to northern Throckmorton County in several decades. He was the only thing that had changed in town the past several years and look at what all was happening.

Allie wished all three of them the best of luck in their ventures and could have personally hugged them for taking some of the heat from the rumors away from her that week. She was picturing three stores on Main Street with clean windows and folks fanning in and out of the new businesses when she came to the end of the baseboards and stood up to paint around the door facing.

She caught a whiff of wood smoke but figured a draft had sent it from the fireplace to her nose. Paintbrush loaded, her hand was headed toward the middle of the door trim when two hands snaked around her waist. It startled her so badly that she squealed, flipped around, and threw up the brush, sending a broad swath of white paint across Blake's face. White went ear to ear, across his mouth, chin, and below his nose, before she dropped the brush on the toe of his right boot.

He pulled her tightly against his chest, tipped up her chin and kissed her, smearing wet white paint all over her face. She tasted wood smoke, cold winter air, and a hint of black coffee mixed with paint. Who would have ever thought that that mixture could be an aphrodisiac?

She rolled up on her toes and then remembered Deke. Sweet Jesus in heaven! She had to get to the bathroom and wash all that paint off her face before he saw it or else he'd have a million questions and at least that many lectures all ready to deliver.

"Deke?" she whispered.

"Is on the way. He wanted to finish up the cord of wood he was working on so that Herman could buy it and take it out of the field. Weatherman says it's going to snow more, starting tonight and going through tomorrow. Never seen winter like this in central Texas before, but when it's cold outside we have to get warm inside, don't we?" Blake pulled her back to his chest.

"You got that right, but first we've got to get the paint off before Deke gets here," she said.

"Hey! This room is almost finished and it looks great." He took a step back and looked around at the fresh sandy colored walls and white trim work. "I can move my furniture back in tomorrow evening soon as we pull up this nasty carpet. That means we've got a date, right?"

"Thursday evening?" she asked.

"I'll pick you up at seven at your place. Should I wear body armor?" He led her to the bathroom and turned on the water in the wall-hung sink.

"It might not hurt. Lizzy is a crack shot with a rifle and she's not budging." Allie stuck her hands under the warm water.

Blake applied soap to a wet washcloth and held it up to her face. "Let me."

She turned her face up so he could reach it better. "You scared the devil out of me."

Blake chuckled. "Then I guess you must be an angel, then."

"Oh, darlin', I got my angel wings the first time we went to bed together."

He wiped away most of the paint from her face and rinsed the washcloth under the warm water. "I scared you when we had sex?"

"No, darlin', you screwed the hell out of me...that gave me my angel wings and my halo," she said.

Behind the white painted-on beard, Blake's face went crimson red. "Your ancestors' blood is rising to the top today."

"Yep, it is." She took the washcloth from him and removed the rest of the paint from her face, then started on his.

"Hey, where are y'all?" Deke called from the living room.

"Cleaning Blake up," Allie yelled back.

"You are what?" Deke wasted no time getting down the hall. He stopped at the bathroom door and leaned a shoulder against the jamb. "What happened?"

"Never scare a woman who's holding a paintbrush," Blake said.

"Good enough for you." Deke laughed out loud. "Be glad she slapped you with that brush and not her freshly painted wall. For that she might have shot you on the spot." He left the bathroom and peeked into the bedroom. "Lookin' good. You'll have it done by quittin' time today. It's amazing what a coat of paint and a new ceiling does for a room, ain't it? I'm going to wash up in the kitchen sink and then I've got something to tell you."

Allie picked up the washcloth again and wiped away more paint. Cupping his chin under her hand sent waves of desire through her body. Did angel wings and halos have to be earned every day? If so, she was more than willing for more of that hell removal business anytime that her halo and wings started to fade.

"I've got the bowls on the table. Y'all going to take all day in there?" Deke shouted.

"Almost done," Allie yelled back. "Be there in two minutes."

"Make that three or four. Get out the cheese, salsa, and chips." Blake raised his voice and bent his head to kiss her again. Her halo was secure by the time he finished the blistering hot kiss that took her breath away.

"Wow," she muttered.

"It never gets old or dull, does it?" Blake whispered.

"Hasn't yet," she said.

"It's on the table and if you ain't here in thirty seconds, with or without paint all over your face, I am eating alone. You've had time to take off the first layer of skin, Allie," Deke called out.

When they reached the kitchen, she sat down in her chair. "You must be hungry, Deke."

Deke got busy dipping tortilla soup into bowls. "I'm always starving by dinnertime. And, Allie, I know y'all are more than friends so you don't have to find excuses to stay in the bathroom and make out."

"What?" Allie sputtered.

"It's all over your face and Blake's been whistling more than usual and well, I'm your best friend, Allie, so I know. Now let's eat before the food gets cold. I'm hungry and talking about hungry"—he blew on a spoonful of soup—"Nadine is having her grand opening tonight. She's serving hamburgers and two blue plate specials. It's not a big menu, but tomorrow she's adding to it. We're going. My treat for all the food I've been getting here and, Allie, this was your idea, so you need to be there."

"So that's what you wanted to tell us?" Blake asked.

"Yep. Now admit it. I'm right. You two are dating," Deke said.

Allie downed the rest of her sweet tea. "Blake and I are more than friends."

Deke reached for the salsa and added a tablespoon to his second bowl of soup. "I knew it. Have you told Lizzy and your mama?"

"Not yet. I thought maybe since we're best friends that you'd do that for me," she teased.

"Hell, no, I want to be out of the county when you tell Lizzy."

* * *

Allie wasn't a bit surprised to see that Lizzy had gotten all dressed up in a cute little pencil skirt, a turtleneck sweater in the same shade of brown as her eyes, and had even added a clunky gold necklace to the getup. She'd abandoned her cowboy boots for a pair of spike-heeled dress boots. Her dishwater-blond hair floated in curls on her shoulders and her makeup was perfect. Mitch expected her to look beautiful when they went out and she did everything to please him.

Lizzy gasped when she saw Allie wearing a snug pair of skinny jeans, a form-fitting sweater that accentuated her curves and her tiny waist, and a pair of cowboy boots that Lizzy had never seen.

"What?" Allie asked.

"Did you change your mind? Please tell me that you did

and you're going with me and Mitch and Grady." Lizzy smiled.

"I'm going to the grand opening, but I'm not going with you. And for the last time, Grady is out of the question. I'm going with Blake Dawson."

Lizzy fell back in the old rocking chair and threw her hand across her eyes in a dramatic gesture that did Scarlett O'Hara justice. "I knew it. I told Mama nothing good would come from you going over there to work. You are weak and you can't say no."

Allie frowned and held up her hand like a little girl in the classroom. "Hello. My name is Alora Raine Logan and I am weak and exactly like most of my whoring ancestors. I fall over backward for any sexy cowboy that pushes on my shoulder. My youngest sister is the smart one. My middle sister is the strong one. I'm the failure."

"God almighty!" Lizzy dropped her hand and glared at Allie. "That is not funny."

"There's the doorbell, so that will be Blake. See you at Nadine's. I hope she made her famous apple pie for tonight." Allie picked up her coat and purse and left Lizzy sitting there speechless for the first time in her life.

Katy had already opened the door and Blake was standing at the foot of the stairs when Allie started down. Her breath caught in her chest at the sight of him there in his bulletproof jeans bunched up over the tops of black boots so shiny she could see the reflection of the foyer light fixture in them. Holding his black hat in his hands, his eyes locked with hers and his smile said more than words could ever get across.

He handed her a tiny stem with a little white daisy-looking flower at the end. "I should have brought flowers, but I didn't have time to go into town so this will have to do. Mama calls them snow flowers because they bloom in the winter. I found it this evening right up next to the house. You are stunning tonight, Allie."

"Oh, Blake, it is beautiful. I'm going to press it and keep it forever," she said. "Hold my coat and give me a second to put it in water until I get home tonight." She hurriedly put the flower in a small glass of water, went back to the foyer, and turned to Katy.

"Are you and Granny going to have supper at Nadine's?" she asked.

"No, she's already in her room and watching episodes of *Designing Women*. I'm going to make myself a sandwich and catch up on quarterly taxes while things are quiet," Katy said. "Give Nadine my best and tell her I'll be there for lunch tomorrow. Lizzy and I are going to put a sign on our doors and take a thirty-minute lunch break. That way all the school kids will go to Nadine's and it will stir up a little more business for her."

"You've cooked your last time at the store then?" Blake asked.

Katy smiled. "Yes, I have, and I won't miss it a bit."

Blake and Allie walked out to his truck, fingers laced together, ignoring the cold weather and smiling at each other. He opened the door for her and settled her into the passenger's seat in his truck. They rode in comfortable silence almost all the way to town and then Deke called to tell her that he was already at the café and was holding a table for the three of them and one of Herman's granddaughters. She was between jobs and came to visit for a couple of weeks.

"Kelly?" Allie asked. "You better be careful. Herman will skin you alive if you mess with her. She's his favorite since she's the only granddaughter."

"It's not a date. It's only a chair at a table. She was waiting. It's a packed house, I'm tellin' you," Deke said. "And Nadine has apple pie. I told her to save three pieces and one of pecan for Blake since he hates apple pie. It's going fast."

Blake had to park all the way down to the end of the block and across the street. Dry Creek usually rolled up the sidewalks at five o'clock when Katy and Lizzy closed up shop and there wasn't another car seen on the street until the next morning. But that night there wasn't a parking place on either side of the wide street.

Blake crawled out of the truck, shook the legs of his jeans down over his boots, and circled around the front side to open the door for her. They walked across the street hand in hand and when he tried to pull away as they entered the café, she tightened her grip.

The place was almost as noisy as a rock concert until they saw that Allie was with Blake and holding his hand and then the only racket that could be heard was the pots and pans in the kitchen area.

Allie marched right over to Nadine's mama, who had held the crown for the biggest gossip in Dry Creek for nearly three decades, and laid a hand on her shoulder.

"Hello, Willa Ruth. Have you met my boyfriend, Blake Dawson? He's been to church a couple of times but I don't think everyone has been properly introduced to him. Blake, darlin', this is Nadine's mama, Willa Ruth. She taught Nadine everything she knows about Southern cooking so this should be written up in the magazines before the year is out."

"I'm right pleased to meet you, ma'am." Blake nodded. "Deke is waiting for us so I expect we'd best get on over there. I'm looking forward to a lot of good meals right here."

Willa Ruth mumbled something that sounded like she was pleased to meet Blake and then threw her hand up over her mouth to whisper something to the women sitting with her at the table.

Between that area and the corner Deke had saved, Allie stopped by two more tables to introduce Blake as her boyfriend. By the time they were seated with Deke and Kelly the whole place was buzzing. Allie didn't need a PhD in rocket science to know exactly what they were saying or that a few of those phones up to their ears were calling everyone else in town to give them the news.

"Well, that was bold as hell." Deke said.

"Did I hear you right? Did you say that Blake is your boyfriend?" Kelly asked.

"I think she did," Blake answered seriously.

"I wouldn't have a bit of trouble crawling up here on this table and telling the whole place if you were my boyfriend." Kelly pushed back her red hair and batted her thick lashes at him. "But I don't mess with another woman's feller."

Lizzy, Grady, and Mitch pushed through the door and Deke nodded that way. "She's liable to tear the place apart when...and there is Sharlene whispering in her ear right now."

Everyone in the place saw Lizzy's expression, but Allie smiled and blew her sister a kiss from across the room. With those mixed signals the poor old gossip hounds wouldn't know what to say or do next.

"So I'm your boyfriend?" Blake leaned around the corner of the table and kissed Allie on the cheek. "I'm lucky to have a girlfriend as beautiful as you are."

Kelly sighed. "Damn the luck. I would've gone to cut wood with Grandpa, but I was lazy and look what it got me."

"I'll be your boyfriend as long as we are at this table," Deke said.

"Why not longer?" Kelly asked.

"Because your grandpa would make sure they never found my body and that would make Allie sad since she is my best friend," Deke answered.

"Quite the charmer, you are." Kelly smiled.

Deke gave her a crooked little smile. "Do my best, darlin'."

Blake glanced at the menu, which was stuck between the sugar bowl and napkin holder. "I like being your boyfriend, but you could have given me a little notice."

"You brought me flowers. Doesn't that mean we are in a relationship?" she asked.

Before he could answer, Mary Jo appeared at the table with a little order pad and pen. "Well, you stirred up things. Nadine says to thank you because gossip is good for business."

"I want a big greasy hamburger with mustard, fries, and a Dr Pepper. Not diet," Allie answered. "Tell Nadine she's welcome. We are glad to be a help."

"Make that two," Blake said. "Double meat and add cheese please. Sweet tea instead of a soda."

Deke nodded. "I'll take what he's having."

"Me, too," Kelly said.

"How long has this been going on?" Mary Jo used her pen to point at Allie and Blake.

"A while," Allie answered.

"Some women have all the luck and just so you know, Sharlene is not a happy camper." Mary Jo rushed across the room to take Lizzy's order.

Blake walked Allie to the porch and then caged her by putting a hand on the wall on either side of her. "As your boyfriend, I do get a good night kiss, right?"

She stood on tiptoe and wrapped her arms around his neck. "I'm sorry. I should have told you I was going to do that. Everyone was staring at us, so I figured I'd give them something to talk about. If you don't want a commitment, then please at least play along with me until after Lizzy's wedding so I don't have to deal with Grady anymore."

His lips came down on hers, sweet and gentle at first, then more demanding, his tongue finding hers and the mating dance starting. Her breath came out in short raspy gasps when he finally pulled away.

"Why didn't you think of this sooner?"

"We can break up after the wedding," she said.

"We'll cross that bridge when we get to it. I'll see you tomorrow at noon and remember, since the room is done, we have a date on Thursday night. I'm thinkin' some dancin' at a honky-tonk."

"Sounds good to me," she said. "Good night, Blake."

He tipped his hat brim toward her and whistled all the way to the truck.

Allie took a deep breath and pushed the door open to find both her mother and Lizzy sitting on the bottom step of the staircase. She exhaled slowly and smiled brightly.

"I guess you heard the news," she said.

"You could have told us yourself," Katy said. "Not that it's a big surprise but to announce it like that, are you crazy?"

"No, I'm weak. Ask Lizzy if you don't believe me."

Lizzy rose to her feet. "Are you doing this so you have an excuse not to go out with Grady?"

Allie put her foot on the first step of the staircase. "I'm dating Blake, plain and simple, and if you would please relay that to Grady so he'll leave me alone, I will love you forever. And Lizzy, the next time you call me weak, you might do well to remember this night."

"I know I've been mean but it's only because I worry about you and I'm sorry," Lizzy said.

"Alora, are you sure about this?" Katy asked.

"I am, Mama and Lizzy, thanks for the concern. Family is always there when friends and marriages collapse and Lizzy, we'll be here for you no matter what, just like y'all are for me," Allie said and then went straight to her room and shut the door. She removed her clothing down to her underpants and pulled on a soft night shirt before slipping between the covers.

She'd made the first call in saying that she and Blake were in a real relationship when she didn't know if they were or not. She'd changed the whole course of her world in a single night and now she had to face the consequences. She turned the switch on a bedside lamp, putting the room in soft shadows. She'd had more fun this past couple of weeks than she'd had in her whole life. What she and Blake had might not last forever but she'd never know if she didn't give it a shot. And besides, Allie liked her life that night. She liked what she was doing and who she was sharing it with and that's all that mattered. She shut her eyes and dreamed of Blake Dawson.

CHAPTER
TWENTY-FIVE

Allie left the Lucky Penny on Wednesday afternoon in a pissy mood. She'd gotten the ceilings in the hallway and the living room bedded and taped, ready for the texturing the next day. That should have made her happy, but it didn't. She'd spent most of the day in the house all alone without even Shooter to talk to. Call it PMS or just plain old bitchiness, but she was in a horrible mood and hoped that Lizzy and Mitch had already left for midweek church services.

There had been a note beside the coffeepot that morning saying that Deke had a couple of cows delivering calves, so Blake had gone to help with the birthing process. Allie had lived in a rural community her entire life so she understood that friends helped friends.

At lunch she had heated up a bowl of leftover tortilla soup from the day before and ate it at the cabinet straight from the pan. While she was washing the pan, she got a text saying that one calf was on the ground but the other heifer was still in labor. Nothing about missing her or a mention of the date planned for the next night.

Snow fell in big fluffy flakes, melting as soon as it hit the warm van windshield on her way home that evening. The clock on the dash said that it wasn't even five o'clock yet, which was hard to believe with the darkness surrounding her. She followed Lizzy's truck and her mother's car down the lane and they all parked side-by-side right next to the gate leading into the yard.

"I hate snow," Irene declared as she held tightly to Katy's arm. "Old people shouldn't be out in this crap. I'm not leaving the house tomorrow, so y'all best make some plans. I could break a hip in this shit."

Allie raced ahead and unlocked the door and held it open for her mother and grandmother. Irene was still grumbling about the cold when out of nowhere a snowball hit Allie smack in the side of the face. She slammed the door and whipped around in time to dodge the second one, which hit the house with enough force to send it flying apart and peppering down into her hair.

Lizzy was scrapping up snow around the fence post and patting it together to make another one when Allie bailed off the porch and tackled her, landing them both in the half inch of snow already lying on the ground. She scraped up all she could hold in one fist and smeared it over Lizzy face. Then her sister did a roll and came up with a leg on either side of Allie's body and pinned her hands down above her head.

"You are right," she panted.

"About what? That this shit is cold?" Allie laughed for the first time that day.

"No, about needing family. Mitch is leaving for three weeks and I have to give up my honeymoon for God and I'm so pissed I'm not even going to church tonight," Lizzy said breathlessly.

Allie freed herself from her sister and leaned against the fence post. "Explain, please."

Lizzy scooted over and shared the post with Allie. "A mission trip to Mexico has come up suddenly and he and Grady are going because they've got vacation time. But that means he won't have time for our honeymoon so I have to sacrifice it for him to do his mission thing. And like I said, I'm pissed."

Allie caught a snowflake on her tongue. "You are kiddin' me, right?"

"I wouldn't tease about something this serious. We were planning a trip to Cancun where the weather would be warm, and I already bought two sweet little bathing suits, and now we'll be going straight to his apartment after the wedding. No honeymoon because his time has to be spent on a mission trip to help build a new school. And I can't bitch about it to anyone because he's doing it for God and you were right. If I didn't have you tonight, I'd be...well, I'm just glad you are here and I don't even give a damn about you liking Blake anymore."

Allie put her arm around Lizzy's shoulders. "I'd be pissed, too."

Lizzy grabbed her sister's hand and squeezed. "Thank you. I'm sorry about being so ugly these past weeks. This is probably my punishment for trying to run your life."

"No apology necessary. Let's go make supper and if it keeps up, we'll make snow ice cream for Granny." Allie hopped to her feet and pulled Lizzy up with her. "You cussed. You fell off the wagon."

"The words I used at the store when he called me and said

he was leaving in two hours blistered the paint on the walls," Lizzy said.

"Two hours! My God, Lizzy! And he bombed you with all this on the phone? That means he's already headed to Dallas to catch the plane, right? What did you say?"

Lizzy slung the door open and led the way into the warm house. "I kept my cool and said that of course God's work should come before our honeymoon. And then I hung up and cussed until I ran out of words and cried until I ran out of tears. I'm glad I didn't have many customers or the gossip would be so hot that it would melt the North Pole."

Both women removed coats and hung them on the rack inside the door, kicked off their boots, and tossed their stocking hats on the foyer table. Pots and pans rattled in the kitchen and the sound of Katy and Irene discussing supper floated out into the foyer.

"Does Mama know?"

Lizzy shook her head. "No, but she will in a few minutes. I might as well 'fess up because it will be all over town by bedtime."

"Why don't you stay home with Granny tomorrow and I'll work the store for you?" Allie said. "That way you can put at least one day between you and the gossip."

"You'd do that for me?"

Allie laid a hand over Lizzy's. "That's what sisters are for."

Blake had awoken in a black mood on Wednesday morning. When Deke called to ask for help, he'd agreed gladly, hoping that being around cattle and new baby calves would get him out of the funk.

It did not!

Thursday at noon, when he went to the house for dinner,

leaving two big piles of mesquite with three inches of snow on top of them, he finally got a handle on his problem.

It was Allie! And he fully intended to straighten it out that night when they were on their first and maybe last date. He pushed back his half-eaten roast beef sandwich, laced his hands behind his neck, and looked up at the kitchen ceiling with all its rusty brown circles. If she quit, he and Toby would have to finish putting up new drywall and they'd have to learn to texture the living room and hall.

"And insulation." The minute the words were out of his mouth his arms began to itch.

That afternoon Herman and Deke showed up to cut firewood. There was at least a days' worth out there piled up and Blake planned on clearing more land that day. Snow on the ground wouldn't keep him from working. Sleet falling out of the sky was a different thing.

The dashboard clock said it was five o'clock when Blake parked the dozer. In another two weeks if this damn weather would cooperate, he'd begin to till the ground, then put in a crop of wheat and one of alfalfa. Not long after that, Toby would arrive with cows and there wouldn't be many days that they'd have the luxury of stopping before dark.

Deke waved and crossed the field. "Hey, the calves are doing fine. Looks like that little bull might be breeder stock. I'll have to decide later, but he's got some fine shoulders and good markings."

"Good. Never knew how much I missed working with cattle until yesterday. I can't wait until the Lucky Penny is in full swing." Blake fell in beside him and together they walked back to the house with Shooter dashing on ahead of them.

"So you and Allie got a date tonight to celebrate your

bedroom getting finished. Where are you taking her? Dinner and a movie?"

Blake shook his head. "We do that all the time right there at the house. I'm thinking about a honky-tonk where we can have a drink and dance."

"Then let me suggest Cowboy Heaven. It's this side of Wichita Falls and it's got a nice dance floor and it's not too loud. I take the women I really want to impress up there," Deke said.

"Directions?" Blake asked.

"You'll see the signs for it soon as you cross the county line. It's right on the highway to the right. Big parking lot and a sign that stands tall. Can't miss it," Deke said. "Have a good time. I'll expect a full report tomorrow. No, don't tell me a thing. If Allie's able to come to work, I'll know by lookin' at her face if she enjoyed the evening. See you tomorrow, but it won't be until midmorning. With this weather, I'm throwing out a lot of hay."

Deke veered off toward his truck and Blake went on to the house, through the back door, and straight to the bathroom. He shucked out of his clothes while the shower water heated and then stood under it for a long time trying to figure out exactly how to approach Allie. He liked her. Hell, he might even be in love with her, but he was a man and he did not stand behind a woman's apron strings for protection.

He dressed in a fresh pair of starched jeans, straight from the cleaners back in Muenster, a plaid western shirt, and his most comfortable black boots. He had already picked up a western cut leather jacket when Shooter whined.

"Fine friend I am. You need to be fed, and I need to stoke up the fire before I leave so you don't freeze," Blake said.

Shooter wagged his tail and headed off toward the

kitchen where his food bowl and water dish stood empty. Blake took care of both containers, then filled a third one with dry food. "That should hold you until I get home and then I'll get out the treats."

The big yellow dog was too busy gulping down the food to even wag his tail.

Allie opened the door at the same time Blake raised his hand to knock and motioned him inside. "I have to get my coat and purse and I'm ready."

He took the dark brown suede jacket from her hands and held it for her. "You look absolutely beautiful tonight. Deke says that we should try out Cowboy Heaven. That sound good to you?"

"I love that place. They make the best cheeseburgers in the state and the dance floor is great," she said. "And you look pretty sexy, yourself, cowboy."

She leaned in for a kiss, expecting something that would knock her socks off, but all she got was a quick brush across her lips and then there was nothing but quietness. For a man who could talk the horns off an Angus bull when they hadn't been together in a couple of days, Blake was too damn quiet. He kept his eyes on the road and his thumbs weren't even keeping time to the music.

Something wasn't right.

For the first time since she met him, she wasn't comfortable. Forget the old proverbial elephant in the room. There was an angry Angus bull standing between them that evening. What had she done wrong? No, she wasn't going there. She'd always figured she'd done something wrong with Riley and then did her damnedest to fix it. She went over the past couple of days and she hadn't done or said anything. She crossed her arms over her chest and looked out the side window. He could open up and talk or it would be one hell of a long evening.

They went from Dry Creek through Elbert and up to Olney with neither of them saying anything except a few comments about the songs on the radio. Allie looked up and saw the Archer County sign and then all chaos broke loose as blizzard-like conditions complete with high winds and near zero visibility hit them head on.

The radio emitted one of those long bleeping noises and then an announcer said that the bad weather had taken a turn and now Highway 79 was now closed at the line between Archer and Young Counties. People were advised to only get out on the roads in case of emergencies.

"How far over that line do you think we are?" Blake asked.

"Five miles, maybe. Sign right there says it's twelve more to Archer City," Allie answered. "I can't even see the white lines on the road."

"Neither can I, but I think we might be the only vehicle out here. Is there a motel in Archer City?" he asked.

"A small one. Not fancy. Not a chain." She gripped the armrest so tight that her fingers ached.

"We don't need fancy. We have to find a place to hole up until this passes through and they clean off the roads."

The radio emitted another bleeping noise and the newest flash was that the storm was heading straight for Throckmorton County. All schools had been closed and again people were urged to stay inside.

"I hope there's a room at that motel," Blake said.

"I hope we make it there without bogging down in this stuff. I've never seen a storm like this before," she whispered. "I feel like I'm in an igloo."

Blake kept both hands on the steering wheel and his

eyes straight ahead, even though the headlights created a kaleidoscope that was constantly moving and came close to blinding him.

"I've been in a pissy mood for two days," he said.

"Me, too. What's your problem?"

"I want to know if you're just using me to get Grady out of your life and off your back until Lizzy's wedding and then planning to end this relationship."

"No, I'm not using you, Blake. And why would you think that?"

"It's doubt creeping in because I'm falling in love with you." He eased up on the gas.

She turned around in the seat as far as she could without undoing the seat belt. "This is one hell of a time to tell me this."

"Why, because we might slide off in a ditch and die?" he asked.

"Exactly."

He turned to face her and his foot leaned too heavy on the gas. The truck slipped from one side of the road to the other before he got it under control and moving forward again at a trusty fifteen miles an hour.

She folded her arms over her chest and said breathlessly, "Let's wait to talk about this until we are stopped at the motel."

Blake glanced over at her. "I wanted you to know in case we do wind up in a ditch and freeze to death in each other's arms." He cleared his throat. "I've flat out fallen in love with you. I think it was love at first sight and I've been fighting it like hell, but it's the way it is and I want you to know."

For a few seconds she wasn't sure that she would ever breathe again. Then she inhaled deeply and said, "Were you going to tell me before we got in this situation?"

One of his shoulders jacked up an inch or two. "I don't know, Allie. I only figured it out tonight and hell, I'm tired of fighting with myself. I know it's only been a few weeks but my mama said that I'd know when the right woman came into my life. And I know so I have to spit it out and say it."

"That's not so romantic for a man who's got the reputation you do," she said. "Look, that sign we just passed said it was only two more miles. We could walk that far."

"Not without frost bite. And my reputation is what scares me, Allie. What if you have second thoughts about someone like me?"

"I won't. I promise," she whispered.

She loved him, too, but she couldn't say the words. They were there but they wouldn't come out of her mouth.

Ten minutes later she pointed to a flashing vacancy sign above a motel and he eased off the road into a parking lot so deep with snow that his front fender pushed it out of the way like a plow. He brought the truck to a long greasy sliding stop in front of the motel and waded to the office where the lady told him that they had three rooms left. One was a king-size, non-smoking room. The other two were double queens. He opted for the king-size bed and asked if there was a pizza hut that might make deliveries in the bad weather.

"A lot of the town is without power so we filled up real quick. Those that do have electricity are takin' in their relatives and all the businesses are shut down," she said as she ran a key card through the machine. "Here are your keys and, honey, right not far from your room is the ice machine and vending machines. Soda pop, juice, bottled water in one. Candy, chips, and those cute little energy bars in the other. That's the best I can do for you tonight."

"Does it take credit cards?" he asked.

She shook her head. "Only takes coins. Need change?"

He flipped a twenty-dollar bill onto the counter. "Turn it all into whatever I need."

She counted out fifteen single bills, then picked up a plastic cup with the motel logo on the side and filled the thing with five dollars in quarters. "That should do it."

He picked up the cup. "Thank you. Do you have complimentary toothbrushes and toothpaste? We were traveling to Wichita Falls when this thing hit us. We don't have anything but what we are wearing."

"Right here, and here's a customer packet with shaving equipment, deodorant, toothbrushes, and such. Holler right loud if you need anything else." She handed him two bubble packs, each containing a toothbrush and a tiny tube of toothpaste. "Oh, and we do doughnuts, bagels, and coffee for breakfast from six to nine in the morning if my husband can get out to the pastry shop to get them and if it's open."

Blake started toward the truck to open the door for Allie, but she pushed her way out of it, stepped out into knee-deep snow, and yelled above the howling wind, "Which way?"

He pointed and bent against the swirling cold chilling him to the bone. He found the room, only a couple of doors down from the office, and slipped the key card into the slot, hoping the whole time that the damn thing worked. He could have shouted when the little green light popped on and Allie hurried into the room.

It wasn't the worst room he'd ever rented, but it lacked the luxury of where he would have taken Allie if he'd had a choice. It was warm, had a television and a big comfortable-looking bed. The warmth and bed were more inviting than anything after hunching over that damn steering wheel for what seemed like hours.

"I'll take that trash can and go get supper," he said. "I'm

going to fill it up so if you've got a preference, holler right now."

"Vending machine?" She removed her gloves and warmed her hands over the wall heater.

"That's right, darlin'. Big juicy hamburger will have to wait until another night. This date has changed course," he said.

"I don't care. Bring me some of all of it and I'll be happy. I'm so glad that we're safe in a room. Oh, I've got to call Mama. I didn't even tell her which way we were going," she said all in a rush.

"You call. I'll be back soon as I spend all my money." He grinned.

Katy answered on the third ring and started talking before Allie could say a single word. "Where are you? If you went north, then find a place and hole up until this horrible storm passes. I swear to God, I've never seen anything like this in our part of the world. It's so bad out there I can't even see the edge of the porch from the window."

"I'm in Archer City and we've gotten a motel room. It took forever to get this far, but I'm safe and warm and Blake has gone to buy out everything in the vending machine so I'm not going to starve," she said.

"Stay put and…" The line went completely dead.

When Allie looked at her phone all she got was a no ser-vice signal. Evidently, the wind had played havoc with the towers between Archer City and Dry Creek. She laid the phone on the nightstand, removed her coat, and hung it in the closet. An extra blanket, tucked away inside a zippered bag, rested on a fold-up luggage rack. She removed it and tossed it on the bed. Then she kicked off her boots and wet socks and set them under the desk.

A shiver running from her backbone to her toes let her know that the legs of her jeans were every bit as wet as her socks. She undid her belt buckle and shimmied out of the jeans, hung them in the closet, and caught her reflection in the mirror across the room. White cotton bikini underpants when she knew she was going on a real date; she slapped her forehead with her palm.

"Allie, open up, my hands are full and I can't knock," Blake called out.

She did double time from heater to door and slung it open to find the abominable snowman on the other side. The wet snow had stuck to Blake's eyelashes and his black cowboy hat had an inch lying on the brim. She grabbed his arm, pulled him inside, and slammed the door shut, but not before a gust of wind blasted her with a face full of cold white snow.

She took the trash can full of vending machine goodies from his arms and set it on the desk. "Get undressed. Hang everything in the closet. I'll put a towel on the floor to catch the drip. Then get under the covers, Blake. You have to be chilled to the bone. Even your jeans are soaked."

His teeth chattered as he reached inside the closet and brought out the rest of the hangers. "I've got a better idea. I'll get undressed in the bathroom and hang all my wet things in the shower, but I will take your advice and get under the covers. I don't think I've ever been this cold and I've ranched through cold winters my whole life. But I do like that outfit. Did you bring it special in your purse in case we had to stay in a motel tonight? This is some first date, Allie."

"I bet we don't ever forget it." She smiled.

The black hat came off first and he hung it on the showerhead. Allie fought the urge to hum the stripper song as he removed one article of clothing at a time. When he pushed his jeans down over a bright pink ass, she gasped and he laughed.

"Didn't want anything to slow us down in case I got lucky on our first real date so I came commando," he explained.

"How did the butt of your jeans get wet?"

He talked on his way to the bed where he threw back the covers and crawled in between them. "It's slippery out there and the soles of my boots don't have the traction that my old work ones do. When I was going to the vending machine, I fell twice."

"Are you okay?" Dammit! What if he'd cracked his head on something and died out there in the snow and she'd been too stubborn to tell him that she was in love with him? He would have died without knowing and she would have never forgiven herself.

"Nothing hurt that a sexy woman cuddled up next to me in this big bed wouldn't heal." One hand came out from under the covers to pat the place beside him. "I need body heat so you really should take off those cute little panties and that sweater and the bra."

"Who says I'm wearing a bra?" she asked. "Maybe I'm going commando in case I get lucky on this first real date."

"I can see the line of a bra under that sweater, but the picture in my mind is damn sure warmin' me up," Blake said.

In seconds the rest of her clothing was tossed toward the desk and she was shivering in his arms. "You could have told me the sheets had been stored in the freezer."

"My love will warm things up real fast," he said.

She looked up into his green eyes. "About that? Are you sure that what you said wasn't..."

He put a finger over her lips. "You know my reputation, Allie. You know what kind of cowboy I've been. But what you don't know is that I've never, ever said those words to a woman before. Not even the girl I married while on a drunken binge after we'd graduated from high school. I stood there and promised to love, honor, and respect her until death parted us, but I couldn't make myself say those three words."

"But you were pissed at me," she said.

"I was." He yawned. "But it was male pride getting in the way and doubts that I could ever deserve a woman like you."

"And now?" She pressed even closer to him.

He buried his face in her hair. "Now, I feel free. I'm happy. I can't imagine life without you in it. I was terrified I'd wreck the truck and hurt you, and I'm exhausted, Allie. Can we take a short nap together before we get lucky? I've got the worst adrenaline letdown I've ever had."

"Me, too. Let's take a short nap." She still couldn't utter the L word.

"Sleep first, then a fancy vending machine supper, then making love, more sleep, and more vending machine food. Sounds like a good plan to me..." His voice trailed off and his eyes fluttered shut.

The phone setting on the nightstand not two feet from her face woke her. At first, she thought it was the alarm and then she felt Blake's naked body wrapped around her and remembered the whole evening. She opened one eye and checked the clock. It flipped another minute making it 11:11. That meant she could make a wish and it would come true. Sure it was superstition, but she and both her sisters had believed it since they were kids. The first person who saw all four ones lined up on the clock got to make a wish.

She brought one hand out and reached for the remote phone receiver. "Yes?"

"This is the front desk. I got a call from a feller named

Deke saying to tell Blake Dawson that he has Shooter at his house. Cell phone towers are down all around us so he couldn't get through to you that way."

"Thank you," Allie said.

"Weatherman says that it's supposed to let up by midnight, but I wouldn't bank on the roads being cleared tomorrow. Y'all want me to pencil you in for another night?"

"Yes, please," Allie said.

"Will do. If you need anything I'm right here all night."

"What was that all about?" Blake asked.

"Deke has Shooter at his place. Evidently he found out from Mama that we're in the motel in Archer City and got the number to call here so you wouldn't be worried," she answered.

"Hungry?" he asked.

"Me or Shooter?"

"You." He grinned.

"Yes, but not for food. I'm reversing the order of the evening. First it's making love, then food, and then we'll talk about the rest. And Blake, I love you, too," she said. The words came out so slick that she didn't realize she'd said them until his lips were on hers.

CHAPTER
TWENTY-SIX

Blake could hardly believe it was already February. Allie had said that she loved him and things had been good since those three wonderful days in the motel when they'd lived on vending machine food, takeout pizza, and lots of sex. Two weeks had passed since then and their relationship had grown deeper with the passing of each day. The next step was to pop the question and open a pretty red velvet box to reveal a ring, wasn't it?

All those sparkling diamonds displayed in a jewelry store window had always made Blake shield his eyes and hurry across the street. But now a ring was all he could think about. He wanted to spend the rest of his life with her, but was he rushing things? Buying the ring didn't mean he had to give it to her before summer. Six months seemed like the appropriate time to wait after the "I love you" to the "Will you marry me?" He would have months to plan the perfect setting and the ring would be ready for that magical moment.

The plan had to be right because thinking the words didn't give him hives. Only the online jewelry stores had so much to offer that he couldn't choose, and then he worried that he might select something similar to her first wedding rings. He worried with it all afternoon and finally decided the only thing to do was ask Lizzy and hope to hell she didn't pull out the gun from under the counter and start shooting.

"Hey, gorgeous!" he yelled down the hall toward Allie as he and Shooter came through the kitchen door. "I'm going to Lizzy's store. You need me to pick up anything?"

Allie's head bobbed down from an exposed rafter in the living room ceiling. "Not a thing. Lizzy is lonely with Mitch away. Want to ask her to join us for supper at Nadine's tonight?"

"I'll ask her. See you later. Be careful up there." He blew her a kiss.

Luck was with him. No one was in the store when he arrived that chilly February afternoon.

Lizzy looked up from the counter and smiled. "Fence posts?"

"Wedding rings," he said.

"I don't sell those things."

"Lizzy, I love Allie and I want to spend my life with her."

"Don't tell me. Tell her."

"I need rings and I need help before I do that."

Lizzy smiled. "I can't believe I'm saying this but I believe you and I'm happy for you both. Now what can I do?"

Allie sat between Blake and Deke in the back pew at the church on Sunday morning. One arm around her shoulders pulled her close enough to hear the steady rhythm of his heartbeat. His fingers interlaced with hers shot delicious little tingles throughout her body. This was the man she'd fallen in love with, part dependable and the other part pure sexy pleasure.

The preacher took the podium, opened his Bible, and looked out over the congregation.

Blake squeezed her hand. "Bet he speaks from that love chapter in Corinthians. Valentine's Day is a week from today."

"As all you folks know, Valentine's Day is next Sunday," the preacher said.

"Glad I didn't make that bet," Allie whispered.

"And the ladies tell me that we're having a potluck in the fellowship hall immediately after church that day. Everyone is invited and I'm sure there will be plenty of food. Nadine has said she's not opening the café that day so y'all best plan on having dinner here with us." He chuckled. "And now if you will open your Bibles to the love chapter in Corinthians and follow along with me while I talk to you about what all love can do in your lives, both in relationships and friendships..."

"Two for two." Blake kissed her on the earlobe and the tingles turned into hot little sparks.

Allie wished they were anywhere but church. But then the pews were wider than the backseat of his truck and longer than the kitchen table and she was still a church pew virgin. She blushed and Blake chuckled.

"Thinking something that will bring down lightning?" Blake asked.

She brought his ear close to her mouth. "More like it would rain hellfire down through the roof. You ever had sex on a church pew?"

"Pick one out. I'm game if you are," he said.

The preacher finished his sermon by saying something about love and then said, "Don't forget the social potluck next Sunday and now I'm going to ask Blake Dawson to end our service with the benediction."

Everyone stood and Blake, bless his cowboy heart, said a two-minute prayer without missing a beat. It couldn't have been easy with the picture Allie had put in his mind, but he managed.

"That was downright mean," he said as soon as everyone else echoed his Amen at the end of the prayer. "I bet he saw us whispering."

"I'm just glad he didn't ask me to do it," Allie said.

Blake was so damn nervous that he could hardly be still during Sunday dinner at Nadine's after church. It had more to do with the ring box in his pocket than the four women sitting around the table with him. Having it in his pocket made him want to put it on her finger. He wondered how in the world he'd ever wait six months.

"So one more week and Mitch is coming home, right?" Blake asked Lizzy.

She nodded. "The day after Valentine's Day, less than a month from our wedding day. The church is planning a wedding shower the week after he gets home."

"And where are you going to live?" Blake asked.

"He rents an apartment in Wichita Falls, not far from the church where he hopes to fill the preacher's shoes in the summer when he retires. Right now he helps out when the preacher needs to be gone or wants a week off."

Blake nodded, his mind on the ring. "And you'll commute to work?"

"It's a distance but..." She shrugged.

"If the weather is bad, she can always stay with us," Katy said.

"Crazy damn notion if you ask me, which nobody did," Irene piped up. "They could live halfway between the two places or he could commute but oh, no, not Mitch. He's got to be in control."

"Granny!" Lizzy exclaimed.

Allie raised an eyebrow in Blake's direction. "Looks like you stirred up a hornets' nest."

"I'll fix it," he whispered, and then said, "Miz Irene, can you believe that it's such a beautiful day when two weeks ago the whole area was covered in a foot of snow?"

"It's Texas. If you don't like the weather, stick around. It will change. And the only thing that's dependable in this place is that in the summer it's going to be hotter'n the blue blazes of hell. I'm hungry. Is Nadine having to wring that turkey's neck and pick the feathers before she can make my turkey and dressin' dinner plate?" she answered.

Katy laughed. "At least it won't be that frozen crap that you hate, Mama. I think the waitress is bringing our dinner right now."

"Well, I hope so. I'd like to live to see my sixtieth birthday."

"Granny, you will be seventy-one on your birthday," Lizzy said.

Mary Jo set their plates in front of them. "Be careful. The plates are hot."

"I'm old, not stupid," Irene said.

"And don't you look beautiful today." Mary Jo stopped to give her a hug.

"Granny, you were rude," Lizzy said.

"For that smartass remark and since you are bound,

damned, and determined to marry that worthless son-of-a-bitch, wannabe preacher, you can say grace before we eat this good food."

Lizzy dropped her chin and said softly, "Father, thank you for this food. Forgive Granny for her dirty language and the rest of us for our sins. Amen."

"That wasn't a prayer. God didn't even hear that short two sentences," Irene fussed.

"It's enough, Mama. Eat your dinner," Katy said.

Irene picked up her fork. "Okay, but if I die tonight and God won't let me in the pearly gates because I ate unblessed food, then I'm going to tell him it's y'all's fault."

Blake chuckled. "I think I'm fallin' in love with her."

Irene's head popped up. "Who's fallin' in love with who?"

"No one, Granny. I hear Nadine made cherry pies and she's got ice cream and chocolate syrup," Allie said.

"I said that I was falling in love with you," Blake said.

"Bullshit! I'm old. You're not in love with me. You are in love with Allie."

Blake nodded. "You are right. I have fallen in love with Allie. I'm downright crazy in love with this woman and I don't care who all knows it."

Irene clapped her hands.

Allie blushed.

"Hey, if you can declare that I'm your boyfriend right here in the middle of this café, I can tell the whole world I'm in love with you in the same place." Blake leaned to his left, tipped her chin up with his fist, and kissed her right there in public.

"Well, would you look at that, Katy? I think he means it?" Irene giggled.

"I was going to wait for a private moment, but this seems

like a perfect place and time." He pushed back his chair and dropped down on one knee. "Allie Logan, I love you. Plain and simple and I can't imagine life without you. Will you marry me?"

He flipped open a red velvet ring box to reveal a brown diamond solitaire ring surrounded by more than a dozen sparkling clear diamonds. "I chose this because it's the color of your eyes."

"Yes!" she said without hesitation.

He slipped the ring onto her finger, picked her up out of the chair, and swung her around the floor several times before his lips settled on hers. Most of the folks in the café clapped. The ones who didn't were already talking on their phones.

* * *

Later that afternoon, Allie held the ring up to catch the sunlight pouring into the bedroom. "I can't believe you proposed right there in public."

Blake wrapped his hand around hers and brought the ring to her face. "That brown diamond is the same color as your eyes. Darlin', it was either propose or explode. I knew I wouldn't be able to swallow that good food until I asked you to marry me."

"We need to talk," she said.

"Oh, no!" He fell back on the pillows. "I hate it when you say that."

"Well, we do."

"Please don't tell me you aren't going to marry me," he groaned.

"Oh, honey, I'm going to marry you, but I'm fixin' to give you a way out if you don't want to be burdened with what

I'm about to say." She swallowed twice and started three times but the words wouldn't come out. "Hell's bells, Blake, this is tough."

Blake propped up on an elbow. "Just spit it out."

"I was married for two years and sexually active for two years before that. We were young and stupid the first two years. After we married we wanted children, but it never happened and Riley said it was my fault," she said slowly.

"And what has that got to do with us?"

She shrugged. "I'm three days late and we haven't even talked about kids because I told you I couldn't have any. But I've never been late and now I'm thinkin' maybe Riley lied to me about going to the doctor to get tested." She stopped to catch her breath.

Blake pulled her into his arms and kissed the top of her head. "I want kids, but I want you more. If you are pregnant, then I hope it's twins so we'll get a jump on a house full. If you aren't and you really can't have them, then someday in the future we might discuss adoption if you want them."

She pushed back and let the tears loose to stream down her cheeks. "I love you with my whole heart and what you just said makes me say yes to your proposal all over again. Let's get married this week."

"Sounds great to me, but don't take the test until afterward. I don't ever want you to feel like I married you because I had to. I'm marrying you because I love you, Allie." He kissed away her tears.

"You are trying to make a ranch here. A wife wasn't in your four-year plan and I know a baby wasn't."

"We'll take them when we get them and if we never get them, then we have each other. Did you have your mind set on a big wedding?"

"Hell, no!" she said loudly. "Let's go get a license at the

courthouse before Friday, get married on Sunday morning after church, and the potluck can be our reception. I want to be a wife, not a fiancée."

He laid a hand on her flat stomach. "I love you, Allie."

"I love you, too, Blake," she said.

CHAPTER
TWENTY-SEVEN

Y ou cannot wear that." Lizzy was absolutely aghast that Sunday morning. "You are getting married, not going to stand on the street corner to solicit business."

"It's Valentine's Day. I like red, and Blake is wearing a red tie so this is it. Besides remember our roots, Lizzy." Allie smiled. "I'll be the hooker bride. You can be the snow white virgin bride."

"I'm not a virgin. Haven't been since I was eighteen," Lizzy said tersely.

Allie leaned in close to the mirror and applied eyeliner. "You might as well be one as long as it's been since you've had a good romp in the bed. When your Mitch comes home, take him to a motel and jump his bones. It'll make you feel a hell of a lot better."

"That wild cowboy has made you as rowdy as he is." Lizzy laughed.

"Yes, he has, and I love it and him for doing it. Now let's

go to church and have a wedding afterward, then we can eat all that lovely food. And Lizzy, thank you one more time for helping me move all my things over to the Lucky Penny. I can't believe I'll be waking up tomorrow in my new home."

Lizzy laid a hand on her shoulder. "Or that it's this close to Mama and Granny. I envy you, sister."

Allie turned around and hugged Lizzy tightly. "I'm not going to think about you having to live all the way up there in the city. I'll miss you so much."

"Don't talk about it or we'll both cry and mess up our makeup. I've got to stand up beside you at the wedding and I don't need to have black streaks down my face. Who is Blake's best man? Deke?"

Allie took a step back. "No, it's his brother, Toby."

"Well, you will have a few months before he moves in to enjoy the honeymoon," Lizzy sniffed. "At least Mitch and I won't have another person living with us."

"But Grady will be there every day, I betcha. And with Deke in and out every day, we're already used to an extra person around," Allie told her.

Allie's hands had started to sweat when the preacher took the podium. He laid his Bible down but didn't open it and smiled out at the congregation. "Today, we aren't going to have a service, but we are going to have a wedding. In my opinion there isn't a better way to celebrate Valentine's Day than to unite two people who are very much in love in the bonds of holy matrimony."

"I thought he was going to preach first," Blake said.

"So did I." Allie nodded.

The preacher's wife hit a few keys on the piano and Lizzy stood up in her cute little off-white lace dress. She pulled a small bouquet of tiny little white flowers mixed with half a dozen red roses from a small cooler at her feet. The white ones reminded her of that tiny little snow flower that Blake had brought her that day and the roses—they reminded her of the roses that grew on the barbed wire fence between the Lucky Penny and Audrey's Place in the summertime.

Folks looked around to see where Mitch was and from the expressions on their faces, Allie could tell that they thought Lizzy was the bride. But then Lizzy laid the bouquet on the altar and took her place on the stage.

Blake and Toby rose to their feet at the same time. Some folks might say they walked up the aisle, but from where Allie sat, there was no doubt that was a Texas cowboy strut or swagger. It definitely covered much more than a walk. She waited until they made it to the front to start down the aisle.

Blake caught her eye and everything else disappeared. She didn't hear the whispers about her tight red dress or the gasps, or even thumbs working frantically as some of them typed in text messages. All she saw was the man she loved, the wild cowboy she'd been waiting on her whole life. She picked up the bouquet and joined him on the stage.

"You are beyond beautiful today. Words could never describe what a stunning bride you are," he whispered.

"I love you," she said loud enough for everyone in the church to hear.

"Dearly beloved, we are gathered here today to unite Alora Raine Logan and Blake Alan Dawson in holy matrimony..." the preacher said.

"I just realized what your initials are," Allie whispered. "I really did fall for a bad boy."

"And I fell for an angel." He grinned.

She handed Lizzy her flowers and held both of Blake's hands in hers. Six weeks ago she hadn't even known this man and now she was standing right there before God and her friends and family saying that she would love, honor, and cherish him until death parted them. Not one doubt filled her heart when she said a loud, "I do!"

The ceremony ended with a prayer and the preacher said, "You may now kiss your bride, Blake."

She wasn't expecting him to bend her backward in a true Hollywood kiss and then sweep her feet off the floor and swing her around the stage twice before he set her down and kissed her again.

But he did and the whole congregation applauded.

"I am the happiest man right now on this whole planet," he said.

"And now the bride and groom and these two young people who have stood with them to witness their marriage vows are going on to the fellowship hall. Give them five minutes to catch their breath and we'll join them," the preacher said.

Lizzy handed Allie the bouquet.

Allie turned around to loop her arm in Blake's but he shook his head. "Not that way darlin'. We are doing this our way."

He scooped her up in his arms and carried her out of the sanctuary and down the short hall to the place where the potluck was set up.

"Would you look at this?" He grinned.

Allie was stunned. Red roses decorated tables covered with white cloths. A gorgeous three-tiered cake decorated with roses and snow flowers sat on a round table with a lovely silver punch bowl.

"Mama, Nadine, Mary Jo, and Sharlene got together yesterday and did all this," Lizzy said.

"It's gorgeous," Allie said.

"I guess I'd best tell you that the church was packed this morning because my family brought campers and RVs and they set up last night on the Lucky Penny," Blake said. "Surprise! You get to meet them all in about two minutes."

Allie was sure she'd faint dead away right then, but she stiffened her legs and made her knees stop knocking together. "Bring 'em on. I tamed the wildest cowboy in Texas. I'm not afraid of anything."

"That's my girl," Blake said.

An hour later when everyone had gone through the buffet line, some more than once, and it was almost time to cut the cake, Allie looked around for Lizzy and couldn't find her. There hadn't been a formal table for the wedding party so she figured Lizzy had opted to sit elsewhere, but something wasn't right. Allie could feel it deep in her bones.

"I'm going to make a trip to the ladies' room, darlin'. I'll be back soon and then we'll cut the cake so folks can have a piece of it," she whispered.

"Don't take that test without me standing right beside you," he said.

She kissed him on the cheek. "Wouldn't dream of it."

She found Lizzy curled up around a toilet in the handicapped stall in the bathroom. Her eyes were swollen and she'd cried so hard that she had the hiccups. She threw her arms around Allie's knees and sobbed.

"What happened? Did Mitch die?"

"No, worse," Lizzy said. "But I didn't want to ruin your wedding day."

Allie sat down on the floor and held her sister tightly. "How much worse?"

"He's not going to marry me, Allie. The preacher's daughter went with them on the mission and he says he's found his soul mate. That after praying…" Lizzy gagged but nothing came up, "about it, both of them praying about it, that they realize God meant them to be together and for them to preach at the little church in Mexico so they aren't coming back to Texas. They're going to be missionaries."

Allie hugged Lizzy even tighter. "Oh, Lizzy, I'm so sorry. That bastard did this with a phone call?"

Lizzy nodded. "He said I was never cut out to be a preacher's wife anyway. And God told him that with prostitutes in my background that he'd never be accepted as a preacher. What am I going to do?"

"Break up with him," Allie said.

"Are you crazy? He broke it off with me," Lizzy said.

"And he's not coming back to Texas for a long time. Give me your engagement ring."

Lizzy pointed at the toilet. "I flushed it."

"That's even better. You are going to get up, wash your face, and use the makeup kit in my purse to fix things as best you can. Then we're going back into the church and we're going to cut my wedding cake. You aren't going to say a word but when people start to notice that your ring is gone you are going to say that your broke it off with him because you found out he had another woman on the line. Do you understand me?" Allie said sternly.

Lizzy nodded. "It's almost the truth and it will save all that sickening sweet pity, won't it?"

Allie pulled Lizzy up and marched her to the sink. "Work some magic in five minutes. The gossip fiends will come looking for me if I'm not back by then."

Lizzy washed her face with a brown paper towel and then applied makeup. When she and Allie walked out of the bathroom, they both had smiles. Maybe Lizzy's didn't reach her eyes but no one would notice.

"And here is our bride and her lovely sister," the preacher said loudly when they reached the fellowship hall. "Let's cut into that cake and see if it's as good as it looks."

Allie reached for Blake's hand and he raised an eyebrow.

"Later, darlin'. More than one prayer got answered today." She smiled up at him as they crossed the floor to the cake table.

"You took the test?"

"Not yet. It's waiting at home and I'll explain the rest later."

"And after the cake cutting," Katy announced, "Allie and Blake will have their first dance as a married couple."

Allie picked up the long knife with a lovely cut glass handle. "The mamas went all out, didn't they?"

"Mamas are like that." Blake kissed her again and the whole crowd applauded. "Don't worry, I chose the song."

"You knew?" Allie asked.

"Not until late last night. Let's get this cake cut and dance so we can go home, Mrs. Dawson."

When the first strands of music started, Allie's eyes widened out as big as saucers. "Is that what I think it is?"

"Not the conventional wedding music, but it's our music and the words remind me of..." Blake said.

Allie put her fingers over his lips and blushed. Blake twirled her out on the area cleared out for a dance floor and danced with her just like they'd done at Frankie's place while Etta James sang "Something's Got a Hold on Me."

"And now for my choice." Allie put her arms around Blake's neck and swayed with him to "I Cross My Heart" by George Strait. "And yes, I knew last night, too. Lizzy told me."

She glanced over at her sister sitting in a folding chair, a smile plastered on her face even though it didn't reach her eyes. That's when Toby stood up and shook the legs of his jeans down over his boot tops and held his hand out to Lizzy.

Allie could have kissed her new brother-in-law as he drew Lizzy into his arms. Lizzy frantically looked across the room to her sister.

Allie nodded and winked. She and her sister might fight. They would definitely argue, but as sisters, they still had the ability to comfort and convey messages with a glance.

Lizzy relaxed in Toby's arms and followed his expert steps around the room as the rest of the floor filled up with folks dancing to the next song on George Strait's CD, "I Swear."

"I do swear to love you with every beat of my heart until death parts us just like George is singing," Blake whispered.

Allie rolled up on her toes and kissed him and hoped that someday her sister found a man just like Blake Dawson. One who, like George Strait sang about, would love her with every beat of his heart.

It was mid-afternoon when Blake picked up Allie for the second time that day and carried her across the threshold into the ranch house. He didn't stop at the bedroom but took her straight to the bathroom before he set her down. "I love you, Allie Dawson, but I can't wait any longer."

She followed the directions on the paper and laid the stick on a paper towel on the counter. With a hand on either side of her face, Blake looked deeply into her eyes. "Neither of us will look until the time is up."

The seconds dragged but finally she covered her hands with his. "Okay, here goes. Oh, Blake, it's positive. Three weeks. Must have happened that first time." She'd wondered all week how she'd feel if she was really pregnant or how he'd feel. And now the answer was there. She was going to be a mother. She was carrying Blake's child. And she was filled with an indescribable mixture of awe and happiness. And his face registered absolute pride and joy.

"Lord, help us if this baby gets your wild cowboy ways and my temper," she whispered.

"Now wouldn't that set Dry Creek on its ear." He chuckled. "Darlin', you have given me the best wedding gift a man could ask for." He picked her up and started toward the bedroom.

"I'm not sure who gave who that gift, but right now I want you to kick that door shut so Shooter stays in the living room and then I want you to make love to me."

"Your wish, Mrs. Dawson, will always be my desire." He closed the door with the heel of his boot, set her firmly on the floor, and slowly unzipped the back of her dress.

ABOUT THE AUTHOR

Carolyn Brown is a *New York Times* and *USA Today* best-selling romance author and RITA finalist who has sold more than three million books. She presently writes both women's fiction and cowboy romance. She has also written historical single title, historical series, contemporary single title, and contemporary series. She lives in Southern Oklahoma with her husband, a former English teacher who is the author of nine mystery novels. They have three children and enough grandchildren to keep them young. For a complete listing of her books in series order and to sign up for her newsletter, check out her website at www.carolynbrownbooks.com or catch her on Facebook/CarolynBrownBooks.

Looking for more cowboys?
Forever brings the heat with these sexy studs.

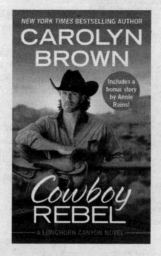

COWBOY REBEL
By Carolyn Brown

After a brush with the law, rancher Taggart Baker has decided to leave his wild ways behind, especially when he meets a beautiful ER nurse worth settling down for. But before he can convince her he's a changed man, his troubled past comes calling—and this time he won't be able to walk away so easily. Includes a bonus story by Annie Rains!

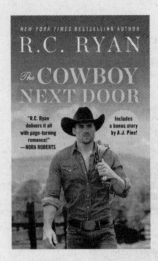

THE COWBOY NEXT DOOR
By R.C. Ryan

The last thing Penny Cash needs is a flirtation with a wild, carefree cowboy. Sure, he's funny and sexy, but they're as different as whiskey and tea. But when trouble comes calling, Penny will find out how serious Sam Monroe can be when it comes to protecting the woman he loves. Includes a bonus story by A.J. Pine!

HARD LOVING COWBOY
By A.J. Pine

Walker Everett has good and bad days—but the worst was the day that Violet Chastain started as the new sommelier at Crossroads Ranch. She knows nothing about ranch life and constantly gets under his skin. But when a heated argument leads to the hottest kiss he's ever had, Walker must decide whether he finally deserves something good. Includes a bonus story by Sara Richardson!

Find more great reads on Instagram with
@ReadForeverPub.

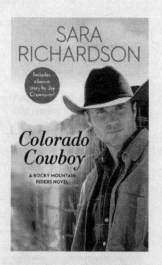

COLORADO COWBOY
By Sara Richardson

Charity Stone has learned to hold her own in the male-dominated rodeo world. There's no cowboy she can't handle...except for one. Officer Dev Jenkins has made it clear he doesn't look at her as one of the guys. He's caught her attention, but Charity doesn't do relationships—especially not with a cowboy. Includes a bonus story by Jay Crownover!

JUSTIFIED
By Jay Crownover

As the sheriff of Loveless, Texas, Case Lawton is determined to do everything by the book—until he's called to Aspen Barlow's office after a so-called break-in. The last thing he wants to do is help the woman who cost him custody of his son. But as threats against Aspen start to escalate, it becomes clear that Case is her last hope—and there's nothing he wouldn't do to keep her safe. Includes a bonus story by Carly Bloom!

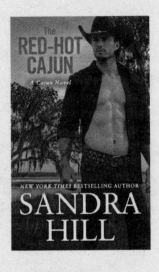
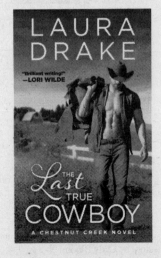